BADLANDS

JACK LIVELY

1
WILD NIGHT

ONE

November 27, 2016
Western Negev, Israel.

A BRANCH BRUSHED against Tom Keeler's left temple and he ducked his head an inch to the right, protecting his eye. Yasmin was beside him, both of them prone in the thicket. The branch had been pushed by her shifting position. She made brief eye contact, like saying sorry. Keeler turned his head to the view of the desert plain down below.

Which was the precise moment that the sun dipped below the horizon, flaring as the last sliver disappeared over the Sinai mountains to the west, on the other side of the border with Egypt. A blue halo rose, flared, and was gone. Keeler blinked twice, the second time slowly, waiting for the retinal traces to die down. When he opened his eyes, a lone hyena had appeared on the hill just in front of them. The beast was upwind of the thicket, unaware of being observed, descending a few yards before tracing the ridge line, snout down and scanning for death.

The hyena hadn't caught their scent, but was certainly

interested in something out there, doing a grid search of the rocky desert outcrop. Keeler watched it work, one of the perfect animals that let others do the killing for them, arriving once the hunter was exhausted, driving the pure predators from their prey and appropriating the rewards.

Keeler glanced at Yasmin, catching her eye again. They both knew what the hyena meant, the truth that its presence revealed about the situation below. She handed him the Nikon binoculars she kept in her Subaru.

Their position was high above a desert flat. About a kilometer to the southwest, two human figures lay as still as lifeless dolls on a desert track a few yards from a white four-wheel-drive vehicle. The wind was coming from that direction. Keeler couldn't smell a corpse from a kilometer away, but a hyena sure can. The fact that the hyena wasn't already closing in on the dead suggested that the animal was deterred by something over there.

Keeler's concern was the possible existence of living human beings, with their smells of tobacco, coffee, oil, urine and sweat. Not much else would deter a hyena from scavenging the kill, but maybe it was the vehicle, the fact that its engine was still ticking or something.

Yasmin had her phone up. She spoke Hebrew in a low voice. A couple of sentences in a cold military jargon. She ended the call and turned to Keeler.

"I told them to hold off a minute."

Them being the Israel Defense Forces Karakal battalion, Yasmin's unit. She and Keeler had been in the area hiking. They'd heard the gunshots and had moved to higher ground. Keeler had stopped her from rushing immediately to the dead, preferring to observe for a while first. The truth was, they didn't know what they were looking at. It could be a politically motivated attack, or the result of a dispute between traffickers. Ambushing first responders was an old tactic.

The hyena was still sniffing around, maybe curious at some small trace of scent. Keeler got the binoculars up again and scanned across the area around the bodies. Sweeping to the right, slowly sweeping back again. Going for depth and letting the landscape lead him along the contours of the desert.

Maybe the scavenging animal had sensed a wounded person, alive but tucked into the brush nearby. The hyena was gone when he lowered the binoculars.

Keeler said, "Let's hike down and around and set up on a likely exfiltration route. We'll get into position and you'll call it in. Get your people to make a ruckus. If there are perpetrators hiding in there, they'll move away from a real force. We'll be in place to catch them when they think they're safely out."

Yasmin said, "Presuming you are correct. How are you going to know which direction they'll take?" She raked her hair back, doing complicated things with a rubber band.

Keeler had examined the terrain. The border was on the other side of the dirt track below, maybe half a kilometer west. A few kilometers north was an Israeli town.

He said, "They'll move to the south-west." He pointed. "There."

"Hmm." She made a clicking sound, tongue against the roof of her mouth.

Six days earlier, Yasmin had been the sector commander in this area. She'd only just finished her army service in the *Karakal* battalion, a mixed gender combat unit responsible for the border zone. They'd met in a hospital room, where Keeler had been recovering from wounds sustained in the Syrian badlands. He'd been in the fight with Yasmin's sister Ruth, who was still hospitalized.

Yasmin had pulled Keeler out of the hospital, taken him south to the desert on a tour of her favorite spots. They'd been camping two kilometers away when she got the call. The current sector commander had been her deputy six days earlier and old habits die hard. The nearest combat unit was still fifteen or twenty minutes out. Keeler and Yasmin were the first responders.

Their position was south of the Gaza Strip, in a barren desert border zone where the state of Israel met Egypt. Keeler could make out foothills of the Sinai mountains to the southeast, the horizon already a craggy line of razor-sharp rock formations in red and purple. He liked this country, a place where things mattered, where every day routines seemed fragile, so obviously in need of protection.

Yasmin spoke into her phone. To Keeler, the Hebrew language was both soft and harsh. She was using a lot more areas of the throat than he was used to hearing, but then again, there were interesting things going on with the vowels, like two of them in a row without a consonant.

She said, "Okay, let's do it."

They crawled backwards out of the brush. Below the crest they both rolled onto their backs, looking at the desert sky, a beautiful purple now in the crepuscular moment.

Yasmin said, "Oh man, I love it here." She had a broad grin on her face, glowing with happiness. It filled Keeler with hope.

He fingered the bolt on the M4 in his hands. rolled back up into a crouch and started moving down, hearing Yasmin follow. They reached the floor of a dry riverbed, a *wadi* in local terms, and moved south. Five minutes later, Yasmin caught up with him. She was 23 years old. Tall and dark and dressed in jeans and some kind of hippy shirt. Carrying another M4 short barrel rifle and holding it like a pro. That was Yasmin. His appreciation of her only increased the more time went by, and showed no sign of peaking.

Ten minutes later, they mounted a hill, crawling to the top and getting belly down. Keeler had the binoculars. He couldn't see the bodies from there, but he got oriented.

He nudged her and chin pointed to the west. She followed his lead, and they moved quietly for another fifteen minutes. The descent was through another wadi, the rocky walls striated horizontally in multiple shades of pink, orange, and red. He figured this would be the best route if you were a perpetrator wanting to stay out of sight and move south.

Keeler led them up the dry riverbed until he found a cluster of boulders screening a shallow cave in the rocky wall. They could stay there and wait. The unspoken assumption was that they were looking for Bedouin traffickers who had infiltrated from Egypt.

Yasmin called it in on her phone. Speaking rapid Hebrew in hushed tones.

Keeler said, "Tell them to make a dramatic entrance."

She nodded to him, a tight smile on her face. "They're going to bring the noise."

It was getting darker. The whites of her eyes flashed at him, excited at the prospect of contact.

He got quiet and let his breathing settle down to low, like a cat relaxing for the hunt. Bedouin were capable of disappearing into the desert. You'd never find them if they knew you were present. Yasmin was only a couple of feet away, sitting with him in the rocky sand, back against the cave wall. They were physically aware of each other. It had been only six days, but those six days had been very intimate, right from the start.

It took fifteen minutes for the heavy bass line of two military helicopters to become apparent. He felt the vibrating tones come up from the stone and sand and rock, and making its way to the small bones in his inner ear. It was like listening to complicated music, like weird jazz or something. Keeler was an aficionado, understanding and interpreting the melody.

It sounded like the choppers had come in low, zipping through desert valleys, rising up fast and synchronized for maximum effect. Keeler pictured the pilots, flight helmets on, heads up displays crawling with data feeds, scanning with thermal imaging gear, and other, less well-known sensors.

There would be an Apache attack chopper in the lead, a Black Hawk troop carrier behind it.

He pictured men in the back of the Black Hawk, ready to go, clutching advanced firearms. Keeler corrected himself. There would be men and women in the back of the chopper because this particular unit was *Karakal*, currently around 70% female.

No sound of small arms fire from below, and no sound of the helicopters opening up with big guns. Just the thumping beat of rotors and the attendant military engine whine coming through in stereo. Yasmin shifted slightly, and Keeler read into it. She was anticipating the opposition coming down the wadi.

Not half wrong. Five minutes later she dug her fingernails into his knee. She already had the binoculars up, scanning to the north.

Yasmin spoke softly. "Two hundred meters, three males."

TWO

Keeler could just about make out the figures moving. They seemed to be carrying bulky packs.

"Armed?"

"I don't see weapons, but it's too dark to really tell." She put down the binoculars and faced him. "I'll break and speak to them, but I'll need you to cover." She pointed up the wadi. "You move up into position first."

He said, "How do you want to kick off?"

She didn't answer immediately, probably running through some options. Shoot one of them in the leg or the head, get their attention somehow. Keeler was up for whatever.

"I'll shout for them to *stop*. You put a round into the rocks, across their path. That way, maybe they'll think a bunch of us have surrounded them. They won't know it's just us two."

Decent plan.

Keeler moved out, keeping the large boulders between himself and the oncoming men, making his way north. The men were a hundred meters away when he settled into a good spot, allowing a clear field of fire while reducing the danger of hitting Yasmin. He watched them come, hiking steadily in a single file down the wadi bed, crunching gravel under what looked like shower slippers, none of them speaking.

The sun had gone below the horizon and the entire wadi was in shadow. One moment the men were trudging south along the western edge, a moment later they were gone. Simply disappeared into some crevice in the rock face. Yasmin moved quickly across the dry wadi bed. Keeler stopped her in the middle, holding her arm and speaking in a whisper.

"Go easy."

He let go of her arm and took point, moving swiftly but quietly across. Keeler had to get close to the rock wall to actually see detail. The residual light from the sunset had faded and there was now only a thin gloom.

Yasmin flicked on her phone light and did the smart thing, looked for tracks. They had overshot by around fifteen meters. The men had entered a slim crevice in the wall, a crack so narrow that it looked unlikely a person could fit through there. She turned the light off.

"There's going to be a tunnel on the other side of that. Bet you a million bucks."

A bleep came from her phone.

Keeler watched as Yasmin spoke in hushed tones. Not many sentences, but the last one came out differently, emotionally. She ended the call and crouched, leaning back against the rock face.

"I know one of the dead back there. He's a friend."

"From your unit?"

"No, from the town up there." She pointed north, glancing up at him.

Keeler saw the hurt, knowing that the community down here in the south was small but tightly knit.

She said, "He's a guy who ran the Friday pub night. Just a dumb thing like that." Yasmin was shaking her head, back and forth, cursing. She stood up. "It's going to take them too long to get here. Those murderers will be gone by then, safe and free on the other side."

Yasmin had been the *Karakal* unit commander here for fifteen months. She was still in the military mindset. Keeler should have anticipated it, but he hadn't. She was closer to the narrow crevice than him and moved into it quickly, squeezing her body through.

It took him a half second to realize what she was doing, but by then it was too late. He darted in and managed to get an arm through the fissure, clutching a piece of her sleeve, but that was it. She tore away from his grasp. Keeler tried to squeeze through the way she'd done, but it wasn't going to work. They weren't the same size.

He had to slow down, lower his body, and get into a contorted position. The lower part of the crevice was wide enough to crawl, or to push bulky backpacks through. A skinnier person could just squeeze through. Keeler had very little body fat, but he wasn't skinny. He was built like a bulging sack of walnuts.

It took him two minutes to make his way through five yards of tight rock formation. The other side was a mini canyon, sky above, steep rock face on either side. Twenty yards in and the canyon dead ended to a hole in the rock, a concentration of black in the darkness. There was no other place that Yasmin and those men could have gone. The entrance was about five feet high. He got in there and started moving, crouching low.

He could see exactly nothing for the first fifty yards. He figured this was a natural cave, not man made. Keeler came around a turn and the passage opened up into a cavern the size of a modest kitchen. A rusty piece of corrugated steel sheeting was set right into the middle of it, Yasmin was crouched there, clearly waiting for him. Keeler stepped in and raised his weapon to cover her.

She lifted the corrugated steel sheet an inch and electric light spilled out. There was an iron rung ladder built into the side of a shaft going straight down into the earth. Yasmin was right about one thing. If they didn't go now, the killers would get away. If the tunnel was here, they'd still have 500 meters to go, getting under the border fence. Presumably the same again on the other side.

He said, "Did you call this in?"

She was looking at him, eyes wide, committed and expecting him to follow. "They'd never agree to it. Let's go in there, get those assholes, and bring them back. Simple. It'll take half an hour and we won't even have to tell anyone what we did."

Keeler looked at her, liking this woman who'd been his intimate companion for the past week. This was do or die time and he probably didn't have a choice. Either he followed her lead, or he lived to regret not doing so.

The men had a couple of minutes on them, but they carried heavy packs. Plus it wasn't a hundred percent clear that they knew Keeler and Yasmin were on their tail. Looking at her crouched there with her weapon ready, itching to get involved. Yeah, she was officially out of the military, but her head and heart were deep in the fight, that was for damned sure.

He nodded at her, not saying the words, but communicating them just the same. *Let's do it.*

THREE

The vertical shaft plunged thirty meters or more into the earth.

Coming down the ladder, Keeler was reflecting on what he knew about the situation. He'd had a week with Yasmin, and she was steeped in it. For one thing, tunnel systems were ubiquitous. This tunnel was deep enough that the stone strata would block ground penetrating radar. There were other ways of finding tunnels, and the Israelis were using all possible means. What Keeler knew: it was whack-a-mole. They'd bomb one tunnel only for another to appear the next week, or month, or day, or year.

It wasn't just the ISIS people in Sinai, or the Hamas and Islamic Jihad maniacs in Gaza, there was big money to be made with cross border traffic. From what Yasmin had told him, it was the Egyptian military brass who got most of the benefit and none of the risks.

This subterranean passage had been operational for quite a while. The cable housing feeding electricity into the lighting system was worn with age. The rungs stuck in the wall were not covered in rust, which suggested constant use. At the bottom, Yasmin dropped to the floor. Keeler landed behind her, putting his hand to the humid sand and stone. There weren't three ways out of there. It was either straight ahead or the long climb up.

The border fence was a half kilometer away. Each step would be a meter, give or take. He counted to five hundred, and nothing changed. The tunnel simply continued. He looked at Yasmin and got a nod. She'd been counting as well. He figured another five hundred meters to the exit. The engineers might have thought to make it symmetrical.

He was wrong.

A hundred steps further in and the tunnel turned sharp right, presumably to the north, but impossible to really know. They arrived ten minutes later at another vertical shaft with iron rungs stuck into the side. Keeler climbed first. The tunnel must have had a hidden incline because the shaft wasn't even half as deep here as on the Israeli side.

At the top of the ladder was a more conventionally hinged trap door with a handle.

Keeler raised the hatch a half inch.

It looked like an empty room in the dark. He swiveled around in a one eighty seeing a closed door, the edged framed with light. Definitely something on the other side. He pushed the hatch up and laid it open carefully. He inched out, covering, as Yasmin followed. There were voices coming from the other side of the door, men speaking in Arabic.

He didn't need to understand the language to know that they were pleased with themselves. Laughter and shouts, rapidly articulated sentences and low murmurs of approval.

Yasmin wanted to return those men to Israel, where the security services could figure out what had happened back there with the bodies. That was the optimal solution. Keeler took the right side of the door, feeling her come up on his shoulder. He stepped back so that she could take point. She spoke the language, he didn't. They made eye contact, and she went through the door, shouting.

Her voice was commanding, projecting loudly in Arabic. Meanwhile, Keeler was getting situational awareness. They were in what looked to be a coffee break room, hence a table with chairs and the sink, a gas stove and coffee making gear, which in this part of the world consisted of a single long handled pot, besides the coffee and sugar.

Three men were seated around a table. Keeler recognized their clothes. The same men as before, wearing shower slippers. If they'd been having a good time a moment ago, the mood had changed. Two bottles of vodka and a torn open carton of Marlboro lights took up space on the table. One bottle had been half emptied already. A white plastic cup took up a sipping position in front of each man.

Yasmin had her weapon on them, was speaking fast and indicating actions she wanted them to perform. Keeler was still looking around. He could smell diesel fuel and oil, a metallic odor as well, maybe the scent of shredded steel. This place was a light industrial facility. He wouldn't be surprised to find a workshop with machinery, say a thing that pressed metal into thinner metal, or some other kind of primary manufacturing process that had blown minds a couple hundred years ago.

Yasmin shot him a look like she wanted some help. He stepped up and did his part. Making the men hand over their phones. The first two slid their phones and ID wallets onto the table, like this was something they were often asked to do. The third man began to argue in Arabic, a language Keeler couldn't understand.

Yasmin said, "The guy's resisting. Take it from him."

Keeler pinned the man by his neck to the table top. There was a momentary attempt at resistance before the guy went slack. Keeler searched him, finding one of those smart phone wallets with compartments for credit cards and stuff in his jacket pocket. The M4 was hanging awkwardly. He slid the man's phone into his back pocket and stepped away, getting the weapon into a more useful position.

The man glared at him with what Keeler thought was unusual malevolence. The other two were docile, but maybe they'd been drinking more. Keeler glanced into the third man's cup and saw only the black opacity of coffee. He wasn't drinking alcohol. One of the drunk men said something that Keeler figured was a joking tone. The others didn't laugh.

Yasmin was examining the identity documents. She glanced at Keeler, chin pointing to indicate the third guy with the coffee.

Keeler pulled the man's phone wallet loose from his back pocket, and a flutter of paper came out with it, spilling out onto the floor. "Shit."

The white paper and cards landing on the cheap tiles. Keeler bent and retrieved them. Three receipts and two business cards. Keeler tossed the phone onto the table for Yasmin and slid the other stuff to the guy, still looking unhappy.

Yasmin was examining a laminated card she'd pulled from the phone case. She read from the card. "Jafar," looking up at him.

Jafar brooded and said nothing.

She began speaking in an enquiring tone, like an interrogator. The guy responded in monosyllables. Yasmin kept going. The guy responded again.

She spoke English to Keeler, holding up the identity card. "This guy has a fake Israeli ID card."

The card looked like an American driver's license combined with a credit card, except all the writing was in Hebrew and

Arabic. An identity card with a chip in it. The man's face was there in black and white. He wasn't bearded in the photograph and was maybe ten years younger. Keeler couldn't read anything, of course.

She read the name out again, looking at the guy. "Jafar Al-Husseini." The guy mumbled something and Yasmin looked at Keeler again. "Fake name too." Holding up the card. "Very good forgery, but it wouldn't pass the biometrics, I guess." She extended two fingers at the other men. "These two are from El-Arish, the main town up in North Sinai. They aren't Bedouin, just Egyptians. Say they've been caught before going across. The army just brings them back to Egypt. The Egyptian soldiers beat the shit out of them when that happens." She tossed the IDs on the table with the phones.

Keeler said, "What about the bodies back on the other side?"

Yasmin said, "They claim to know nothing about it. We'll see what they say to the police in a proper interrogation."

No weapons in sight. The men hadn't been armed.

Keeler had them squat against the wall near the door to the tunnel shaft. It was time to get out of there, bring the infiltrators back over the border, and figure out what had gone on with the killings. But Yasmin was in the next room, looking into boxes.

She said, "Discarded table saw blades. A box full of tangled wire." She came back in with a shrug. "Nothing crazy."

Which Keeler interpreted as 'nothing related to terrorism'.

The men's backpacks had been set on a large stainless steel kitchen work top. He walked over and examined them. The packs were full of bottles of cheap Israeli vodka and cartons of Marlboros. Alcohol is illegal for most people in Egypt. This looked to have been a shopping trip. So what was the deal with the bodies?

Keeler said, "These guys crossed over for vodka and cigarettes."

Yasmin said, "Well, they *came back* with vodka and cigarettes." She gave him a look. "That isn't the same thing."

Which was a hundred percent true. At that point, there was no way of knowing what had taken place and who these men were. They'd need to be interrogated.

He was going to make a comment, but the sound of something metal and heavy falling onto a concrete floor came from some other part of the warehouse, resounding and echoing for a second. Keeler's weapon was up and he moved, leaving Yasmin with a look that said, 'keep these guys under control'. The three men watched him as he went, faces suddenly tight as terror crept in through the alcohol haze.

The M4 rifle was set up with aiming lights and optical gunsights. This was Yasmin's sister's weapon. Since Ruth was currently recovering from wounds sustained in Syria, her little sister was taking care of it. Which meant that Keeler hadn't dialed the gear in since he'd been handed the weapon an hour or two before. Not that it was hard to improvise. He flicked on the gunsight, looking through advanced optics that offered up an infrared reticle with 2x magnification. Scanning and walking, keeping close to the walls, being a shadow in the shadows.

Something changed, like a kind of electric charge in the air. Keeler stopped moving, not breathing, and simply let himself listen. A scuffle of boot around the corner. Someone was trying to creep up on them. What he didn't know, how many men he was facing. It's one thing to come blind to one guy, but if it's three, the advantage of surprise would last a third as long. Or maybe the probabilities moved logarithmically. Keeler's math was rusty.

Across the corridor was another room. He stepped through and backed into shelves. Keeler got the weapon up. Through the infrared scope, he saw two men creep past the corner in tactical formation. For a moment he thought he was looking at a special tactics JSOC squad like his own. A third operator came after them, all three of them scanning through scopes mounted on weapons very much like the M4 he was holding.

But these weren't Americans. It was an Egyptian special forces squad.

FOUR

Keeler took his eye from the scope and lowered the weapon. He backed out of sight and started thinking. This was going to kick off and there were any number of ways that it could go seriously lopsided. You don't just shoot at Egyptian operators on their own soil. While Egypt and the USA were technically allies, he didn't know a single American operator who would enjoy partnering with these people.

But if he wasn't going to kill them, he'd have to meet them.

The trick was going to be making it, so they didn't get startled and kill him. At the same time, he was an active service US Air Force officer in a special tactics unit. It would be complicated if the Egyptians found out. A quandary. Keeler enjoyed puzzles. Don't get shot, don't be identified as a serving American officer. He had one thing going for him, a fluent command of the French language, thanks to his mother.

Keeler called out in French. He wasn't trying to communicate anything more complicated than 'don't shoot me', and at the same time, signal the ploy to Yasmin.

"*Je suis Francais. Ne tirer pas, s'il vous plaît.*" He followed that with its English equivalent. "Don't shoot, I am French."

What followed was a torrent of excited Arabic and three laser dots spinning over the wall in his direction. No bullets were fired, thankfully. Keeler leaned the M4 against a shelving unit and walked out of the alcove with his hands first, waving them in the air slowly.

"French. Don't shoot. Je suis Francais. Ne tirer pas, s'il vous plaît."

He didn't get far, clearing the opening to find a masked soldier moving aggressively at him. There was a second and a half of furious action. The soldier raising his rifle, swinging the thing around to hit him with the butt. Keeler ducked instinctively to avoid the blow. Kicking into the man's groin and making contact, feeling the soft parts squish under the hard sole of his hiking boot.

The soldier squawked and fell back. Other men were on Keeler, beating him down furiously with fists, feet, and rifle butts. He protected his head and endured several seconds of frenzied pummelling until someone shouted. The violence stopped and Keeler was able to hear Yasmin speaking loud and clear in Arabic.

She was trying to sound both reassuring and commanding. Two men lifted Keeler by the elbows and threw him into the room where the three infiltrators were clustered. He stabilized himself against the wall, watching the masked commandoes descend upon the three unfortunate men, beating them with rifles until they cowered in the corner.

Yasmin was still speaking, hands up, as if trying to be reasonable. She was moving to Keeler, putting a palm against his shoulder and keeping herself between him and the soldiers. He wasn't that concerned, taking a look at the gear, scanning and making inferences in the space of a second and a half. The tactical vests weren't so different from what Keeler's team might wear, but instead of a muted American flag badge, these men sported the green, red and black Egyptian flag.

He already knew their unit insignia, an eagle killing some kind of monster. These were *El-Sa'Ka forces*, tier one Egyptian operators known for brutality towards political prisoners and extrajudicial killings.

The gravelly bass octave of a male voice barked from behind the soldiers. It was enough to make the *El-Sa'Ka* men turn. Yasmin stopped talking. The soldiers parted to make way for the man, striding through in civilian clothes, making the wonderful sounds of the Arabic language.

He was in his forties, dressed like he'd just come from bingo night at an Egyptian coastal resort. Jeans, blue-collared shirt open at the neck and a black leather jacket. The shoes were shiny brown. The man's face was tanned and handsome, his body just beginning the process of expansion that would peak after a few years of middle age.

Yasmin began to speak calmly in Arabic, some lengthy monologue that Keeler had no hope of understanding. He got the tones though. She was speaking like a professional, the way a good lawyer faces a judge.

The man responded with a monosyllable, and she nodded. The cologne hit Keeler then, a sharp acrid smell of animal glands that was supposed to be seductive. The guy looked at Keeler and spoke in perfect French.

"You're the Frenchman?"

"Oui."

The man indicated Yasmin. "What are you doing here with her?"

He said, "We're on our honeymoon."

Which shocked the guy into complete physical paralysis for a second, before he burst out in an ugly laugh. Pointing at the tricked out M4 rifles collected by the commandos. He said, "Let me ask you again. What are you doing here in my country, armed and accompanied by an Israeli military officer?"

Keeler working on his French accent, channeling mom. "I'm not permitted to say."

An improvised response. Instinctive, and maybe stupid. He figured, make the guy think he was a French spook, that might throw him off balance, force him to think twice before doing anything rash. Looking at the Egyptian, a member of the elite ruling caste, dressed like he'd just come from the polo club. He'd be some kind of intelligence officer.

The man lost interest in Keeler, uttering a long growl of Arabic to Yasmin. She seemed to agree and responded, after which the man fired off verbiage thick and fast. She glanced towards Keeler, obviously saying something about him. The intelligence officer turned and examined Keeler again, head to toe.

He said, "I lived in Paris as a child. My parents had a villa in the 16th arrondissement. You French are pigs, but you know how to be rich." He snorted and spit on the floor.

The man barked a command to the soldiers. One of them responded in a short barrage of Arabic and ran out of the room. Another soldier stepped forward with a smart phone and took pictures of Keeler and Yasmin separately. The officer stepped into a photo of Keeler, which was weird, like he was a trophy catch.

The other thing Keeler did notice was that neither the *El-Sa'Ka* operators nor the intelligence officer seemed to have the slightest interest in the three men who had infiltrated in and out of Israel. They were still there, squatting by the wall with their hands on their heads, looking frightened for their lives.

The soldier returned with a handful of zip-ties and white cloth strips. One of his buddies barked commands to the men sitting at the table. They scrambled to their feet. The soldiers blindfolded the infiltrators and zip tied their hands behind their backs. Pushed their faces up against the wall.

The officer jerked his head at Keeler and Yasmin and growled. Two *El-Sa'Ka* men approached. Yasmin began speaking quickly in Arabic. She was going for a commanding voice, but it wasn't working on them. Keeler noticed that she was surprised, maybe even a little shocked. She gave him a look, and he tried to nod subtly, telling her to submit.

At the moment, there was no other option.

Yasmin turned away, her shoulders dropping as the soldiers blindfolded her. Keeler's arms were pulled behind his back and he submitted to the procedure, a full body search and the binding of his wrists.

Keeler was frog marched out of the warehouse, a type of accompanied conveyance that hadn't happened to him for years, maybe since one of the many trials and tribulations on the way from boot camp to being a member of the killer elite. It seemed like the *El-Sa'Ka* guys either side of him thought it was amusing to make him bump into things on the way.

The breeze and the ground surface told him they were outside. A couple of seconds later, the tailgate of a pickup truck hit Keeler just above the knees. He folded and allowed himself to be shoved into the vehicle's bed. Yasmin was pushed in beside him. The *El-Sa'Ka* men screaming at them, Keeler not understanding a word. Feeling Yasmin shuffle up towards the cab. He could feel her legs against his shoulders. A heavy boot was placed on his neck, pinning him to the bed of the truck.

Keeler didn't like that.

FIVE

THE COLONEL WATCHED the Israeli woman and her friend being led away, his commandos forcing them to bend forward uncomfortably. He jerked his head at the cowering peasants in the corner, zip tied and blindfolded. The El-Sa'Ka in the room were watching him.

He said, "Take them to the front room and wait for me."

The three were led away, strong hands at the nape of each man's neck, one commando for one prisoner. The colonel tapped the last soldier on the shoulder and put up a single finger. *Wait*.

He let the two others leave the room and observed the prisoner for a moment. Jafar Al-Husseini stood, hunched by the pressure being exerted on his neck. The white blindfold and the hands zip-tied behind his back. Probably not the first time he'd had this experience.

The colonel said, "Cut him loose."

The soldier obeyed and released Al-Husseini, who stood straight while the zip-tie was snipped. The colonel allowed him to remove the blindfold himself.

He looked at the soldier. "Go with the others. We'll be a few minutes." When the man had gone out of the room, he pointed to the table. "Sit."

Al-Husseini was massaging his wrists. "That wasn't very nice."

The colonel said, "What comes next will be even worse, but luckily you won't be around for it."

Al-Husseini moved to the table and retrieved his phone wallet and identity card.

He said, "Who the hell was that?"

The colonel sat down and found a clean plastic cup, poured himself a couple fingers of pure vodka. He lit a cigarette.

"I don't know exactly." He exhaled a thin stream of tobacco smoke. "Why are you carrying your identity card? Did they see it?"

"They saw it. What did you want me to do, leave it under a rock in the desert?"

The colonel hadn't considered the question before because it had never come up. He said, "You always bring your ID with you when you come?"

Al-Husseini said, "Yes."

"So next time you won't."

Al-Husseini examined the phone in his hand. "There was something back over the border. A fight among the Bedouin. Nothing to do with us, if you can believe it. I think those two infidels came over because of that."

"Chasing you?"

Al-Husseini nodded. "It's what you call a surprise." He quoted from the *Quran,* "Never will we be struck except by what Allah has decreed for us; He is our protector."

The colonel wasn't a believer, unless believing in opportunity counted. This however, was not a good situation. There would be a cleansing needed. First of all, the two scum bags whom Al-Husseini used for cover as a simple smuggler. The Israeli and her friend needed to be more carefully eliminated.

In the meantime, he wanted his stuff.

"Gimmee."

Al-Husseini slid the phone out of its case and set it down on the workbench. He fiddled with the back of the device and removed the SIM card. Behind it was a second slot with a micro-SIM. He pried it out with a fingernail. The micro-SIM was a quarter the size of his pinky nail. He let it sit on the pad of a finger, waiting for the Egyptian Colonel.

The colonel retrieved a fancy pen from an interior jacket pocket. He removed the nib and feed, accessing a recessed slot behind the ink cartridge. He produced a pair of tweezers, took the micro-SIM from Al-Husseini and inserted it into the pen. He reset the nib and feed without the ink and pushed the pen's clip, holding it in for three seconds.

It was semi-embarrassing that they needed to do this physically, like a World War Two movie or something. Two agents huddled over a dead drop. Fact was the Americans and Israelis dominated the electromagnetic spectrum so thoroughly that no wireless communication was safe.

He said, "Tell me about what I'm going to find here."

Al-Husseini said, "You gave me fifteen addresses on the list. I got into four of them. I don't remember the names but it was Rishon Le Zion, Petach Tikvah, Bet Shemesh and the place in Tel-Aviv."

The colonel said, "In the Old North."

"Right."

"No issues?"

"No. The place in Rishon was good. That's one very organized guy, everything filed correctly. I think you'll be happy."

"What did you get, just paper?"

Al-Husseini tapped his head. "Got a lot of paper, including

some in French, which I can't read, but I scanned it anyway. I also put your thing into his laptop and it seemed to work. I hope it makes you happy."

The colonel didn't respond, except for another exhalation of cigarette smoke. Al-Husseini was essentially a common thief. An Israeli Arab guy who had a little burglary crew. The Egyptian Mukhabarat ran him as a low level agent. They had his crew breaking into the homes of retired and active Israeli security officials. Al-Husseini was trained to look for interesting documents, the mundane and not so mundane material that might be used to build up the Egyptian Security Service profile of their Israeli counterparts. These people were part of a bureaucracy, and like anyone else they developed a paper trail. Some of them had Swiss bank accounts, that kind of thing. If they were on a job, travel expenses needed to be claimed. Retirement benefits interrupted by the occasional temporary contract were also of interest.

And sometimes they kept official files at home.

The Rishon Le Zion address belonged to an active member of the Shin-Bet, Israel's internal intelligence agency. But the colonel was not going to reveal his hopes to Jafar Al-Husseini.

A soft bleep signaled the completion of the transfer operation.

The colonel removed the micro-SIM with the tweezers and fumbled it, snatching it as it fell to the floor. He bent and pressed the pad of a forefinger into the micro-SIM, letting the natural oils from his skin adhere to the chip. He took the tweezers and held the SIM by a corner, taking a disposable lighter to it, letting the chip drop to the worktop in flames, watching it immolate.

When it had finished burning, the colonel swept the ashes to the floor with a hand.

He said, "I guess we'll have to get you back through a different tunnel."

Al-Husseini said nothing, which meant he wanted money. The colonel unstrapped a large money belt from his waist, which required pulling out his shirt and getting in there. He unzipped the main compartment and counted out eight thousand dollars. Two grand for each successful burglary. The amount of reward seemed to be sufficient to keep Al-Husseini at it.

He slid the cash across the table and remembered the vodka that he'd poured. The colonel picked up the plastic cup, throwing the cheap alcohol back in one go and letting it burn down his throat.

He watched the other man put a hand over the stack of cash and carefully fold it into something he could pocket.

The colonel said, "I'll have a couple of men bring you to another crossing point."

"I don't want to go anywhere near Gaza."

"Who does?"

He left Jafar Al-Husseini sitting at the table in front of the vodka, looking nervous. Walking out of there, the colonel felt his chest constrict, like a steel band was closing around the top of his rib cage. Like a heart attack was imminent.

He was already involved in complications, now he had more complications. Once the complication turned into unmanageable complexity, he'd probably just die, at least that's what a cardiologist friend of his told him in Cairo.

Luckily he had Anastasia, his Russian treasure up in El-Arish. Although, *had* wasn't exactly true, and not only because she was a prostitute. He could dream though, and the colonel did. Another consequence of his relationship with the lovely Anastasia was a marked increase in the colonel checking his phone.

He did so once again, finding no new message from her. He tapped into the thread, skimming over the last one, dated a few days earlier. He was up in the Sinai pretty often, and there was usually a flurry of communications preceding each trip.

She'd texted, 'I've been counting the days my colonel. We'll make memories.' The words were in Arabic, intermingled with heart emojis in pink and red.

In the front room the two unfortunate smugglers squatted zip tied and blindfolded, facing the wall. Five heavily armed El-Sa'Ka commandos stood around smoking cigarettes. The colonel made a hand gesture to their commanding officer.

He let them leave the room before making the phone call.

The major answered on the first ring. "Where are you?"

The colonel said, "We'll have to have the meeting elsewhere, there's a new problem to discuss. I'll send you coordinates."

"What problem?"

The colonel lit another cigarette, futzing with the pack. He spoke with his lips around the filter. "You'll see. Nobody's going to like it, prepare the general for that."

The major made the lip smacking sounds of a cigarette being smoked. He didn't even bother to speak, just letting the call hang there like an unwanted acquaintance. The colonel ended the call.

SIX

THE BOOT WAS LIFTED from Keeler's neck.

The *El-Sa'Ka* soldiers stopped yelling and screaming and a kind of quiet settled over the situation, viewed from inside the blindfold as a milky darkness. Voices came from inside the building, approaching and then spilling out into the yard or wherever the truck was parked. Keeler listened to someone moan and the sound of scraping over sand, people moving, heavy breathing and stern commands followed by hoarse shouting, which Keeler figured came from two or three people. A thin cry of pitiful pleading cut through the ambient noise, words spoken in Arabic, incomprehensible to Keeler. The whining tone was abruptly cut down by a rude and sustained rattle of semi-automatic weapons fire.

Keeler mentally wrote those three infiltrators off, despite the blindfold, imagining how they'd look, slumped against a wall now, executed and surely dead. He was trying to interpret the fact that he and Yasmin were in the back of a pickup truck. Maybe that meant that they weren't going to be shot just yet.

But he couldn't help from wondering why the *El-Sa'Ka* commandos would need to execute those men. What did they gain, what were they afraid of? Was it just what they did with people, maybe for fun?

The truck set off, jolting and bumping over pitted roads, Keeler's skull vibrating with it. The soldier's boot was off him now, so he rested his head on Yasmin's leg, while she did the same on his, both protected from continuously slamming into the steel truck bed.

It gave him a little space to think.

Yasmin had been hasty pursuing the infiltrators into Egyptian territory. That had been a rash and unwise thing to do. He knew it and knew that she knew it. Right now wasn't the time to dwell on that. His operational assumption had to be that they were being transported to a military base. This would probably be the administrative procedure, given the situation. They'd be processed there, documented and dealt with, maybe even interrogated by the Egyptian security service, the *Mukhabarat*.

That was going to be annoying.

At the same time the Egyptian government had a peace treaty with Israel, and depended upon its western allies like France, the UK, and the United States for money and weapons. The simple version was that the western allies held their noses and paid, figuring better a brutal military dictatorship than a brutal Islamist caliphate, a wise choice in Keeler's opinion. Which is why he was optimistic. He figured that any *Mukhabarat* officer who jeopardized the flow of cash was borderline suicidal, since the dictators and cronies enjoyed their villas, luxury cars and beach club memberships.

Keeler estimated 24 hours at the most. Holding them further would make it potentially political. In the end they'd be handed over to the Israelis at the border. This was his assumption, but he was aware of other possibilities, the unknown unknowns. He wasn't carrying any identification,

Yasmin had understood his gambit. He'd play a dumb French guy all the way, riding the legend like the bad cover story it was.

An hour later, the truck skidded to a halt, throwing him violently against the back of the cab. He managed to tuck his chin into the chest and took the hit on the shoulders.

Yasmin yelped beside him and was pulled away. He heard her body hit the ground outside. They'd pulled her off like a sack of potatoes, letting her fall, hands bound behind her. His boot was gripped and yanked hard. Since he'd had the warning from Yasmin, Keeler was able to twist onto his back and aim his other boot where he estimated the soldier's head would be. The heel landed on something solid and Keeler wasn't being pulled anymore. He came upright, swinging legs over the open tail gate.

Being in a fight blindfolded with hands bound behind him wasn't a new experience, but it was never a great one. This time it was over fast. As soon as he sat up a heavy fist like object slammed into his face, knocking him back and coming close to giving him whiplash. He was working on the next idea when Yasmin's voice cut through the grunting and pounding sounds.

"Cut it out. There's no point."

Totally correct, and exactly what he'd told himself in the beginning, when they'd first been zip tied and blindfolded. Keeler stopped struggling and two men grabbed him roughly, yanking him to his feet. He was marched a short distance on rough gravel and sand. The two men holding him stopped, gripping his shoulders and elbows hard. A chill wind swept in, whipping at his hair and making a rushing sound as it came through desert and low brush.

At least two large engines purred nearby. Keeler corrected that thought. Three large engines, most likely corresponding to the same quantity of militarized vehicles. More tires rolling over sand, slowly. A fourth engine purring back there, only slightly less aggressive than the others.

～

THE COLONEL SAT in the back of his Toyota Land Cruiser. The driver up front nothing more than a closely cropped haircut to him. It's what he called the guy in private, *the haircut*. The general's glossy black Chevy Suburban rolled past, joining the melee of military vehicles making a circle around the captives. If there was one thing that the El-Sa'Ka were very good for, it was intimidation.

The colonel came out of the Land Cruiser and made the walk over hard sand to the huge Chevy. He opened the rear door, revealing a beige leather interior, highly customized according to the general's preferences and delivered like a gift by the Americans.

Inside were two of the colonel's Mukhabarat colleagues. They weren't friends, more like co-conspirators. In other words, ambitious rivals. The interior was setup like a limousine. Two large bench seats facing each other. The major was facing backwards, looking at him from underneath the dark curls of a young and ambitious man. The colonel vaulted into the vehicle and sat beside him.

The general was in the rear seat facing forward, a clean-shaven face below a cleanly shaved head, the totality of the man above the neck like a polished oak knob. The colonel handed the pen gadget to the major.

He said, "Apparently some good material there."

The major made a humming sound. He said, "Okay."

The general was on the phone, looking out the side window and listening to someone on the other end of the line. He hadn't even looked at the colonel yet.

The major said, "How much did you pay Al-Husseini?"

"Eight."

"Fine. He's happy with that?"

"Apparently."

The major made his face into a surprised expression, like, 'who would have thunk it.' The budgeted funds for running Al-Husseini were at least double that, which meant more for them to embezzle.

The general ended his call with a grunt. He looked at the colonel, eyes deeply recessed into the skull, dark orbs always in shadow.

The general and the colonel were the same age.

The general said, "Speak."

The colonel told them about the Israeli woman and the guy pretending to be French. The colonel told them his plan, what he thought they should do with the two of them.

When the colonel had finished speaking, the general looked at the major. The major smacked his lips and raked his fingers through oiled hair. The two of them always seemed to communicate without speaking, making the colonel feel left out of the loop, even though he did most of the leg work.

The major said, "I think you ought to verify that he's French, or not French, just so we know of course." He shot a look at the general, who this time nodded his head. "Then, like you said. Take care of them and make sure it's not us."

The colonel said, "Do you have any ideas on how to verify that?"

The major said, "No, but I'm sure you do."

Which happened to be the truth and led to a second uncomfortable truth. The burden of competence is that the competent are almost always the ones who stick their necks out the most. The colonel was often suspecting that strategic incompetence was actually a higher form of performance, he was just unable to do it.

The major handed him a portfolio folder, closed with an elastic band.

"This is for the Americans."

The colonel said, "I thought you were going to give it to them?"

The general said, "He's a major. The Americans will be more impressed with a colonel."

The major shrugged, a little smirk lifting the corner of his mouth.

The colonel walked back to his Land Cruiser. He handed the documents to his driver through the window. The major was too junior for the CIA, and the general was too senior. Therefore, the colonel was just perfect, like goldilocks and the porridge.

It made him think that his entire rank and position had been engineered simply for the purpose of being a useful idiot. He put that thought out of his mind because it was ultimately not useful.

SEVEN

THE BLINDFOLD WAS REMOVED and Keeler blinked into total whiteness, resolving in a couple of seconds to three sets of bright halogen lights mounted on militarized pickup trucks. Yasmin was right beside him, eyes squeezed shut. They were harshly lit and exposed, subjects of attention in the center of a circle made by the vehicles. He could make out the silhouette of soldiers standing up on truck beds, watching. Others were faintly outlined leaning against the vehicles, maybe a dozen men in all. From the silhouettes Keeler could see that they were outfitted in full combat gear, helmets and tactical vests and weapons.

Someone was moving behind him and he felt the zip ties being clipped, his hands came free. The Egyptian officer from before entered the circle. The back light from the halogens revealed an ambitious black hair dye and comb-over job. He was looking at Keeler intensely, ignoring Yasmin.

The man spoke in French. "Have you ever trained with our Egyptian soldiers?"

Keeler had done one joint training exercise in Cyprus with Egyptian and Jordanian special forces. On a thing like that, you figured the country would send their finest soldiers.

He said, "I have."

"What did you think of their quality, as soldiers?"

Keeler said, "You're asking me to give you an honest answer?"

"Yes."

The Egyptian had a leer on his face, like he was looking at something pornographic. Sometimes people ask you something and don't want an answer, their question is rhetorical. Other times they're actually interested to know what you think. With this guy, he wasn't sure.

Keeler said, "Nice guys as individuals." Which was true. The men he'd met were almost too nice, like all they wanted to do was please you.

"Yes, but as soldiers. Please."

As soldiers the Egyptians lacked unit discipline without severe authority. The worst thing was their inability to take initiative. What they'd told Keeler was how recruits get the shit kicked out of them and forced into doing dumb disciplinarian stuff all the time. Not that dumb disciplinarian stuff didn't exist in every army, but for these guys it was over the top.

He said, "Excellent soldiers, the best in the world."

The guy was smiling, as if Keeler's words had made him happy for some reason. He walked close and clapped him on the shoulder. The man winked and spoke in English.

"I got you." Grinning from ear to ear. "You couldn't help but say it. We've never done a joint exercise with the French military. You're about as French as a French fry my friend. As French as me. Anyway, your American accent is obvious."

The man looked at Yasmin. "And you, tell me about the Egyptian soldier's qualities, in your estimation."

Keeler saw Yasmin and knew that she was thinking, calculating, maybe hoping for the best. She said, "From what I've seen colonel, the Egyptian soldiers are very competent."

The man looked disappointed. Keeler figured that colonel was his military rank in the Egyptian services. Maybe Yasmin had picked up on how the men had addressed him.

Two soldiers approached on either side of the colonel. Each held one of the M4 rifles that Keeler and Yasmin had brought over the border. The soldiers cleared the weapons and removed the magazines. Each weapon was laid down, the magazines were emptied of ammunition and placed alongside the rifles.

The colonel walked back to the vehicles. The two soldiers hadn't moved. They stood silent, watchful and alert behind their face masks, doing their best to give off hooligan vibes. Engines began to growl and men mounted, putting weight onto suspension springs. A guy got behind one of the heavy machine guns and pointed it at Keeler. What a joker, these people had no manners.

Keeler wasn't sure what was about to happen. He waited, flicking his gaze over whatever presented itself as information. The weapons lying there on the hard desert floor. Two Israel Defense Forces issue M4 rifles with a variety of attachments, some only available to the IDF. Two empty magazines. If Keeler and Yasmin were about to be machine gunned, the setup wouldn't be correct. He figured they weren't about to be executed. He felt his body relaxing a little.

Keeler looked at Yasmin, caught her eye. She seemed concerned. He winked, which produced a quick laugh from her. She was saying something but he couldn't make it out over the engine roar, big tires skidding in the sand. After about a minute and a half of vehicular noise, halogen lights and dust clouds, the Toyota trucks had become small red tail lights disappearing into the distance. Half a minute later the desert night had completely closed in. The bright stars made visibility high, which Keeler was on the fence about, if it was a good or a bad thing.

He picked up one of the M4s and retrieved the magazine, inspecting it and blowing off any detritus that might have entered the action. He snapped the magazine into the rifle just so it all kept free of sand and dust. Yasmin did the same with the other weapon.

Keeler said, "I guess we stepped into some shit."

EIGHT

YASMIN LOCATED THE BIG DIPPER, made a little diagonal line from the dipper's lip to find the North Star and the east. Keeler was already tilting his head in that direction.

He said, "Let's move. No point in remaining static."

He set off at a fast clip, Yasmin trailing Keeler's longer legs and catching up.

They needed to move east, that's all she knew. Sunrise wasn't until maybe six. She was still hopeful, thinking maybe the man from the Egyptian *Mukhabarat* was just sending them on a long hike to the border, simply hassling them because he could. Keeler stopped moving. At which point a set of headlights flicked on about fifty meters to the east. An engine growled, and the vehicle approached. She glanced at Keeler, saw his profile in the hard light, mouth clamped shut and a murderous glint in his eye.

She said, "Keep your hands off the weapon."

Another pickup truck, this one more battered and poor looking than the military vehicles. The driver, plus a passenger in the cab, three men in the back clinging on. All of them wearing keffiyeh headscarves, bedouins maybe, affiliated to one of the north Sinai militant groups. The three in the back leapt off the truck and began jogging towards them, weapons up.

The man in front had a red keffiyeh, screaming at her. Yasmin had her hands raised. She didn't want to just obey, because that would let them know she spoke Arabic. She played dumb, trying to look confused and helpless. One of the other guys came around and pushed her down to her knees, pulled the weapon away from her. She turned her head, seeing Keeler undergoing the same treatment.

Yasmin had a weird feeling, the fact that she was essentially helpless distanced her from the action. The men had strong body odor, like they'd been out here in the mountains living feral for a while. Outside the cone of bright light coming from the vehicle, the desert was an endless black. The surface of the hard sand was cold through her jeans.

They were hustled and pushed towards the back of the truck. Keeler seemingly relaxed, walking with his hands held loosely in the air, nodding and speaking in English to a guy wearing a dirty white keffiyeh. The man's face was fully covered except for a slit for eyes, obviously not understanding a word that Keeler was saying, but attentive in any case. What Yasmin realized, it was all about the tone. Using a pleasant tone of voice had psychological effects on the recipient.

The man in the passenger seat closed the door carefully. He examined her with deep-set eyes. In the hard glare she could still make out that they were a light hazel shade, striking against his deeply tanned skin and grizzled white beard. An older guy walked over, adjusting his keffiyeh. He barked at the men, using a hand gesture to shoo them away, all the while staring at her like he was looking at a piece of meat, an indifferent yet fascinated gaze. Like she was some mysterious object or something.

He got within spitting distance and Yasmin was anticipating what might happen. The man abruptly turned to Keeler and began speaking to him in Arabic.

Of course Keeler wasn't understanding the man, but she was.

The man said, "We're bringing you to the border where you will be allowed to cross."

Keeler said, "English."

The man dug deep into his English vocabulary, pointing to the east, using a gesture like washing his hands and sprinkling the residual liquid towards the border. "Israel. You go."

Keeler said, "Outstanding. Excellent idea."

The guy broke off his one-sided conversation and gestured for them to climb into the back of the truck. One of the men who'd been riding in back had the two M4s and carried them over and placed them in the cab.

Yasmin climbed up into the bed, she and Keeler shuffling to the rear and putting their backs against the rectangular window looking into the cab. She turned her head, seeing the white bearded passenger get in and say something to the driver. This striking older guy with a handheld Motorola, now lighting a cigarette from a soft-pack of Cleopatra.

The three other men jumped onto the truck bed and took seats on the edges, weapons up. One of them banged twice on the side of the truck and the driver peeled out. Yasmin fell against Keeler for a second before getting her balance back, feeling his hands on her, putting her back upright. She was noticing how the guys had to hold on to the truck when the driver swerved. Her head had knocked against Keeler's shoulder. Yasmin brushed hair back from her eyes.

She said, "Apparently driving us to the border."

Keeler said, "Who do you think these guys are?"

"Bedouin." Looking at the weathered faces, poor nutrition, wind, sand, and sun making a twenty-year-old man look forty. "I don't know why we're getting a ride with them though, that doesn't make any sense. The military should have chaperoned us."

Yasmin felt Keeler shrugging his shoulders next to her. "What makes sense is that this officer guy is washing his hands of us."

She said, "The guy's *Mukhabarat*, Egyptian intelligence service."

"Mm, hmm."

The passenger in the cab raised his voice to the point that she was hearing him argue with the driver but couldn't make out what it was they were discussing.

She said, "What do you think they're going to do with us?"

Keeler said, "My guess? They're planning on taking us to some spot and putting two rounds in each of our heads, arranging the corpses in some particular way to try to sell a story."

Which was along the lines of what she had been thinking. Arrange a story for when the Egyptian military accidentally finds their bodies. She looked out into the bleak dark. The wind had kicked up from the north, spraying sand at them as the truck rumbled onto a desert track. The ride smoothed out and Yasmin felt Keeler shifting position.

Operational assumption was that Keeler was correct, in which case they'd need to fight.

The closest of the men was a young guy with a white keffiyeh, sitting perched on her side of the truck, holding on for dear life with the AK-47 slung over his shoulder. Across from him was another man wearing a white keffiyeh, older, with a thick beard. This one perched further back, maybe two meters from Keeler.

Since they were holding on for balance, their hands were not ready with weapons.

She said, "Are we going to do this?"

"We could."

Yasmin was thinking about what that would entail, leaping up and pushing her guy over the side for a start. If she did that, there was no doubt that Keeler would be right behind her. No doubt that he'd take out the other man clinging to the edge of the truck.

The issue would be the third man, sitting in the rear with his weapon in his hands, an older AK-47 the steel worn down in some places, wooden stock with a big chip in it. This guy wasn't holding on to the truck, but squatting comfortably and staring right at her. He shifted his eyes from her to Keeler. Yasmin glanced to her left, seeing Keeler's profile again, staring right back at the guy, alpha male predator stuff going on there.

He said, "This guy's my favorite."

Yasmin looked again at the third man. It's true that for some reason he was exuding a kind of weird malevolence, like they'd done something to insult him. Very strange.

She took a deep breath, getting ready, planning to go for it, launch up at the man nearest to her and knock him over. She'd let the velocity of her movement and the truck's acceleration take her to the back and just run into the third guy, use her weight to mash him against the tailgate. Hopefully Keeler would do the rest. She could feel him there beside her, muscles coiled and ready. What she'd known about him since the beginning, a perfect killing machine, having had plenty of opportunity to get her hands on those arms and the barrel chest.

The truck slowed. She looked over her shoulder into the cab, seeing their direction of travel through the windshield. Headlights illuminated a low concrete structure, the truck now crawling towards it. The passenger spoke into his Motorola, looking over at the driver and saying something. There was a bang from the back of the truck. Yasmin turned to see the third guy who'd been crouching. He was up now, having kicked the tailgate open, speaking in Arabic, calling on her and Keeler to come down, making motions with his hands.

The other two had already come off the sides and were roaming to the back with their weapons. It was pretty cold out now.

Yasmin got to her feet. The passenger door opened and the guy with the grizzled white beard came out in mid-sentence, speaking roughly to the driver. The Bedouin dialect here wasn't the easiest for her. He was saying something about '*them*' being a bunch of thieves, not specifying who.

The driver came out and pulled an AK-47 from the cab, setting it for a moment on the roof. He spoke to the older guy. "Fifteen thousand each, not total."

The passenger snarled a kind of complicated curse about '*scum from Rafah.*'

The driver said, "You have ten minutes to think about it."

Which is how Yasmin understood that these Bedouin were planning to sell her and Keeler to someone in Gaza.

Keeler was abreast of her now, coming down off the truck bed. Yasmin grabbed his arm and made as if to lean against him getting off the truck. The three Bedouin were arrayed in a semi circle waiting for them.

She said, "They're selling us to people in Gaza for fifteen thousand Egyptian dinars. Probably to Hamas. They're coming to get us in ten minutes."

Keeler glanced at her and made eye contact. He was cool as a cucumber. "Is that a lot?"

"Ten minutes?"

"Fifteen thousand dinars."

"It's like five hundred dollars."

"That's all we're worth?"

She said, "To these Bedouin. Hamas could get a thousand prisoners exchanged for me, after I'm raped in a dungeon for the next decade."

Keeler was casual. He said, "Yeah, that's not going to happen." He nudged her. "Fall down when they grab you."

NINE

Yasmin let the man with the red keffiyeh put his hand on her arm, tightening his grip a little as he began to push her around. She let her weight take over, dropping like a sack of bricks. The man did exactly what most people would do, he tried to hold on to her. Which meant that inevitably he ended up bent over.

Hitting the ground, she felt the man's grip loosen and then he was over her in a spasm of frantic motion. For a brief moment she felt the weight of him pinning her until he lost balance, grunting as he lurched. Keeler must have kicked him in the ass, no doubt. Yasmin used the man's momentum to yank him to the ground, rolling on to him and ramming the edge of her hand into his windpipe. His hands flew to the throat. She kneed him hard in the groin, eliciting a groan. There were gunshots, loud pops that she ignored. The man was squirming and writhing with pain, the red keffiyeh slipped down over his eyes.

She scanned quickly, found the man's AK-47 over to the left where it had fallen. She leapt to the weapon, aware of the man's urgent movements, getting his keffiyeh away from his eyes. She glanced at him, seeing the guy up on an elbow and looking to move. By then she had the gun up and aimed. She squeezed the trigger and found it blocked by the safety. The man was charging at her now. Yasmin flicked the heavy safety lever and pulled again. This time, the gun chugged mechanically in her hand, set on full auto for some reason. Five rounds stitched into the man's body, tearing flesh and bone and clothing, some of the hot metal going into the dirt.

She was up, looking at Keeler straddling another man and doing something fast and violent to his head. Another two gun shots and someone was yelling. A guy with a white keffiyeh moved to her right, fumbling with his weapon, like he was panicked and needed a minute to get the safety lever adjusted. Yasmin was faster, the training and experience making her a smooth mover, putting her weapon up and controlling the rate of fire this time, sending two rounds into his chest. The pattern was tight, satisfactory.

A burst of gunfire came from behind her and the dirt twitched three feet to her left. She moved in a crouch, turning to the threat. Keeler was over by the truck, using the side of the vehicle to steady a weapon. He put three shots at whatever it was he saw and then turned to look at her, nodding. Eye contact. He jerked his thumb to the other side of the truck.

Yasmin went running alongside the vehicle, seeing a white-robed keffiyeh clad figure running, visible in the headlights. She took a knee and put a single round down at him, clipping the man's leg. He fell and made a tough target, so she sprinted at him.

It was the old guy, the man with the grizzled beard, rolling onto his back, eyes wide and mouth aghast, trying to get his weapon into operation. The thing looked heavy in his hand. Maybe the man was injured in the arm. Yasmin stood over him with her rifle pointed at his head.

She spoke in perfect Arabic. "You think I'm only worth fifteen thousand dinars?"

The man was catching his breath. He grimaced, sweat popping on his forehead.

"Only because you're a Jew. If you were just a woman, you'd be worth nothing."

She shot him twice in the face, the rounds ripping into the nose and the mono brow between his eyes. The flat angle directed the projectiles to tear through the flesh and bone, into his brain, the centrifugal force of rifling ripping and whipping through gray and white matter, tearing it up. Scrambled gore passed out through the top of the man's skull and wet the dirt behind him.

KEELER UNCLIPPED A MOTOROLA radio from the driver's tactical vest. The device crackled, and a voice asked a question that he couldn't understand. The driver would have been in command, chubbier than the others and maybe older, but not as old as the passenger, who Keeler figured for an experienced second in command. The other men had been young, what they call *shabab*, the guys. The leaders had been the first to flee of course. None of them were carrying phones.

Over here in the Middle East, Keeler was aware that in general, he didn't know shit. Things were different, was the simple way of putting it. *Complicated* didn't even begin to describe it.

Bedouins and Egyptians of different persuasions and tribal affinities were out here in the Sinai peninsula, Palestinians from Gaza, plus whatever ISIS or Al-Qaida elements might have sought refuge in the desert wilderness. Different clans and customs, this desolate landscape where women were kept out of sight, only males permitted to act in the public space. Yasmin had told him a Bedouin guy could have four wives, if he could afford them.

An entire way of seeing the world, a universe in itself.

Keeler knew it from guys he'd worked with, Iraqi special forces, Syrian militiamen, or whomever. You'd be in a conversation with someone and suddenly a huge gap would open up, like you're both looking in the same direction but seeing different things. Keeler wasn't any kind of anthropologist and didn't pretend to be one, but cultural differences were real and profound. He wasn't a big strategy guy because he'd seen that the world was a chaos, essentially unpredictable. Best you could do was try to straighten out the squiggles.

He did three quick squats, right there, surrounded by the corpses of five men leaking body heat into the cool desert. Keeler's joints crackled and popped.

The mysteries of nature.

Yasmin emerged from the dark. A natural predator. Her weapon was ready, gait assured and relaxed. A tall slim figure in motion, the sharp triangle of her eyes and nose making perfectly symmetrical shadows in the headlight glare. Now, walking over, recognizing that the fight was finished. Keeler mentally added her to the anthropological mix. A woman like her, *people* like her from only just across the border, but a quantum leap away from this place, like the difference between reality and a science fiction movie.

She said, "Phones?"

He held up the Motorola radio. "Just this."

She nodded and looked at him. "So we get out of here or what?"

The Motorola spurted noise and a voice, asking a question again. Yasmin took the radio from him and turned a few knobs, focusing on the words. Someone speaking again, the same question.

She looked up at him, exasperated. "If you spoke Arabic maybe we could fool them with your manly voice, but you don't and so we can't."

"Sorry."

Yasmin grinned and shook her head, looking up at him. Pointing to the vehicle. "Do we take that?"

"Might as well."

Both of them froze at the same time. The sound of vehicles approaching had become apparent all at once, a low hum of tires rolling fast across rough ground.

Yasmin said, "Shit, I forgot about the people from Gaza."

Keeler chin pointed to the low building, twenty yards away and began to sprint for it. The structure had a set of stairs going up to a second level. He mounted the stairs to the landing, stepped up on a ledge and found a foothold at a window to reach a drain pipe. It took his weight, and he hauled himself up to the roof.

Yasmin was right behind him, dropping to the hard smooth surface and getting low, one hand on the AK-47 she'd slung over her shoulder. Headlights washed over the area. Keeler risked a glimpse over the roof's parapet and saw two of the militarized Hilux pickup trucks laden with *El-Sa'Ka* forces.

He said, "Not the people from Gaza."

Keeler rolled onto his back, the AK he'd appropriated lying against his chest. He looked at the desert sky, what seemed like a million stars, all of them brilliant and clearly defined, like being on the inside of a gigantic marshmallow that had been shot through with bullet holes.

TEN

Yasmin snuck a look over the parapet, checking out the soldiers below, pulling her head back after a second or two. She lay on the roof next to Keeler looking up at the stars with him, hearing the bustle of movement. *El-Sa'Ka* forces again. The accents of the soldiers were different from how the colonel spoke. The foot soldiers recruited from poorer parts of the country, down south between the Nile and the Red Sea. The military class were either from Cairo or up north on the delta, Alexandria or Damietta on the banks of the Nile.

She didn't see or hear the colonel, only the soldiers below discovering five Bedouin corpses, and not sounding too emotional about their find. Hearing them calling to each other in their country bumpkin accents, exaggerating the vowels and using harsher consonants than the colonel might have.

Radio squawk and soldier's commands, the laconic turning to routine matters. Yasmin figured they were dealing with the bodies, reporting up the chain of command and getting instructions. These *El-Sa'Ka* troops showing up like this in the middle of the desert was weird and hard to explain.

Yasmin listened carefully to the activity below. The voices

changed suddenly, the straightforward conversation elevating into higher pitched commands and loud shouts.

Something was happening.

A chattering burst of gunfire cut the night, shrill and abrupt. Initially it was a few shots, but quickly devolved into a riot of smalls arms fire, until overtaken by the chug of a heavy machine gun. The rounds boomed and chattered for a good ten seconds and stopped just as suddenly, leaving only the steady bleat of a car horn.

Keeler was looking at her, mouthing words. "The people from Gaza."

Yasmin risked another look over the edge, her eyes seeking information. What had just happened? Answers lay in the smoking ruin of a Russian Lada 4x4, the clear target of heavy weapons fire. The windshield was a cloud of spidered glass, a hole drilled through on the driver's side. Human beings inside only visible as dark blood stains. The remnants of the driver's head must have fallen against the horn, given the never-ending honk. The tires and exterior parts of the vehicle ripped apart by the metal rounds.

She pulled herself back. The men down below were now bellowing at each other in excitement.

Yasmin moved close to Keeler. She said, "Looks like the *shabab* from Gaza got shredded."

The horn honking ceased.

She was working it out, why had the *El-Sa'Ka* forces arrived first? Yasmin wasn't surprised about the crew from Gaza, Hamas, or Palestinian Islamic Jihad, come to fetch their new hostages. But she didn't understand why the Egyptian military had shown up on the scene. How had the *El-Sa'Ka* known to come? Only one possibility, because of the short battle she and Keeler had fought against the Bedouin. Which was either a total coincidence, or the *El-Sa'Ka* force had been nearby, maybe even shadowing them.

Keeler was peering over the parapet. He pulled back and sat against it, looking at her.

He said, "The Egyptians were monitoring us."

She said, "Now they're going to come up here."

Keeler didn't respond at first. He looked away and then returned his gaze to her. He said, "They should but they won't."

Yasmin watched him lie back again, looking at the sky, understanding what Keeler meant, and kind of accepting it. The soldiers wouldn't do a proper search because no senior officer had told them to. She'd been operating on the border for more than fifteen months, enough time to get to know the Egyptian military a little. She'd thought the *El-Sa'Ka* were different.

Sounds were coming up from down below. Operational conversations happening between grunt soldiers. Noises of objects moving and landing, relatively heavy things thudding into sand. Vehicles starting, moving, engines rumbling, brakes being applied, gear boxes grinding, tires rolling over hard packed desert.

The sound of a door breaking just beneath them. Maybe they'd had to go find a heavy object to use. She glanced at Keeler beside her, raising an eyebrow. More stuff was happening downstairs, immediately underneath them. It was enough to make her examine the roof a little more carefully. They were up on the main flat part of it. An access hatch was over on the other corner. What was this building anyway? Maybe an administrative compound, possibly filled with files and a desk with not much more than an old computer on its surface.

Keeler poked her. He was crawling ever so slowly across the roof towards the access hatch. She figured, better safe than sorry, and followed him. By the time they made it over to the opposite corner it had become urgent, since there were sounds of scraping just below the hatch, someone was coming up. Keeler pointed at something, she couldn't tell what. He was already over between the hatch and the wall, sliding into the narrow space with only room for a single body.

A loud snap came from the other side of the hatch, a pair of bolt cutters being introduced to a padlock. She saw what it was Keeler had been pointing to. The hatch was coming up. He'd been pointing to the hinges, having set himself down between hinge and parapet. Yasmin crawled on top of him, making it just in time to get the hatch banging onto her back as an *El-Sa'Ka* commando poked his head up to take a look at the roof.

She let her face drop into the hollow of Keeler's shoulder. Having been there before it was at the same time comforting and weird, given the circumstances. He put a hand on her back and held her close. The man on the other side of the hatch said '*la shay*', the Arabic word for nothing. She couldn't tell immediately if he'd gone away, because the Egyptian soldier didn't bother to close the hatch.

They stayed there like that for a long time, unmoving, caught in the improvised embrace while they listened to the *El-Sa'Ka* men moving around below them. Ten minutes later vehicles rumbled into motion and a little while after that there was silence, leaving them alone on the roof of that building. Yasmin rolled off Keeler and leaned over the parapet, verifying that everything was now clear. She looked up at the sky, the light from the stars almost as bright as day.

Keeler had a humorous look on his face.

He said, "What'd I tell you?"

She said, "You told me they wouldn't come up to the roof."

"I was wrong."

"Well, the issue now is the weapons. I'm going to need to find some reason why I've lost two IDF issue M4 rifles."

Keeler grinned. "One thing at a time. Let's focus on the task at hand, staying alive."

He descended first, hanging from the ledge, dropping to the balcony and spotting her as she came after. They picked their way between the drainpipe and another narrow ledge. She misjudged the final drop and rolled her ankle, coming up seated and massaging it. No harm, no foul, as Keeler liked to say.

The vehicles and corpses were gone, only stains remaining of the scene. Blood and engine oil and .50 caliber casings spilled in the dirt and sand.

She said, "This like some kind of sick game right? They know we're here?"

Keeler was scanning the area, operational. She watched him checking the distance between stars or whatever, calculating their position.

He said, "I don't know. Let's move east and see what happens. Maybe those *El-Sa'Ka* people didn't know about the boys from Gaza."

Yasmin nodded to herself. That was probably correct. The Bedouin had cut a side deal with Hamas or whoever, in Gaza. They started hiking east, up a draw until they were walking among strange mounds created by the sand and the wind, Keeler always a couple of steps ahead, setting the pace.

ELEVEN

THE COLONEL'S PHONE RANG. He looked at it for a long moment, recognizing the number, even though it was not on his contact list. He was sitting in the back of a Toyota Land Cruiser. The armored exterior acted as a sound proofing mechanism. Consequently, they were riding in silence.

He answered the phone.

"Yes."

The voice was easily recognizable. It was the *El-Sa'Ka* officer he'd rented. The man's plaintive tone, almost begging all the time. Now he was making excuses, saying that the Zionist whore and the American were loose in the desert.

The colonel cut him off in mid excuse. "The desert is vast. Find them."

It was important to maintain a polite and respectful demeanor, even though he fully intended to do terrible things to the man if he failed again.

The vehicle slowed at the entrance to El-Gora airport. The driver lowered his window. A guard moved in, examining the driver, his eyes seeking the colonel in the rear seat. The colonel's head was leaned back against the soft leather rest. He was doing breathing exercises that the yoga instructor back in Cairo had taught him.

"Identity."

The colonel handed over his heavy leather wallet, embossed with the seal of office, a serious piece of equipment, given that he was an officer with the *Mukhabarat*, Egyptian security services. In other words, someone you don't mess with. The guard had to do his job though, tough it out. He looked at the identity card and examined the colonel carefully. It was one thing to unintentionally piss off a *Mukhabarat* officer, quite another to be incompetent on the job.

He read slowly. "Hisham Al-Masri."

The colonel said, "Are you trying to prove that you're able to read my name?"

The wallet returned through the window and the colonel snatched it. The guard stepped back, his face hadn't divulged any emotion, from the beginning to the end of the interaction. Good.

The vehicle passed through the checkpoint and the driver cruised the kilometer or so to the cluster of buildings. El-Gora had a landing strip and the attendant buildings, but it wasn't strictly speaking an airport. The complex was home to the Multinational Force and Observers, the peacekeepers who were supposed to guarantee the terms of the Egyptian - Israeli treaty.

Basically a pit of corruption now, like everything else.

The complex had swimming pools and a library, living quarters and other facilities for the multinational force. It was certainly the most comfortable place in Sinai. The colonel hummed to himself as the driver navigated the grid of roads and buildings. It wasn't their first trip to El-Gora.

The colonel was the point man for a small group of young Mukhabarat officers who had a special thing going on with the CIA. He was the one carrying the goods, in this case a folder with pages and photographs related to Egyptian intelligence on a man the Americans very much were interested in killing.

The CIA really seemed to believe that their little cabal was the future of an uncorrupt Egyptian deep state complex. They called the colonel and his compatriots 'Young Turks'. They were investing in the future.

The American was in the MFO dining facility, eating grilled fish and French fries. He looked up at the colonel and grunted something. Chewing and finishing his mouthful and clearing it with a gulp of Stella out of a can.

He said, "Sit down."

The American was delicately removing bones from the fish, a Red Sea grouper sourced from Bedouin fishermen, no doubt. The best fish in the world. Split open and filleted, grilled over charcoal and served with a squeeze of lemon and a sprinkle of salt.

The colonel wasn't crazy about beer, he preferred white wine with fish.

He sat and slid the folder across the table. The American wiped his fingers and removed a compact Sony camera from beside the plate. He powered on the device and began flipping through the folder, taking photos of each page, barely paying attention to the contents.

He said, "No surprises?"

"No. It's just confirmation, new photo I believe.

"Okay." The American looked at him with watery blue eyes. Turning pages and documenting. "This shit is going to happen, huh?"

"That's the idea isn't it?"

"Mmmm hmmm." The American smiled. "Yes, that's the idea."

The colonel said, "What is it?" He decided that the American didn't look like an American, he looked like an Iraqi or something. Which was the problem with Americans, you couldn't pin them down, they didn't look like anything but they always *acted* like Americans. Drinking coke, dedicated to an idea beyond the family and tribe.

"Nothing." The American smiled, showing the teeth again. "If you have the slightest doubt, now's the time to tell me."

The colonel kept a good poker face. He'd done his research on this man, a junior level CIA agent working out of the embassy in Tel Aviv. The Americans were rightly concerned with leaks from the Cairo station, same as he was. The situation was borderline ridiculous, both of them coming up here to the middle of nowhere because Cairo was so inherently unsafe.

He said, "It's pure gold man. Definitely."

The American nodded and kept looking at him strangely, like he was seeing something that irritated him. It wasn't pleasant.

The CIA man said, "When you say shit like that, colonel, I get a funny feeling."

TWELVE

THE COLONEL LEANED FORWARD and put his hands together, making eye contact and mobilizing his suggestive qualities.

"What's on your mind, Bill? that's your name, right?"

The CIA man didn't rise to the bait. He said, "I look at you, I'm being honest here, I don't like you. I don't get good vibes from you. I'm not sure why exactly. I'm trying to get past the cultural issues, the instinctive discrimination you know."

The colonel said, "Unconscious bias."

"Exactly." The American looked surprised.

The colonel knew that this man was only a junior officer in the CIA, so his instincts were meaningless.

The colonel pointed at the fish remnants in the plate, charred tail fin and bones. "Do you eat frog's legs Bill?"

The CIA man said, "No."

The colonel smiled. "I didn't think you would. I'm surprised you can deal with a whole fish, being an American."

The American said, "It's all they had. Kitchen's closed and I had to get my driver to cook. Guy's a Bedouin and brought me a fish like it was some gift."

The colonel didn't like this scene. He was waiting for money.

The American ate a French fry. He wiped his hands again and smiled, revealing very white teeth, reaching into his jacket for an envelope and sliding it over. The colonel looked at it for a moment, judging the thickness.

The CIA man said, "That should chill you out, colonel."

What the colonel knew: Americans trusted money. If they thought he was ideological, they wouldn't believe in him and his co-conspirators. And the Americans were a hundred percent correct. He'd come to believe that money equaled power, despite the abstract nature of the stuff. Money and power were very good companions.

THE CIA MAN waited for the colonel to leave. He let the man go out the way he'd come and then counted to one hundred.

"One hundred."

He stood from his chair and wiped his mouth with a napkin, throwing it down and turning away. The back of the dining facility accessed the gymnasium directly. The basketball court's glossy wood flooring made a soft percussive sound, resonating as he walked. He switched on the lights and got a ball out of the ball cart. He took off his jacket and draped it on the cart. The ball felt good in his hand, genuine leather, just like in the NBA.

The CIA man shot hoops for forty-five minutes, practicing his three pointers, mid-range jump shots and free throws. He did a series of exercises focusing on ball control, both hands, dribbling straight and crossovers, flipping the ball behind his back and setting up a rebound sequence.

A door at the far end opened and the cool air came in. An airman stood in the door looking at him.

"It's ready."

The airman walked away, leaving the door open. The CIA man returned the ball to the cart and grabbed his jacket. He was sweating, which didn't concern him too much. The door opened directly to a runway. The airman was waiting for him, seated just under the canopy of a maintenance shed.

The CIA man removed the Sony camera from his jacket pocket. He ejected the SD card. The pilot had a payload canister ready. He opened the compartment and the CIA man placed the SD card inside. The airman filled in the remaining space with foam pieces and snapped the compartment closed.

The payload canister fit into place beneath the drone's main brain, snapping in there with a satisfying click. The airman got the control panel set and tapped the screen. The quad rotors spun up from zero to full rotation in a quarter of a second.

The airman glanced back at the CIA man for confirmation and got a nod.

He swiped and tapped and the drone shot off. Initially vertically, up into the night sky. Altitude was convenient. That thing would get seven thousand feet up before it zipped north, and there wasn't any way to detect an object that small moving so fast at that altitude.

The airman said, "And there she goes."

The CIA man said, "Yup." He nodded and removed a phone from his pocket. He swiped and tapped until he was in the clandestine messaging network, telling the Tel Aviv station chief that the package was on its way. In a few minutes it would be approaching its destination at an American facility in the Israeli desert.

THIRTEEN

Jafar Al-Husseini crawled out of a narrow tunnel entrance located in a thicket surrounded by cluster of prickly pear. He'd have to be careful getting out of there. The horizon was simply dark, the desert visible only thanks to the bright stars.

Hopefully, he was in Israel now. He'd been crawling for maybe an hour on his hands and knees. Al-Husseini had never felt so exhausted.

At least his phone worked with like, twenty-five percent battery remaining. He sent a message to his buddy, currently hanging around a shitty town called Be'er Sheva, trying not to be too obtrusive, too Arab. This was difficult if you were in fact an Arab Israeli, it necessitated what the Kardashians called a *'glow up'*.

Basically, the best thing you could do as an Arab Israeli petty criminal who wanted to avoid attention was to dress like an Israeli hippy, which is what Al-Husseini and his little group of burglars did. Nothing extreme like dreadlocks, it was only a question of a few subtle changes. Hippies could look poor, but they were poor in a very specific way which allowed his friend to hang out in Be'er Sheva, as long as he didn't actually speak to anyone for very long.

The message he sent was simple. 'Come and get me,' along with his current location as a pin dropped on a phone map. He was five hundred meters from the nearest road. Which meant he had time to kill, since his friend was an hour away.

Al-Husseini jumped up and down, trying to get blood into his limbs and muscles. Once he was no longer feeling like a compressed animal, he sat down and looked at his phone. His sister had called while he'd been jumping. She'd left a message.

'What's up?'

Al-Husseini tapped into the phone. 'Not much. Hanging out in the south.'

He owed her money as usual. Thinking for a second if he should offer to pay it back.

She wrote, 'Are you okay?'

He loved his sister, the only member of the family who'd stood by him over the years.

He impulsively wrote, 'Oh by the way, I can pay you back now.'

Feeling his heart beating in his chest, realizing this was pretty emotional. Al-Husseini understood that it was a heavy thing for him, the fighting with his family and how he was never really managing to get his shit together financially. She was typing something, and he waited for it.

'You don't have to.'

He wrote, 'But I'm going to.' Thinking about it. 'It's about the principle of the thing. A man needs to pay his debts.'

She typed back immediately. 'Proud of you brother. Don't listen to the haters.'

He typed back in English. 'why you gotta be a hater?'

She sent back a LOL emoji. Both of them were big Kardashian fans.

FOURTEEN

Tel Aviv, Israel

Mike Hershkowitz was about to capture the last piece of Alaskan crab sashimi, currently lonely on the black stone plate between him and the girl. His chopsticks were poised, but the phone rang and he looked at her. A pretty face with smoky eyes, watching him, aware of the dynamic, who he was, and her place in this dance.

Hershkowitz stood up and took the phone outside, watching her through the window as she waited for him to be gone before finishing the sushi. Allenby street was a riot outside Nilus, a focal point for the rich artsy crowd in Tel-Aviv. Hershkowitz was there to impress the girl, a young curator of contemporary art.

The call was from his assistant. Not a good sign.

"Yeah."

"Sorry to interrupt your date."

He said, "What?"

His assistant said, "El-Gora sent a ghost-fish to the *Midreshet* facility."

Our facility, Hershkowitz immediately thought. *Ours* meaning, on Israeli territory. Only Americans had clearance for that and the El-Gora multinational peacekeeping force were all Canadians now.

He said, "No Americans at El-Gora?"

His assistant said, "What I understand: one thousand and three Canadians, four hundred and thirty-two Egyptians, and three Dutchmen. No Americans."

"Shit, they sent a ghost-fish to Midreshet?"

"Correct."

Hershkowitz was the deputy head of an intelligence agency without a name, it had a number, 201. Nobody knew what that number referred to, including Hershkowitz. His operational assumption was that the number had no relation to any chronological order, the unit wasn't the two hundred and first on some list, it was just three digits picked at random.

Unit 201 was running an operation against El-Gora. The Egyptian airbase was sixteen kilometers from the Israeli border. As far as they were aware, the Canadian soldiers currently serving at the base had been using UN aircraft to smuggle raw opium to Italy, so why the ghost-fish drop to a secret US facility in Midreshet?

Hershkowitz said, "Anything else?"

She said, "Well, yes. The drone was preceded by a visit. An Egyptian security vehicle arrived at El-Gora one hour before the drone took off."

"Who, what kind?"

"We don't know who. The vehicle's registered to the *Mukhabarat*, not assigned to anyone in particular."

"Motor pool out of where?"

"Cairo."

"So, none of the usuals."

"Exactly."

Meaning, the usual Egyptian security officials of the

Northern Sinai were accounted for, and this wasn't one of them, although the vehicle was of the security services more generally. How they knew this, Hershkowitz wasn't sure, but to ask was to admit so.

He said, "And now?"

"The vehicle just arrived at the coast. Some cheesy Egyptian resort."

Hershkowitz said, "You've told them to walk it back right?"

"Yeah."

"Okay so we'll see."

His assistant would now arrange a liaison with the other imaging team. Feeds would be mapped and built out. Satellites, and drones, and hacked CCTV feeds if that was deemed necessary. Truck dash cams often worked, so did gas station cameras, if you wanted to track past movement of a vehicle. Hershkowitz would have to get to *Palmachim* eventually. In a few hours they would have walked back the mukhabarat vehicle's journey from Cairo. Maybe they'd even know who was in it.

Which meant that now was the time with the girl. Sitting there where he'd left her, minus one piece of expensive sushi. She'd ordered another vodka, which Hershkowitz took to be a good sign. Since he needed to work later on, he'd have to go a little faster with her. He figured skipping dessert could help. But he was wrong.

Skipping dessert turns out to be a bad idea when you're on a first date.

FIFTEEN

North Sinai, Egypt

After an hour of walking and not coming across a single object of human artifice Keeler and Yasmin arrived at a steep banked dry river bed, a *wadi*. They followed the wadi east, winding eventually towards the north. By the light of the stars Keeler saw large puffy shapes of marsh grass ahead. They were approaching an area with at least some water beneath the surface. He wasn't sure if oasis would be the right term for it.

Something acrid hit his nostrils, and he stopped moving. Yasmin was behind him, taking a knee.

Keeler stayed still for a long while, letting the northeasterly wind blow into his face there and thinking and listening, a whiff of tobacco smoke tickled at his nostrils again. Human life up ahead, since that's where the wind was coming from. He turned again to Yasmin, getting a nod. She'd caught the scent.

A shuffling noise carried on the wind, not just the tall marsh grass, something more agitated. Like someone reaching into a pocket, or adjusting position. Or a sentry posted to watch the approach up the river bed. Keeler motioned Yasmin to get down. She leaned into the shallow bank. Because of the wind's direction he risked whispering.

"I'm going to take a look."

She said, "We could avoid the contact, go around them."

He shook his head, no. She looked at him a second and nodded agreement. They couldn't afford a discussion about it and he'd decided that they needed to know what was up there. He could see the contours of Yasmin's face, trusting him.

Keeler turned and loped down the wadi towards the tall grass. He got up to the edge of the riverbank, nestling himself into the reeds, settling and waiting and listening and smelling. The scent of tobacco smoke was stronger, the man was very near. The marsh reeds made swishing sounds with the wind, masking his approach.

A cough came from close range. The man was maybe twenty feet away, higher on the bank. Keeler wondered for a second why the guy hadn't seen them earlier. He realized the sentry might not have been looking. Maybe dozing off with the cigarette, doing his time and impatient for a comrade to take over.

Keeler inched his way around, crawling on his belly so slowly that he made no sound at all. It took five minutes to get behind the sentry. Once he rose, the man's silhouette was visible against the lighter portions of the starry sky. A young guy wearing a head wrap and smelling of tobacco and sweat, maybe a teenager.

Slipping up on an enemy is always surreal.

Keeler stepped slowly towards him, an inch at a time, placing the heel first and rolling down to the balls of his feet, watching the back of the guy's head, alert to the tension in his muscles, noticing the way he moved, his expressions. Some people act naturally when they know they're being watched, others are more self-conscious. This guy looked like he was self-conscious even when he didn't think he was being watched.

By the time the sentry was paying attention it was too late. Keeler was tightening his arms in a vice around the man's neck and head, controlling his body and restricting the oxygen transfer to his brain. The man struggled and Keeler got his legs wrapped around like a python in a full body hold, keeping him still until he was out. He rolled off the limp body and crouched, fingers dancing rapidly, searching for interesting items. The sentry carried a short range Motorola radio clipped to a tactical vest, a basic AK-47 model from the 1980s with one extra magazine tucked into the vest. He had small plastic bottle of water and a crumpled half filled bag of roasted nuts.

Unfortunately, no car keys.

Keeler wanted a vehicle, but if this man wasn't carrying keys, someone else would be, and the sentry would know who. He slung him over the shoulder and crept back to Yasmin's position to the south west. He lay the man down as quietly as he could.

He said, "We need to get keys to a vehicle. This guy will know who has them."

The man was already regaining consciousness. Keeler pinned him back against the river bed with a large hand around his throat. The man's eyes began bulging when the business end of Yasmin's AK-47 was pressed to his forehead. Yasmin whispered something in Arabic. The guy swiveled his eyes, trying to see her, but not making it. She leaned closer and began whispering dense Arabic phrases into his ear.

The guy began to nod convulsively, as if he *really* agreed with her. He looked at Keeler and grinned broadly, exposing unhealthy gums with only a couple of teeth.

The man said, "Zidane number one," his English heavily

accented. He pointed at Keeler and expressed at least six syllables.

Keeler looked at Yasmin for a translation.

"They've been told to hunt for the American and the Zionist whore." She looked at him significantly. "Literally what he just said."

"Like what, a bounty?"

Yasmin nodded.

SIXTEEN

Keeler crouched, keeping guard while Yasmin held a whispered interrogation. He was liking the way she operated, focused in on the guy like she cared about him. After a while she nodded and said something that sounded sweet. The guy blinked twice and Yasmin came over.

Keeler felt the heat of her breath whispering in his ear, plus her hand resting casually on his leg, reminding him that they were lovers. It took a little concentration to listen to what she was actually saying.

This was a five-man squad from a splinter group of disaffected Muslim Brotherhood supporters who'd now pledged allegiance to ISIS. The kind of Islamists who had fled to Sinai after a hard core army crackdown in Egypt six months before. They'd only posted the guy as a sentry because he was the youngest. The rest of them were back at the truck. The young sentry said they were sleeping.

He was wearing a sweater and dirty gray robe, what they called a *dishdasha*. Keeler made him take it off and tore the robe into pieces, making fabric strips. He did the best he could with what he had to bind the man's arms and legs and stuff a rag ball into his mouth. Duct tape would have been a luxury.

Keeler glanced at Yasmin seeing her watch him constrain the prisoner. The young guy was cold, shivering in the wind. She made eye contact with Keeler and looked away. Life sucks and then you die, basically true if you're going to sign up to be a member of *Wilayat Sinai* in the year 2016.

The rest of the crew were fifty yards back, on the other side of the thicket and a hill. A battered pickup truck was nosed in by the ground spring. Two guys slept under the vehicle, the other two were curled in blankets on the truck's bed. Keeler didn't trust the captured man's account of things, so he made Yasmin wait while he did a tour of the perimeter. The man had been telling the truth, his friends really did leave him alone on sentry duty.

Keeler observed the four sleeping men, how their weapons had been left out of reach. Two AK-47s leaned against the back of the truck's cab. Another two leaned against the truck itself. The men sleeping under it would need a good 20 seconds to get their weapons operational in case of an attack. They were severely unprepared. Looking at them lying there in their comfort zone, he almost felt sorry for them. The fact that the Egyptian military couldn't defeat an enemy like this didn't say much for their capabilities.

He began by collecting the weapons. Slowly, inch by inch, creeping up and trying his best not to make a rattle of any kind, like where the metal clip of a strap might hit the rail of a weapon. The wind in the rushes was on his side and in a few minutes they had a little pile of armaments. Keeler began taking the men one at a time, while Yasmin covered the others.

The two under the truck were first. Keeler crouched down and got stable, looking at the man sleeping on his back breathing through a gaping mouth. Another guy was on the other side, back turned, curled into a foetal position facing the other way. The mouth breather was snoring heavily.

Keeler stuffed a ball of torn cloth into the man's mouth and gripped his head hard, pulling him out from under the truck. By the time the guy was conscious, Keeler had straddled him with one hand against his mouth, a forearm pinning his chest to the ground. The man's eyes bugged for a few seconds. Yasmin approached and put an AK-47 barrel into his right nostril, which softened his attitude. She held her finger to her lips while Keeler simply glared at him.

The guy nodded in complete agreement.

Keeler stripped the man's clothing before binding his hands and blindfolding him. He pushed him to kneeling position in the sand, facing into the marsh grass.

The next two men were captured in the same way. One of them taken from under the truck like his sleeping buddy. The third was pulled from the truck bed. That was trickier, and there was a commotion. The fourth man, sleeping up on the truck bed must have heard the struggle and feigned being asleep for a minute or two. Keeler was binding the third man's limbs when there was a fast scrambling noise from the truck.

Yasmin stepped clear of the vehicle to a firing position. She took a knee and aimed her weapon.

Keeler said, "Don't do it."

She didn't immediately respond, looking down the sight at the guy running like a madman. Finally she lowered the AK and stood up, facing him.

She said, "I hope you're right."

The captured men had phones, with battery power. They divulged passcodes. Yasmin quickly got a mapping app up on the screen and located them. Middle of the desert, maybe sixty kilometers from the Israeli border, smack in the flat area between the Mediterranean and the mountains.

She jerked a thumb to where the fourth man had run off. "He can run as much as he wants. He won't make it anywhere anytime soon."

The truck had two full twenty-liter jerry cans and a second Motorola radio on the front bench. Yasmin crouched to the captives and spoke long Arabic phrases. In response she obtained a couple of frequencies that the group in question were using for communications. Currently there was no radio traffic.

Yasmin, looking at him with a grin, said, "They're all asleep back at camp. Some military organization, huh?"

Keeler was searching for the car keys. Nothing under the sun visor, same in the glove box. He said, "Malnourished, most likely." He jerked his head to the captured men. "Look at them."

Yasmin was pulling a *dishdasha* robe over her clothing. She nodded her head slightly in agreement. The men were thin with prominent bones. Two of them had the initial signs of fluid swelling in the belly and face. They'd need to get decent food soon.

She walked over and threw him a robe. "Put that on over your clothes."

Keeler got out of the truck and put it on. The white head wrap thing was a little puzzling, but he did what he could. Figured they'd look legitimate at a distance. After that, it wouldn't matter. The night was chill but clear. Yasmin tucked stray hairs back under the head wrap.

She was looking at Keeler. "They said no keys."

Keeler was busy with an examination of the wiring beneath the steering column, which was exposed and tangled. He looked up, seeing only her eyes. He said, "Yeah, I think they were telling the truth, it's a hot wire operation over here."

Yasmin laughed. "This is all my fault. I was really stupid. We could be back at the camp site you know.. doing, you know."

Keeler said, "That's true, but I think this is your twisted idea of a date."

She laughed. "You're a sick man."

Keeler got the two wires crossed and started the vehicle. Something banged hard in the distance. He killed the engine. "Did you hear that?"

A single shot cracked, the sound skipping over the flat desert surface, coming at them with a little echo.

The blindfolded men were still kneeling naked in the sand. Murmurs rose from their gagged mouths. Yasmin hissed at them and they quieted down for a moment.

A second later an extended burst of heavy machine gun fire drilled the night. The shooting had come from the direction the fourth man had run off to, desperately sprinting away from the truck. The weapon fire couldn't have been from him, since his AK-47 was bundled into a blanket in the back of the Toyota with the others.

The captured men began to panic.

Yasmin jerked a thumb at them. "You see, they're all terrified of the army here."

SEVENTEEN

Keeler started the vehicle again and got out of the truck.

"We're going up there. You drive. I'll ride up top."

Yasmin slid over to take the wheel. He got up on the truck's bed shoving the bundle of captured weapons against the cab with his feet so that they wouldn't move around too much. Keeler took a wide stance and settled his forearms and AK-47 rifle over the cab's roof. He tapped once and the vehicle moved. Yasmin flipped the headlights off, running in the dark in the direction of the gunfire.

The escaped man hadn't made it far. Keeler saw the body as a small speck in the darkness, getting closer. The crumpled figure wore a black jacket over his *dishdasha*, dark textile contrasting with desert tones. Yasmin stopped the vehicle. Keeler came down over the side and began hunting around, making a circular tour with the corpse as the epicenter. He crouched low, scanning for tracks and found the tire marks thirty yards south west of the body, tucked behind a low rise.

A truck, or 4x4 had stopped there and then turned out. Cartridge casings littered the scrubby terrain. The men who had done the shooting were now gone. Yasmin was examining the body. The heavy machine gun had torn the fleeing man to pieces so that he didn't appear to have ever been human, more like an avant-garde sculpture, a three-dimensional puzzle that escapes solution.

Killing happened in combat, all the time. But shooting an unarmed and defenseless man who was clearly out of the fight wasn't anything that Keeler could countenance. The *El-Sa'Ka* squad were playing a sadistic game, party to this colonel's little exercise. This killing was a message to Keeler and Yasmin. The *El-Sa'Ka* people were playing hunter seeker. They were shaping the envelope of movement, trying to get him and Yasmin into a funnel.

Yasmin said, "You get that bad feeling?"

"Very much. They're moving us east." He cast a hand towards the north. "They've got roaming units keeping us penned between here and the mountains to the south."

Keeler couldn't quite figure out why.

Theoretically there would be limits to how far this colonel asshole could go. It was hard to believe that he'd get his men to directly attack. That wouldn't be within any official Egyptian policy, it would be a total aberration against their most strategic ally. At the same time, it was true that if some fringe bunch of militants killed them or sold them to Hamas in Gaza, the Egyptians wouldn't have to claim responsibility.

Worse, they might ask for more money from the USA to fight ISIS. A thought that made him laugh out loud.

Yasmin looked at him. "What?"

Keeler wasn't smiling. He said, "Only thing I can think of is that we caught that Egyptian intel officer doing something back by the tunnel entrance that he doesn't want anyone knowing about, so his plan is to eliminate us in a deniable way."

Yasmin, watching him, looked pretty serious. She said, "Like what, something to do with the infiltrators?"

Keeler said, "Your guess is as good as mine."

She said, "We should have searched them more thoroughly."

"But we didn't."

Keeler walked back to the truck, scouring the horizon for a moving silhouette. The driver's side door was open, Yasmin leaned against the seat. He could see the small pile of phones she'd collected from the Islamists, stacked on the seat behind her. She had one of them in her hand. He could guess what she was thinking.

He said, "You want to call it in and get help from your people? What are the scenarios?"

"Yeah, I've been thinking. Scenario is, my people coordinate with the Egyptians and they hand us over at the border. Back home I get court-martialed. I don't think I'll get much jail time but it'll be a bummer."

"Jail time's a bummer."

"Plus my chance of a military career will be done."

Keeler glanced at her, not having entertained the thought of Yasmin as career military.

He said, "So what's the other scenario?"

Yasmin shrugged, looked at him. "If the Egyptians make an issue out of it, or aren't quick enough to respond, it's possible that some idiot at Southern Command will send in a team. Then it either goes smoothly, or turns into world war three, depending upon how the principles of unintended consequences unroll." She laughed and swept a hand towards the bright stars above.

Keeler made a noise, between a grunt and a hmm. He didn't immediately answer her, fingering one of the .50 caliber bullet casings he'd picked up, out where the truck had been positioned. He was looking at the corpse, thinking about the panicked ISIS men abandoned over by the marsh grass, getting themselves all tangled and hysterical, the emptiness of the desert with its sudden surprises, the way you could never truly get to know it.

He said, "Plus you still get a court martial."

"Plus I get the court martial."

"Bummer."

Yasmin wasn't smiling, looking at him like he was being a dick. Truth was, Keeler was enjoying himself. What the enemy wasn't entirely aware of yet was that they'd decided to try to hunt the hunter.

The other thing preying on his mind was slightly trivial, but that didn't make it go away. The fact was that he still had a week and a half of rest and recuperation leave before he was required to report for duty. After that, it was anyone's guess where they'd be deploying him. Probably inserted with a team of hooligans in Iraq or Syria again, given the current JSOC areas of focus. A week and a half wasn't nothing, and it would be more fun to spend it with Yasmin than without her.

Which meant the court martial would be a double bummer.

He said, "Don't call. This colonel has full deniability and we've got nothing except the dumb move coming under the border. We can make it back over ourselves, take it from there." Watching her turn to the front and look through the windshield. He could tell the reassuring effect those brief words were having on her. Yasmin took a deep breath, like she was at a yoga class. He said, "Do you know of any other tunnels under the fence?"

She was looking out the passenger window, to the other side. Her voice coming a little softer than before. "There's a tunnel in my sector that we've got under observation. The Bedouin know it's compromised and avoid it but sometimes we get Egyptian guys crossing."

"How's it monitored?"

Yasmin said, "Ground sensors and a trail cam. The area's

vast enough that we always catch them. The tunnel's too narrow to bring any kind of vehicle through. At least a kilometer crawl in the dark, another reason why we always get them, they're too tired to run."

"But it's monitored."

"From a base a couple of kilometers back from the border. I know some of the girls there. Maybe I can get them to look the other way for a minute."

He grinned. "You know the girls there."

She was nodding. "I think they'll do it, if I ask the right way." Yasmin glanced at him. "Let's get to the coordinates and I'll try. Worst-case scenario we go over and the army finds us. At least we'll be alive."

KEELER DROVE THE TOYOTA HARD. The desert coming on like an endless blue gray carpet with an unchanging dark horizon. The rolling hills turned into a flat, which continued for what seemed like an eternity, but was only fifteen minutes. It was the kind of driving where your mind could drift. A part of him was alert, ready for whatever was coming, prepared. The other part of his mind was in a state of deep relaxation, enjoying the edge that danger brought.

Yasmin said, "Stop."

He brought the vehicle to a halt. She was looking at him, all intense and aflame about something.

He said, "What?"

"We forgot about those guys back there. We left them defenseless, without weapons. You saw the one they mutilated. Don't you think they're going to kill them all?"

She was right that he'd forgotten about them, hadn't actually cared about them was more accurate. He wasn't in the habit of concerning himself with the fate of ISIS fighters. But she was also correct about the high probability of them being killed by the *El-Sa'Ka* squads.

He said, "And now you want to go back for them."

"No, I don't want to, but we need to." Looking at him with that expression he'd come to know, deep confidence in a decision.

Those were ISIS zombies back there, but they were currently unarmed and defenseless. It wasn't a difficult calculation and Yasmin wasn't wrong.

EIGHTEEN

KEELER TURNED NORTH, seeking the dry riverbed as a landmark, figuring it would take them back to the marsh grass area. He found the wadi, and the truck wobbled precariously as he navigated a descent into the river bed. He estimated that the shallow depression would at least provide them a modicum of cover from casual surveillance.

He ran the Toyota dark, but the *El-Sa'Ka* squad didn't feel the need to hide. Coming around a turn in the wadi Keeler saw lights up ahead on the right. He pulled the vehicle into the bank and killed the engine. He looked at Yasmin, her eyes wide and alert. She was already feeling that edge, a kind of high you get before battle.

He said, "You ready for this?"

She nodded.

They came out of the truck and began making their way up the wadi, hugging the shallow bank. As they got closer, what had begun as indistinct sounds from afar, clarified. There was harsh shouting and barked commands, and whimpers. Occasionally this was pierced by a shriek of agony.

Keeler signaled Yasmin to a stop by a large mound of thick

marsh grass. The soldiers and their victims were on the other side. He began to crawl in through the tall grass, stopping half way through to be able to see what was going on while remaining in cover. Yasmin inched up beside him.

The military vehicle was parked a way off, halogens illuminating the scene. Two of the *El-Sa'Ka* team were standing around watching a colleague torture one of the ISIS men. The commandos were laughing and giggling at the poor man's contortions. The victim's face was easily recognizable in the harsh light. It was the first one they'd found, the young sentry who hadn't been very good at his job. An *El-Sa'Ka* soldier was straddling him and doing something with a combat knife.

Two of the ISIS men were still on their knees, bound and naked. A third was dead, tossed like a limp rag by the side. Something had happened to his torso and Keeler realized that a large hole had been made at the level of the upper rib cage, which had been gouged out, the ribs cracked open. He turned his head slowly to look at Yasmin beside him. She was staring at the scene, horrified. The ISIS man's heart was literally hanging out of his dead body, resting on the sand.

He struggled to figure out exactly what the *El-Sa'Ka* commando was doing with the knife. Hard to believe, but it looked like he was skinning the kid alive.

Three soldiers, one vehicle. That's not how these guys played. They'd have a driver and passenger in the cab and two riding up on the truck's bed with the heavy machine gun. Where was the fourth soldier? Keeler signaled to Yasmin, two fingers apart poking out from eyes, two fingers together tapping his wrist, the numbers six and zero. She crawled back out of the grass, her job was to find the fourth man and be in position. Keeler had given her 60 seconds.

He didn't spend the next minute watching the ISIS man die slowly. He spent it making a plan, that he would put into motion rapidly, and hopefully effectively. Because they weren't going to have two chances. The *El-Sa'Ka* soldiers were wearing ceramic armored vests. Those could stop a bullet, but the force of a solid hit could buy a second or two.

Another thing he noticed, the two spectators hadn't removed their helmets, and he realized why, they were using the helmet mounted cameras. Keeler had a shock realization that these men were streaming live video of the torture scene. Of course, no way to know if it was streamed privately or to an internet platform.

The man straddling his victim had removed his helmet, which was in the dirt by the marsh grass. Keeler noted the camera, turned in the direction of the wadi.

Those things needed to be taken into consideration, incorporated into a plan. It would be better if his or Yasmin's faces weren't streamed live online just yet.

60 seconds were up.

He drew a bead on the first *El-Sa'Ka* soldier to his left. The man had his back to Keeler, crouched with his head tilted to the action, presumably so that he could better capture the scene on the helmet cam. The position left the back of his neck exposed. Keeler let his breath out easily as his finger put smooth weight on the trigger. He shot the man once in the neck, bullseye. He shifted the weapon immediately to the second standing man, who was in motion, whirling and frantic, getting his own weapon up and operational.

Keeler put a carefully aimed round into his upper thigh, near the groin, watching him spin and fall.

The first man he'd shot in the neck was face down, his helmet cam filming an intimate portrait of sand and dirt. The man with the groin wound was on his back in agony. Keeler dispassionately observed that the helmet cam would be facing to the sky, maybe catching stars, but more likely a shaking blur of darkness.

He rose up out of the marsh grass, moving laterally for three steps. The torturer with the knife had left his weapon barrel up, leaning on his helmet. He'd leapt off his victim and was in the process of making a mad dash for the AK. So far, the entire episode had taken two seconds.

Keeler shot him once in the back, hearing the sound of a bullet thwap into a ceramic plate. The impact was flush, the force of the shot pushing the man off balance. By the time he was scrambling up again, Keeler was standing over him with a foot on his chest. He pulled the trigger on the AK-47, putting a heavy round through the man's forehead into his brain pan. This guy wasn't going to be torturing any more defenseless prisoners. Someone should have taught him the basic rules of warfare.

Keeler saw in his peripheral vision that the man with the groin wound was getting a weapon up. Moving, weapon coming up. Searching for the target and then the target's head went into a weird kidney bean shape. Yasmin had shot him from the side.

She jogged over. "The fourth man was by the vehicle. Neutralized."

Keeler pointed at the two survivors cowering helplessly by the grass. "I want you to convince them to get into that Hilux truck and drive the hell out of here, up into the hills as fast and as far as possible." He swept a hand across the grisly landscape of dead *El-Sa'Ka* operators and their victims. He said, "Watch out for the helmet cams, I suspect they're streaming live."

Yasmin seemed a little taken aback by this idea, but it was pretty clear that he was right. She cursed and began moving to the panicked living captives.

Keeler had another idea. "Let's use the cameras."

They each put a helmet on, using them to film the awkward

corpses of the *El-Sa'Ka* heroes, doing their best to make it captivating viewing back wherever the *Mukhabarat* base was. They did that with both helmets before setting them strategically in the Hilux truck's bed. War had become strange, the battle zone had merged with media. Now, even a camera was a kind of weapon.

Keeler started moving bodies. He watched Yasmin with the captured men. It struck him that the men really listened to her, a kind of availability bias where, in their state of panic, Yasmin became the most reliable source of information. She seemed good at that kind of thing. Maybe a future in advertising loomed.

She came back, assisting him with the remaining corpse. "So tell me your plan. We're trying to distract the other *El-Sa'Ka* squads."

Keeler said, "Create a spectacle for them, drive them nuts so they lose their cool. If the other units pursue our friends here, we can use that to penetrate into their rear."

One of the *El-Sa'Ka* men wore a sidearm. Keeler removed the weapon, what looked like a Beretta 92, but had the words *Helwan 920, CAL 9mm, made in Egypt*. Helwan 920, the Egyptian copy, with the magazine release on the bottom of the mag. The pistol hadn't been fired in a while. The mag was full, fifteen rounds plus one in the chamber.

Yasmin was staring at him. "You want to get behind their lines?"

"Obviously." Keeler slipped the pistol into his waistband, liking the heft. He said, "Guy tries to have you killed, maybe putting him down first is a good idea, instead of wasting energy on his pawns." Keeler checked his weapon for dust and sand, clearing it and resetting the magazine. "The best defense is an active offense. Didn't they teach you that?"

∼

THE TWO ISIS survivors took off in a jabbering panic, engine screaming and tires kicking up plumes of gravel. Keeler gave them maybe an hour before the *El-Sa'Ka forces* caught them. But an hour was going to be enough to get north and breach the enemy line.

Keeler said, "I figure their base isn't so far away from here. Bet you five bucks that asshole's still at work."

"The colonel."

"Yeah. Bet you he's been called back from dinner or bed to deal with this. The man's probably apprehensive." He grinned. "Bet you he's not expecting a visitation though."

Yasmin was looking at him now, frowning. Like she was actually concerned about something. It took Keeler a second to understand it, that she thought he was insane.

Keeler was curious about that. He said, "A guy like that tries to toy with you, aims to kill you maybe, or get you kidnapped into the Gaza Strip by the most dangerous bunch of zombies in the world, you don't think he deserves hooligan treatment?" It didn't look like Yasmin had much to say about that. Keeler nodded at her. "Believe it. I'm taking him out."

He wasn't about to tell Yasmin the real reason. He wanted to improve their chances of making it back across the border, figuring that instead of defense, going straight up the chain of command was the best way of guaranteeing their return. Take out the leader and the chess pieces fall apart. Usually that meant a bullet in the leader's head. Keeler was okay with that.

The colonel had made his choices.

NINETEEN

It was research time.

Keeler had stopped the vehicle in a depression tucked behind rocky hills. A great spot for observing the desert to the north. Almost a hundred and eighty degree view while remaining out of sight themselves. Yasmin had her feet up on the dashboard, both of them tuned into the screens of smart phones they'd pilfered.

They were waiting to see if the El-Sa'Ka maniacs would pick up the bait they'd set by sending the surviving ISIS men into the mountains with high end Egyptian military vehicles. For sure the Hilux trucks were fitted with GPS tracking devices. The military would never allow them to get away without a fight.

Keeler had said 'the best defense is an active offense' and now similar expressions were populating Yasmin's mind. Her dad was an intellectual, so she'd read the classics.

She said, "He who strikes first, strikes twice."

Keeler grunted.

She said, "Control the conflict, and you control the outcome."

He said, "I like that one better."

Yasmin was looking at a mapping app, using her fingers to zoom in on satellite shots of nearby settlements, trying to decide which one looked most like a place where an intelligence officer in the feared Egyptian *Mukhabarat* might be hanging out. Keeler was beside her, looking for the same thing.

But then she remembered what the colonel had been wearing. The kind of clothing an Egyptian man would wear to something fancy, like a high-class dinner party. He wasn't dressed for work.

She nudged Keeler with an elbow. "Remember what he was wearing?"

Keeler said, "Cologne and hair oil."

"Yeah. You should check social media. keywords, colonel, stylish, and Egypt and maybe Sinai, and El-Arish. Maybe you'll get him. The stylish Egyptian colonel."

Keeler didn't raise his eyes. "You do that, I'm looking at the maps. Plus it'll be in Arabic."

"Right."

Yasmin started a rapid-fire sequence of tapping and swiping and pinching. She included his rank, colonel, handsome bachelor, Egypt, and then added keywords relating to the local area, the town of El-Arish on the coast. She was remembering the research. Sports clubs are hugely important for the upper classes. She ran a couple of searches, looking for private sports clubs from Port Said near Suez, to Rafah on the Gaza border. If the colonel lived in the area he'd be involved with a sports club. Some of the provincial clubs had affiliation with larger ones out of Cairo and Alexandria.

Keeler looked fascinated by something and she glanced at his screen. He was spreading finger and thumb to examine a small complex of buildings that seemed to have a significant antenna array, a separate installation away from the buildings.

She watched him stab a finger into the screen at a specific building.

"Right there, bet you a million bucks."

Yasmin didn't answer him, she was inside two social media platforms at the same time, getting hits on her search terms, adjusting and refining. Things were coming into focus.

Keeler jabbed again at the satellite image he'd found. "They've got Hilux trucks parked in the compound, at least they did when that picture was taken." Showing her the map image. "Let's do it."

Yasmin said, "He's not at work, he's out partying."

"How do you know that?"

She raised her phone, showing him the screen. Specifically, a social media post from one hour earlier. A girl making a pouty face selfie at a party. Like a red carpet affair with guests arriving. The colonel was recognizable behind the girl and her friend. He was coming out of a glossy black SUV, his mouth twisted as he said something to another man who might have been his brother.

Yasmin tapped the screen with a sky blue painted fingernail. "This is half an hour ago, up by El-Arish." She poked and swiped more, showing him. "The Palm Oasis Resort." Holding the phone so he could see the messy cluster of grids on a map at the coast.

Keeler said, "A party?"

She was reading and swiping, gathering information. "Looks like a birthday party for the Governor of North Sinai."

Keeler said, "Whoa there." Pointing through the windshield, which was too dusty for her to see much.

Yasmin got out of the truck. Looking out into the desert, seeing what looked like headlights coming at them. Keeler was next to her. They watched the headlights approach, turning into two sets.

She said, "You think it's them?"

"Wait and see."

They waited half a minute until the vehicles were identifiable. The headlights of the rear truck illuminating the one in front. A small convoy of militarized Hilux vehicles with mounted machine guns, kicking up dust.

Keeler said, "Looks like they're in a hurry. Outstanding."

She looked at Keeler nodding and staring at the death squad convoy passing below. She and Keeler were secure in their hidden position. No way the *El-Sa'Ka* troops could see them.

He turned to her. "Feels like a drive-in movie."

She said, "You want me to get the hot dogs? You want both ketchup and mustard?"

He grinned. "I like the hot onions. Maybe the colonel's got the grill going up in El-Arish."

They waited for the vehicles to pass. Keeler got in the vehicle and started the engine. The beat-up old truck teetered and tottered out of the wadi and down to the desert flat. Keeler steered around a few mounds of sand and got them moving in a straight line north.

YASMIN WAS NAVIGATING, telling him about routes and roads and intersections and likely points where they'd meet a check post. She was enjoying herself, liking Keeler, liking the weather and the smells of the desert going by, window open and elbow resting on the door. He was definitely having a good time, like a born commando. Watching him put his head out the window and holler into the night made her feel glad.

He was yelling the word *muqaddam*, with his atrocious American accent.

TWENTY

The *El-Sa'Ka* officer stank of sweat and bird shit. At least that's how the colonel associated the smell. He'd seen videos of the commandos undergoing their initiation rituals, which were disgusting. They'd force themselves to eat chickens and snakes alive, as if that somehow contributed to making an elite soldier.

Looking at the guy, watching the sweat on his face as he stared into the phone while holding it so that the colonel was able to see the screen. The video started off pretty steady, standard stuff of Egyptian *El-Sa'Ka* men toying with malnourished jihadist fighters they'd captured. Pretty distasteful if you were at a dinner party or something, but entertaining in the military context.

The colonel thought that one of the secrets of life was being able to balance the unavoidable shit you needed to do with the good stuff.

The game was all in service to *the big plan*.

Anyway, the unpleasant stuff was inescapable, but getting the balance right was important. In this case, the party. The Sinai desert was a shitty waste hole, but there was a single, shining, beautiful perk to the entire thing. Her name was Anastasia, and she was the most perplexing and complicated piece of perfection that the colonel had ever had the pleasure of holding in his hands and mind.

Since the colonel had finished his chores, it was time to chill. He figured he'd down a couple of drinks and get a little light so that by the time Anastasia showed up at the bungalow he'd be cool. But he was only one cocktail in when a bodyguard had tapped his shoulder and said that there was a visitor.

And now, instead of being out on the beach with the others, he was stuck with this *El-Sa'Ka* officer with his rotting bird stink.

Glancing at the guy again. The man's simian features, heavy lipped but clean shaven. Darkened by genetics and the desert sun. What were the necessary qualifications for this man's position, besides the family connections, sadistic tendencies maybe? An ability to put up with shit, for sure.

The officer was holding a large tablet device with two hands, currently showing an edit of video captured by *El-Sa'Ka* commandos wearing helmet mounted cameras. The scenes were at night, out in the desert and lit by strong halogen lights from their vehicles. While the video had been funny at first, when the commandos were torturing ISIS affiliated *Wilayat Sinai* men, it wasn't quite so funny to see the mangled corpses of expensively trained special forces soldiers unceremoniously piled into the back of their own Toyota Hilux truck.

The colonel got hot and heavy and had to breathe for a moment. When he'd calmed a little he said, "You're tracking the barbarians into the mountains now?"

The officer said, "Yes sir. The *Wilayat Sinai* scum are not aware that we track our vehicles."

The colonel thought about that for a few seconds. "Well, they probably are aware of that, unless you think they're stupid." The officer just looked at him blankly. "Because if they were simply stupid, you'd have an easy time wiping them out, isn't that correct?"

The officer said nothing. The colonel blinked and things blurred for a half second. He went into a weird fantasy mode, like watching a movie. In the movie he slapped the officer in the face, hard, knocking him back. He blinked again, back to reality.

The colonel said, "Am I correct?"

"Yes sir."

"Where's your second in command?"

The man said, "Sir, he's out there with the rest of the force."

The colonel said, "And what about the Zionist whore and the American?"

"What about them?"

"Where are they?"

The officer shrugged and puffed out his chest, like he was proud of something. "We'll come back for them when we've had our revenge."

The Palm Oasis resort had extensive grounds, irrigated and designed so that the landscape resembled someone's idea of a golf club, minus the golf, but with perfectly green grass and water features connecting multiple pools, bridges arcing over chlorinated streams that twisted among palm fronds and fresh beds of desert succulents and cactus.

They were about a hundred meters from the club house, tucked back into a quiet area under a sunshade canopy. The music from the party had gone up a notch in tempo, some kind of Brazilian beat. The colonel felt rage flowing up from his feet to his head and exploding out the top of his skull.

The blurring thing happened again. Blinking and then a half second of blur, going into movie mode. The colonel punched the officer in the face as hard as he could. Which was hard since his fitness club had boxing on Sundays, after the yoga session. The colonel's meaty fist landed somewhere between the man's chin and cheek bone, a knuckle glancing off the soldier's first molar.

The officer staggered backwards. In his fantasy, the colonel had prepared for that. He stamped on the man's knee and shoved him to the ground. The soldier went down and the colonel stepped on his head, grinding his face into the paved footpath.

The chlorine stank.

There was a female voice from behind him. The *El-Sa'Ka* man gone, and the colonel was leaned over the banister, looking into the chlorinated stream below, illuminated by submerged LED lights. The colonel stood up, realizing as he did so that the violence had not been real. He'd been in movie mode again.

Anastasia came into the light. She was about twenty-eight years old, the colonel had guessed, and a real blonde. Not only a real blonde, but a seriously real woman. The presence of this person was almost overwhelming, coming as she did into the most intimate proximity in a matter of seconds. She had her hand up at his cheek, concern in her intelligent eyes. Anastasia might be Russian, but she spoke perfect Arabic.

"Are you alright my colonel?"

"I'm fine."

His mouth was dry. Anastasia wore some kind of dress made out of a fabric that seemed visually to have substance, but materially was nothing more than a kind of cotton candy, or a fluff. His hand moved through it, almost immediately landing on her firm flesh. The hip substantial but not soft. She wore scent, and he breathed it in.

Her left arm came around his neck, pulling him to her. The colonel felt her hot mouth brushing against the skin below his ear. Her voice a whisper.

"You're fine now honey."

Anastasia was a little taller than him, the height even more exaggerated with the heels. Her thigh moved against his crotch.

She said, "Oh, sorry."

He said, "What?"

She was moving against him now, her mouth finding his and kissing him long and slow. The colonel was almost out of control, but this was Egypt and he couldn't just take her here and now. As usual Anastasia could read his mind.

"Oh, my colonel. I've got just what you need."

He managed a few incoherent syllables, feeling her hand on his sex now, taking his measure. He was effectively mute.

She said, "I got the key to the bungalow."

AFTERWARDS THE COLONEL lay on the king-sized bed, naked and feeling like royalty. Anastasia stroked his chest with her fingernails, trailing them through the thick hair. One of her long legs was entwined with his and in a constant if barely perceptible undulating motion.

She said, "Debrief me my colonel."

He began speaking, looking directly into the ceiling fan, telling her everything that had happened. He didn't know if Anastasia was really a prostitute, but she was definitely an intelligence operative. The fact that she was his case officer had never been discussed, but as an intelligence operative and case officer himself, he knew that to be a correct description of their relationship. He was her agent, and she was running him.

He assumed that she was Russian, but he'd never asked the question.

Anastasia held onto her questions until he got to the El-Gora situation, giving the folder to the CIA man, Bill.

She said, "And Bill seemed to be happy about it?"

"I think so, although he was pretending to play it tough."

She nodded to herself, gazing into the air. "What did the general say about the American and his Israeli girlfriend?"

"He's only interested in money."

Anastasia stopped stroking his chest, and he had an almost immediate reduction in oxytocin.

"What did he say?"

Her eyes were piercing his, which felt like being in the grip of a vastly superior creature.

"The general said to get rid of them. He's onboard."

"But that's not working is it my colonel?"

Her fingernails began working however, and the good times returned, relaxing the colonel into a perfect stupor. He was even beginning to feel himself ready again, almost.

He said, "The El-Sa'Ka will find him."

She purred. "They'll try and they'll probably fail, since they've failed so miserably until now." Anastasia yawned, her entire body moving beside his, skin on skin. She threw her leg over him and mounted. Long blonde hair flowing into his face. "They don't deserve you here habibi. They really don't."

Her breasts were perfectly round and firm, resting on his chest.

The exact dimensions of heaven.

TWENTY-ONE

THE APPROACH to El-Arish was a narrow track winding around desert foot hills. The city lights appeared quite suddenly from the darkness. Resembling a moderately advanced civilization emerging out of pre-history. The truck rocked on uneasy springs, the inside smelling like stale tobacco and cardamon.

Keeler said, "Civilization."

Yasmin said, "Some form of it, yeah."

Keeler said, "Civilization is a diner open twenty-four hours a day, with a menu that consistently delivers, plus good coffee mugs that hold the heat."

She said, "You can get KFC in El-Arish."

"A poor substitute."

A string of bright orange lights came into view from a distance, running east to west, parallel to the sea. Yasmin drew the line with a finger. "Coastal highway, feeding towns and terminating in Rafah, a city split in half by the border between Egypt and Gaza."

She was making geopolitical commentary, but Keeler was thinking about KFC. A bucket, with fries, ketchup all over it.

Maybe barbecue sauce and an orange soda, preferably Fanta. He was okay with limited civilization.

They dipped into a hollow, the track winding around desert hills before cresting at a higher elevation. El-Arish came into view as a riot of cheap concrete block housing on the other side of the highway. Up on the right was a driveway marked by a broken sign showing a faded image of a child eating a date.

Keeler instinctively pulled the truck in, driving a minute into what turned out to be an abandoned date palm plantation. Yasmin didn't remark on the move. He stopped eventually beside a rotting date palm. Fifty yards down was a gaping ruin of a building. Beyond that was a steep drop and the coastal road. They could access El-Arish via a descending track to the highway. The other thing was a feeder road, visible now, reaching down into the city.

Keeler was happy with it, a great spot from which to observe the approach to town. Looking at the road into town, Keeler wondered if there would be check points further in. Messed up parts of the world like this, it was likely to mean nervous soldiers checking cars.

Yasmin looked out at the view, the starlight casting a highlight to her cheekbones. Keeler liked her, more than that he was into her. She looked at him and he knew that she was feeling the same.

She said, "Not now, cowboy."

He said, "Ok."

Yasmin said, "If we gussy up a little we might pass as guests at the birthday party." She chuckled. "As long as I do the talking and nobody's looking for us."

Keeler said, "I'll have to check my wardrobe."

She said, "Ask your stylist."

The kidding around was a poor substitute for sex. Keeler wasn't into delayed gratification.

He said, "Cowboy says bullshit."
"Yeah?"
"Yeah, bullshit."

Clearly, she felt the same. The rush. Something weird and magnetic about it. They came together in a kind of hyperreal choreography. No fumbling, everything sliding into everything else in perfect unison and harmony. Like a kind of love, even though Keeler would never say it. The clothes were there, and then they weren't. Yasmin was sitting on the other side of the pickup truck cab's bench, and then she wasn't. She was straddling him, taller than she could be in the confined space, making do with the situation.

Skin was like silk. Her mouth was like a perfect furnace, as was her sex. Perfectly hot. The best place to be. He felt his rational mind slipping away for a while, giving into the human animal. Then there was an intensity, a grinding plateau that could have lasted forever. The thing you want to maintain, a heightened pleasure that should last, but can't.

Afterwards Keeler was outside of the pick up truck, taking a piss.

A single headlight became visible at a distance, a two-wheeled vehicle, speeding in their direction from the town. Looked like a moped. A couple seconds later Keeler made out the guy riding it, shorts and a t-shirt, a delivery man, judging by the large box on the back.

Keeler got into the truck and closed the door. He pointed at the incoming moped. "There's your KFC delivery."

She looked up. The moped pulled onto the coastal highway for a moment and then came off-road onto a dirt track, winding uphill towards their position. The delivery driver was oblivious to their presence, seated there in a beat up old pickup truck, blending into the dull landscape. The guy came up a winding path into the palm plantation.

Keeler was thinking about the guy, and how it was pretty likely he'd regret this detour, if he lived.

Yasmin said, "He's going to stop and eat a pizza. Bet you a million bucks."

Keeler said, "Not a pizza, a kebab."

The moped parked in front of the abandoned building. Keeler figured the driver might be hiding from the road, didn't want to be observed. The rider balanced his helmet between the handle bars and walked back.

Yasmin said "Pizza."

The delivery man pulled a paper bag out of the large box behind the seat.

Keeler said, "Not pizza."

Yasmin giggled. The guy walked into the abandoned building and disappeared from sight. Keeler looked at her in a significant way.

Yasmin said, "What?"

Keeler tilted his head at her. "You know."

She said, "What?"

He jerked his head at the abandoned building. "Guy's chowing down."

She said, "Uh huh. Yup."

He said, "Dice are falling, Yaz."

"You've never called me that before."

"Doesn't change the way the dice roll. Know what I mean?"

"Yeah."

They were on the same page. The delivery guy was about to become collateral damage. His moped and helmet were simply too useful, too timely, given the mission.

Keeler opened the driver side door and didn't bother to close it, moving down to the abandoned building in the shadow of the sharp rocky hillside. Aware of Yasmin doing the same, using the date palms as cover. He came around the side of the squat building and vaulted through a punched out hole in its side, what had once been a window.

He landed lightly, making only a slight scratching sound. The room was dark, concrete rubble and garbage in the floor. He avoided the detritus, stepping to the doorway. No door. Just a hole in the wall and the kid about thirty feet away eating fried chicken with earbuds stuffed into his head. The audio leak was profound, filling the place with the shrill echo of a soccer game announcer screaming in Arabic.

The delivery guy was maybe 16 years old, wholly occupied by the game and a large chicken thigh he'd pulled out of the KFC bag. His eyes were glued to the phone, seeming to Keeler as captivated as a soft prey animal might be, chewing on the high savannah grass.

By the time the kid noticed him it was too late. Keeler wasn't even moving fast, just walking quietly from the spot where he'd entered, staying in the shadows as much as possible. He detached himself from the darkness and entered the kid's peripheral vision. The boy made only a quick gasp, wide eyed in fear and trembling. Keeler was crouched behind him within a second, thick arms squeezing the consciousness out of him, careful not to restrict the blood flow for long.

Yasmin was there when he eased the delivery boy to the ground. Together they stripped, bound, and blindfolded him. The clothes were a size too small in either direction. Keeler pulled off his own clothes and started trying to get into the kid's. Yasmin was looking at him.

Keeler said, "What?"

She said, "What are you going to do?"

The t-shirt was an ancient white cotton souvenir with a faded print of a city skyline and the words: *Dallas, Texas.*

He shrugged, thinking that it didn't matter exactly what he did, as long as it worked. He said, "I'm going to take the colonel's head off his shoulders, is what I'm going to do." Keeler pulled at the hem of the t-shirt, trying to get it stretched. Luckily baggy clothes were in fashion.

Yasmin said, "You didn't like what the colonel did, huh? Took it personally."

Keeler glanced at her, wondering what it was she didn't understand. "I didn't like it, but that's not the important thing. The important part is us getting out of here, Yasmin. Taking this guy's head off means the body will cease to function. You get what I'm saying? It's a metaphor."

He put a hand on hers and she linked fingers.

Keeler jerked his head back into the desert. "I don't know what else they've got waiting for us out there. So I figure it'd be better if we just took off the head. Maybe the rest of the body will die all by itself, if you know what I mean."

Yasmin looked away. "Good hunting."

He knew what she wasn't happy about, staying around to babysit the kid. Nothing he could do about that. Women didn't just ride around on mopeds in this part of the world. Yasmin knew that better than he did.

TWENTY-TWO

The moped's engine had been derestricted, the motor tuned to a high pitch, capable of making a screaming whine when he cranked the throttle. The seat vibrated uncomfortably beneath him, the machine stinking of oily two stroke fumes.

The AK-47 didn't fit into the delivery box, so he'd left it behind.

Good thing the Helwan 920 pistol fit nice and snug at the small of his back. Fifteen rounds plus one in the pipe.

Keeler had to wait before entering the main road, holding the bike steady on an incline, front brake helping out. A large truck came past kicking up dust, moving east, in the direction of Rafah, in other words the Gaza Strip. Looking at the load, a tarp covered trailer, Keeler was wondering what it carried. Humanitarian aid maybe, or utilitarian stuff, like cement or weapons.

What else did people send to Gaza?

The truck gone, Keeler steered the bike onto the highway, zipping away from Gaza and making a right off the coastal road onto the lumpy track to El-Arish. Just as he'd predicted, a military checkpoint appeared after the second twist of road.

He thought: What would the kid do?

The driver might be delivering to that check point, or coming through several times a day. The soldiers would be from out of town, Keeler guessed. The kid would be a local. Maybe the locals would resent the Egyptian military. He might even be afraid of them. Which meant the kid would try to avoid them.

By the time Keeler found himself thinking about that, he was already headed full speed at the checkpoint, sort of over committed. The barrier was down, and wasn't the automatic kind, rather an object that required a person using body weight and strength to lift it. Which would mean the soldiers rising from their current positions, leaning back against concrete breeze blocks smoking cigarettes, AK-47 rifles slung back.

Plus they were stoned. It was obvious, the way they moved and their reactions to his appearance on a fast moving moped. He could get the pistol out and kill them all before they understood what was happening. Three of the four men were looking in his direction, the other one was trying to light a cigarette, futzing with the lighter.

The kid would never stop, Keeler realized in a flash. He'd blow through.

Keeler carved left at the last moment, coming around the side of the checkpoint. He steered off-road and into rough sand and pebble, balancing with one foot dragging the ground. The rear tire kicked left, skidding out. Keeler nosed back up on the asphalt and took a look back. The men hadn't moved yet, they weren't even watching him. One of them tossed a butt, another guy looked like he was talking and a third laughing at the joke.

Keeler twisted the throttle, keeping track of the grunts in his side mirror, pretty much kids themselves.

The road ahead was just flat desert scrub. El-Arish coming on as a mess of dispersed shacks and Bedouin tents, dusty camels in the head lights and then he was into the first concrete structures, residential things looking half abandoned. Orange lights cast a weak glow over cats and garbage, old cars and a few people out on the streets. Three burka clad shapes moved out of a darkened doorway. A couple of streets later he caught a glimpse of a bent man leading a donkey.

The town got busier, and then it got crowded. A few dense minutes of that was enough for Keeler. He got trapped in a cluster of people, slightly concerned that he'd run into the friends or family of the delivery driver tied and bound back at the date palm plantation.

The weapon snug in his waistband helped psychologically.

Keeler got out of the center. The rutted road arrived at the beach. He took a right, out of town in the direction of Rafah. The Palm Oasis resort was about a kilometer from the center of El-Arish.

A minute of beach riding and the streetlights gave way to full darkness, punctuated only by the occasional headlight. Like the other side of town, most buildings seemed abandoned. A caravan of camels blocked the road and Keeler went around them, getting dead looks from a group of teenagers dressed in rags, the moped raising dust in their faces. An old beggar appeared out from behind a tin shack. The man put out two hands unconvincingly and Keeler made brief eye contact.

He said, "No one can help you buddy."

The entrance to the Palm Oasis was an impressive check point embedded into a pillared arch, like a prop in a stage play. High walls painted salmon pink ran either side of the entrance, illuminated by spot lights planted into the dirt.

Keeler took the moped past, stealing a good look at the security. The men at the check point were not stoned and bored Egyptian soldiers. They were alert military aged males in black suits with tight geometrically shaped beards. But to Keeler's critical eye though, these guys were a little too well fed. In his view, the only attribute most proficient operators shared was that they looked consistently hungry.

Keeler followed a dirt track running alongside the wall, inland towards the coastal highway.

At first the sea presented itself as the best option for infiltration, and Keeler was always up for a bracing swim. But, on closer examination the wall had more potential. It was longer and therefore made a greater attack surface.

TWENTY-THREE

The wall ended at an embankment and cornered ninety degrees into an area thick with old palms, basically the far end of the Palm Oasis Resort's property. The dirt track ran into a tunnel, bored out of the embankment, a dark hole with only dim light at the end. Keeler pulled into a narrow residential street and parked the moped. The apartment blocks were uniform, three stories. The streets were unpaved. Local kids had been practicing spray painting their names on a wall using the Latin alphabet, *Ehab, Khaled, Shash, Amro*. The humidity from the sea was casting a haze, made dull orange by the street lights.

Keeler felt *watched*. The operative assumption being that behind the closed doors and windows, frightened people hid and spied. He didn't know El-Arish. The place looked temporary and fragile.

Walking back towards the Palm Oasis compound, a bearded man appeared out of a doorway, stepping from absolute darkness into orange tinted shadow. The man looked unfed and unbathed, growling something in Arabic, making a hand gesture. Keeler grunted back at him and raised his hands trying to mirror the gesture and kept on moving. The man didn't follow.

Keeler took a left along the wall, looking for some excuse to loiter. A kid's bike had been discarded by the side of the road, tossed into the landscaped verge. He squatted to examine it, like was interested in scavenging the thing. Keeler wasn't the first to have had that idea, the brake and gear mechanisms were missing.

The good news was that nobody seemed to be paying any attention to him. He didn't spot surveillance cameras or lookouts, or guards. Possibly they'd be running mobile patrols along the perimeter.

Keeler walked to one of the old palms and slipped between the tree and the wall. He shimmied up until his butt was at the top of the wall. Still nothing moving except stray cats, no activity at all. Maybe he wasn't being watched.

The shadow made by the palm tree kept Keeler out of the light. He spun around, looking out over the resort's grounds. It took a moment for his eyes to adjust. Within the walls the park was a soft velvety darkness punctuated by dapples of warm light, where water features had been highlighted.

He dropped down into cool grass, touching it with the palms of his hands. The sounds of El-Arish were gone, leaving a low hum of pool filtration systems and drip irrigation. In the distance he could make out the clatter of silverware and glass clinking. laughter and an insistent oriental beat.

Keeler kept to the dark patches, moving normally, like a person would if they were strolling at night. The party was happening by the beach. There were buildings between the grounds and the action, muffling the music. Two men moved along a parallel footpath, deep in a hushed conversation. They were around twenty yards away. Keeler avoided them. He made a wide arc around the cluster of club house buildings, staying clear of the silhouetted party goers.

He found a good observation point inside a beach pagoda perched up on an artificially grassy verge.

Below him, the dance floor was a torrent of movement. Limbs and thick bodies convulsed. Tables had been set up on the hard packed beach sand. No colonel in sight. Keeler waited two minutes, just watching and thinking about the scene.

It wasn't an adult only party, the whole family was invited. Keeler was looking at groups of teenagers and tweens. The kids were divided by gender. He noticed the female tweens were engaged in an eating activity, scooping something out of cardboard cups with plastic spoons, delivering the delicacy to hungry young mouths.

He tracked it back to a guy handing the cups out of a cart over by a club house building, spooning stuff out of steaming pots. Keeler approached. There was no verbalizing necessary, the guy knew why he was there and simply handed over a cardboard cup and a spoon. The stuff was hot and milky and very sweet. A kind of custard flavored with rose water and cardamon, sprinkled with crushed pistachio. Pretty good.

Nobody seemed to find Keeler out of place, which was fantastic. No doubt if he got inside, closer to the VIPs, that could change.

For now he strolled easily, enjoying the milky custard, on the lookout for signs of the colonel, excited at the prospect of getting his hands on the guy. He walked through a group of middle-aged men with tans and manicured fingernails, smelling of cologne. More of them and their wives were seated at the tables. Closer in Keeler could see that alcohol was being consumed.

Getting involved in the table situation would be tricky, it

was dense, the interactions occurring at seated level. You'd have to wade through it. Still no colonel.

Up in the club house he could see more middle-aged men in suits. Keeler strolled around the back of the building, thinking maybe he'd find a service entrance or something. Thinking about how he'd do it, separate the colonel from the rest and take him out.

Improvising.

The club house was a round structure, Mediterranean chic. The walkway stepped up to a wrap-around deck. Between that and the building was a sunken space with air conditioning units and a pallet of used beer kegs. Keeler took a final spoon full of the custard, chewing crushed pistachio and hitting a kernel of pomegranate, hot and good. He scooted down the steps, slipping behind the kegs to a service door. The knob turned, and he was looking into a back of a kitchen. Shelving units and a long steel table with a sink.

People were in there, busy with kitchen tasks. The resort was busy with workers, the layout designed to facilitate discreet movement while hiding their presence from the guests as much as possible.

Keeler slipped through and closed the door. A pair of blue dishwashing gloves were draped over the faucet of a sink. He tossed the cardboard cup into a trash can and pulled the gloves on, finding the fingers a little tight. On the way out he grabbed a pile of white linen napkins, stacking them on an empty platter. He'd never worked in hospitality, but carrying a platter piled with fresh folded linens and wearing dishwashing gloves seemed a decent camouflage.

The Helwan 920 at his back was cool and heavy.

The kitchen was large, with maybe a dozen men sweating over the grills and ovens. Some seared and steamed, others were stirring and chopping. Still more of them were occupied with slicing and plating, putting the finishing touches on dishes and moving them towards large double doors swinging in and out. Black and white clad male waiters retrieved the final product from where it rested beneath heat lamps. They banged in and out through double doors.

Keeler avoided eye contact and took a position by a stack of champagne glasses, piled up three glasses high.

The traffic through the door was relentless. Through them, he was able to examine the crowd. Maybe a couple hundred guests packed in there, swaying and partying. Keeler picked up the platter of champagne glasses and walked backwards through the swinging doors, spinning to enter the crowd.

The music was intense, booming middle eastern beats, swallowed by a computer and spit out with glitches. It took a moment for him to get used to the hustling vibe, get comfortable with it. Faces moved past, flushed and excited. Five steps in and he saw the colonel, deep in conversation, in front of a promotional stand for beachfront real estate. The Egyptian intelligence officer's tanned and handsome face shone with sweat, eyes gleaming.

Keeler maneuvered the stack of champagne glasses between himself and his target. The platter balanced on his left shoulder. Guests were coming in from the beach, laughing and falling over themselves. It was a good party. Keeler moved closer to the colonel, recognizing the man's false laughter, a kind of deep fake guffaw.

TWENTY-FOUR

A couple of yards from the promotional stand was a trestle table laden with *hors d'oeuvres*. Pastries and meat kebabs on sticks with cut vegetables and fruit and bowls of pureed chickpea and other bean related substances. A half dozen guests were in there, using fingers and fists. Piling edibles onto small plates, grabbing and clutching.

Keeler set the tray of champagne glasses down at the end of the table, his back now turned to the colonel. He hooked a boot around one of the table legs, discreetly lifted the table a little at a time until it reached its tipping point. Nobody watching, nobody paying him any mind. The guests were in a feeding frenzy, oblivious to the table's slight tilt.

He pushed and lifted while releasing his boot from the table leg. Keeler turned away right as the tipping point was exceeded and the entire edifice began its downward trajectory. By the time the glasses hit the floor, he was well away and moving on target. A cascade of shattering glass was met by howls and surprised squeals.

Which meant that the colonel didn't notice danger approaching, busy rubbernecking like everyone else.

Keeler went in hard, quickly getting deep into the colonel's personal space and putting a lighting quick double knuckle jab into the man's windpipe. The colonel went still and Keeler grabbed him with both hands, one at the collar, the other at his belt. He moved the man back. The colonel gagged and choked.

Keeler said, "Hello old buddy. Looks like you've swallowed something down the wrong pipe. Let's go get you some air."

The colonel made panicked eye contact. His face registered shock, the muscles going rigid, lips drawn back over shiny white teeth. His eyes bulged, swiveling in sockets, seeking body guards or security. But the guardians were distracted and Keeler had already propelled him behind the promotional stand, out of sight mostly.

Potted indoor palms screened the main party space from an exit door.

Keeler elbowed the door open, frog marching the Egyptian through it, dragging the man three steps to a walkway sunken into beds of desert vegetation. On the other side of that was the beach and the sea. The party music bopped and people laughed and screamed.

The Mediterranean breeze was cool after the muggy interior of the club house. The colonel tried to wrench free of his grip, like he was annoyed. Keeler put a fist into his gut, palm slapping the nape of his neck. They walked the rest of the way in silence, the colonel having given up the fight. Keeler's arm looped through his armpit, his right hand holding the man's neck, fingers dug into the generous flesh. After maybe a minute of fast marching Keeler stopped, satisfied with the relative seclusion.

The colonel looked at him and Keeler kicked the man's feet out from under him. He guided his prey to the ground, the grip relentless on the man's neck. The colonel's face smashed into hard sand. Keeler ground it in there, hoping to do damage. The

Egyptian made a muffled sound, between a hiccup and a groan. Keeler searched him, finding only an embossed leather wallet in his pocket.

Flipping it open revealed an official identification card with the colonel's photograph. Unfortunately everything written was in the Arabic language. Keeler couldn't even read the guy's name. Obviously an official of some kind, the seal was an eagle messing with a snake, an eye floating above it, a lighting bolt in the background.

Keeler tossed the wallet into a bed of succulent plants and cactus.

He got down so the colonel could hear him. "You're trying to have my friend and me killed. It isn't working. You did succeed in making me come after you." He lifted the man's head by his hair and slammed his face deeper into the sand. "Why are you being a threat?"

The Egyptian said something incomprehensible. Keeler pulled him up again.

The colonel spat out sand and blinked. His face was a little messy with blood. He spoke perfect English, "You're what, an assassin. I'm not completely understanding our relationship, Frenchman."

The colonel was smiling.

Keeler fished the Helwan 920 out from his waistband. He pushed the pistol into the colonel's forehead. "Shooting you in the head won't be a novel experience for me."

The colonel did a good job pretending to look bored. Under the circumstances it couldn't be easy.

He said, "I've dispatched my fair share of killers. The real ones don't talk about doing it, it just gets done. You aren't a regular killer, just like you aren't really French, Frenchman."

Keeler said, "That's probably correct. I'm cursed with

curiosity. I guess I want to know why you want us dead. You could have let us go back through the tunnel."

The colonel spat more sand out of his mouth. His tongue ran over teeth, ejecting hard grains. He said, "Why what, why bother, why have you killed?" He looked up at Keeler with hooded eyes. "Because I felt like it. I won't lie to you. I just felt like having you and your arrogant Israeli girlfriend die in Gaza. Like that was a suitable continuation. Is that good enough? I liked the idea of it aesthetically."

"You know she wouldn't have simply died in Gaza."

The colonel shrugged. "The Israelis are always saying it's a tough neighborhood."

Keeler punched him hard in the nose, crushing cartilage. The colonel's head snapped back on his thick neck. He steadied himself and smiled, wiping the blood away with a sleeve.

The colonel raised an eyebrow. "I can understand you don't like me, Frenchman. I'll tell you what, out here a man with a little power always finds ways of pretending he's got more. This is a crazy place, believe me." His laugh was wild. "You're fitting in perfectly."

Keeler had been around. He knew how insane it could get out in places like the North Sinai. He thumbed the safety lever on the weapon. He said, "This is what kind of gun?"

The colonel said, "Beretta 92 copy, made in Egypt under the name Helwan 920. Shitty pistol. Welcome to the third world. You're taking your life into your hands if you fire that thing. Mostly it'll blow back in your face." He laughed. "I don't know where you got that, I'm guessing from one of the soldiers you killed, who must have been low ranking since he couldn't afford something better. Bet he never actually fired it."

But the Egyptian's own face had become red. The man was perspiring freely now, soaking through his suit.

Keeler said, "You're sweating so much I'm almost embarrassed for you."

The colonel's expression fell, eyes darted behind Keeler, looking at something up the beach.

Keeler turned his head to look and saw a flash of light, like a storm coming in from the east. He ignored the lightning.

"I want to know what you were doing back there by the border." He pushed the barrel into the colonel's sweaty forehead. "You're such a high-class guy. Why were you hanging around those infiltrators?"

The colonel wasn't paying attention, he was looking over Keeler's shoulder to the storm out there. Keeler glanced back, keeping the pressure on the pistol. Another flash of lightning.

The colonel mumbled to himself. "Gaza."

Keeler dug the pistol harder into the flesh, trying to make a mark. The man grunted and looked at him, dull confusion in his eyes.

He was illuminated by another flash of light. He said it again, to himself. "Gaza."

TWENTY-FIVE

The barrel hurt, digging into the colonel's forehead. But being six cocktails deep, he was effectively anesthetized. He giggled and looked away from the distant flashes strobing up the coast.

He looked back at the American and said, "Shit."

The American said, "I asked you a question."

The colonel didn't remember the question, because he'd just realized the complexity of his problem.

Essentially, he was between a rock and a hard place, as Americans like to say.

The American might shoot him in the head, right here and now. That was one outcome. Call it the rock. The colonel had been around the block a couple of times, and he didn't think the American would pull the trigger.

The new thing was this lightning, the storm. Call it the hard place.

The American didn't know it yet, but this was no storm, and the flashes weren't coming from any weather-related incident, they were coming from exploding munitions up in Gaza, the Israelis bombing tunnels again. Something must have happened up there, maybe the psychos in Hamas or Palestinian Islamic Jihad were firing rockets into Israeli population centers again, drawing retaliatory fire right on schedule.

What the Israelis called *mowing the grass*.

This was now a regular occurrence, as was the frenzied reaction of Egyptian military brass. Something the colonel hadn't entered into his operational calculus, the greed of his own people. The richest Gazans always got desperate to buy their way over the border into Egypt. The price went up from the usual five grand a person to ten. Entire families became desperate to get away from there. Hence, competition for the bribes became fierce among the Egyptian military elite.

Which meant screaming generals and big shots angling for their cut. The pile of gold was always going to be finite, so it became very cut throat.

This was going to be complicated. If he had to guess, the general was already blowing up his phone. Luckily it was back at the bungalow with Anastasia.

Now, the American was digging the pistol into his forehead again, drawing blood, insisting that he answer the question. The colonel remembered what it was, *why he'd been down by the Israeli border earlier*. The American was dangerous.

He said, "I'm here for the party, Frenchman." The colonel waved his hand to the south east. "I was checking up on smugglers at the border. We use them as informants. If they're not terrorists, we sometimes allow it."

The American said, "Yeah, bullshit."

There were more flashes from up the coast. The colonel smiled.

"Weather comes in from the sea here." He pointed out to the Mediterranean. "Do you see weather out there?"

The sky above the sea was velvety black, and studded with stars, not a cloud in sight. The colonel licked his lips, buying time. With the situation kicking off in Gaza, someone was bound to come looking for him. Given the number of security officers here tonight at the Palm Oasis Resort, the party would be over within a half hour.

The music had stopped. Now, instead of music there was the sound of shouting. People were moving out.

The American had noticed. The pistol was down now. He said, "What's going on?"

The colonel bent to blow blood from his nose into the sand. He pointed towards the east. "The shit has hit the fan over there again."

"Over where?"

"Gaza. They'll be looking for me now so you'd better leave."

He saw the comprehension in the American's eyes. That the lightning wasn't from a storm.

The colonel said, "The Israelis are bombing the tunnels again. Which is a bummer, since I get a good passive income stream. They'll rebuild, but it might take a while."

A bodyguard was coming up the footpath, heavy set and out of breath. He stopped as soon as he saw the colonel, waving his hand to beckon. "Sir, come with me now please."

The American put the pistol to the colonel's head. They made eye contact. The colonel was surprised, as he hadn't believed that the American would do it. The big man squeezed the trigger, and the colonel felt a thud as the pistol misfired. The hammer had hit, but the round didn't ignite. His first thought was faulty ammo, or a messed up firing pin.

The colonel coughed. He couldn't believe it. He'd identified the gun, a Helwan 920, Egyptian made copy of a Beretta 92. Home-grown incompetence had saved his life.

The bodyguard was standing there like an idiot, paralyzed. The colonel screamed. "Kill him!"

The American moved too fast for the colonel to track. Like a beast. He'd seen videos of lion attacks. A hunter with a rifle and the lion comes at them out of the bush. The American was like that, all thick muscle and intent.

The bodyguard was caught reaching into his suit blazer. The American leapt at him, kicking his knee. The man fell, and the American was on him, striking him with the pistol, the contact accurate and forensic. The colonel looked around him, getting desperate. The plant beds had stones. He found a big one, red and beige and the size of a grapefruit. He picked it up and ran over, fast as he could.

The American was doing things with the pistol. Crouched over the unconscious bodyguard. He was working out the issues, ejecting the failed round and checking the magazine. In a second he'd be ready. The colonel crashed the rock down on the back of the American's head, failing to get a solid hit, but the glancing blow sufficient to temporarily stop this man.

The American lost his balance, tipping over onto the unconscious bodyguard, a hand out to stabilize his fall. The pistol fell, still unassembled.

The colonel turned and ran. As fast as he could, a kind of zigzag through the beds of cactus and succulents. He didn't think twice, or look back. At the beach there were people. The guests were all out now, rubber necking at the flash and bang of JDAMS or bunker busters, or whatever else the Israeli Air-Force was using to collapse arms smuggling tunnels from Sinai into Gaza.

Now the clap and bang of heavy munitions was coming through loud and clear. The border area was getting ripped, that was for sure. The colonel turned to look back, feeling more secure in the crowd. The American was gone, and the bodyguard hadn't stood up or anything, so he'd still be out cold.

Which was almost the best outcome possible. Now the colonel wouldn't need to explain anything at all to his own people. It was like nothing had happened, yet. The bodyguard would remember something, being hit by someone. He wouldn't know anything else and the colonel could say that he didn't either.

He went right into the sea and washed away the blood. Getting all traces of the fight off him, not caring about the soaked clothing. He came back up from the beach, avoiding the club house and going straight to the bungalow.

TWENTY-SIX

Anastasia was on the bed, sitting upright and naked with a phone in her hand.

She watched him come in, expression not so much disapproving as curious.

"My colonel. What happened?"

He spoke all in a rush, mumbling words that fell out of his mouth all mixed up, ranting and raving about the American. The colonel couldn't help it, hadn't yet calmed sufficiently to get his head together. As usual, Anastasia helped.

She sat him down, clucking over him like a mother goose. The clothes came off. The bath was run. The colonel was treated well, his wounds cleaned. Anastasia went away for several minutes and returned with fresh clothing. He didn't speak, just lying there in the warm bath water, looking at his toes. He leaned his head back and looked at the ceiling.

The colonel could hear her in the other room, speaking softly on a phone. What he didn't completely understand was how her communications network was secure if his wasn't. Some Russian technology no doubt. She never seemed concerned about that.

Ten minutes later he was out of the bath, getting dressed in the clothing she'd brought. Anastasia patted the bed beside her, and he sat down. She took his hand and looked into his eyes.

"You know that I've been there for you, helping you always."

It wasn't always, but it was real. He said, "Yes."

Anastasia was already nodding, as if she knew that this was the only possible answer. She said, "Luckily we're not alone. *You* are not alone. What we think is best, is that you convince the CIA man at El-Gora, Bill, that they need to assign this American to the operation that you and your friends have helped them put together."

He looked at her, expecting more. The colonel didn't understand the connection between Anastasia and the project he and his Mukhabarat friends had going on with the CIA. He'd told her about it, but that was all.

"Why would I do that?"

She kissed him lightly on the forehead, running her fingers over the nape of his neck and giving him chills. Her eyes bored into his, steel gray. "Trust me, you don't need to worry about the why. Just focus on the how."

"Alright. How am I going to convince the CIA to take him?"

She smiled and a million roses bloomed. "I didn't choose you by accident. I chose you because of your many qualities. You're going to find a way. I believe in my colonel."

The colonel let his head sink to his chest, focusing on breathing correctly. By the time he'd made a little plan Anastasia was gone, only her scent lingering.

TRYING to convince the CIA to bring the American into their

operation would be a last resort. He had options available before going there.

The colonel managed to get his *El-Sa'Ka* officer on the phone and explained the situation. There were new rules of engagement. They were to shoot on sight and disappear the bodies, whatever it took.

The officer asked for a hundred thousand dollars extra but the colonel was able to get him down to seventy grand, which was still fifty more than the original plan.

He summoned his driver. The party was over and he was sobering up. It was time to get involved and make sure things turned out correctly.

He almost ruined his carefully trimmed nails by chewing on them, thinking through the situation. The Sinai road network wasn't the most complex, unless you had a true off-road vehicle, and then whatever. But he was guessing that the American and his Israeli woman didn't have such a vehicle. Maybe they had some shitty thing they'd taken from the jihadist scum.

In which case their options were limited. If the *El-Sa'Ka* didn't catch them, he could send a few Mukhabarat men up to the junction south of Rafah just in case. The colonel got a mapping app up on his phone, tapping and swiping. *Al Qassima* was the place. In order to access the border zone they'd need to deal with the military checkpoint there, or bypass it, which was in effect the same thing as dealing with it.

He lay back on the bed and tried to think, the alcohol and adrenaline making his mind into a fog. But even incapacitated his brain was superior, just as Anastasia had said. The *El-Sa'Ka* were fine as a first line, but he needed more. He hit the number of a Mukhabarat guy he knew based in Rafah. The man was busy, but the colonel mentioned ten thousand dollars cash for a quick trip down to Al Qassima. Just stick around there and observe. Interdict only if necessary.

Ten grand, no problem.

With the Land Cruiser he could be at Al Qassima in an hour and change. The road to Rafah was going to be cleared of any traffic other than security vehicles. The American and the Zionist bitch would need to be evasive if they wanted to survive. In any event they'd be funneled into the checkpoint.

He'd be there to make sure they died, and to supervise the distribution of their body parts into various mountain hollows and crevices, to be picked apart by vultures and hyenas. The skulls would have to be crushed into dust. It would take money, and luckily he had an envelope filled with dollars, like holding a winning hand in a high stakes poker game.

TWENTY-SEVEN

Keeler returned the way he'd come, crossing the landscaped gardens, impossible creations in the arid climate. Pools of light and snaking pathways. He vaulted the wall, hauling himself over, same place as before. Coming down the other side, going on pure adrenaline now. The moped was parked where he'd left it. The helmet stashed inside the delivery box. He wanted to avoid the military check point, navigating the bike through the embankment tunnel and finding his way along a dirt path snaking through an agricultural zone to the coastal road.

Armored vehicles rumbled past in a tight convoy of three. A police car followed, flashing blues and a screaming siren. Keeler caught the eye of the passenger, a fat cop with a thick mustache, the whites of his eyes reflecting the blue lights. Keeler gave him a thumbs up, but the car was gone, the guy turning away.

Keeler let them get out of sight before joining the coastal highway for thirty seconds or so. He turned off, zipping the moped up the hill to the abandoned date plantation. Yasmin was sitting on a stone wall in the dark, watching him cruise in and park the bike.

She walked over to meet him. Keeler noticed her eyes, roaming over his body, looking for wounds. She came close, putting a hand to his face. This felt really good. Yasmin tugged Keeler by the hair, bringing him in for a hot kiss before pulling back, face flushed. She said, "And?"

Keeler said, "And it got complicated."

She held up a phone. "We're bombing Rafah up there. You've seen the flashes?"

He said, "Is that something that happens a lot?"

"It happens. We bomb their tunnels, how Hamas and Islamic Jihad smuggle weapons and stuff into Gaza."

They watched an ambulance screaming in from the west accompanied by three police vehicles.

Keeler said, "Let's get out of this mess."

He went back inside and released the delivery driver from his bonds. The kid was scared, rightfully so. Yasmin spoke in Arabic, a long string of words. He nodded, eyes glued to her, a trusting look. Keeler went out and removed the battery from the kid's moped. He put it in the back of the truck. Whatever delivery he was supposed to make next was going to be very late.

Shit happens, call it collateral damage.

A DIRT TRACK ran parallel to the coastal road. Driving through the old date plantation, the trees all inexplicably chopped off at the base, leaving a grid of obstacles. The main checkpoint into El-Arish came into view, east of their position, to their left. Keeler continued for another half kilometer and stopped the vehicle behind a low abandoned building.

More orange and white flashes lit up the horizon. Gaza was being pummeled.

Keeler said, "Explain this to me."

Yasmin was busy on the phone she'd taken off of one of the ISIS men.

"There's been an attack on Kfar Azza." She looked up at him. "A village on the border with Gaza, north of the Egyptian border. A terrorist infiltration. They're saying fifteen dead but that must be an exaggeration. No way." She watched the APCs moving along the highway. "If it's true, we're going to beat the shit out of them." Yasmin's eyes were wide and her face flushed. Keeler saw real emotion in there.

She said, "We're going to take those zombies out."

Keeler said, "No doubt." He wasn't so sure. One of his mottos was 'hope for the best, prepare for the worst.' He said, "Where are those people going?" Meaning the armored personnel carriers and police.

"The Egyptians seal the border, making sure that nobody can leave Gaza for Egypt. Last thing they want is Hamas in the North Sinai."

Keeler was wondering who would want Hamas anywhere.

Looking at Yasmin, "You said something about a tunnel?"

She showed him the map on the phone in her hand. They needed to avoid the main roads, so they could keep going across the desert, feeling their way through and arriving at a spot 30 kilometers to the south of Rafah where the mountains met the road, a place called *Al Qassima*. This would be a choke point. Hopefully they'd avoid the *brouhaha* up in Gaza and wouldn't get caught up in any military dragnets on the highway.

Keeler pinched and squeezed on the map. That bottleneck was unavoidable for vehicular traffic, a natural place to set up a military checkpoint. He gave Yasmin the phone back. The words of Woody Allen coming to him, *eighty percent of success is showing up*. Keeler agreed with that wise sentiment, you show up and then you find a way.

. . .

AFTER AN HOUR and a half of driving in flat darkness, rock formations began to appear to the south, foothills of the Sinai mountains, forcing them further north. A half hour later a bundle of lights appeared on the horizon. Yasmin was alert, staring hard into the distance and multi tasking with the map application.

"Al Qassima. It's not exactly a town, maybe a military garrison." She showed him the screen, with a satellite image of the topography. The mountains went right down to the road. It would be impossible to avoid that stretch, unless they hiked into the wilderness.

Keeler said, "What about going straight north and around it?".

"Negative. Up north there are population centers. We're going to run into people, plus with whatever's going on in Gaza. The Egyptians will have security mobilized. We'll be conspicuous."

Keeler drove until they were maybe a kilometer from the lights. The hills had edged them even further north, funneling their path into the road presumably ending in the bottleneck where he was expecting the military presence. He slowed the truck and killed the engine.

"Decision time."

Yasmin was looking out to the distant glimmer of electric light. "Straight ahead or what?"

"Up into the hills would be one possibility."

The mountains rose steeply on their right, hard black shadows cutting jagged edges into the starlit sky. They'd be facing the possibility of a long hike through hard terrain. Climbs and descents, in the kind of country where things could easily sneak up on you. The Bedouin had cannabis and poppy plantations in the high valleys, they'd be on guard for trespassers and would certainly shoot first and ask questions later.

Yasmin cursed. She was looking to the left, which was the north. Keeler saw it, two sets of headlights coming right at them across the desert, small pin pricks in the darkness now. The vehicles would be at their location in a minute or two.

Yasmin said, "You think it's our Egyptian friends."

Keeler focused on the incoming vehicles for a moment. He said, "Who else? I'd bet the farm on it."

He was thinking they might have sensors this close to the border, devices to detect off-road vehicles incoming. They would have sent out a squad. Keeler was sort of amused at the whole messed up situation.

Picturing the Toyota Hilux trucks, painted desert beige with heavy .50 caliber machine guns mounted in the back, speeding over the desert, armored tires crushing gravel and spitting up a plume of dust into the night. Four guys in each, nestled in their own thoughts and fears and emotions, cocooned for the moment in safety.

The heavy weapons were a problem. It isn't possible to run from .50-caliber machine guns, even if the guys shooting are a bunch of maggots.

He opened the door. "Come on, let's go."

Keeler removed himself from the truck. Checking the AK-47 in his hands without thinking, muscle memory working on its own. He was aware of Yasmin coming out and joining him on the other side of the vehicle. A steep wadi went up into the hills. Keeler guesstimated they'd need to move another 200 yards to get into cover. He figured they had a minute before the Egyptians were close enough to see them.

It was dark, so hopefully that'd give them enough time.

They jogged up the wash until it became rocky about half way and they had to climb methodically, stepping around the larger boulders and picking their way carefully where it became steep. The vehicles were not fifty yards out when he and Yasmin found cover behind large boulders. He could hear the tires on the gravel. Once out of sight they turned to look. Her hand was casually resting on his shoulder, warm.

He watched the men below, discovering the truck and the bundle of weapons in the back. Gesticulating to each other and glancing around apprehensively. There wasn't a tracker among them. Keeler put his hand on Yasmin's, held it there for a couple of seconds and then started up from where he was crouched.

"Let's move."

He had formulated a plan.

Keeler didn't want to go up into the mountains. They did that, it'd be a day or two before reaching the border. They'd have to feel their way around up there, try to avoid running into more locals, all of which was a serious hassle. Plus, he was getting hungry and if that was the case, Yasmin would be running low on energy as well. He noticed her timing her footsteps with his, synchronizing their movements so that any listener would hear a single person. She was a trooper. He had a rush of feeling for her. When did you ever get to meet a girl who did that? Probably trained into instinct, no conscious thought necessary.

Keeler took a step and realized that Yasmin had stopped moving. He paused, looking back and caught her in his peripheral vision, completely still, head cocked as if trying to hear something. He stilled his breathing and listened. Nothing, for almost a minute, glancing at Yasmin, the shadows covering her face, some deeper than others, giving him an impressionistic view of her deeply concentrated expression. Another minute went by and a small stone rolled down from the ridge above, passing them and continuing on its way until out of earshot.

He made eye contact with her. It was quiet up there, pretty

much total silence except for the low hum of wind through the wadi. Another stone tumbled from above, knocking against other stones and stopping.

TWENTY-EIGHT

Keeler had mentally prepared the path up to the crest, maybe a fifteen yard climb. He executed immediately, left foot using a flat solid stone to launch him to the next chosen step, reaching the ridge line in four strides. His weapon came up as he lowered into a crouch. So far he had only made the slightest noise, possibly covered by the gentle wind up there. Nothing moved in front of him but his eyes quickly picked out a shape that was different from the others. Less hard edged than the stones, something round and organic.

It took him a few seconds to realize what he was looking at. When he did, Keeler first scanned his surroundings for more, but this one was alone. He reached forward and pulled the boy up from where he was huddled under a brown wool shawl, trying to blend in with the boulders and rocks. The boy looked at him, the whites of his eyes flashing in the dark. He was holding something to himself, clutched protectively in his arms.

Keeler couldn't see what it was until the boy stood up and the shawl fell off. The thing in his arms was a newborn goat, still wet and glistening in the starlight. Yasmin had followed Keeler and pushed forward. She crouched to the boy's height and spoke calm Arabic. The word for yes was like 'ah' in English, and that's what he said a couple of times to Yasmin's questions. "Ah, ah."

The boy's eyes darted between Keeler and Yasmin. The presence of a woman seemed to reassure him. He began speaking quickly, in a soft voice. Yasmin listened to him, nodding and saying 'ah'. She turned to Keeler, pointing north east, along the ridge line.

"The mother goat is sick. He says they'll punish him if she dies."

The boy was cocked in that direction, looking and listening and clearly upset. Keeler heard the weak bleat of a female goat. He moved towards a mass of large boulders clustered below the jagged hill crest. The huge stones made a natural system of caves. The bleating came from deep inside the boulders and Keeler found three other goats hanging around the entrance. Inside, a female goat was moving restlessly, her cries the desperate sounds of an animal without strength.

Keeler had seen a goat give birth before, and he was a trained combat medic.

He said, "She's not sick, she's giving birth."

The boy simply hadn't known what to do. He was maybe eleven years old. If the doe died, it wouldn't be his fault, it would be the fault of his elders. They had left him out here with a tough situation.

"Give me some light."

Yasmin flipped on a phone light.

Keeler said, "Tell the boy to calm her down. Show the mother her newborn."

The boy presented the kid to the mother, and she licked it, sniffing and a little distracted from her problem. Keeler was getting involved, examining the situation, crouching there with Yasmin over his shoulder with the light. The vaginal canal was dilated and all he could see in there was the tip of a little tail. The newborn kid was turned around in the birth canal. Keeler reached in and pushed gently, allowing the small body to slide in, releasing the hind legs until they rose into view. Keeler was aware that the umbilical cord might be wrapped around the kid's throat, but he was betting otherwise. He could smell the amniotic fluid and figured that the umbilical cord had burst. The issue wasn't the newborn animal being strangled; it was the danger of the kid being drowned in amniotic fluid.

He gripped the hind legs and pulled hard. The doe bellowed, the boy making soothing sounds and Yasmin holding the light. Keeler pulled again. He put his right boot down for the doe to push against with her hind legs. In the meantime he kept up relentless pressure, helping her own pushing efforts. A minute later the second newborn came out in a rush of goo and fluid and a soft sucking sound.

He got free of the mess. The mother seemed satisfied, if exhausted, dropping to her knees and then onto her side. Keeler set the newborn in front of her. She began eating the goo still attached to her newborn and got busy licking it clean.

The boy crouched by the goats, speaking to them. Yasmin turned the phone light off.

Keeler was already moving to the cave entrance. On the way in they'd been focused upon the animal in distress, but he'd also noticed that the terrain changed up ahead. Now he was standing in the entrance looking out over a small plateau stretching no more than five hundred yards to the next desert rise. The interesting thing was that he was able to see the plateau covered by a field of poppy flowers, standing out in the bright starlight.

A trail led into the field. Standing either side of it were three Bedouin men looking right back at him. The men were distributed along either side of the path. The closest one wore a red Adidas jacket. He was crouched with an AK-47 rifle across the knee. Behind him, the others had taken more active postures.

Keeler grinned. "Hey there."

The boy came out with one of the newborn kids in his arms. He spoke to the crouching man in their language. The man asked a question. The boy responded, and the man stood up. He was looking past Keeler at Yasmin. She spoke, and the man said nothing. The second guy down the path said something, and the boy said something.

Yasmin said, "They're going to show us a way down past the Egyptians."

The men turned and walked through the opium field. Keeler and Yasmin followed to the other side of it. A narrow ravine wound along a mountainside. They came around a turn and saw lights below. The man with the Adidas jacket turned to Keeler and walked into his personal space, maybe two feet away. Keeler watched him, speaking to his face for more than a minute. The man had strong body odor. He got that the Bedouin knew he couldn't understand what he was saying, but also that Yasmin would translate.

Keeler figured that the issue was cultural, the man wouldn't speak directly to a woman who was not a member of his family. The guy stopped talking and stepped away.

Yasmin pointed to the lights. "That's the checkpoint." Her hand drew a dark line on the plain below, tracing a road. "He says the Egyptian soldiers all drove out a little while ago." She looked at him. "Must have been the ones who came for us back there."

Keeler said, "So what, we just walk in?"

She shrugged. "That's what he said. Said there's nobody on guard there except for a crazy old guy who makes tea."

TWENTY-NINE

The Bedouin leader in the red Adidas jacket accompanied them until they were out of the hills, right on the edge of a steep mountain descending sharply to the checkpoint below. A hundred yards from the checkpoint the man stopped. Keeler walked by him, turning and seeing the man lowering into a squat. The guy was planning on watching to see what happened, maybe hoping for entertainment.

The mountains ended in a steep incline twenty yards from the road. Concrete blocks were laid across it so that cars would have to zig zag slowly through the checkpoint. The glow of a fire was clearly visible on the other side of the barricades.

Yasmin said, "Interesting situation."

Keeler looked at her and lifted an eyebrow. "Sometimes you can't think too far ahead."

They both wore the *dishdasha* robes from earlier. With the AK-47s their silhouettes wouldn't be remarkable.

The walk into the checkpoint became hairy when they got within easy range of small arms fire, at least for Keeler. He'd been in that situation many times and always felt an uncomfortable itch. Yasmin was behind him and he couldn't guess her thoughts. He just walked in like he was supposed to be there, waiting for someone to shout, a light, a warning shot, something. But the only thing that happened was the sound of their boots crunching over rock and sand. A couple of minutes later they were walking through the checkpoint.

The huge concrete blocks had been painted light blue, the color since faded and cracked. Either side of the check point was sturdy fencing. On the right side, the enclosure ran south up the mountain. On the left it stretched north as far as he could see. A tall security fence topped by rolls of rusted razor wire.

Keeler carried the AK-47 across his body, finger along the trigger guard. He was ready for whatever. Which turned out to be an old man sitting on an ancient steel gas can, looking into the flames of a small fire. His weathered face was a web of deep lines in sharp relief from the shadow cast by the fire.

He didn't even look up as Keeler and Yasmin approached. When they were almost within touching distance, the man spoke clearly, a husky voice making an Arabic phrase. Keeler had operated in enough middle eastern battle zones to recognize the hospitable offer of tea. A blackened pot rested at the edge of the fire.

The man reached forward abruptly and came up with two clean glasses. Without waiting for their response he lifted the pot high and poured. Amber liquid arced into the receptacles, swirling immaculately without the slightest spill. Keeler had thought the guy was staring into the fire, but he was wrong. The man was blind, his eyes sightlessly oriented to nothing.

FOR A MINUTE they stood around the fire with him, sipping at hot and sweet tea. Closer up, and from the new angle his eyes were cloudy, like a silky gray skein had been pulled over them.

He was mumbling to himself, a low liturgical murmur. Keeler didn't understand the language, but he could see Yasmin paying attention. She turned to him with a smile, shaking her head and making a hand gesture that Keeler understood meaning that the man's words were not operationally interesting.

Just the poetic ramblings of a blind sentry at a checkpoint in the Northern Sinai desert, 2016.

Technically Egypt, but way out of control. They passed the tea ceremony in silence. Yasmin took Keeler's empty glass and placed it on the concrete block serving as the man's side table. She put a hand on the old guy's shoulder in thanks.

Another word that Keeler understood. "*Shukran*".

The man's gruff voice spit out the reply. "*Afwan.*"

Yasmin was ahead of Keeler, walking away. The area on the other side of the concrete blocks and the old guy was open ground. Keeler caught up with her. A motorcycle engine whined a short distance away and abruptly halted. Other than that, there was no sign of human activity.

Up ahead was an incline and a cluster of low buildings, geometric shapes in the dark. A light glowed weak orange. Keeler jogged up the road, looking for a way off it, Yasmin just behind him. A man walked out of the darkness, jeans and a leather jacket, another behind him. The first man said something in Arabic, looking directly at Keeler. The tones were questioning, hostile even. Keeler smiled broadly, hands off the weapon and out in the open.

A problem opened up right in front of his eyes. The kind of issue that can't be solved by diplomacy. A military problem.

The second man was raising a stubby black firearm from under his jacket. The first guy still coming on, speaking, facial muscles shifting and tight. But Keeler wasn't paying attention to him anymore. The man behind him looked intent on using the thing in his hand, which was a Skorpion submachine gun.

From behind Keeler came the sound of Yasmin's AK-47 popping off. The man holding the Skorpion developed a stain in the blue-collared shirt under the black leather jacket. The man in front of Keeler leapt back, getting his own weapon operational. Keeler dropped to a crouch and put a round at him, aiming for the chest. The man had been in motion however, so he took it in the neck, going down and flailing, hands grasping at the life-sustaining liquid streaming hot into the chill night sand.

Unavoidable.

The man was making noises. Yasmin moved in and dead checked him with a bullet through the forehead. Keeler watched her face, eyes widening as she pulled the trigger. She saw something on the man, bent down and retrieved a coiled plastic key chain, examining the keys and holding them up for him to see.

"Honda. I think it's the bike we heard."

There had been three gunshots. Someone was going to come running. Keeler pulled Yasmin up by the arm but she resisted. She was looking for identity documents on the man Keeler had shot. He went to the other one and did the same, coming up with a very official-looking identity wallet in black leather. Opening it he saw the man's face, unsmiling, but in better days. There was a large Saladin Eagle crest and all kinds of things written in Arabic that Keeler couldn't understand.

He showed the ID to Yasmin. She was already reading the other one.

She said, "*Mukhabarat.*" Looking up at him. "This sucks."

Keeler nodded. "Let's go."

A motorcycle was parked along with several battered older vehicles in a graveled area.

The sound of another vehicle came from up the road, where the two mukhabarat men had come from. An SUV coming around the turn, between buildings. Keeler moved up, the AK-

47 ready and aiming. There was no more messing around here. The vehicle was a Toyota Land Cruiser, beige. Keeler had his finger on the trigger, slightly pulling it back. The vehicle stopped, illuminated by the weak orange light coming out of a second-story window.

He waited. Nothing happened.

Keeler walked closer, weapon up and trigger finger now indexed. The driver wasn't moving, his hands on the steering wheel, fingers flexing. The head just a silhouette. The back of the Land Cruiser was dark. Keeler couldn't see if there was a passenger or not. He thought of putting rounds into the tires.

Behind him, the Honda motorcycle started. Keeler started walking backwards, still looking at the vehicle. Sure, they were probably hostiles in there, but they weren't getting involved.

Yasmin spun the bike around, coming up behind him. Decision time.

The Toyota just standing there, the driver watching. Keeler had a feeling about it but he wasn't going to fire first. He climbed on the back of the bike, a low powered Honda CG-125 model. He held the seat strap behind him with his left hand while Yasmin skidded out of the gravel, onto the road. He couldn't hear anything at all over the sound of the motor.

The Toyota Land Cruiser didn't move. A minute later they were zipping the other way, out of the village.

THE COLONEL CAME out of the Toyota Land Cruiser. The driver opened his door, but the colonel snapped at him to stay. He walked over to the bodies. The first guy was the colonel's friend from Rafah. Luckily, he hadn't been paid in advance. The second man was an underling.

A convoy of military vehicles came roaring through the border. The *El-Sa'Ka* commandos.

The commander came down from the lead truck, looking at the bodies.

He said, "We found their vehicle."

The colonel said, "Good, well done."

The commander was confused pointing to the dead Mukhabarat men. "Who did this?"

The colonel was improvising. "Bedouin scum, they killed these two and went back into the mountains. Probably *Wilayat Sinai*."

The commander cursed and began organizing his men for the hunt. The colonel was already walking away, already detached from this bullshit. He'd find another way of neutralizing the American. Now he'd have to deal with his own people in El-Arish. They'd be sitting in the conference room scheming about the situation in Gaza.

THIRTY

Keeler got settled behind Yasmin, the engine running at a high pitch. The road straight and empty, a single lane highway running alongside the foothills. He estimated that they were riding parallel to the Israeli border.

He yelled into Yasmin's ear. "You sure you know where you're going?"

She nodded vigorously. "There's a landmark on the Egyptian side, we'll be looking out for a mountain crag they call the goat's head. We find that and we're home free."

"Looks like a goat's head?"

"Yes."

After twenty minutes of hard riding Yasmin pointed up to the right. The moon had been rising, now showing behind a mountain peak with complicated sharp edges that didn't look to Keeler like a goat's head, but he figured that's what it must be. Fifty yards further on she pulled the bike off-road and took it as far as she could. She stopped the bike and killed the engine.

"Let's walk from here. Not a good idea to make noise."

Keeler knew what she meant. Yasmin wasn't as concerned with alerting the Egyptians as her own people. After five minutes of fast walking the flat land turned into brush filled rolling desert hills.

Some startled animal bolted from a deep wadi filled with thickets of bamboo. On the other side of that the tunnel's mouth was accessible only by belly crawling through a passage of wind bent stalks. The excavation looked rudimentary, the tunnel unserved by electric lighting. Keeler leaned in and examined what he could by the light of one of the phones they'd taken. The low subterranean ceiling was propped up by the occasional wood planks, otherwise he saw a few plywood boards pinned by the struts, beyond that was just dirt.

Yasmin fell back against a stand of bamboo and settled comfortably. Keeler saw her tapping and sliding and sweeping fingers in various directions over a phone screen. Probably finding a web browser and logging into her account on some communications platform.

The thicket had a damp feel, pleasant given the arid context. Keeler could smell the trace of animal excrement, this would be a source of water in the desert. The bamboo capable of tenaciously digging in and surviving, kind of like the people around here.

Yasmin had said it might be possible to make contact with someone working at the sensor monitoring facility.

Keeler watched her tapping on the phone.

He said, "You're going to tell your friend that we're in Egypt?"

Yasmin muttered, deep in concentration. "No, are you insane? I'm going to tell her we're operating in the area of the tunnel entrance, Israeli side, so they can ignore signal activity that the sensors report."

She glanced at him, the look saying *did I really need to tell you that?* Keeler liked it. Seeing her gaze shift back to the phone and tap furiously. She let the device drop to her thigh. "Okay now we wait."

The sky was littered with bright stars with almost no light pollution. Keeler liked the desert, the way it seemed simple at first, getting more and more complex as you entered into it. Every living creature here had its intuitive systems honed and streamlined, sharp and rapacious. As if the desert was a purification filter for biological adaptation.

Something shifted in the sky, hard to know what it was, maybe a star had blinked out for just a moment.

The phone in Yasmin's hand lit up.

She was reading. "We're good."

Keeler visualized the person Yasmin was communicating with. A young female soldier, back in one of those military bases where they monitor the system of electronic border protection, the ground sensors, cameras, microphones, drones, and up on the Gaza line, remote controlled machine guns mounted on high towers. Yasmin's friend would be in her early 20s maybe, sitting in front of a bank of computer screens. Not a job that Keeler would enjoy, that's for damned sure.

Yasmin slipped the phone into her pocket.

"Yalla."

Keeler went first, crawling through the thick smooth stalks and sliding into the tight tunnel. It opened up a little wider further down, but not much. They had to move forward bent in a crouch, maintaining that for at least a kilometer. It was necessary to stop several times during the crossing and lie on their backs to straighten up and avoid cramp. The end of the tunnel was a steep incline for a dozen meters. It was necessary to scramble up it, the passage becoming claustrophobic. Keeler emerged first, a big man, squeezing through the tight gap, agonizingly slow. He felt born again.

The opening was screened by two large stones which he

grabbed, pulling himself out. He tumbled down the slope and lay panting for breath. Looking back up the hill, the entrance was invisible from fifteen feet away.

Yasmin had an easier time coming out. She stood up stretching.

She said, "Welcome to Israel. The road's another three kilometers from here. Let's rest for five minutes."

Keeler dropped to a squat beside her, feeling muscle and ligaments get loose again after that insane underground haul.

THIRTY-ONE

The Egyptian Mukhabarat headquarters in El-Arish had been separated from the general military facilities a few years earlier, after a bombing attempt. Now, they operated out of a building in the Health Affairs Directorate complex. The colonel opened the door to the conference room and walked into a cloud of cigarette smoke and the stench of competing male perfume.

His face had been messed up by the American. People were staring at him, which wasn't necessarily a bad thing. His presence was going to be noted and transmitted, as was the condition of his face. The generals around the table wore collared shirts and Rolex watches. The more junior officers had to take chairs lined against the wall. The colonel saw an empty one and placed himself in it. It was simply important to be in the room.

He watched the big guys operate, speaking with low growls, discussing minutia of their deals with Hamas, or the Israelis, negotiating over the plan. Which wasn't complicated. Control the border with Gaza. Nobody was going to be allowed out without paying, except a few of the Hamas billionaires who paid their monthly dues. They controlled the tunnels and made huge piles of cash.

The men around the table were a mix of mustaches and no mustaches. The clean shaven ones were invariably men who'd had close contact with American or Israeli allies, having adopted the managerial style of those institutions. The colonel had no mustache, and neither did *his* general, currently amidst his peers at the big table.

The colonel recognized himself as a particularly intelligent man. The issue was everyone else.

You go out there to do something and you have excellent ideas, and make a success of yourself. Then everything gets screwed up because of other people. Here the problem was the way it worked, nepotism. You were always dealing with someone's son or cousin or nephew, put in their position by dint of the family connection.

His general stood up, the knob like head rising above the others, turning minutely in his direction for a furtive glance. The mukhabarat was organized in a cell structure, each unit having some degree of autonomy. Much of the activity involved the control of turf, like opium trafficking in the Sinai, or the trafficking of women from Sudan in the south.

Now the general was approaching the colonel, a big smile on his face. The colonel stood and made a small bow of respect. All of this was theater for the others.

"General."

They exchanged the conventional double kiss greeting, the general's cologne was very strong. The colonel felt the man's soft skin against his day-old stubble. The general held both of his shoulders and examined his face.

"You look terrible *habibi*, what happened to you?"

The colonel averted his gaze. He said, "There was an attack in El-Arish. I fought with the terrorist."

The general, nodding. "Yes, we heard. Nobody was killed."

"No. The man escaped."

The colonel snuck a look at the general, examining him again. The knob head knew, of course, that the terrorist was this American. Knew that the colonel wasn't managing to keep the situation under control and had, indeed, lost it completely.

The general said, "The wounds look superficial."

"Yes general."

"Mmm hmm." The general patted the colonel on the cheek. "I believe our friend would like to have a word with you."

"What friend?"

The general smiled and tilted his head to the right. The colonel followed with his gaze, seeing the major standing by the door. The general nodded and departed, probably going to the bathroom.

The colonel stood up and said "excuse me" to nobody, and nobody responded. The major was already out of the room and the colonel found him waiting in a corner of the large entrance hall, taking up one of two plush chairs arranged around a small mosaic topped table.

The colonel sat, straightening his shirt.

The major looked at him and nodded, like there was something to agree upon already.

The colonel said, "What?"

The major said, "Complications."

"As always."

The major shook his head. "Not exactly, no."

Which was the truth. The colonel had a bright idea all of a sudden.

"So, what do you want?"

"It's not what we want colonel, it's what the Americans want. The CIA has requested that we send someone to verify the target we have provided."

The colonel felt hot around the collar. "What do you mean? That wasn't the deal."

The major said, "Well let's just say, it is now." The last three words spoken with force.

The colonel leaned back and softened his tone, maintaining composure. "Okay, what changed?"

The major shrugged. "There's a legitimate request for verification. It's our intelligence in the end, so they want you there to sign your name to the product." The man grinned. "I mean, you've already made the trip up here from Cairo. Flight leaves tomorrow oh five hundred hours. Takes off from right here in El-Gora, no customs no nothing. CIA aircraft listed as an MFO routine flight transiting through Wiesbaden. They'll bring you back once the operation's complete."

The colonel was on the verge of losing his shit, keeping it together. Him being involved in the field had never been part of the equation.

But now, what Anastasia had told him came back. She'd said he needed to demand that the American be included in the operation. Now, if they wanted him there as well, he suddenly had leverage.

The colonel nodded to the major. "Excellent. Thank you major."

The major smiled. "No problem. I'm glad that you agree."

The colonel found a quiet spot on the outside stairwell. He tapped the phone number he had for the CIA man at El-Gora. It was just before two in the morning but the man answered on the third ring.

"Yes, colonel."

The colonel tapped and fiddled with his phone. He said, "I've just sent you a photograph. Do you see it?"

It was a picture of the American and him, taken by one of the *El-Sa'Ka* commandos back at the tunnel entrance. The

American standing with him in that sordid workshop break room with the stench of vodka and cigarettes.

The CIA man said, "Who's that?"

The colonel said, "One of yours."

The CIA man spoke slowly, "Okay," obviously not meaning what he was saying. "So, what about him?"

The colonel said, "I want him for the operation. I want him there."

The CIA man said, "I don't think we can do that, colonel. The operation is already in the execution phase now that we have the confirmed data points. We don't make demands on a team in the field, that's just not how it's done."

The colonel said, "Then I don't go."

The first precept in 'The Art of the Deal', discussing negotiations. The strongest bargaining tool you have is the ability to walk away.

He could hear the CIA man breathing, the rhythm steady but a little more intense than before. The colonel imagined him looking again at the photo of the American.

He said, "I hear you colonel. I'll need to send the picture up and we'll get a decision. It's all I can tell you right now. You're hitting me with this out of left field."

Just like they'd hit him by requesting his presence.

The colonel said, "Fine. I'll wait."

The call ended. The colonel went back to the conference room. Nothing had changed, except for new cigarettes being lit and a tray of hot sugary tea that had arrived. He lifted one of the small glasses from the tray and carried it to his seat in the ridiculously ornate chair.

The colonel's phone vibrated in his pocket.

Almost two in the morning, sitting here in some bullshit meeting. Four hours before he was supposed to fly out to join the American mission he'd been instrumental in setting up.

The CIA man had sounded as if he'd been in bed. The colonel hadn't been so lucky. He'd been up all night, plus the alcohol, and plus the shit he'd had to deal with. The expression from America was great, life's a bitch and then you die.

The colonel remembered the buzz of his phone. He pulled it out, looking at the screen as a message from Anastasia revealed itself.

'Bravo my colonel.'

He typed back, thumbs flying over the smooth glass. 'Why?'

'The City of Love.'

The colonel didn't remember telling Anastasia about the city of love.

2
UNINTENDED CONSEQUENCES

THIRTY-TWO

PALMACHIM AIRBASE, *Central Israel*
Mike Hershkowitz was standing in the intelligence collection center just south of Tel Aviv. The room was dark, lit by a wall of screens. He was watching the live video feed from a remotely controlled Heron drone. The aircraft currently in rotation over the Egyptian border, a spot a hundred and fifty odd kilometers away, roughly a two-and-a-half-hour drive with no traffic.

He'd been in bed a half hour before, at his ninety-year-old mother's apartment where he was staying while trying to hire a new live-in nurse for her. But he wasn't sleepy, just calm and calculating, trying to make dispassionate judgements about what he was looking at.

Which was an overhead view of two figures reclining against a desert hillside, having just emerged from the mouth of a tunnel known to lead under the border into Egypt. The images were sharp and clean but they came from an infrared sensor, showing inverted colors and shades. As a consequence, facial features were unfamiliar to the naked eye, failing to engage the human pattern recognition elements of his brain.

The drone was at a sufficiently high altitude that the people down there would neither see nor hear it.

Moving image reflections from the large screens played over his eyeballs and face.

Hershkowitz was one of maybe two dozen people in the room. The majority of them female soldiers in uniform, operating computers and technical interfaces. His palm rested on the back of an ergonomic office chair, a young conscript sat in it, moving her head. His knuckles were brushed by her blond ponytail and he retrieved his hand.

The uniformed shift commander stood to his left, a stocky lieutenant, stirring a spoon in her cup of black coffee. On the other side of her was the base commander, a small guy with a sharp nose and glasses who'd had to get up out of bed too. Hershkowitz's assistant lurked by the door, busy with her phone.

The shift commander pointed a stubby finger at the screen. "What do you want to do?"

Hershkowitz ignored the question and closed his eyes for a moment.

He opened his eyes again and addressed a second soldier, sitting in the chair to his left. "Rewind. Show me what happened earlier, on the other side of the border."

The soldier manipulated the controls and a large screen played back the recorded video. Two figures below, a man and a woman, young and moving well, easily visible thanks to the infrared sensor.

She said, "This is where we picked them up." The camera operator had pushed in on the two ditching a motorcycle and beginning to move towards the border. "Here they begin to hike towards the entrance of the infiltration tunnel hidden in the bamboo." She looked up at Hershkowitz.

The intruders were armed. He leaned forward. "That's an AK-47."

The soldier adjusted a dial and punched a button, spinning a second dial. The image zoomed to a close shot of the weapon. Obviously the standard AK-47 model used by militants. The operator sat back and lifted her plastic cup of black coffee.

Hershkowitz considered the AK-47, an unremarkable object in the hands of a male Egyptian, Palestinian, or Bedouin, but certainly unusual for a woman, given the locality.

A third soldier said. "Oh yes, they've gotten into my favorite position."

Hershkowitz's attention moved to her screen, showing the figures now collapsed onto their backs, looking at the sky. The soldier rotated the camera's point of view and captured a perfect image of the two faces, still inverted by the infrared sensor. She punched a couple of buttons and swiveled a knob. The image was split in two, one for each face, quickly isolated against black. She clicked and swiped three or four times until the black and white inverted images were recognizable to the human eye.

Now there were two clearly visible young people.

Hershkowitz didn't know the man, but he did know the woman. The Israeli intelligence community is small, the dinner parties intimate. That was Ruth Shoshan's sister up on the screen. He was forgetting the name, but

he knew her well. Outwardly he expressed no emotion, not wanting to let on to the assembled analysts and commanders. It came to him in a flash. The name was Yasmin. Her sister Ruth was a Mossad officer. Yasmin Shoshan's identity details flooded the screen with data, matched by the facial recognition program.

Hershkowitz and the dozen or so others in the room were quiet, watching Yasmin Shoshan and her friend having a conversation, then chilling out, then they just left on foot, walking away from the scene. Weird. Hershkowitz became aware of his assistant in the doorway. She registered his attention, her fine eyebrows arched ever so slightly.

Hershkowitz said, "Let's run it down."

His assistant said, "There's no such thing as a coincidence."

"Right."

She said, "The ghost-fish from El-Gora to Midreshet. Then this."

Hershkowitz said, "Let's go over the walk back from earlier. The Egyptian vehicle."

His assistant opened the cover to her tablet device. She set it down on a worktop at the back of the room. Hershkowitz was thinking about the Egyptian mukhabarat vehicle. They hadn't identified its occupant.

His assistant was tracing a route. Up from the El-Gora airbase to El-Arish on the coast, some resort called the Palm Oasis.

She said, "After that the vehicle went to Al Qassima and stopped for a short while."

He said, "Before going back up to El-Arish, mukhabarat headquarters."

"Right, but that was their big Gaza powwow."

"So Yasmin Shoshan and her friend got involved with whoever's in that Toyota Land Cruiser."

She said, "And she managed to get away from him."

Hershkowitz said, "Maybe." Thinking about the vehicle. "That's one busy guy if it's a single occupant."

His assistant was deep in the screen now, swiping and tapping. She pulled back, finger pointing.

"Look at this."

He leaned in, saw lines and a map and things in red. "What am I looking at?"

"The Land Cruiser's moving again."

Hershkowitz was staring at screen, not really looking at it.

He was thinking about barbecued chicken. It was currently Friday morning, before sun rise. He was getting the feeling that his weekend was no longer going to include an occasion to schmooze at some tech billionaire's garden party.

The Egyptian mukhabarat vehicle was on its way back to the El-Gora airbase. Now, a suspicious military installation. Unit 201 wasn't only interested in the little Canadian opium poppy smuggling scheme, it looked like bigger things were afloat. The Egyptian mukhabarat intelligence service, and possibly an American connection.

He said, "I'll need to speak to Gabi."

His assistant barely nodded, fingers already flying over her phone's screen to find the deputy head of Mossad's direct contact.

THIRTY-THREE

Hershkowitz's assistant handed him a phone. He put it to his ear without taking his eyes off the large screens in front of him.

"Gabi."

The deputy director of the Mossad made one of his low practiced growls. "What?"

Hershkowitz said, "Exactly my question. What is Ruth Shoshan's sister Yasmin doing with an unknown male, crawling into Israel through a terrorist infiltration tunnel from Sinai?"

"Who?"

"Ruth's sister, Yasmin."

"Yasmin Shoshan."

Hershkowitz said, "Right."

Gabi said, "Crawling into Israel, what like right now?"

"Just happened to see it Gabi. I want to know if it's yours, that's all."

"Hold on."

Since Ruth Shoshan was a Mossad officer, her sister was their property. Unless she wasn't, which was what Hershkowitz needed to know.

One of the analysts in the room said, "Bingo!"

Hershkowitz watched as the screen filled with the boyfriend's face.

The soldier turned slightly and said, "What we have here is an active duty American soldier."

Hershkowitz coughed, mildly surprised, maybe the first time that had happened in a while. He said, "What kind of an American soldier is that?"

The analyst was looking at him directly in the eyes, an uncommon procedure. She wore glasses over striking blue eyes and had a smirk on her face. "The non-Israeli kind of American soldier, *sir*."

Hershkowitz found himself momentarily paralyzed and had to force himself to look away from her.

Gabi, the Mossad man had come back on the line but Hershkowitz's phone was dangling from his hand now, no longer the object of interest it had been. Data began populating boxes on one of the screens in front of the pretty analyst. A name, *Tom Keeler*, with the relevant recent details of his visit to Israel, alongside more permanent details of his US military affiliations.

The information was rich and unusual enough that the base commander uttered a four letter word.

Sounds came again from the phone. Hershkowitz lifted the device. "Gabi, Tell me."

The deputy director of the Mossad said, "Not us. You need to go to Irma. They're the ones who've been busy last night."

The reference to the Gaza situation, kicking off last night in a limited way. Irma was deputy head of the AMAN, military intelligence. It'd been their gig.

Hershkowitz said, "Obviously, but if Yasmin's clean with Irma I can have her?"

Gabi almost sounded humorous. "Sure, and the chief rabbi's

eating pork chops for dinner. We'll share her. Ruth's ours, her sister keeps at least one foot in the family, Mike."

Hershkowitz grimaced involuntarily. "There's American involvement. A whole knot that needs to be seen to. I'll send you details."

Gabi grunted, and the call was over.

Hershkowitz's assistant was looking at him, having overheard the last morsel of that conversation. She was jutting her chin at the screen with the soldier's face and his military details. Tom Keeler, some guy in the Pararescue unit, the USAF version of IAF's 669. His assistant was silently asking if those were the details to send over.

"Yeah, do it. Send him everything." Watching her make three swipes on her phone and look up at him again. He said, "And get Irma."

He handed his assistant the phone he'd been using and looked again at the analyst who'd made eye contact. Watching her, clicking and clacking on the keyboard, speaking to a colleague. Dimples and freckles, maybe twenty years old. His phone was returned into his hand and his assistant's mouth was close to his ear.

She said, "Irma will be on in a minute, she's pretending to be busy."

The hot female breath went away, leaving him bereft of the minty scent and slightly lost. A voice on the other end of the line said something, and he raised the phone to his ear.

"Hershkowitz."

Irma's scratchy voice. "You called me."

Hershkowitz adopted a tough guy tone. "I need to know if you have anyone tunneling in and out of Egypt today, Irma, say, thirty kilometers south of Rafah?"

A thousand cigarettes rasped in her voice. "No."

He was thinking, 'good'. He said, "Okay, so tell me what's going on in Gaza?"

Irma began to speak, a steady stream of precise details, delivered in her smokers croak, clipped and succinct, one reason she'd been elevated in the ranks of AMAN, the woman could summarize. In this case, it was about Gaza and not about Yasmin Shoshan getting up to no good on the Egyptian border. Irma knew nothing of that. The Gaza story was exciting enough, a dozen rockets fired from the southern strip last night, Khan Yunis, nine of them intercepted by Iron Dome, the remainder landing on empty ground. But, the Islamist maniacs firing randomly into Israel was always an occasion to hammer them back, what everyone was now calling 'mowing the grass'.

Hershkowitz loved to hear about action, it never bored him. Irma's narration was great, a smoky drawl telling the story of how under cover of IAF missile fire, AMAN had managed the IDF's insertion of two forces into the southern Gaza Strip, one entering from sea, the other from the area near the Egyptian border. They'd been composed of undercover Mista'arvim elements from Duvdevan, along with a Sayeret Matkal team for the finish.

The plain clothes Duvdevan units had used the general confusion generated by airstrikes to blend in and identify targets, tunnel entrances and command structures. The Sayeret Matkal teams had done the heavy hitting. They'd managed to capture three high level Nukbah commanders and sent two dozen of their best fighters to their 72 virgins. On top of that, the boys had all returned home. Hershkowitz listened to Irma tell it proudly, she deserved the minor success.

The grass had been mowed. He'd seen a funny sign up in a barber shop in New York a couple of years ago, 'you grow it, we mow it.'

Bottom line, neither AMAN nor the Mossad knew anything

about Yasmin Shoshan and her American friend. Hershkowitz would get with the Shin Bet to confirm that Yasmin was at least partly an orphan. After that he'd have to organize a meeting with the deputy heads of agencies, Shin-Bet, AMAN, Gabi from Mossad, and maybe a few others. Whatever was going on would require a fully integrated approach.

There was also a possibility that the brouhaha in Gaza was a smokescreen for another operation.

Once that was completed, he'd need to get with the US ambassador, an ex-marine with a rigid schedule who could reliably be intercepted between his pre-dawn jog and the grapefruit and pomegranate juice he ordered every day from the same street vendor.

THIRTY-FOUR

The United States ambassador to Israel was a guy name of Steve Chambers.

Chambers had been summoned to the embassy earlier than his usual four am wake up. At that moment he was standing to attention, getting taken to the carpet by Undersecretary of State for Politics Vicky Neuman, her florid face up on screen one right beside screen two, shared by the CIA Director and the current commander of Joint Special Operations Command.

He had a strong feeling that today was not going to be a routine day in his life. He wasn't going to be jogging, or sucking fresh squeezed fruit juice through a straw. Vicky Neuman made horrible sounds, shouting over the remote conferencing system, her voice cracking and distorting. Putting up with her and standing to attention, Chambers was thinking about his career.

He was the kind of ex-marine who'd been assembled by the corps and forged in combat. He'd won the United States Marine Corps Scout Sniper Competition twice. He was aware that some people said he'd won the second time on a fluke, on account of the target of his stalking task having suffered a cardiac arrest during Chambers' approach. The ambassador knew that this wasn't true, so the idle talk didn't bother him. He also knew that adherence to a strict routine was the secret to all success in military and other affairs.

Which is why he could filter out Vicky Neuman's voice and turning ever slightly to seek the attention of his secretary. The secretary made eye contact and Chambers mouthed the word 'coffee'. The young man jumped from his desk and it wasn't twenty seconds before the ambassador had a hot mug in his hand.

He took a long sip and winced. Another slug and things seemed better. A third and he was at an even keel.

Neuman had been talking non-stop but the words out of her mouth were alien to him. He'd been stationed in Tel Aviv for almost three years and knew very well what the word 'relevant' meant. This place was relevant, decisions made meant life and death, every day. And here's Vicky Neuman going off about beltway politics.

Everyone knew that she was going to be replaced by some other predatory bureaucrat within a week. It was very likely that Chambers was also going home soon.

He said, "Madame Undersecretary, I'm sorry to interrupt you."

He'd had enough political nonsense about administrations and whatever it was that people thought about in DC.

She stopped talking and said, "What?"

Chambers said, "No disrespect intended Madam Undersecretary, but I'm hearing what you're saying without any idea what you're talking about." He pointed the mug at the second screen. "Maybe CIA can fill me in, because at the moment I'm not following the source of urgency."

The CIA Director said, "The Undersecretary is talking about *Kaleidoscope* Steve."

Chambers coughed involuntarily. He had a handle on the local political atmosphere, which is why he was good at his job.

The politics of US - Egyptian security ties were complex. On one hand you had the governing military class, sort of like *Cosa Nostra* on the Nile. The top guys were cynics with hands in the cash pots, pulling out as much as they could, hand over fist into offshore accounts, trying to cash out before the Islamic takeover that everyone feared.

On the other hand, you had a smattering of true patriots and professionals among the cadre of younger officers. Egypt's not like Jordan, or Lebanon, it's a real country with a real national history. The CIA's strategy was to hand pick the less corrupt patriots and cultivate them in the hope that one day Egypt would become a democracy.

As far as he knew, Kaleidoscope was a joint intelligence operation that CIA was running with this handpicked group of trusted officers from the *Mukhabarat*. Because you couldn't trust the Egyptians to keep a secret, the project was run out of Tel Aviv instead of the US embassy in Cairo.

Chambers had his doubts about the project, but optimism was the American way.

He said, "I am briefed on *Kaleidoscope*. What about it?"

Vicky Neuman said, "Oh shit."

Chambers felt himself getting hot. He was aware that his face might be turning red. Looking at the CIA man and trying to stifle the catch in his voice and refrain from cursing. He said, "Would you like to catch me up, Trevor?"

His secretary, a young blonde man straight out of Yale was hustling up to him with a folder marked top secret. "Sorry sir, I forgot to hand this to you."

The commander of Joint Special Operations Command smirked. He had a skeletal face made more pronounced by the darkness surrounding his illuminated head. Chambers ignored the papers in his hand, he wasn't going to be seen studying them like some kid who'd forgotten his homework.

The CIA Director said, "Forget it Steve, shit happens. Our top guy over there's a *muqaddam*, equivalent of a colonel in our system."

Chambers knew this. He nodded. "Yeah. I'm read in."

The CIA Director said, "Right. So, we're involved in a project with this guy. I can't go into what it is exactly, okay?"

Chambers sipped coffee. "Okay."

"Now the colonel has a request, Steve. It's screwing us up."

Vicky Neuman said, "Correction, it's a demand, not a request."

The CIA Director said, "Right."

Vicky Neuman said, "It's blackmail."

The CIA Director said, "The colonel's request involves personnel currently under your purview Steve. This guy has apparently embarked upon a full-on invasion of a strategic ally's sovereign territory, and in doing so, somehow made the acquaintance of our man in the Egyptian *Mukhabarat*."

He clicked a button in front of him and the screen was filled with an image of two people standing in what looked like the break room of some light industrial facility. The colonel dressed for an Egyptian beach club party, standing next to a military aged male who Chambers recognized as the Pararescue operator they'd hosted up in Haifa at RAMBAM hospital, recovering from combat injuries sustained in Syria.

He said, "Keeler, that's our guy's name."

The commander of JSOC said, "Tom Keeler, a PJ attached to my task force. Supposed to be on R&R. Go get your hands on him Chambers. Whatever plans he's got have now changed."

Vicky Neuman was chewing the neckline of her sweater. She said, "Just please don't screw it up Steve. I put you in Tel Aviv for three years. Don't make me regret it."

Which meant to Chambers that whatever these people were cooking up was emotionally important to them, like a legacy defining thing. That was his cue to disengage and remove himself as far as possible. Emotional attachments, politics, and military affairs didn't ever amount to warm and fuzzy outcomes, in his experience.

He said, "Will do," and killed the connection. Chambers turned to the assistant, now very alert to his attentions. "CIA station chief and security officer in my office, twenty minutes."

He'd brief everyone and send them on their pre-dawn missions. After that he'd take a nap in his chair. Once the sun was up, Chambers was going to stroll outside and acquire his grapefruit and pomegranate juice, despite there being no chance of getting a beach jog in today. Getting screwed once is okay, twice is unacceptable.

In his line of work one crisis blurred into the next, a perma-crisis is what they were calling it.

The world in a perma-crisis.

The weather in Tel Aviv was good this time of year, the beach loaded with tanned young flesh and one could even ask for a *macchiato* without fear of some ungodly horror being served in return.

THIRTY-FIVE

Western Negev, Israel

Down by the Egyptian border, the rising moon hadn't yet reached its culmination. Keeler looked at it, thinking to himself, two thirty in the morning, maybe two twenty-six. He and Yasmin collected firewood on the hike back to the campsite. Not so much wood as dried vegetal growth from shrubs and the occasional hardy desert tree. They didn't need much of it, since dinner was going to be quick.

The tent was still where it had been when they'd left it. Keeler got to work organizing the combustible materials into a good pile and lighting it up. Yasmin lay back on a blow-up mattress and stared into the sky.

There wasn't much to work with, just dried lentils and rice with garlic and spices and some herbs he'd clipped from desert bushes. He had a little bag of cured beef, like some kind of middle eastern version of jerky.

Yasmin dragged her mattress closer to the fire. She said, "Make it spicy."

He threw in two chili peppers.

She said, "So what's the plan?"

He knew what she meant. Keeler said, "Plan is we eat and sleep and then we'll have to communicate with the deep state."

"You mean this is it."

"Pretty much. The shit's hit the fan."

Yasmin said, "No ignoring it, huh?"

Keeler didn't respond because the idea of ignoring it was obviously ridiculous. What they'd been through, the coincidental run in with the deranged Egyptian mukhabarat officer, had to be reported, by them both.

She said, "I'll drive into southern command. You can come with me."

He said, "You know the one about Sir Walter Raleigh and the Spanish armada?"

"No."

Keeler stirred the pot, making sure nothing was sticking to the bottom. The aluminum pot thin against the hot flame. He said, "Spanish armada's coming to invade England. Sir Walter Raleigh's finishing a game of bowls up on the bluffs, the whatever you call it."

"White cliffs of Dover."

"The white cliffs of Dover. He's up there on the grass playing bowls and an aide comes running up in a panic. 'Sir Walter, the Spanish armada is coming!' Sir Walter Raleigh doesn't even look at the kid. He's weighing the ball in his hand, lining up the shot. He says, 'There's time to finish the game of bowls and defeat the Spanish armada as well.'"

Yasmin clapped. "He kept a cool head."

"Exactly. Finished the game of bowls and then went and burned down the Spanish armada."

"That's a bullshit story, right?"

Keeler said, "Not any more bullshit than other stories."

Later, they sat around the fire eating from bowls and staring into the flames, silent and wrapped in their thoughts. When they'd finished, Yasmin retrieved a half filled bottle of whiskey that they'd been sipping from for a week. She took a slug and passed it on.

"Here's to the dead. May they rest in peace."

She wrapped her arm around Keeler's waist and snuggled close, digging her hand into the back pocket of his jeans, pulling him tight in the desert chill.

He said, "Amen", and took a mouthful, letting the Johnny Walker burn in his mouth before swallowing.

Yasmin's fingers wriggled in his back pocket, like they were uncomfortable in there. She pulled something out of it with two fingers. Holding the thing up and looking at it in the fire light. "What's this?"

Keeler examined the object in her hand, a photograph of a woman with two children in some tourist spot. He took the picture from her and realized what it was, remembering the situation. The infiltrator with the fake Israeli ID. Keeler had taken his phone, which had been cased in some kind of fake leather wallet thing. He remembered the papers falling out in a flutter to the floor when he'd pulled it out.

He said, "It fell out of that guy's phone wallet, back over there." Pointing towards Egypt.

Yasmin took the photograph again, looking at it by the firelight and handing it back. "It's his family I guess."

She rose from the fire, took the dirty dishes and disappeared into the darkness. Keeler heard her scraping the utensils and pots and bowls with sand. When she was finished, she went straight into the tent. After a few minutes of her fumbling around in there, he heard only silence.

Keeler looked at the picture. A woman with a kind round face framed by an Islamic hijab. Two children, a boy and a girl, maybe five and eight years old. A body of water behind them. He almost threw the photograph into the fire but stopped himself and returned it to his pocket. He took another pull from the whiskey bottle and rose. Out here there was no reason to kick sand on a fire, you just let it burn out by itself.

He slipped into the tent naked. Placing his clothes at the foot of two sleeping bags zipped together. Yasmin's body was warm and cool at the same time. Smooth and hard and soft in all the right places. He pressed lightly against her back, feeling the bump of her push back against him, having an immediate effect. He bit her ear lobe.

"Was it spicy enough?"

Her hand snaked back and took him. He let his right hand drift over her body to cup her breast, finding evidence that she was already getting into the vibe. Keeler threaded his left arm under her, lifting her gently and feeling her adjust, giving herself. He moved his hand downwards brushing over her abdomen to the inner thighs, feeling her parting, the warmth and readiness there.

Keeler woke at some point, roused by Yasmin moving around. She'd settled back into the sleeping bag and had a head torch on, looking at something. He adjusted his position to see her looking at the photograph he'd had in his jeans pocket. He rested his chin on her shoulder.

"What do you think?"

She said, "I think it's strange." Yasmin held the picture for him to see better. "Something was bothering me."

The photograph of the woman and her kids posing against the backdrop of what looked like a calm sea.

He said, "What's strange?"

She pointed at the photograph. "What's weird is the water behind them." Tapping on the photograph. "This is lake

Kinneret, the Sea of Galilee. It's in Israel, not Egypt, or Gaza. You remember that guy who had the fake Israeli identity card." Yasmin shifted in the sleeping bag to look at Keeler with large question marks in her eyes. "Maybe it wasn't a fake ID. I think the first name was *Jafar*. I don't remember the second."

"Hell of a name." Keeler said, "What's the concern?"

"I'm just wondering, what was he doing there with the Egyptians from El-Arish?" She shifted a little against him. "It's totally abnormal. An Israeli Arab guy with a couple of Egyptians coming in and out of an infiltration tunnel."

Keeler didn't have the slightest idea what normal was supposed to mean in this place. He did know that this colonel had been disturbed enough to try to have them killed. Maybe that was why.

He said, "What about the dead guys, the one you said was a friend who ran the Friday pub night?"

She went still against him. "I don't know."

He settled back down into the sleeping bag and felt Yasmin shifting around for a minute before her breathing became deep and regular. Jackals were yelping out in the desert. Keeler realized he'd left the beef jerky out by the fire.

THIRTY-SIX

Yasmin woke first, or at least she thought that she had, until she realized that she hadn't. She could see the sun's position from inside the tent. She estimated 6:30 am, which meant they'd slept less than four hours.

She said, "Are you awake?"

Keeler said, "No."

She had never actually caught him sleeping. He definitely slept, but seemed to have a built-in sensor that didn't just detect movement, Keeler knew when she was awake even if she hadn't moved. His system was sensitive to mental activity, which was ridiculous. What happened now was she'd get up and let him sleep, and any time she checked on him he'd be awake.

A strange person, but that was par for the course with those who worked with her sister, Ruth.

Ruth and her friends might be eccentric in some ways, but none of them engaged in idle rumor, speculation, or gossip. So when they'd told her that this guy Tom Keeler had saved her sister's life, she knew it wasn't an exaggeration. Ruth had been shot point blank in the chest and lived. Partly that was because of luck, the way the bullet had gone in, the type of ammunition, and what it had touched in her body, and the way it had exited. But mostly her survival was down to Keeler's quick thinking and bravery.

Yasmin understood this was all she would ever know about the episode. Ruth was Mossad.

She slipped out of the tent and stretched as tall as she could. Huddling in that tunnel had been intense. Her Subaru was parked about a kilometer back, on the nearest navigable trail. She'd left her valuables in there, including a bluetooth speaker and right now she felt like listening to music.

There was no footpath, but she knew the direction, knew the whole area like the back of her hand. She came down through a boulder strewn desert gorge, leaping between rocks and sliding down through the gaps until she came out near the spot where she'd left the car. A white Hyundai sedan was parked behind her Subaru. Two men were looking in the dust smeared windows of her car.

The Hyundai had a white license plate with red lettering, which meant that it belonged to some military branch.

The men were in plain clothes and older than conscription age, in their late thirties or early forties. She thought, *Shabak*. The Hebrew acronym for the Shin Bet internal security service.

One of the guys saw her first and waved. He came over and met her near the vehicles.

"You're Ruth's sister?" He was holding up an identity card.

"What's that? I can't read it."

He looked at the card. "It says right here. Prime Minister's office."

She nodded. Mossad, not Shin Bet. That's how they knew her sister.

The guy still had his face in a question mark. "Where's the French guy?"

"What's the French guy?" Yasmin was a little puzzled

until she remembered Keeler's little game, pretending that he was French with the Egyptian *Mukhabarat* guy the night before, but only those present at that incident would know this. The two Mossad guys looked at her like, Yasmin thought, not exactly pit bulls, but some kind of animal that won't ever let go of anything. Creatures like that, it's better to be friendly.

The other guy said, "We're going to need the French guy."

She said, "Back at the camp. He hasn't eaten breakfast."

The two Mossad men relaxed. The first one approached Yasmin and clapped her on the shoulder. "Don't worry, Your French guy will eat breakfast. It's a long drive to Tel Aviv."

The two Mossad men helped them break camp. They were decent and friendly once they were reassured that Yasmin and Keeler were cooperating. Apparently, Keeler had an appointment with someone in Tel Aviv. Where exactly, they wouldn't say. She didn't seem to be invited.

Keeler threw the pack and tent into the back of Yasmin's car. He looked at her, eyes clear and wide awake.

He said, "You think this is it?"

She put on her best scowl. "Let's play it that way. If it isn't the end, we'll have surpassed expectations."

He came into her personal space. "You've already surpassed expectations."

She felt heat rising to her face. "I know."

Keeler grinned and nodded. "Yeah, you do."

Yasmin went in for a kiss, figuring screw it. Keeler's hand went to the small of her back and she felt his easy strength. She adjusted her position, getting close to his ear and whispering. "Don't let them rip you off. I didn't get my fill of you. They owe you a week and a half of R&R and I'm expecting you back, you hear?"

Keeler put his forehead to hers. "Roger that."

Her phone had been lost over there in Sinai. She'd have to figure out getting a new one, maybe she could keep the old number, maybe not. Keeler didn't have a phone at all. He'd claimed an allergy to them.

She said, "How do we stay in touch?"

Keeler said, "I'll buy a burner and message your sister." He tapped his head. "Got her number up here."

Keeler and Yasmin's sister Ruth had history.

Yasmin said, "Code word *cluster*." One of her favorite English words.

Keeler nodded. "Cluster's good."

Pulling away from him. Watching him turn and walk back to the Hyundai. The two men were already in the front, the engine running. Yasmin watched them drive away.

Cluster. Practicing the word, feeling the combination of sounds that involve many parts of her mouth.

Yasmin held the photograph between thumb and forefinger, photo paper with its plasticky feel at the back, glossy image. The woman and her kids in front of Lake Kinneret, what Christians call The Sea of Galilee. The photograph had been taken in summer, the grass yellowed, the kids wearing tank tops and floppy hats against the sun. The woman wore the hijab, framing her plump and pretty face, now red with the heat. On close inspection Yasmin noticed a fine gold chain necklace on the woman's neck. The precious metal circling reddened flesh and disappearing underneath a loose long-sleeved t-shirt.

A moment of clarity occurred in Yasmin's brain. The fact of the hijab didn't have to mean that the woman was a Muslim. The gold chain could easily be a cross, worn under her shirt as the Christian Arabs sometimes do.

The questions were occurring to her because she recognized the location, the site at which this woman and her children had been photographed. They were seated on a low stone wall overlooking the Sea of Galilee, a vantage point that Yasmin knew as the *Beit Tsaida Zachi* Reserve, a historical site dear to Christians, a place that Jesus was said to have miraculously fed 5,000 men from five loaves of bread and two fish.

The photograph might have been taken by the man who carried it in his phone wallet, presumably her husband, now a curious character in Yasmin's mind. Who was this guy? Perhaps an Israeli citizen, an Arab Christian from a village in the Galilee, like Nazareth or Fassuta. What had he been doing in Egypt?

The dust was settling from the Hyundai's departure. Her last image of Keeler, stooping to slide into the backseat of the car. The two Mossad guys in the front. The vehicle and contents not long down the road, leaving her on her own. A feeling she enjoyed now, free, winged, unbound.

Keeler would take care of himself, that was a certainty. Yasmin had met many fighters in her young life. Some had died, most had lived, many had been brave and more had not. Keeler was different. This man whose attention never wavered, alert and relaxed and at the same time capable of being funny, attentive to her and basically kind, if she was honest about it.

The thing about the photograph and the Egyptian intelligence officer needed to be reported. She'd been out of the military for a week and a bit, but her ex-battalion commander was still the first person she could think of getting in touch with. Problem was, Yasmin had the phone she'd kept from the night before, but the SIM card was Egyptian. Not only Egyptian, she realized, taken from a dead man.

You don't just call the IDF Southern Command headquarters from an Egyptian phone that had recently belonged to a deceased Wilayat Sinai man without someone paying attention.

She'd have to just show up there in person.

THIRTY-SEVEN

Keeler watched the sky go by, his head leaned back against the Hyundai's rear seat cushion. The vehicle's movement lulled him into a meditative mental state. The two Israeli security guys up front were silent. One of them had opened a pack of local potato chips that smelled like falafel. Which reminded him, thinking about falafel, places like Iraq had different variations. Best falafel he'd had was in Israel though. No special place, a bus station maybe. Yasmin waiting in her car while he took a piss, washing his hands and seeing the falafel stall up by a newsstand. Waving over to her in the car, pretty there behind the wheel. Some hot girl, for sure.

That was like, the second day he'd known her. The falafel again, the smell hitting him hard as a memory bomb. His first Israeli falafel at the bus station. They'd crushed the fried bean balls into the bottom of a fluffy pita. Threw in some tahini sauce over that, pickles, and hot peppers. They'd stuffed in chopped tomato and cucumber, more fried falafels and more stuff, something yellow called amba, like a pickled mango sauce.

Amazing.

Keeler was about to ask the guys up front if they could stop for falafel, but the car was turning off the highway and slowing down. He came up to sitting position. The vehicle was descending an off ramp, winding down into more desert. To his right was a bright flash, making Keeler turn his head rapidly, seeing a burning white light on the horizon, something man made. Realizing what it was, the concentrated solar power station at *Ashalim*, a place with mirrors in a circle, robot controlled on servo motors, computers optimizing their angle to the sun, focusing its power onto the central tower, and transforming that concentrated energy into steam.

They were now down into another dip, a series of small hills. He put his head between the passenger and driver seats.

"I thought we were going to Tel Aviv."

The passenger turned, not unfriendly. "Sorry man, we had to say that for your girlfriend."

The driver sought eye contact in the mirror. "Got to love her and leave her, buddy."

Keeler said, "Where are we going?"

The two said nothing, and the Hyundai came around another bend. Directly in front of them was the ugly beginnings of the kind of military facility with which Keeler had an intimate familiarity. An airbase from the looks of it. Already he could see a section of tarmac with curved hangars, under one of them the very familiar silhouette of an MQ-1 Predator drone.

They were coming up to the guardhouse, Keeler noticed the cement blocks strategically located to prevent a vehicle borne attack on the base. Thinking about the Predator drone, particularly how it wasn't something that the Israelis used. They had their own drones. The Israeli military guard waved them through, and the car stopped in front of a gate.

The passenger turned and looked at Keeler. "Welcome to the United States of America."

The gate was a cluster of cold steel, high and complicated in its asceticism, not only a portal but a skeletal barrier of beams and tubes with sensors. Beyond it was a wall of some flat material with a large opaque rectangle of glass set into a slab of concrete. There would be people behind that glass, scanning the arrivals and following protocol.

The passenger was anticipating something from Keeler, looking at him.

Keeler said, "What, I get out here?"

The man nodded. "They'll open the gate for you my friend, not for me."

"No Tel Aviv?"

"No Tel Aviv."

Keeler had been imagining the beach, across the street from the US embassy, sunbathing and ice cream, not this stark looking facility in the Negev.

He said, "I didn't know we had bases in Israel."

The driver said, "You don't, but here we are."

The passenger smiling, liking it. Keeler cracked a grin and opened the door. Stepping out onto the hard asphalt. He approached the gate, and it clicked open like some invisible hand had touched it, allowing him to walk through. A door in the wall clicked open an inch. Keeler pushed lightly, the heavy slab of steel swinging easily in. A man wearing the uniform of a United States Air Force Command Chief Master Sergeant waited on the other side.

Keeler approached, and the man stepped forward.

"Captain, I'm the Command Chief Master Sergeant here. Please come with me, they're waiting for you."

The man walked away rapidly, striding down an absurdly clean corridor, literally shining with wax. The place was lit by a wall of windows looking out to the tarmac. The Predator drone sheds sat closer to the entrance, beyond that the airfield opened to a wide horizon. An enormous C-17 Globemaster III stood hulking a hundred yards from the building, almost blocking out the light.

The Command Chief Master Sergeant opened a glass door and held it. He pointed down a steel staircase to an aircraft maintenance guy waiting below.

Keeler said, "Thanks."

The man nodded curtly. "Captain."

Keeler went down the stairs, the Globemaster's engines already roaring, making it impossible to hear anything. The maintenance guy wore a noise cancelling headset over his ears. Keeler inserted fingers, the wind whipping at him as the man uselessly screamed something. The aircraft's rear loading door was open, the airman pushing Keeler ahead of him, up the steps into the enormous cargo hold. A cluster of loaded pallets was strapped down tight, just inside the doors, the contents concealed by tarps.

The airman pointed to a seat in the back, one among many empty places. He handed Keeler a head set, plugged by a looped cable into the wall. Keeler put it on, the guy already speaking.

"You hear me?" He nodded. The guy said, "Strap in and sit tight, we're taking off immediately."

"Where to?"

"RAF Mildenhall sir, in England. I'll alert you when it's alright to come up front for coffee and sandwiches."

Mildenhall airbase in England was home turf to the 321st Special Tactics Squadron, Keeler's unit. He nodded and got himself strapped in. Maybe they needed him back home for a mission. A need urgent enough to require an emergency recall from injury leave was bizarre, given that the 321st was a large unit, maybe a hundred operators total, with a mix of Combat Controllers, Pararescue Jumpers, Special Reconnaissance, and Tactical Air Controllers. Why him?

Time would tell.

The headset dampened the relentless roar and shriek of the engines and ventilation equipment. Keeler was thinking that it might get cold when something moved in his peripheral vision and his hand darted out on its own to catch an insulated parka the airman had tossed at him. Which meant they'd be flying at a high altitude, maybe to a place with mountains.

Keeler closed his eyes as the Globemaster lifted off the tarmac. A smooth powerful push and they were into thin air. No windows available, just his imagination of the view, looking out over the Negev desert. He'd probably be able to see Egypt from there. The aircraft's left wing lowered, sending them in a swooping turn. Maybe headed north or east.

Like many aspects of military life, you could never know where they'd send you next. It was better not to speculate, better yet to get some sleep while he could.

THIRTY-EIGHT

YASMIN KNEW the Southern Command headquarters well, which is why she was surprised to see her battalion commander in the lobby, in uniform and sucking down a small paper cup of coffee, a Marlboro red clutched between knuckles. When the woman saw Yasmin she dumped the butt in an ashtray and blew out the residual smoke from the side of her mouth.

"Let's go."

Yasmin stood for a moment, looking at her, unprepared to just accept the command. "How did you know I was coming in?"

The commander crushed the coffee cup in her fist and tossed it for three points into the waste basket. She looked at Yasmin with sly eyes. "I knew, that's all, yalla."

She swiveled on one foot and marched into the building. The left turn to the Karakal battalion office came up but the Lieutenant Colonel stormed past it. She strode ahead and then surprised Yasmin by taking a right towards the secure entrance to Southern Command's Intelligence Unit office. Two guards in blue short sleeve shirts were positioned either side of a secure entry system to the Intelligence Unit. The armored doors slid open, revealing yet another fluorescent lit corridor. If you closed your eyes, you'd be in a hospital, or a low rent corporate headquarters.

A boring conference room. The door open, the interior anonymous and institutional.

A man lounged at the end of a table, swinging the rotating chair in an arc and then back again, looking up at them coming in the door. The guy was in his forties with managed stubble on his face and close-cropped salt and pepper hair. He wore plain clothes and had the aspect of a well-practiced killer, not a look that Yasmin disliked.

A woman twenty years his junior was leaning back against the wall and doing things to a phone. The killer's assistant or something of that nature. She looked up, raised a hand, eyes drilling the Lieutenant Colonel.

"Just her. Thanks." Jerking her head towards Yasmin.

The commander scowled, looked at Yasmin. "Good luck."

A second of discomfort passed, as the Karakal battalion commander removed herself from the room. Yasmin's eyes met the assistant's, a coldly beautiful woman with the unsettled look of a raptor. She closed the door.

The man said, "Sit down, Yasmin." He didn't wait for her to settle. "We're all happy that your sister is recovering. I met you once, I don't know if you remember. I knew your father pretty well."

The guy had a folder in front of him, closed with no markings visible. She realized it was probably her file.

In fact she did remember him, not his name though, just the face and bearing. It had come to her a few seconds earlier. She'd been younger, pre-army age. Coming home drunk from a night out with friends. This guy had been in the back yard with her dad and some other veterans from *the unit*, eating sausages from the grill.

The guy said, "I'm not with *Duvdevan* anymore. I'm heading up something new." He glanced away. "New, but not new, if you know what I mean."

Duvdevan was her father's old military unit, mostly composed of Israeli immigrants from middle eastern origins, now into the second and third generations. Essentially Jewish Arabs whose family backgrounds permitted them to speak the language fluently, having learned it at home from their mothers and grandmothers.

Just like Yasmin.

Duvdevan specialized in undercover operations penetrating Arab areas in the Palestinian territories or abroad. They did dirty war, kidnappings, targeted killings and arrests. Of course there were other things that they did which nobody knew about. It was their father's path that Ruth had followed.

This guy seemed to be trying to dig into the little emotional crevice between her family tradition and the path Yasmin had chosen. Which was smart but mean, in her opinion.

The Shoshan family circle had been predominantly right wing and Sephardic, with Ruth serving initially in Duvdevan and going on to be tapped by Mossad. Contrary to that, Yasmin had chosen Karakal, with its left-wing Ashkenazi roots in the Nahal brigade, gender equality, and all that socialist kibbutz shit that Yasmin found so alien.

She said, "What is this, some kind of Godfather rerun?" Making the Brando voice. "Just when I thought I was out, they pull me back in."

The man with the killer smile said, "What's bred in the bone will come out in the flesh."

Yasmin rolled her eyes, but nonetheless had the sinking feeling that this was going to ultimately lead to one of those places, the kind of thing that you did but could never talk about for the rest of your life.

She thought, Shit, this is where I'm going to end up. Like Dad and Ruth.

The truth was that she didn't know what she wanted to do next in life. She was one week out of the army and had spent it with an American special forces operator showing him the terrain that she'd been navigating for the past year. Most people her age would be setting off on a long trip around the world, Thailand or India, but for some reason that didn't appeal to her.

She didn't even want to get away.

Yasmin said, "What do you want from me?"

THIRTY-NINE

Mike Hershkowitz laughed.

Looking at this young woman in front of him, liking her for now.

He said, "Well, what do you have?"

She gave confused guilty vibes. "What do you mean?"

"I mean what do you have, let's see it."

Yasmin pulled the photograph from her pocket.

"You mean this?" She pushed it across the table. "You're following me."

Hershkowitz raised his eyebrows theatrically, looking at the thing on the table, not actually having expected an object to appear like this. He swiveled back and forth in the chair, not touching the photograph yet. Glancing at Yasmin.

"Following you." He smiled. "Like you're going to sneak across to Egypt with a US pararescue officer and infiltrate back through a known attack tunnel and we aren't going to pay any attention to you?"

He cracked a smile as wide as possible and crossed his arms.

Yasmin Shoshan rolled her eyes. "Well, if you put it like that, right."

He nodded, liking the attitude. "Right." Hershkowitz put a finger on the photo, pinning it to the table. He beckoned to his assistant. "Analysis, please."

The assistant came over to the table with her smartphone, one of those ridiculous devices with maybe five cameras on the back. She got the angle right but wasn't happy, glancing up at Yasmin. "You mind blocking the light? I'm getting glare."

Yasmin stood and used her hands to block the reflection from overhead lights. The assistant snapped the photograph and did something with her phone, retreating at the same time to where she'd been leaning against the wall.

Hershkowitz said, "Yasmin, tell me the story, from the beginning." Pointing at the picture, he said, "Put that in context for me, so I know what I'm looking at." Looking up at her with curiosity that couldn't be faked.

He watched the young woman, pushing back the hair over her ears and putting both elbows up on the table. She told him the story, what had happened the night before. Hershkowitz interjected questions here and there, taking his time, allowing her to take hers. An hour later Yasmin was done with the telling, seemingly happy to have gotten it off her chest.

She was mostly concerned with the fact that she'd lost two $M4A1$ carbines. As she told it, buried over there in the Sinai somewhere. She'd wanted to get that off her chest right away. The truth was that losing control over your service weapon is a serious offense in any military, worse in the IDF. But in Hershkowitz's reading, that's not what happened.

He said, "You didn't lose your weapon. You buried it, okay? That's different."

Yasmin said, "Tell that to Keren." The battalion commander who'd brought her in.

The last thing Hershkowitz wanted was for her to be distracted by petty bullshit.

"I'll deal with Keren; you leave it with me." Giving a significant nod to his assistant, who responded with a micro gesture of acknowledgment. He said, "Another thing you should know. The murders you and the American friend were alerted to initially."

Yasmin said, "Yeah?"

He said, "Your friend was murdered, but it wasn't by those infiltrators. Just so you know."

"Who did it?"

"Your friend got mixed up with one of the crime families from Rahat. Smuggling weed and hash over the border."

Rahat was a Bedouin city in the Negev, home of multiple competing crime clans who fought over access to Sinai based networks bringing stuff over the fence from Egypt.

Yasmin said, "How do you know it wasn't the infiltrators?"

"Because the police found the murderers, like I said, guys from Rahat. I'm sorry about your friend. The infiltrators were in the area, but uninvolved, as far as anyone knows."

"Ok." Yasmin was leaned back in the chair, hugging herself.

He said, "You cold?"

"No." She released her hands.

He looked at his assistant, who made another micro-gesture. Hershkowitz raised his phone from the table. "Let's see what we've got."

The photograph had come through processing and he'd received the relevant details.

He read from his phone. "The woman in your picture is Zeina Ahmad Makhoul. Forty-three years old, resident of Nazareth, Melkite Christian. *Only* three children." He indicated the photograph. "That's from a few years ago, maybe now she's got more."

Yasmin said, "Probably not. Three children is a lot for a Christian. Muslims usually have three." She leaned forward and pulled the photograph back to herself, looking at it carefully. "Didn't you hear? We're beating them in demographics these days."

Yasmin's father had been a big dude in the Duvdevan, responsible for setting up their undercover mista'arvim units. Later he'd been an amateur historian with a couple of published books. Looked like the intellectual streak was running in the family.

Yasmin said, "What about the husband?"

Hershkowitz scanned the details on his phone. "Married to a guy name of Mikhail Samir Makhoul." He swiped and tapped for a photograph of the man and got his latest identity card pic. The husband was heavy set and clean shaven, thin hair trimmed tight, maybe fifty years old. He held the phone up for her to see. "You think that's the guy you met last night?"

"No."

Hershkowitz grunted, suddenly not so happy. He pinned the photograph to the table again with his forefinger. He spun it to face himself, leaning in to take a good look. Nice looking plump woman from Nazareth, three kids, apparently more than she should statistically be having. Some guy across the border carrying this married woman's photograph in his phone wallet. The run in with an Egyptian intelligence officer. Several options were populating his mind. Makhoul could be having an affair... the photograph could have been planted by Egyptian intelligence for some reason...

All the above, none of the above. Hershkowitz's mind switched gears, burying the previous thoughts into a compartment to the back and to the left side above his ear, how he pictured it, what the geniuses called a memory palace. He chin pointed at Yasmin.

"Let's talk about you now."

"What about me?"

He said, "Sector commander for the past year. Top of the class with firearms and combat stress tests. Five combat engagements. Two confirmed enemy kills." He looked up at her trying to see if Yasmin was impressed that he'd memorized her file. "Tell me about the incident up near Rafah with the Hummer."

She pointed to the folder Hershkowitz had in front of him. "It's all in there. We got shot up, we shot back. One of us died, and four of them died. What else do you need to know?"

He leaned back in the ergonomic chair. "You didn't just fight back in defense, you pursued the enemy over the border. Some people say it was insubordination."

"There are always some people."

Hershkowitz smiled for the first time. "I call it initiative and aggression. It's the number one thing I'm interested in." He pointed at her. "And last night you did it again."

"That was stupid."

"Yes, it was, but stupidly brave. Now you've opened the can of worms we might never have known existed." He pushed the folder across the table to her. "Before we go any further, you'll need to open that and put some ink on it."

Watching Yasmin open the folder and examine the single sheet of paper and a pen that it contained. Surprised, he could guess, to find it wasn't her military personnel records, but a legal document that stated in stark and simple terms that if she ever spoke to anybody about the nature of their conversation and the actions and events that might follow, she'd be buried alive in a black site for the rest of her life.

Yasmin's face flushed. She looked up at him. "What is it you want me to do?"

Hershkowitz pointed at the document. "You need to sign that anyway, regardless of doing or not doing anything."

Which was true, she couldn't be talking about what had happened the night before, not ever. He saw Yasmin realizing this and signing. She shoved the papers across, not unkindly. The rule of law was important, but in Israel there was always the rule of law during wartime. Only morons thought they lived in a country like Belgium.

She said, "What do you want?"

Hershkowitz looked at his assistant. "Did you get the Egyptian file?"

She nodded.

Hershkowitz said, "First thing I want Yasmin, is for you to look at some photographs so that we can identify your new Egyptian friend, this colonel."

The assistant slid a laptop in front of Yasmin and adjusted the screen to her height. She said, "Use the arrow keys, take your time."

Yasmin said, "Oh, I already found a picture of him online."

FORTY

HERSHKOWITZ and his assistant crowded around the screen. Yasmin made way for them to look at the social media post she'd found of the colonel. Turned out he was in several of the pictures taken by one of these Instagram beach bunnies.

Hershkowitz said, "The Palm Oasis Resort."

His assistant snickered. "So cheesy."

She leaned in and copied the url into another application, along with a screenshot and sent that up to a secure server. The word came to him, *cloud*. He knew that it wasn't really a cloud, but more like a warehouse sized room full of blinking machines tended to by a small army of uniformed geeks down in 8200 grooming and coaxing whatever AI robots had been created for this purpose. The programs, like spiders, were crawling over the image of this man, ripping apart features and sucking ancillary information, contextualizing, changing worlds. The machines feeding on the metadata and making connections and models, which altered other models and machines, an endless chain of complexity.

Hershkowitz was on the fence about technology like that, if

he didn't understand it, what good was it? Half of him was pretty sure that it made the world more complex than it already was, a conundrum in any case. The machines were apparently decent because within a minute the screen was populating with all kinds of interesting information.

Yasmin said, "That's the guy."

Exactly why people like Hershkowitz would never win the battle against the robots, besides everything else, they really worked.

His assistant reached in and enlarged one of the images that the machine had found of the colonel, bringing up further details. A decent looking Egyptian man in his late thirties when the picture had been taken, not in military uniform, dressed in a pink polo shirt with a sweater tied around his shoulders, smiling, and tanned. Some Red Sea beach club, maybe in south *Sinai* or *Marsa Alam*.

He read the name aloud. "Hisham Al-Masri," cocked his head to Yasmin. "Does that name fit the face for you, Yasmin?"

She was bouncing back in the ergonomic chair. "Names are arbitrary. Everything fits and nothing fits."

Hershkowitz skimmed the file. "Born 1974, father connected to military people, manages their corporate interests overseas." He looked up at his assistant, playing to her as usual even though they'd never had sex, and never would. He said, "Family spends some time in Russia early on, interesting, plus France and Germany later. Parents put him in French schools wherever they're living. *Lycées Français*." Looking at Yasmin, making sure she was paying attention and winking. "You know, going for the international *Baccalaureate*. Blah blah blah." Skimming over details, finding the interesting stuff. "Hey now, Al-Masri gets into a very decent business school in France. Combined a bachelor's in finance with a masters in management." He waved his hand around. "Some kind of accelerated program."

The assistant said, "Living the dream."

"Indeed. Right out of the gate he starts a financial services company with two buddies, real actual French people mind you." He glanced at his assistant.

She said, "Shows ambition."

Yasmin yawned.

He said, "Exactly, that's ambition for you. Or you could say overreach. What's the story, Icarus, flies too close to the sun and his wings of wax melt, bringing him down to earth."

Yasmin said, "That's cynical."

"You think so."

His assistant said, "Just wait, we've seen this before."

Hershkowitz was skimming. "Blah blah blah. They go hard, seeking funds, venture capital rounds for a couple of years. That's decent." He scrolled, sucking in data and processing, getting to the good part. He nodded his head enthusiastically, jabbing at the screen. "Here we go, Icarus. The problem is with his partners." Looking at his assistant. "Can anyone ever trust the French? Oh look, some juridical process and it's getting dirty. Six months later and our man is back home." Addressing his assistant, "What do you think, he got on the unemployment line?"

"No, his dad found him a soft landing."

"With his buddies in the *Mukhabarat*."

His assistant said, "Classic."

Yasmin said, "I'm not following you." Looking at them angrily. "You guys sound like assholes. What's so obvious and classic about this? It's a sad story is all. Now I'm feeling sorry for this guy."

Hershkowitz looked at her. "You're still pure. It's cute. Connected Egyptians have a single dream that animates them, that's making it overseas and escape that shithole. Hisham Al-Masri here had more opportunity than most and still failed. He had to come back with his tail between his legs and accept a position with his father's old friends in the security services." He tapped the picture of the colonel. "This guy's rotten."

Yasmin said, "Hmmm. Because he came back and made a career in the *Mukhabarat?*"

His assistant butted in. "Most of them go straight into the security service and live satisfying lives. You don't need to believe Mike. But this guy's past is different, he had real opportunities and squandered them. And then of course there's last night."

Hershkowitz was looking into the screen now. "Unmarried." Glancing at his assistant. "True?"

She checked, verified. "Never been married."

They looked at each other, a grin spreading on her face. Both saying the word at the same time, "Playboy."

Hershkowitz looked at Yasmin, nodding his head like a sage. "You add in what you've told us Yasmin and there's a greater than zero chance that our colonel, Al-Masri is playing against the house."

Yasmin said, "Greater than zero."

His assistant said, "That's our threshold Yasmin, all we need, in terms of a threat analysis."

Hershkowitz said, "How do you feel Yasmin. You're interested, am I right or am I right?"

She said, "Of course I'm interested."

"Yeah, alright." He dragged the photograph of Zeina Makhoul and her children back to the edge of the table, spinning it around. "What we need right now is to find the guy who was carrying this photograph. Our operational assumption being he's connected to Al-Masri, and the connection is not kosher."

Yasmin said, "Why do you think I can help? I assume you've got sufficient resources."

He spun the photograph. "This is different. You're the only person who's seen the bearer of this photograph. This *Jafar* person. We're going to operate simultaneously along several vectors, but I want you up in Nazareth with this Makhoul woman. Just be yourself, but different. We've got a whole legend for you, sticking to some truth about your Syrian family. You have perfect Arabic and you'll look great in a hijab. The eyes are important and yours are so very expressive. They won't know shit, okay? It's an unusual situation but you'll have a team backing you. Just go in there and play it real. You did theater in high school right?"

"Pirates of Penzance."

Hershkowitz smiled. "Perfect."

She said, "I played Mabel."

He shrugged. "So now you're Frederic joining the pirates, it's an upgrade. The world's just getting better, right?" Hershkowitz leaned forward, suddenly impassioned to be discussing one of his pet theories about life. "Don't you have the impression Yasmin, that everything's always improving?"

Yasmin said, "I guess you need to be an optimist in this business." She put her elbows on the table again, suddenly confident. "I'm *not* going up there in a hijab, man, that's just a terrible idea."

"You aren't?"

"No. I'll go up there another way, if you don't mind."

Hershkowitz nodded, adapting. Whatever she wanted. Yasmin Shoshan was an intelligent woman in the prime of her life, already making decisions at the edge. He'd let her lead, often a good idea when you've got an agent in the field, until it isn't a good idea anymore. Like Mike Tyson said, everyone has a plan until they get punched in the mouth.

His assistant was looking at him, with that look. He said, "What?"

She said, "Gabi."

"Right."

They now knew the Egyptian *Mukhabarat* man's identity. He'd need to update the Mossad man.

FORTY-ONE

Keeler was jolted awake twice on the flight. The first time was when everyone on board suddenly started getting extremely busy, not agitated, just professional and determined. He'd been dreaming about free fall as usual, this time falling through the sky surrounded by happy dogs.

He'd come out of that dream and back to reality, a dozen men in flight suits and headgear buzzing around the tarp covered load. The cover had been removed, revealing a whole bunch of JPADs, a parachuted airdrop package with its own guidance systems and stuff. He'd been on the receiving end of a JPAD drop many times. The thing kind of *found* you by itself.

The back of the Globemaster was opening, mouth sinking ajar like a whale all ready to start skimming for plankton. The cold air came shrieking in, blasting everyone back a couple of inches. The light from outside was intense, blinding and blue, and very cold, they were above the cloud cover, and maybe a lot higher. Keeler was seated, strapped in, bemused with all this activity around him. Guys checking strap connections, making sure the skids were clear.

After a few minutes, many hand signals and flashing lights, the JPAD loads swished out into the nothingness. One after another the blunt containers slid down rails and disappeared, maybe a dozen of them until the huge doors closed, the harsh sucking sound ceased and the airmen disappeared back up front.

Keeler mused on the destination. They couldn't have been airborne much longer than an hour. He'd know if it was longer. His first thought was that they'd just dropped munitions and other gear to the Kurds in northern Iraq, which made a kind of sense. Problem was, those areas were reachable by other means, so why do it this way? Could just as easily have sent a load of weapons to some insurgent group in Iran nobody knew about. JPADs were expensive devices designed for high altitude delivery, which meant they were only usually sent places where you couldn't fly low.

The second time Keeler woke up was four or five hours later, when they were turning for landing. The enormous aircraft sweeping in a lazy arc as they made the approach to Mildenhall airbase, north east of Cambridge England.

AN AIRMAN HAD BEEN WAITING for Keeler on the tarmac. English weather wasn't on the same level as the Negev desert. They sped towards the terminal in a modified golf cart, rain lashing at them from all directions, the November cold biting. The airman was chewing gum and getting the rain sideways into his face. Keeler had the advantage of the parka, the hood pulled over his head.

The golf cart curved around a loading dock. The airman slipped the nimble little vehicle under the arched roof of the cargo terminal and brought them to a halt in front of a picnic table. He turned to Keeler, pointing at the table. "I'll be back in a minute."

Keeler dismounted and watched the golf cart speed away. He'd been expecting the chow hall, followed by a fresh OCP uniform and a bunk. The picnic table was clean and painted a glossy olive drab. He'd never been in the cargo terminal before, some place where other people did other things for other projects. Now there was nothing going on except the damp wind blowing through this cavernous place. Five minutes later the golf cart returned, whining around the loading dock and speeding at him.

Keeler recognized the sharp outlines of Jodorowsky's face, moving into profile as the airman made the sharp turn. Jodorowsky was a Lieutenant Colonel, and the commanding officer of the 321st. Not knowing exactly what was expected of him, Keeler did something very unusual and stood to attention. The golf cart squeaked to a halt and Jodorowsky jumped down, already cackling with mirth.

"Never thought I'd see that. Please stop, it's out of character." The airman smirked. Jodorowsky reached back into the golf cart and retrieved a foil covered dinner tray, thrusting it at Keeler "Better scoop that in, son." He looked at his watch. "You've got six minutes, chow down."

Keeler didn't need to be asked twice.

He got into position at the picnic table and got busy removing the foil covering. A full meal from the cafeteria. Chicken fried steak with gravy and mashed potatoes. Green peas and a bowl of green Jello. A bread-roll with an icy square of rock-hard butter. The beverage selection included a carton of chocolate milk and a cup of coffee, sealed and hot.

Jodorowsky came around and took the opposite bench. He said, "You eat, I talk."

Keeler grunted and dug in. The chicken fried steak was a

favorite. If the Lieutenant Colonel wanted him to verbalize, he'd ask. Jodorowsky had been the Chief Instructor for Keeler's special tactics indoctrination cohort, back in the day. As an enlisted man it wasn't an easy thing for Jodorowsky to switch up and maneuver himself into the position he now held. Along with the rest of the team, Keeler had watched him weave and duck in the political battlefield of military command, taking body blows and head shots on the way.

Jodorowsky yawned, looking around the place, eyes moving back to Keeler.

"You got a tan."

Keeler nodded, making affirmative noises around a mouthful of chicken fried steak.

Jodorowsky said, "Yeah, out in the desert, huh? Good times."

Keeler said nothing, kind of glanced up at Jodorowsky and ate.

The Lieutenant Colonel said. "So, what I'm asking myself is, did Keeler screw somebody's mother, or somebody's sister? That's what I'm wondering. What kind of asinine thing did you do out there Keeler?"

Keeler kept his head low, ducking down to address the bowl of green peas, finding them salty and buttered, just as he liked it, hard to get more than a couple of them onto a fork, like a puzzle to figure out. When it looked as if the Lieutenant Colonel was actually expecting a response he evaded.

"It was somebody's sister, sir."

Jodorowsky grunted. Keeler chewed peas.

Jodorowsky rapped his knuckles on the olive drab painted wood. He said, "Okay bud. You're probably wondering why we've had to hide you out here. Fact is, you're not here, and never were. You're still on convalescent leave and will remain so until this is done, at which time you'll receive the relevant OPORDs."

The cargo terminal had a couple of bad leaks. The water, infiltrating the roof layer, running through the nooks and crannies of the substratum, found its new shape in a droplet, forming and finally falling. One such liquid unit splattered into the middle of the picnic table, equidistant between Keeler and his commanding officer.

Keeler said, "Outstanding sir."

Jodorowsky said, "You're being inserted into some CIA spook shit, I'm not read into the file. They've asked for you in particular and nobody said please or thank you. The team's already in place, so you'll be doing a solo insertion."

"Any idea where I'm going sir?"

"Some place in the Middle East would be my bet."

"Okay."

Jodorowsky said, "You're going back with the Globemaster, so I'd guess it's somewhere on that flight path. They'll drop you out the back and hopefully nobody notices."

Keeler jerked a thumb in the direction of the airplane he'd come in on. "Back on that thing?"

"Correct. It's a monthly round trip, they'll be hiding you in the routine. Dropping you out in the stratosphere so nobody knows."

Meaning the insertion was a HALO jump. Whoever was in charge didn't want him going through passport control. They'd push him out the door and get him into the game without an opposing spook force any the wiser. Keeler finished eating, mopping up the tray with the remaining bread-roll. Only the butter remained uneaten, sitting there like a frozen rock. Keeler contemplated putting it in his pocket to melt a little. The five point seven grams of fat contents might be useful under certain circumstances. He decided against that route and leaned back with the coffee, looking at the commanding officer.

Jodorowsky said, "I don't know shit, but so far the communication on this one has been, let's say even more lacking in irony than usual."

Keeler said, "A *special* situation sir?"

Jodorowsky stared at him, maybe trying to figure out if he was kidding.

Because, back in the day Jodorowsky had a favorite phrase: *You are not special*. Keeler could still hear the guy screaming *You are not special, because to be special would be an unacceptable coincidence*. He'd always liked that concept. Now he kept his face expressionless.

Jodorowsky's eyes bored into him for several seconds, before swiveling to the empty tray and up again at the waiting airman. The enlisted man shuddered from a seated position, resting on the golf cart's steering wheel, and began the short journey from the golf cart to the picnic table, retrieving the platter and returning to the vehicle. Jodorowsky waited for the airman to push the electric start button. He rose from the bench and nodded to Keeler.

"Good luck."

The golf cart zipped away. Ten minutes later the airman was back.

THE GLOBEMASTER LIFTED off and Keeler was soon drifting into a deep sleep, the images in his dream, vivid and somehow hyper real.

Yasmin was there. Beautiful, moving in the desert, her habitat. The vision not exactly related to any specific memory, more like fleeting images of her in the tent, the red fabric filtering hard sunlight. Squatting at the fire, showing him her method of setting up a camp kitchen. Her laughing in the car. White teeth in a tanned face, young and still carefree, despite all that she'd seen and been through.

Her sister Ruth was there at one point, the way Keeler had seen her in Syria, a good combat soldier, fearless and aggressive, even while wounded and pretty much dying. After that the inside of his head was a blur of star streaks and strange cosmic formations. The dream was short but intense.

Broken abruptly three hours later by the airman coming for him. Time to jump.

Keeler broke out of the slumber and oriented himself to the mission, which was nothing more than a HALO jump into an unknown location. This was the first time anything like this had happened to him. There were stories though, of guys getting dropped into shitty places, like a test to see if they'd survive, but without even telling the operator that he was being tested.

Hard core.

Keeler had a half thought that this was one of those occasions, some deeply secret unit was putting him through an exam. Maybe they were dropping him in Haiti or something, without a weapon, seeing if he'd survive. The key was to go beyond mere survival. It was important to thrive.

So, he figured he'd be up for whatever.

The crew helped him suit up. Helmet on, oxygen mask working, jumpsuit and boots tucked in and cozy, GPS unit operational. Three guys buzzed around him, helping with the prep. The airman from earlier approached carrying an entrenching tool, a strange object to see on a military cargo aircraft. He pushed it at Keeler, mouthing something that he couldn't understand, two words. Keeler took the foldable shovel and examined it. The thing was known as an E-tool, this one made from steel. The blade was serrated on one side, normally used for digging trenches, or any other such attempt at geo forming.

At that point Keeler had no access to the aircraft's communication system, so he couldn't ask questions.

The airman winked at him and gave a thumbs up. He started looking for a place to put the E-tool, but the Globemaster's door began to open and lights were flashing. No good place to strap it down on his body, so he'd just have to hold on to it. There must have been a reason the guy had given it to him, like doing him a favor in some way.

The rear cargo door lowered its mouth, seeming now to have a kind of animal form. The story of Jonah and the whale came fleetingly to Keeler, as it had before in a similar situation. He couldn't remember what exactly they'd said about it at church one time, something about the futility of avoiding divine will.

An airman to his left started flapping his hands, making frantic gestures, like get the hell off the plane.

Keeler walked down to the lip. They were still high over the cloud layer, a pillow of dark gray. The cloud contained weather, hopefully only rain. Turning his gaze to the horizon, seeing its curve, a layer of cloud as far as the eye could see. A couple of airplanes whipped far below in as many directions, tiny specs above the cloud line, so far away that they probably hadn't even detected the military aircraft up in the stratosphere.

At that altitude international law didn't apply. He'd asked the airman if there was any kind of specific destination that he was supposed to be aiming for. The guy had looked at him with his half amused face. "The man said you're supposed to head for the place by the windmill."

Keeler allowed himself to fall off the Globemaster's lip, turning back and hurtling away from the gigantic aircraft, loving how it looked as he fell away, the thing was pretty much the material embodiment of American power. It gave him a thrill every time. He let it get small in the sky before allowing his body to tilt slightly, spinning him the other way, horizontally splayed, arms and legs spread out into a good structure, his right hand clutching the E-tool, constantly trying to be ripped out of his hand. The heavy cloud rushed up from below and enveloped him, after which he saw nothing at all.

FORTY-TWO

The cloud broke with no warning and Keeler found himself plummeting over a tight pattern of green and brown blotches, a messy grid of agricultural fields as far as the eye could see. He adjusted his arms and legs, allowing himself to make a controlled spin in a 360-degree circle. This was Europe, but it wasn't possible to guess exactly where from that altitude, the fields being divided by country lanes and mediating areas of vegetation. The rain didn't help and would become dangerous if it increased. Once deployed, the parachute might become heavy with water.

But that wasn't what Keeler was thinking about, too busy scouring the landscape for a windmill and finding nothing because the altitude was too great to make out exactly what was down there. He spotted a body of water over to the left, northeast by his calculations, perhaps a small lake or large pond. A river of some kind seemed to be snaking along the contours of the countryside.

The airman had said to look for a windmill. The message was that someone would liaison with him there.

Keeler's practiced eye made note of the topographical

features, hills and ridges that might get windy, descents and inclines that were tough to spot from the nearly vertical angle. You had to look for signs of depth in the valleys. All the same, he was dropping fast, turning with well-practiced gestures to examine the other directions, finding another snaking river as everything started getting closer.

It didn't look like windmill country, which is often flat land.

He glanced at the altimeter, two thousand meters and falling fast.

Keeler deployed the chute at a thousand meters, bracing for the hard jerk. Now, drifting, he needed to spot a landing zone. Manmade objects below were still lacking detail. As the ground elements clarified, agricultural structures came into focus, spread out around large fields. Still, it could be anywhere in Northern Europe. Closer yet and the buildings became more distinct, gray stone structures for the most part with that particular architecture that made him think of France. Not only France, but specifically a style of building that he associated with what was called the Paris Basin.

Which was a relief, Keeler knew where he was. Some place in the vicinity of Paris, probably anywhere in a 300-mile radius around the city.

He noticed a mill at about five hundred meters, a white structure at the edge of a river, an old school French *moulin,* but not a windmill, a water mill. This could be the wrong mill, or the guy who'd given the instructions might have made an error. Keeler could easily see it, guy number one says *mill,* guy number two repeats it to someone else and says, *windmill.*

Hope for the best, prepare for the worst.

Keeler allowed his body to turn slightly, directing himself closer to the mill, spotting a large field on the other side of it, the edges of which were dense with tree cover. The descent was faster than he anticipated, preoccupying him with the necessity of avoiding landing on one of the boulders interspersed with grass and mud that were suddenly rushing up to meet him. The dark soil loomed, and he hit hard, boots touching down and his roll technique basically working, although a little messier than usual.

Keeler ended up sliding ten meters on his ass, looking up at the wet parachute canopy gathering around him, realizing what the entrenchment tool was for. The thing was still gripped in his right hand, the fist having formed an unbreakable bond with the object. They'd given him the tool so that he could bury the parachute gear.

At that moment he understood what the airman had been mouthing to him, the two words that he couldn't hear. Pooper scooper.

A HALF HOUR later Keeler had disposed of the gear in a hole dug three feet deep and as narrow in width as he thought he'd get away with. He'd noted the GPS coordinates before burying the device.

Now he was a little impatient, vaulting a nearby stone fence and hiking uphill for a while before coming to a wooded area that he hoped would be closer to the mill, the forest descending sharply to a wooded valley. He wedged the E-tool deep into a cluster of large boulders on the way down, navigating between tree trunks in a controlled descent until reaching a tow path on the banks of a small river.

He squatted to wash his hands and face in the small river, seeing the dark soil below his boots, letting the dirt from his hole digging activity come off, muddying the downstream flow, towards the mill he assumed. The water was cool and fresh and flowing abundantly, very different to the parts of the Middle East he'd recently visited.

When Keeler stood he felt physically strong and very hungry. Mentally he was hopeful and optimistic, and slightly elated. Surprised but not upset to find himself in this place all of a sudden, like magic. Feeling as if the world was a kind of cornucopia of abundance. Good things were always out there.

Six minutes later the mill and its outbuildings came into view around a turn. It looked like the kind of establishment that lived off day hikers and the occasional overnight guests in the old mill itself.

The original buildings were connected to a newer structure that served as a bar and restaurant, with a gravel forecourt and parking in the back. Three vehicles sat in the forecourt, a red sedan, a people carrier with three rows of seating, and a silver Peugeot convertible. The license plates were French alright, the sedan had an older plate with the 92 suffix, denoting a Parisian suburb. The people carrier's plate was newer, but still had the departmental suffix, from the city of Dijon. The Peugeot convertible was an old school 75, a bullseye for central Paris.

The hood was warm on the sedan, not the people carrier. The silver Peugeot had its roof up. Glancing inside Keeler saw a pair of sunglasses between the front seats. A yellow scarf with a fancy pattern lay tossed on the passenger seat.

The airman had mentioned a liaison. But nobody was volunteering yet. Maybe it was going to be the woman with the scarf.

Keeler opened the front door and walked into a dark and low-ceilinged place. Old Europe, dingy, like they thought the past was something to celebrate. Keeler couldn't understand that attitude. He assumed that the past had been worse than the present, in almost every way. For one thing people had been smaller, evidenced by the way he had to be careful stepping through the door.

The good news was that he'd entered a restaurant, and it was lunch hour.

Examining the setup: just inside the door two tables had been shoved together for a party of seven adults, whom Keeler decided were passengers in the people carrying vehicle outside. Four men and three women, a range of ages from thirty to sixty. No coats on the backs of chairs, which suggested a coat room. Two wine bottles on the table and heavy cutlery knocking against porcelain, forks laden with flesh and other culinary matter, rising into ready mouths. The buzz of quiet conversation emanated from this table, the French chewing politely with closed mouths, conversing in low tones.

Further in he was looking at a family unit seated in the corner by an active fireplace. Two hetero-normative adults with faces bent to their young boy, currently sucking down coke with a straw. The male adult had a coat on the back of his chair, indicating the avoidance of the coatroom, with the potential implication that his coat contained something valuable. Lunch was yet to arrive for them, the cutlery still organized on top of folded linen napkins. The adults did not seem overly concerned about timing and the coke was only half consumed.

A woman was bent over her plate by the window, carefully using the provided utensils to separate the pale flesh of a fish from skin and bones. Keeler estimated that she'd received her plate no more than seven minutes earlier, given the state of the fish. The woman was approximately 70 years old, tastefully dressed with a white bob of hair and jewelry flashing from her fingers. A small leather handbag hung from her chair, no coat.

The kind of person who'd wear a fancy yellow scarf.

Stepping in further he found himself in front of a chalkboard scrawled with specials of the day. Snails and frogs, most likely cooked in butter and garlic, desserts with cream, soups made from root vegetables and leeks, various pork pâtés followed by more standard things like steak and fish and ice cream. Keeler's eyes zeroed in on the word steak, which in French is not different from the English, almost like a tunnel between the cultures.

He was so distracted by the menu that the manager's voice came as a surprising interruption.

"For lunch monsieur?"

A woman, forty years of age, medium height with dark hair pulled into a ponytail, wedding ring on the finger of her left hand. Dressed in jeans and a sweater and looking at him expectantly.

Keeler said, "Absolutely."

FORTY-THREE

The restaurant manager marched Keeler to a window seat for two. She removed the unnecessary place setting and turned to depart. Keeler was aware of how long service could take in a French restaurant, so he tried to fast-track the situation by preventing her from leaving so quickly.

"Excuse me ma'am."

The woman spun back. "Yes."

"I don't need to agonize over the menu, I'm going to have the steak, rare, side of salad and fries. Coffee, large and black."

She didn't like it, the formalities hadn't been conducted. "We only have an espresso machine."

He said, "No problem, make three espressos and put them in a mug, that'll be fine."

"But you haven't seen the wine menu."

"I'm not a daytime drinker." Looking at her pursed lips, knowing how French people can be starved of compliments in a tough culture, letting out some rope. "I like your glasses; they suit your face perfectly."

The coffee came sooner than expected.

Keeler sipped at the bitter black brew and made plans. The

small key the airman had given to him was currently occupying a position in the change pocket of his jeans. Other than that, he had no further instructions. He assumed that those were not necessary, that by solving the riddle of the key he'd be directed to the appropriate path. He needed money.

The restaurant's proprietress emerged from the kitchen banging backwards through swinging doors, followed by an adolescent boy with a blonde mop. Both carried large platters requiring two hands, both backing through the doors into the restaurant space, spinning to face front and accomplish the delivery of large bowls of soup to the family unit in the corner.

Things moved in Keeler's peripheral vision. His head swiveled to the right, looking out the window. New customers were arriving, a trio of middle-aged men in walking clothes, among them a younger adult male, in his thirties and prematurely bald, the pate shining. Something about the way the group walked, at an unnatural speed, like they were pacing themselves. He got it, the younger one wasn't quite right, an overgrown kid who'd been born with developmental impediments that he'd never gotten past. That, or he'd acquired problems during a severe illness, or he'd suffered brain damage.

They were walking directly past the window now. He could hear the soles of shoes and sneakers crunching on gravel. The young man's face was chubby, the color of cotton candy. He had his mouth open, tongue lolling. The eyes were baby blue, looking skyward, cheeks rosy. As Keeler watched, the cherub adjusted, coming back to a horizontal tilt, tongue retreating into his mouth and the eyes focusing.

Looked like what people called a *functional disability*. Something going on in there that wasn't what people considered normal, but not enough to check him into a facility. Maybe the prospect of lunch had focused the guy's unsettled mind.

Keeler got back to the task at hand. The fancy handbag on

the lady's chair wasn't more than twelve feet away. The thing was pink leather, in the shape of a kidney bean. The gold chain seemed firmly connected to the bag, partly wedged between the white-haired woman's body and the chair back. He'd need to dislodge her somehow, maybe bump into the table and spill something on her. Between bites she was drinking from a glass of chilled white wine, taking small amounts of the liquid between her teeth. It looked good, Keeler admiring her technique, wishing for a second that he had that kind of restraint.

There was nothing complicated about the situation. He needed money, he'd take that purse. Keeler put the flat of his palms on the table, planning to rise. Act like he was visiting the bathroom and improvise. Whatever happened, the lady's bag was his target.

Too late.

The kid with the blonde mop backed out of the kitchen, banging through swinging doors. Heads swiveled in his direction. The kid spun to face front, acrobatically balancing a brown platter with his right hand, the serving dish laden with crockery.

Eyes in the room focused. Keeler recognized it as his order. The steak and fries occupying one white plate, a bowl of green salad and a pot of sauce staying put. The boy carried a basket of sliced baguette in his left hand, placing it on the table first, before unloading the dishes with a flourish.

"Et voila."

He plucked a fry between thumb and forefinger, squeezing gently to test the technique, finding sufficient crunch and evidence of a soft warm interior. He dipped the fried potato into the pepper sauce pot, chewing evenly and lifting his eyes at an abrupt noise.

Something was happening up front, visible signs of agitation and the sound of breaking glass. It wasn't immediately obvious what was going on. The seated party of seven were in their chairs, eyes up and looking at something blocked from Keeler's view by a thick vertical beam between counter and seating area.

He cut off another slice of steak and fed himself, pushing two fries into his mouth after the meat. Something moved quickly across the table up front, airborne and maybe a wine glass. The stocky woman at the end jerked her head back, making a sharp screech. The tablecloth rippled and wine bottles and plates shifted five inches to the left. Glasses toppled and the murmurs of shock became louder and more chaotic.

An altercation of some kind, but its nature unclear. The perpetrator stepped to his right, out from behind the vertical beam, clarifying the situation.

Keeler was looking at the younger bald man with the cherub face. The functionally disabled guy was now in a violent frenzy, not attacking people directly, but totally out of control, limbs twitching, sweeping plates and glasses aside, basically unleashing his inner maniac. Things were flying, shards of broken glass bouncing off walls. The cherub faced guy was methodically displacing objects on the table, shoving glasses and plates and jugs and cutlery and bowls left and right in his fit.

The situation was non-lethal, but a menace regardless.

Keeler took a final bite of steak, mindful of the flying glass shards. Each bite could be the last, so he'd have to devour as much as possible in the ensuing ten seconds. He chewed diligently, looking into his plate.

When he looked up, the teenage waiter was approaching. He carried a navy blue backpack that looked very new. Keeler watched as the kid draped the backpack over the chair across from him. He hadn't finished the mouthful of steak yet and resorted to a grunt when the kid bobbed his head in a little courtesy move.

"Monsieur."

The kid spun away, moving to the commotion up front.

Keeler grunted again. He reached across and pulled the backpack to him.

Inside was a wallet, containing a French driver's license in the name of Jean-Francois Peillex, several hundred euros in cash, a single credit card and train ticket folded in half.

FORTY-FOUR

CENTRAL *Israel*

Yasmin had a window seat on the left side of the train, hurtling north along the Mediterranean shore. She was on the beach side, currently passing Hadera on the right, already halfway to the terminus at Karmiel where she'd change to a bus. The timing was lucky, not too many soldiers commuting. She'd fallen asleep on the journey, but now simply gazed at the bright surf out the window. Forehead leaning against the cool glass, watching birds, the odd surfer making do with the small Mediterranean waves.

There was something slightly funny that the man had said, after he'd asked her to 'call me Mike'. The name had come to her then, not Mike, but Hershkowitz. That's how her dad and the others had called him. They'd been bending heads over the conference table by then, checking out what they'd gleaned of Zeina Makhoul's biographical details. What Hershkowitz's secret unit had come up with.

The picture forming was detailed, the contours of Zeina Makhoul coming into view. Yasmin hadn't thought that information could have a geometrical form, but there it was, hard to define in physical terms yet present, a kind of shape.

Hershkowitz was looking at Makhoul's university records, including the unofficial ones collected by the Shin Bet. He'd said, 'That's not your standard Mary.'

Yasmin was still trying to figure out exactly what he meant by that. Thinking in the end that the *Mary* part of it referred to Zeina Makhoul's photograph with her kids, like an average-looking Arab woman from a place like Nazareth, hijab and jeans, kids wearing cheap clothing.

What they'd discovered about Makhoul wasn't a secret, but she wasn't any kind of average person, regardless of ethnicity or religion. She'd received her bachelor's in chemistry from the Technion in Haifa and worked for three years at a pharmaceutical tech startup in the Herzliya area. Clearly she hadn't enjoyed that experience, pivoting a year later to do a Masters degree in musicology at Ben-Gurion University in Be'er Sheva.

Hershkowitz had particularly liked Makhoul's thesis title, *Tradition and Identity in Cornwall: Exploring Folk Customs and Mannerisms.* That had been fifteen years ago. Zeina Makhoul now worked at something called The Polyphonic Project in Nazareth, a small but high brow institution that brought Arabs and Jews together through classical music. Makhoul directed a 'music appreciation' program for Arab youth and ran the outfit's polyphonic singing group with monthly public performances.

They had searched the term polyphonic and singing in YouTube, which elicited some kind of religious classical music, like ancient church songs from Christendom.

Yasmin was going to check it out. She'd go up there as herself, just a little different. They'd given her cover as a journalist for a trendy Tel Aviv website. There was no choral performance planned until next week, but a music appreciation session was scheduled for the next day. Her plan was to get in there and introduce herself somehow, like she'd just happened to be in the area and was a fan. If Makhoul was in the building that might work, worst case she'd be busy or elsewhere.

The backup plan was to just show up at the kids' session tomorrow.

∼

NAZARETH IS a hilly town and the hike from the bus station got Yasmin's heart rate up. The institute was high in the northern section, housed in an old monastery. It wasn't exactly the kind of place a regular tourist would just happen upon, but there she was.

The entrance gate was open, cars parked in a cedar lined lot out front of the main building, a beautifully made structure of large stones built in the Ottoman period. A set of stairs ran through to the double wide entrance. The door opened and released music, the sound of a pianist rehearsing, horns and strings from upstairs, hushed voices and the grating sound of a violin being tuned. The lobby was polished stone, functional with a seating area but no concierge.

Yasmin opened the first door she came to, interrupting a group cello lesson, a room full of kids with instruments and a bearded man in his thirties caught in the middle of a demonstration. He looked annoyed.

Yasmin said, "Sorry to disturb you. I'm looking for Zeina."

The guy rolled his eyes. "Which one? I know a million Zeinas."

One of the kids said, "You don't know a million Zeinas."

He said, "Not a million, but at least three."

"Zeina Makhoul." Smiling like, shucks. Yasmin said, "Sorry to bother you."

He said, "Zeina's not here."

Yasmin nodded. "Okay, she's not working today?"

"No."

"Thanks."

She retreated from the room, closing the door behind her. Turning her back to the wall and facing the front door, across the stone floor, thinking about her next move. A shadow flittered in the stained-glass window set into the door. The knob turned, and a woman peered in, holding the door half open. Her seeking eyes found Yasmin.

She spoke in Arabic. "Can you help me please?"

The language kind of threw Yasmin off, not that she *should* have expected Hebrew, this was an Arab city in Israel, people here were both Israelis and Arabs, and she spoke fluent Arabic.

She said, "Sure. What's up?"

The woman beckoned. "Come. The driver won't help. It's too heavy for me." Holding up an arm to show Yasmin a splint from hand to forearm. "Carpal tunnel syndrome, we all get it."

They were out the door, looking at a taxi with a large thing wedged into the back, most of it sticking out, the hatchback jammed against it, bungee cords holding the ensemble together. The driver sat in his seat, window open, chewing on sunflower seeds and dropping the shells to the ground.

He looked apologetic. The woman said, "He has a slipped disk."

Yasmin understood, the object in the taxi was a musical instrument in a case, a harp. She helped the woman wrestle the thing out of the back, gently setting it down on its wheels. The taxi drove away and the two women maneuvered the instrument inside.

She was in her forties, hennaed hair cut chin length. "Thank you for helping me." She was looking at Yasmin and making an abrupt critical appraisal. Yasmin knew that look, this Arab woman examining her and inferring crucial information from the clothing and style, maybe other attributes and signals identifying her as an Israeli Jew. The woman switched to Hebrew. "Thank you. That was very kind."

Yasmin continued in Arabic. "No worries, and this is my mother tongue." She forced a smile and extended a hand. "My name is Yasmin by the way."

The woman took her hand limply. "Basima."

"Really good to meet you, Basima. I'm looking for Zeina Makhoul, she's supposed to work here?"

Basima's smile remained in place a moment too long. Forced, the word coming to Yasmin involuntarily.

Basima said, "Of course. Do you have an appointment with her?"

"No, sorry. I'm a writer with Y48." The confused look was expected. "It's a contemporary culture magazine in Tel Aviv." Basima's gaze blank, having no clue what that meant. Yasmin chose an informal Arabic register. "Don't worry if you haven't heard of us, not many people have." Smiling, trying to be charming, to make up for the earlier suspicion. "I saw the polyphonic singing choir last year." Her hand went to her heart. "I loved it. I'm just in Nazareth for the day. I was dreaming of a short interview with her for the magazine."

Basima's face relaxed, actually becoming apologetic. "My dear, Zeina's not here. She's at home cooking, it's Friday."

"I see." Yasmin nodded.

Basima placed a hand on Yasmin's arm. "Listen my love, help me get this big harp into the other room and I'll take you up myself. I live near Zeina. We'll stop by and see if she can give you a few minutes of her time."

Nice. Yasmin knew where Makhoul lived, but she hadn't wanted to show up there both uninvited and alone. This was going to be much better.

Twenty minutes later they were walking up a set of outdoor

stairs to a second-story apartment near the Polyphonic Project. Basima was knocking on the door and Yasmin stood off her right shoulder by the balcony, trying to look trustworthy.

The door opened and there was Zeina Ahmad Makhoul, just like in the picture but maybe ten years older, still easily recognizable. She wore an apron and greeted Basima with kisses, glancing to Yasmin and back again. The scent of Arab home cooking hit Yasmin, cumin and anise and cinnamon and rose. She was struck by a memory bomb, home on a Friday afternoon, coming back from school when her mom used to cook a lot, before Ruth went into the army.

The two women were looking at her strangely, amused. Basima said, "Are you alright?"

"Yes, sorry," glancing at Makhoul. "The smell from your kitchen, it just hit me." She made a gesture, like being pleasantly struck. "I was reminded of my mother's cooking. We're from Syria."

Zeina Makhoul's face softened. "Memory travels through the nose, darling."

Basima said, "And the stomach."

Hershkowitz's team had given Yasmin a necklace that did an excellent job of recording audio. They'd be listening carefully to the proceedings. A team was nearby, probably in a vehicle, she didn't know.

The two older women laughed, covering their mouths. Gentle hands ushered Yasmin into the warmth of the kitchen. The door was securely closed and coats were taken. It had been quite a while since Yasmin had experienced Arab hospitality. Army life was a serious cultural mixer, plus it made you pretty rough around the edges. Her parents had mostly lost contact with their relatives from the old country, some grown elderly, some dead, and others no longer interested in what life had been like before the traumatic escape out of Syria and the immigration to a new life in the land of Israel.

FORTY-FIVE

Yasmin acted all apologetic, playing the part of the young Tel Aviv girl out of her element in an Arab town far from the Metropole. The women ate it up, at least twenty years her senior and matriarchs in their own rights. These two were community stalwarts, ladies whose lives were bedded in family, extending out to their work at the Polyphonic Project, an underfunded treasure that each of them clearly felt was a calling rather than a job.

Zeina Makhoul made tea, not like Yasmin would have, by throwing a bag in a mug, rather combining loose dry tea leaf with herbs she said she had collected on 'the mountain'. Basima was clearly at home at the Makhoul property, preparing a plate of homemade cookies and cake. When the formalities were complete and the three of them sat around a low table. Zeina Makhoul laid a warm hand on Yasmin's arm.

She said, "Before anything else, please, I'd like to hear about you. You said earlier that the family is from Syria?"

Yasmin nodded. It was an interesting moment that she hadn't exactly been prepared for. The issue of Jewish emigration from Arab lands during the 1950s and 60s was not something that Palestinian Arabs seemed to discuss much, at least not as far as she was aware.

"I only know the story on my father's side. The family was from Aleppo." She made a gesture in the air. "I don't know how many generations, maybe forever. I think they liked it there, that is, it was life, right?" Zeina Makhoul's house was obviously Christian, crosses and icons prominently displayed, in some ways it made Yasmin feel more comfortable. She said, "You know how it is. We were *Dhimmi* to them." *Them* meaning Muslims. "Tolerated but second class." Both women murmured, not words, but sounds of agreement.

Makhoul said, "I know exactly what you mean," smiling at her with a half-eaten cookie in one hand. "We are also a family from Syria and Lebanon. My great grandparents took the family from Damascus after many Christians were massacred in *Simele*." She put a finger in the air. "They came here and built this house."

Basima said, "There were economic reasons for coming as well."

Makhoul nodded, looking at Yasmin. "People were moving here from Europe and from all over. Mostly Jews, but stuff was happening here, business activity, money coming in from abroad. That's something nobody ever talks about."

Yasmin said, "It's something nobody knows about."

Which stopped the conversation momentarily, each of the women sipping tea and nibbling biscuits, at a loss for words to speak about general ignorance. Yasmin wasn't going to bring up the subject of what had actually happened to her grandfather and his friends trying to escape Syria in the early 1960s. That would probably be a conversation ender, since it involved rape and murder.

It was Zeina Makhoul who broke the spell, shaking her head as if to get rid of dust and impediments. "Let's talk about something else." She looked brightly at Yasmin. "You want to know about the music program, is that right?"

Yasmin brightened. "Absolutely, if you have the time."

∼

LATER, the team met in a safe house in the *Nof Hagalil* neighborhood, above Nazareth in the hills. They huddled around a coffee table, listening to a recording of the episode. Hershkowitz and his assistant sat on dining room chairs, while two men who could be brothers were seated on a sofa. Yasmin had the armchair, a glass of white wine in her hand.

The 'interview' had been sufficient, Yasmin asking Zeina Makhoul questions about a subject of which she knew next to nothing. Thankfully they hadn't needed to go into depth about polyphonic singing or anything, since the most important element of the Polyphonic Project was the attempt at creating pluralism between Arabs and Jews in Israel.

Zeina Makhoul's husband Mikhail had come home briefly. What Yasmin already knew: Mikhail worked as a kidney dialysis technician at 'The Scottish Hospital'. The women hadn't stood up in honor of his arrival or anything, so Yasmin had remained seated watching him come in, a good-looking middle-aged guy with thinning hair and a cropped salt and pepper beard. Smiling, good teeth and courteous when he was introduced to her, walking over to give her hand a modern shake. Mikhail all smiles and good nature, discussing the kids' schedule with his wife before picking up a cased musical instrument from its place on the living room floor, and leaving the house again.

Yasmin recognized the shape of the instrument, an oud, like a middle eastern guitar.

She said, "You're a very musical family."

Zeina Makhoul said her husband was part of a musical

ensemble who got together Fridays. Stranger things were known to happen to musical families.

She'd used the toilet twice during her stay. The first time, she'd poked her head into rooms accessible from the direct route, tea station to toilet, via corridor. The second time she'd gone off the beaten path some, taking three large steps to peer into the master bedroom, not that there'd been anything special to see in there.

The overall impression she had was of a cultured family who liked music and books. They also seemed to be having a good life, if she was honest about it. You could do a lot worse than Mikhail and Zeina Makhoul in Nazareth, 2016. Something must be going right in the world. Musical instruments littered the place and bookcases lined much of the wall space. Blank space was filled with framed family pictures, also strategically set up on book shelves.

Sipping wine and listening to the recording was weird, particularly her own voice. She was a little anxious to know if she'd sounded fake when speaking to Zeina and the other woman, but she hadn't. A good thing because she'd made a conscious decision to keep it real.

Once the recording had been played and another bottle of wine opened, Hershkowitz turned to his small team, the two guys and the assistant. He jerked a thumb at Yasmin and said, "Now work her."

Which surprised Yasmin, who'd begun to feel a little warm and cozy with the alcohol. In her mind the whole thing was over.

She said, "What do you mean?"

The two guys on the sofa were digging in. One of them topped up his glass, and hers, set the bottle back on the coffee table.

He said, "Let's talk about the visual part of your visit Yasmin, what you saw."

"I already told you what I saw."

The guy leaned forward. "Sure, but let's go deeper. For example, you said there were many books in the house, which books did you see?"

Yasmin blew through pursed lips, followed by screwing her face into an amused expression. "You think I actually looked at the books, like read the title on the spine?"

The other guy was leaned deep back into the cushions. He said, "Close your eyes Yasmin, visualize it."

Hershkowitz's assistant threw back the remains of her glass and went in for more. "You'd be surprised. Let it come to you."

Yasmin closed her eyes, let the mind wander, and took another sip of wine. That's why they'd opened the bottle, why they were being cool. The whole thing was a calculated attempt to get her into a suggestible state. These people were weird, but they weren't stupid. The images started coming to her.

One of the guys said, "You need to tell it out loud."

She said, "Okay, there were a couple of books on the coffee table."

The assistant said, "Be specific."

"A National Geographic book about the savannah with antelopes on the cover, underneath that was a book with Arabic script, gold lettering, but not fancy, another coffee-table book.

The guy on the couch said, "Read it for us."

She laughed. "I can't read it for you. I assumed it was about Ottoman classical music. The nat-geo book was actually on top of it, so I could only see the end of the title but the picture was of some ottoman guy playing a clarinet." Yasmin opened her eyes. "You know, an old picture, like an engraving from back then."

The assistant said, "The instrument is called a *Zurna*."

"Whatever," said the leaned-back guy on the couch, "Yasmin, take us on a walk through the house. Show us, I don't know."

His friend said, "The bathroom."

"Yeah," the guy said, "Show us the bathroom."

Yasmin let her mind flow. "Alright, I'm getting up and walking away from the place where we sat drinking tea." She actually saw it, pointing her finger into the air, eyes squeezed closed. "I see a bookcase right there between the seating area and the entrance to a corridor, kitchen's on the right, there's a pot on the stove and something covered in foil. Smells incredible."

The assistant said, "Nice. Focus on the bookshelf, what's written on the spines?"

"I'm looking at a family photograph actually, on the bookshelf." She cursed in Arabic. "It's the same picture." Yasmin opened her eyes wide, looking at the people in the room, each of them staring at her. "Shit! I forgot about that. The same picture we found on that guy in Egypt. Right there on the bookshelf in the living room."

Hershkowitz rolled his eyes and reached for the wine bottle. The others didn't react.

The assistant said, "Good. Hold that thought. Now what about the books?"

It took Yasmin a few seconds, the books that she saw in her mind looked different from books that she'd have in her room, or that her parents would have. She said, "They aren't novels or anything, they were bigger."

The assistant said, "Bigger than novels, but what exactly?"

"I don't know, there's pottery and stuff in there too, maybe they're art books." She opened her eyes for a moment. "They could be more coffee table books on musicology or something?"

One of the guys said, "Don't invent, see it. What do you read on the spine of these books?"

Yasmin said, "I don't know. Maybe gold writing again, like a bible maybe. Can I move on?"

She moved on, going through the house, examining objects and letting the whole visual picture come to her. There had been novels in the master bedroom, where she'd snuck a look at the end. Also in the kids' room, bookcases packed with novels, textbooks and comic books. Basima had caught her looking into the kids' room, what she remembered. No big deal. It wasn't more than two steps from the toilet.

The assistant held up a hand. "She caught you snooping."

Yasmin thought about it. "Not exactly."

Hershkowitz said, "What exactly?"

"I just looked inside the room and Basima was behind me. It startled me is all."

One of the guys said, "Basima was alert to you snooping."

Yasmin shrugged, not able to deny that this was a possibility, even though it's not how she'd felt.

Hershkowitz said, "Okay brush it off. The room was cute?"

What had made the biggest impression on Yasmin had been the photographs framed on the walls.

She said, "Family pictures, but I didn't look carefully at them." Yasmin leaned forward and tipped the last of the white wine into her glass, feeling loose. "You know what I just realized?" Everyone looked at her. Hershkowitz with an amused curve to his lips. "I've realized what those other books were, the large ones in the living room."

The assistant said, "What?"

She said, "Family albums. There was a whole shelf of family albums."

The more eager of the two guys on the sofa said, "Like, from when people actually took physical photographs that they'd print and keep in albums."

Yasmin was nodding. "Exactly, like my parents. But the Makhoul's are in their forties, so they'd have used analogue cameras." Knocking back the end of her glass. She swept her hand wide around the room. "Think 2007 or something, like before the iPhone. Everyone's using actual cameras, right?"

Hershkowitz caught her gaze, his eyebrow raised, nodding. "Right."

FORTY-SIX

Family albums.

Hershkowitz let the *feels* of that idea circle rapidly around the contours of his brain. He liked it, refreshing to think of people still holding onto a tradition where photographs of loved ones were kept in physical albums. The clean mineral taste of good wine from the Golan trickled from the rim of his glass to his mouth, cool and dry. He swallowed.

According to the conceptional framework currently fashionable in the Israeli Intelligence Community there were a couple ways that he could handle the Makhoul family. Whichever direction he chose would have to be optimized for the *iron triangle*.

He wanted a thorough investigation of the family's social ties and he wanted it immediately, couldn't be fast enough for him. But he also needed it to be clean. No question of banging those good people up in an interrogation center and extracting information that way. Not a chance. These were Israeli citizens with no history of security violations, on the contrary, they were perfect examples of what the state was hoping they'd get from the twenty percent of their citizens who were Arab.

Which left him with several combinations of his three desires: thorough, clean, and fast.

The iron triangle says that you can only ever have two of them.

Thorough and clean, but not fast.

Clean and fast, but not thorough.

Thorough and fast, but not clean.

Thing was, he needed thorough and fast more than he needed clean. Hershkowitz thumbed into his phone's screen and produced the photograph of Zeina Makhoul and her children. Nice picture, nice people. There were multiple definitions of clean, a gray concept.

This nice family in Nazareth now had two big problems.

Number one, a photograph of Zeina and her children had been found on the person of an unidentified Arab male, possible first name 'Jafar'. This person of interest had been in the possession of an Israeli national identity card. Number two, the unidentified Arab male had made a clandestine journey via an infiltration tunnel to Egypt.

Problem number three compounded the first two points, a potentially rogue Egyptian Intelligence officer had been seen roaming the border region below Gaza. Rogue because he had allegedly attempted to have Yasmin and her friend killed obliquely, in some way that would give him and the military deniability.

According to Yasmin Shoshan that is, currently sipping a glass of wine, seeming fatigued but holding on. Privately, Hershkowitz had his doubts about the experience, the notion that the Egyptians had intended to have her and the American guy killed. That didn't matter anyway because points one, two, and three were impossible to ignore.

Hershkowitz said, "Family albums, I like it." He leaned forward to place his wine glass on the coffee table and stood up.

He stretched, gave his little team a once over. "That's it right? Family photographs." The guys and girls looking back at him, smart operators with deadly backgrounds, a great team. He said, "You all know what to do right?"

The guy on the sofa was nodding vigorously. "Absolutely, boss."

The two agents rose from their seats and got busy. Phone calls, text messages and the unloading of backpacks.

The assistant made a circle with her hand above her head. "We're here tonight?"

"Yes, you and them here." Pointing at Yasmin. "Put her somewhere close. Figure it out."

He turned to Yasmin and looked at her. Behind him he knew that the dining room table was fast becoming an operational command center, with cables and laptops and other specialized boxes and things. Yasmin's eyes were roaming over the activity, glazed with fatigue, a small smile playing over her lips. He could see that she was exhilarated by the work.

THE NEXT MORNING, ten minutes after the last member of the Makhoul family had departed the house, three sanitation workers came up the driveway pulling a garbage can on two wheels. Nobody paid any attention to the men in municipal outfits, people who nobody actually saw anyway. Two of the men gained access to the house within a minute.

A van had parked down the block, its interior a small office where two young women operated an impressive bank of electronic signals gear and computers. They'd been on site for two hours, already deep into every surveillance camera, doorbell, mobile phone or other connected devices within 400 meters of the targeted property.

Inside the house the first two entrants removed their shoes and set about systematically documenting the Makhoul family's photograph collection, harvesting imagery both from family albums and framed pictures on the wall. Reference photographs had been taken, so that anything removed could be perfectly replaced.

The third man was still outside, finding and accessing the home's sewage pipe. He took trace samples of the feces, urine, blood, spit, and other human waste habitually flushed out of the abode. Once that task had been completed, he entered and removed his shoes like the others. His first mission was to use a specialized sensor to canvass the home for any device capable of digital storage. Phones, computers, tablets, watches, thermostats, oven, fridge, smoke detector, whatever. The same device was able to wirelessly access their contents and suck in data, sending it into the system via a remote link to the van parked down the road.

When he was finished doing that, he spent the rest of his visit scanning the premises for chemical traces. He wasn't looking for anything in particular, just taking a chemical profile of the premises that would populate a model.

Like with the photographs, the analysis would happen at a separate facility, and in fact was already underway. When the agents had finished working, they retreated out the way they'd come. The third man's final task was to do a last tour of the house with a spray can. The stuff was able to eliminate 98.9% of trace DNA that might have been shed.

~

JAFAR AL-HUSSEINI DROVE past on his moped, seeing two men come out of the Makhoul residence. He knew for a fact that the family wasn't home, which only confirmed what his sister had said, calling him the day before in a weird fluster.

He hadn't actually believed her suspicions, but now these men coming out of the house. The van parked down the road. He was careful not to rubberneck, just continuing on his way and out of there.

Inside the helmet Al-Husseini was actually sweating, even though it wasn't particularly hot. He had to pull over at a scrappy olive grove. Stopped the bike and got the thing off his head. He walked into the green area, which was not exactly an olive grove, more of a wasteland, and found a pile of dumped building materials to sit on. A disgusting place actually, but with a view over the city.

He was done, screwed, completely busted. That was a fact.

If they knew about what he'd been supplying to the Egyptians, it'd be twenty years in a black site, or maybe life, or maybe they'd just shoot him in the head. You could never totally believe the conspiracy theories, but since there wasn't any better source of information you were left with nothing else.

Shit.

He'd tell them about the break-ins, and they'd get him for worse. That's how these people rolled. They find your weakness and then exploit it, make you into an informer and then toss you away when you were blown. He lit a cigarette and tried to think clearly.

Three cigarettes later he had an idea.

The people in the north, Lebanon. Maybe they could help him. Lebanon is a beautiful place, so they say. He could get across and live there. It was a poor country for sure, and completely messed up, but life there would be better than solitary confinement in some Jewish black site in the Negev.

He looked at his phone, the number he had for a guy up there. Not exactly a top-of-the-line drug smuggler. Not exactly clued into the Bedouin clans and the best routes. The guy was a small-time dealer who didn't mind throwing shit over the fence once in a while.

What Al-Husseini knew for sure was that up there in Lebanon there was no such thing as a dealer who was not connected into the Hezbollah network in some fashion. It would be the price of doing business. Maybe they'd like to meet an Arab Israeli like him. Give him a task in exchange for asylum.

FORTY-SEVEN

T*ROYES, France*
Keeler came off the bus at the *Troyes* terminal.
It looked, felt, and smelled like France. Not the place he thought he'd be HALO jumping into. Good thing he felt comfortable in France, speaking the language thanks to his mother being a native. She'd moved to the United States of America and never looked back, but she had brought him and his sister up with an excellent grasp of both language and culture.
Troyes seemed pretty typical, viewed from the bus station.
Keeler's left leg had a slight cramp from the way he'd landed earlier with the parachute, sliding through the mud and hitting his hip on something. He shook it out by taking a tour of the station's exterior.
There were outdoor tables at a cafe near the park, across the street from the station. He jogged over and took a chair at a two-seater. The waiter came eventually and Keeler ordered a hot chocolate. He nursed the sugar and cream, no marshmallows, wondering what would happen next. He paid in advance, just in case.

Ten minutes later a battered old Peugeot 206 honked at him from out front of the park.

Keeler recognized the driver, a JSOC operator named Rodriguez, first name no idea. He jogged over the street to the car. Rodriguez was an officer in the clandestine part of their service, originally something else, like a Green Beret. He was in his early forties now, maybe a colonel. Keeler figured he'd be the Task Force Commander on this thing.

Rodriguez had an earbud inserted and tapped it once, speaking to someone on the other end of the line. "Pick up complete." He looked at Keeler. "Nice of you to drop in."

Which sounded like a complaint. Keeler said nothing, just looking at Rodriguez, curious. The corners of the officer's mouth remained horizontal, the man dead eyeing him. Neither of them blinked. The older man finally nodded.

"Alright."

Keeler thinking, right. None of this was his idea. If Rodriguez was going to have a beef, he could have it by himself.

Rodriguez got the vehicle into gear, navigating out of the town center, handling the manual transmission roughly, grinding through the gears, the clutch burning hot. The officer stared straight ahead for around ten minutes, before glancing at Keeler abruptly, like he was thinking of saying something. Keeler looked into intelligent eyes set deep into a strong face. Rodriguez seemed concerned, or anxious, not a good look in the clandestine service, even worse pre-op in a foreign country.

As in, something interesting was going down, and they weren't going to talk about it in the car.

Rodriguez piloted the Peugeot into an industrial park. Beside the warehouses and light industrial workshops, the area had fast-food outlets and big box stores, that and a vast expanse of empty parking lot. He pulled into a Burger King drive through.

"I like Burger King better than MacDonalds." He glanced at Keeler. "Hope that's not an issue for you."

Keeler said, "No problem. You think it's flame broiled but you know that's bullshit, right?"

"Might be bullshit, but it tastes better that way. Plus I like the lettuce and tomato they use on the Whopper."

Keeler was already hungry again. He went standard and ordered the Whopper with medium fries and a chocolate shake. Rodriguez was into the fact that the menu included French specific specials, sandwiches that contained brie cheese and French sausages. He pointed at the menu. "They've got their own shit here. Like it's Burger King but French."

Like it mattered. Keeler said nothing, watching the man order a burger with crunchy onions, special cheese and mustard mayo. He looked at the photograph of the burger on the menu card, an impressively constructed thing.

Keeler said, "You know it's never going to look like that."

"Yeah, I know. Disappointment comes free here."

Which Keeler thought was a pretty good comment.

They ate, sitting on a small grassy knoll between the Burger King playground and a parking lot the size of three football fields out front of a massive supermarket. Good location, a lot of wind and a 360-degree view.

Rodriguez unwrapped his sandwich. He said, "What the hell happened back there in the restaurant?"

The brouhaha, someone had been observing. Probably a CIA over-watch crew, making sure nobody was interested in the newly arrived American. Keeler grunted and popped a fry. Chewing and speaking at the same time. "Some guy spazzed out."

Rodriguez said, "For real?"

Keeler nodded. "Yeah. No indication that it was a setup or anything."

Rodriguez laughed. "Truth is stranger than fiction."

A cliche, but definitely pointing to the inherent weaknesses of fiction.

Turned out that Rodriguez wasn't the Task Force Commander on this operation. He was the Operations Officer, one step down. The Task Force Commander in this case was CIA, but a decent man, as Rodriguez told it. Keeler threw three fries into his mouth at once, not reacting to that statement. Thinking he'd be the judge of that.

In any case the rank situation meant something. All clandestine operations had consequences, but once in a while a project had particularly high stakes. That's when they'd bring in a Brigadier General to be the Task Force Commander, and need a Colonel to actually run it as Operations Officer. Maybe that's why Rodriguez was stressed out.

Rodriguez tore open a ketchup sachet with his teeth and squeezed whatever he could get out of it onto his sandwich. He tossed the packet into the paper bag, looking at Keeler. "You haven't done wet work for us yet, right?"

Wet work, the euphemism for killing someone, an assassination within a civilian environment.

Keeler had done plenty of work involving weapons and death, but no, he hadn't yet been sent as an assassin. Rodriguez would already know this, therefore it was a rhetorical question and didn't require a response.

Keeler said, "What I really want to know is why you're the first person I'm talking to about this." He popped a fry into his mouth and chewed. "Not that I mind, but I'm curious about the interesting insertion, HALO jump to the mill. What are we doing here, starting a war against French onion soup?"

Rodriguez chomped burger. "No, we aren't. Word is that we're here to take advantage of a special opportunity. The snail eaters aren't in the game because they're a pain in the ass. The president didn't want to ask please because if he had they might have said no. You feel me?"

Keeler said, "So what exactly?"

"This is a settling of accounts brother. We're taking the score line back. We'll brief back at the house." Rodriguez took a bite of the burger and chewed silently; mouth closed. He swallowed and sipped coke. "Regarding the frogs. Someone might have decided to teach 'em a lesson. I really don't know and neither do I give a shit." He pointed at Keeler. "You're the sharp end of the stick, the kill team. Besides your team we've got several other squads, all zipped up and compartmentalized."

Keeler said, "Reconnaissance, security, target verification?"

"Yeah. Something of that nature."

Keeler hummed a tune he'd heard in the restaurant, just before that guy had gone apeshit. Thinking about the set up and the command structure. A big operation involving compartmentalized teams for the major aspects of the mission, with Keeler on the kill team. A target verification team so they'd get it right.

Rodriguez was looking at him. "You good?"

Keeler said, "Outstanding."

Rodriguez chewed burger, dipped a fry and ate it. He said, "You ever think that what we do is a little weird?"

Keeler almost choked on a French fry. "Understatement of the decade."

Rodriguez said, "You don't know shit, huh? Why they dropped you out of a plane in the stratosphere just now."

Keeler looked at him, eyes widened. "No idea."

Rodriguez nodded, like he was accepting the truth of Keeler's innocence. "Okay. Some days the job is weirder than others. Yesterday we were all set to rock. Had the teams out here a week already. The kill team's in seventy-two hours already, all acclimatized, rehearsing routes and routines and shit, right?"

Keeler said, "Right."

"Only thing we're waiting for is target verification. We've got the location all wired up and modeled, but we're missing the target."

"Uh huh."

"Yesterday morning the Task Force Commander sends over the dossier on the target." Rodriguez eyed him. "You know how they do it. Some spook shit happens, the process they go through for target vetting. I guess it gets sent up the pipe and back down. Takes time, whatever, we get the green light and start working through the end game. Figuring out the kill."

Keeler had been there before. "That's how it works."

Rodriguez said, "Except last night the Task Force Commander yanks my point man and sends you in to replace him. No reason given, no excuse, no nothing. Not even twenty-four-hour notice."

Keeler said, "I didn't request to be here."

"How could you, since not even the president's girlfriend knows about it?" Glancing up at Keeler and wiping his fingers on a small square of napkin.

They chewed burgers and fries for another six minutes. The Whopper lacked ketchup, consequently a little dry. Keeler ate it anyway. You never knew when you'd be getting another chance at so much protein. He and Rodriguez sucked milkshakes in the car, Rodriguez keeping to the speed limit, still looking unusually anxious to Keeler's mind. The milkshake was chocolate, light on the cocoa but still good.

~

THE DESTINATION WAS AN ISOLATED HOUSE, set behind high hedges in a dismal wasteland of fallow fields. Mid November and gloomy, wind driving in the face with a spit of rain. Keeler liked that kind of weather, but a better jacket would have been nice. Inside the door was a farmhouse kitchen with a big oak table. A man and women were seated, eating what looked like pasta and red sauce. Rodriguez stood examining them.

"Who called lunchtime?"

The woman shrugged. "You weren't here, we got hungry."

Rodriguez relaxed walked into the living room. "That's alright, we ate on the way, Burger King."

The man sat at the table laughed, sucking a thin strand of spaghetti into his mouth. "Flame broiled, right?" He had a tattoo on his right forearm, some kind of diamond pattern. Looking at Keeler. He said, "I'm Chet."

"Keeler."

The woman nodded at Keeler, holding her hand over her mouth, currently occupied with spaghetti.

Chet said, "We call her Billings."

Rodriguez fell back on a sofa in the other room, pulling a laptop from the table. He said, "I'll give you people five minutes to eat." Pointing a finger at Keeler. "You're upstairs in a room with that dangerous character. You don't have any belongings, so there's no reason to visit your quarters. Might as well make coffee."

Keeler found the coffee and located the filters. He set up the drip machine with a sufficient quantity of crushed bean. Seven minutes later the four of them sat around the table with hot mugs. Laptop computers had appeared, cables were connected to black boxes and other data security devices.

Rodriguez started the meeting. Scanning the faces around the table, settling on Billings and drifting. He jerked a thumb at Keeler. "This is for his benefit. You people bust in with your own ideas anytime." Rodriguez chin pointed at the woman, "Why don't you kick off."

Billings nodded. "Right." Addressing Keeler in a matter-of-fact tone. "It's you and me going in to do the dirty. They've established pattern of life for the target. He comes back to his room every afternoon and takes a nap."

Keeler interrupted. "One sec. The target's been here how long?"

Rodriguez said, "Four days."

"But you've only just made him as a verified target."

"Correct. The other teams would have been dealing with his movements. They clued us in once it was verified."

Keeler sat back.

Billings said, "Okay." She chin pointed at Chet. "This one gains entry and secures the door. You and me go in. The plan is to inject the target with succinylcholine. I was thinking between the toes, but whatever. He isn't small. You'll control him while I administer the drug. Then you'll suffocate him with his pillow." She shrugged. "I mean, that was the plan me and the guy you replaced agreed to. I'm open to adjustments."

Even though they hadn't told him anything about the target yet, Keeler had no problem visualizing. Seeing the initial entry, some large man surprised and getting up off the bed, maybe in a state of panic. One of them would jam a stun gun into him. Keeler would hold down the convulsing body, guiding it to settle on the bed. Billings would be removing the target's socks if he was wearing any, and she'd insert the sharp end of a syringe between big toe and index, unloading the neuromuscular blocker into the man's blood stream.

The guy would struggle, but he'd fail. The concentrated muscle relaxant would be dosed generously, any signals from brain to muscle would be blocked and he'd be immobilized within a minute, unable to move, but fully conscious. Keeler would throw a pillow over the man's face, put some weight on it and the guy would be dead within two minutes.

They'd clean up the room and that would be it. Guy like that, if he was middle-aged and died in bed, they'd write it up as a heart attack.

Everyone was looking at him. Keeler nodded. "Sounds like a plan."

FORTY-EIGHT

Rodriguez started with the location and context. They'd be operating within an upscale convention center East of Paris. The *Marne La Vallée Expo Center*. The complex was busy with the usual corporate boondoggles, catering to both French and international clientele. Which was one reason the place was good for the mission, foreigners fit in. The *Expo Center* had facilities, three Hotels, swimming pools and saunas, tennis courts and fitness rooms.

The target was on his own, traveling under an assumed name, staying in a fifth-floor suite at one of the hotels. The reconnaissance team hadn't spotted a security detail, which was interpreted to mean that the target was trying to keep a low profile and could even be dealing on his own behalf.

Keeler said, "Who's the target."

Rodriguez clicked keys and turned the laptop around to show an overweight middle-aged man with a mustache. He had thinning hair in a comb over. Maybe forty-five years old. The photograph had been taken on surveillance. The target held a plastic shopping bag and was wearing a suede brown jacket. The tail of his button-down shirt stuck out on one side. He looked like a regular working guy, a small business owner, or maybe a teacher.

Keeler leaned forward and looked at the photograph. "What's he got in the bag?"

Chet said, "Shoes. He went to a discount store and bought a pair of shoes, fifty percent off."

Rodriguez smeared a finger on the screen. "That image was taken three days ago, it's the first verified photo of this man in fifteen years that the service has managed to procure. This is confirmed to be *Farid Tabrizi,* an Iranian national. You're looking at the Islamic Revolutionary Guards Corps officer who planned and directed the Karbala attack." Rodriguez took a breath and sucked coffee. Looking at Keeler, letting the significance sink in.

Everyone knew about Karbala, 2007. The most successful attack on American troops in the Iraq theater of operations. Iranian Revolutionary Guards forces successfully raided a US military outpost and got away with it. They'd gained access posing as a team of US Security Advisors at an Iraqi military police headquarters. The IRGC team wore US uniforms, carried US weapons, and spoke American.

They'd come in five black GMC Suburbans, same as the US Security Advisors used. The Iraqi security guards had opened the checkpoint gate. Once inside the base the IRGC commandos had murdered five American officers and taken four more Americans hostage. They hadn't hurt a single Iraqi, the armed military conscripts and officers not getting in the fight, standing back and allowing their American advisors to be captured and slaughtered like animals.

The four hostages had been found a short distance from the raid, corpses thrown into a garbage pile out by the desert, their hands zip tied behind them, bullet wounds indicating they'd been executed point blank. Taking out *Tabrizi* was going to be an honor. Being chosen for the hit made Keeler feel good.

He said, "So what's he doing in Paris?"

Rodriguez didn't immediately respond, his eyes doing a little rotation

Billings said, "Good question." She looked at Rodriguez.

Rodriguez said, "Well we guess he's doing some bad guy shit. What do I know?"

Chet said, "All they tell us is who to hit, where." He was swirling a finger up in the air. "The why of his being here is a matter for those guys."

Keeler said, "Which guys?"

"Intelligence people, you know, the analysts."

Keeler said, "Office worker type of people with laptops and touch typing skills."

Billings said, "Latte sipping yuppie scum."

Rodriguez said, "Guy entered France on the identity documents of some Iranian journalist who lives in Istanbul."

"A real person?

Rodriguez said, "Apparently so, a real journalist with a fatwa over his head, like Salman Rushdie."

Billings said, "Asshole's using some dissident journalist based out of Istanbul as a sock puppet."

Keeler said, "No French involvement, huh?"

Rodriguez said, "Strictly 'ghost protocol', as they say in the movies." He coughed. "Like I already said, it looks like the brass stopped giving a shit what the snail eaters think anymore."

Billings said, "Amen."

Chet had a set of earbuds for Keeler and a device that looked like an iPhone to go with them. They did a short and successful test of the equipment.

THE REST of the briefing focused upon execution.

Rodriguez went down a long list of items, getting deep into the details. There were architectural plans to memorize, staff schedules and their routines. There were medical histories of adjacent guests who could conceivably interfere with the execution, as well as security camera coverage in the operational zone and planned infiltration and exfiltration routes.

Keeler absorbed it all, a professional. At the same time, his mind was roaming. Something was making him uneasy, but he couldn't put his finger on it. All military operations are in their essence arbitrary, someone up there decides and your job is to execute. Tabrizi was a bad guy and taking him out was going to be more than acceptable. Keeler wasn't in the habit of feeling uneasy.

Rodriguez finished the briefing, looking at him directly. "You got here in an unconventional way. Anything you need?"

Keeler said, "I could use a better jacket."

The Operations Officer tossed him car keys. "There's a supermarket down the road. Turn left on the departmental and you'll see signs for it in a couple of clicks."

Chet said, "Get me some fruity gum."

Keeler took the Peugeot, enjoying the drive. The supermarket was what they called a *Hypermarche* in France, not the size of a Walmart back home, but as big as it gets in Europe. The clothing section was full of options, overcoats and blazers in wool or more resistant materials. He found himself at the hunting section looking at the French version of something he'd probably be happy to wear back home for the winter.

The other inner voice said, no, the only place you'll be hunting is a corporate convention center, get with the program. You'd think the clandestine service would include a stylist for missions like this. In the end he got a regular medium weight parka in blue, in addition to a pack of fruity gum for Chet.

Next door was a technology store. Keeler bought a burner phone and a pay-as-you-go SIM card. He sat in the car and took some time to set up the phone. He needed a fresh profile for messaging apps, keeping it as anonymous as he could. He downloaded a call forwarding app and paid for a disposable phone number. Anyone he called would see a Bulgarian caller ID.

It wasn't rock solid, but he thought, *good enough for rock and roll*.

Keeler sent a message to Ruth Shoshan's phone back in Israel.

'K for Y. How you doing Cluster?'

The code word he and Yasmin had agreed upon. Keeler sat back, expecting a response. Yasmin would have notified her sister to expect a message. Ruth would know. He waited two minutes and put the burner phone in his pocket, only a little disappointed.

Keeler switched on the car radio, getting a French ballad through the speakers, not very satisfying. A minute of intense radio seeking later he was listening to Don't Fear the Reaper, by the Blue Oyster Cult. He got the vehicle on the road, warm in the new parka, feeling good.

That tune had been the theme song at his high school prom. That had been a place called Artesia, New Mexico. He hadn't lived there long enough to get very social, so he'd ended up going to the prom with the class nerd, a shy girl with bad acne and glasses. She seemed immune to fashion, like Keeler. They ended up having a pretty good time, finishing the night out in the desert, leaned back on the hood of her dad's truck out by the Pecos River sipping from a bottle of Southern Comfort, drunk and laughing about stuff.

The burner phone started beeping and buzzing in the front pocket of his jeans. He turned off the music, pulled off the road at the first opportunity. A building and a parking lot. Keeler wasn't paying attention; the phone was pretty insistent. He parked and pulled the burner out, pressing the call button to receive.

"Yeah."

"So, you got with my sister, huh?"

Ruth, Yasmin's sister.

Keeler said, "True. Am I in trouble?"

Ruth said, "You might have to marry her is all. We're a traditional family. You'll need to convert."

Keeler said, "Take it easy on me Ruth, I'm just an innocent American."

She laughed. "You're not actually in Bulgaria, are you?"

"No, I'm not."

"Okay." She said, "Unsecured line, right?"

Keeler said, "Right."

"Y is fine, but she's busy. It's related to your honeymoon trip the other night. I'll also just say that I'm involved now. What's up with you?"

Keeler said, "Not sure yet. Just wanted to get in touch, see how you're doing."

Ruth said, "I'll pass on the message. Take care of yourself."

Keeler ended the call.

Ruth's tone at the end had been slightly cold. He reminded himself that she worked for an allied service. The Mossad was known to spy on its allies, and so was the CIA. Friends, but also competitors in a crazy world.

So Ruth was involved in the repercussions of his and Yasmin's night out in Egypt. Which meant what? Mossad involvement indicated a foreign intelligence interest, Egypt related. Yasmin being busy with something related to that would possibly mean something else, unless she'd been tapped by Mossad.

He looked up and noticed that he'd happened to pull the car

into the forecourt of a motel. Keeler sat for a minute, looking out at the motel building, but not even seeing it, thinking about the situation.

Four teams on this mission. Rodriguez had said it. One team each for reconnaissance, security, target verification, and the kill. The teams were compartmentalized, no one group in contact with another. This by itself was not a problem, it was the way these things were done. A weak link in the chain could only jeopardize the links it directly attached to. That was standard operating procedure for clandestine missions.

Keeler got the vehicle started again. The motel lot was almost empty. Three cars in it and a van up by the office building. *M'sieur-Dame*, written in faux hand script with a cartoon snail sitting on the final letter *e*. The place had four outbuildings, with two rooms each. On the other side of the parking lot a raised berm indicated the highway. He rolled the window down, hearing the shriek of tires on asphalt, unseen but sounding dangerous.

FORTY-NINE

When Keeler got back to the house, he found Billings watching TV on the sofa. Rodriguez and Chet had gone out.

He went upstairs to the room he was supposed to share, having forgotten to ask which one it was. Presumably the room would contain two beds. Keeler opened the first door he got to, realizing fast that it wasn't the right one. This room was dark and filled with equipment. Three flat panel screens were spread out on a makeshift desk made from a couple of side tables and a door. Other machines with discreet lighting hummed. A mustachioed blonde guy was in there, face lit up by the electronic glow of surveillance imagery, fingers busy manipulating controls of some kind. He swiveled his head to look at Keeler and they recognized each other.

The guy was an intelligence officer name of Neilson.

Keeler closed the door behind him and sat on the edge of a single bed shoved up against the wall.

"Neilson, long time no see." He gazed at the screens, seeing images of the surrounding area and the interior of the house itself. "What's all this?"

"Keeler." Neilson nodded to him, indicating the screens.

"We seeded sensors and cameras around the perimeter. They got me running force protection now." He grinned and winked. "I heard about your dramatic entrance. Who'd you piss off?"

"I don't know." Keeler raised his eyebrows and shrugged. He said, "Tell me something. How did they verify the target?"

Neilson said, "What do you mean?"

"Whatever his name is. Tabrizi. This guy hadn't been photographed in 15 years."

"Yeah?"

"So how'd they know it was him? The call must have been made by someone who knows him currently."

Neilson was interested now. "That's highly likely, yes."

Keeler said, "So who would that be?"

Neilson swiveled on his stool for several seconds, back and forth, thinking. He said, "The target verification team's been here for a week. Who specifically made the call? I do not know."

He brought up images on his screen, flicking through videos and photographs of Farid Tabrizi going about his daily business at the Expo Center. One of the still photographs showed Tabrizi seated in the food court of what looked like a shopping mall. The target eating a hot dog with a man in his late thirties.

Keeler said, "Who's he meeting with?"

"Guy from the Iranian embassy in Paris." Neilson managed a simulation of an Iranian accent. "*Behzad Faravahar*, no middle name. He's on the books as sports and culture advisor."

"Which you figure is a spook role."

"Correct. They think he's the Al Quds guy at the embassy."

"Did we get a recording of the convo?"

"No." Neilson said, "He made contact and had a conversation. That's all we have on it. No voice recording."

Keeler was wondering about this. "Why are they meeting in Paris if the guy's living in Istanbul?"

Neilson shrugged. "How should I know?"

Neilson was looking at him. Keeler knew what he was thinking, the same thing drummed into all intelligence officers when faced with a potentially complex situation. You always assumed that the simplest answer sufficient to explain the facts in front of you was the correct answer, a principle known as Occam's Razor.

Keeler said, "So this most wanted IRGC guy comes to Paris posing as a journalist from Istanbul, meets with an Al-Quds guy working out of the embassy."

Neilson leaned back on the rotating stool, balancing. "Even more complicated than that brother. The assumption going around is that Farid Tabrizi became a Quds Force covert officer." He pointed at the screen. "Could be they're planning something for France, why Tabrizi had to come over covertly."

Which made sense. The Quds Force were the Iranian version of the CIA, a covert operations arm of the Islamic Revolutionary Guard Corps. That would have been a natural transition for someone like Tabrizi, a successful IRGC warrior with notches in his belt, now keeping a low profile from infidel assassins sent by the Great Satan.

Keeler said, "Who's this Iranian Journalist, the identity he's using for cover?"

Neilson had a good time pronouncing the name. He said, "Pejman Kazemi."

"Yeah, but who is he, what's the profile."

"Oh. Dissident journalist who's supposed to be close to some regime players."

Keeler said, "A guy with access, a pain in the ass."

"Yeah."

Keeler pointed at the screen. "You read his stuff?"

"No." Neilson looked at him. "You want to read his writing?"

Keeler shrugged. "Yeah, let's check it out."

Neilson's fingers clicked and tapped and swooped over trackpads, on keys, and mouse buttons. Two minutes later he had three of the guy's articles translated into English. He pushed back from the desk.

"There you go."

Keeler leaned forward. They weren't too long. He got the phone out of his pocket and waved it to Neilson. "Can you get that on here?"

Neilson nodded and clicked a couple of things.

Keeler extended a hand to the man. "Good to see you, brother."

He walked down the hall, found a bed and lay down on it. His fingers and a thumb made movements over the phone's glass surface. He got up one of the articles Neilson had transferred. Some opinion piece about an Iranian election. The writer had opinions, but it was impossible for Keeler to tell if he was an idiot or a genius, since he knew nothing about Iranian politics.

He switched out of that app and Googled the writer's name, *Kazemi*. Keeler looked at random stuff about him on the internet. There wasn't much information. Keeler put in search terms related to Iranian elections, picking up on keywords that were often used, putting those back into the search and reading about that stuff.

Another of the journalist's articles was about local politics in Fars province, Iran. The writer criticizing the National Iranian Oil Company's handling of negotiations with municipal authorities in Shiraz. The writer alleging corruption within the Iranian Oil Company and the Ministry of Petroleum. This article mentioned names. Probably why the guy was considered a dissident, he was a dangerous man.

Pejman Kazemi.

He tried out the journalists name and liked it. *Pejman*

Kazemi rolled off the tongue smoothly, something pleasant about this specific combination of syllables.

Keeler spent some time on the internet, looking into the deal in Shiraz and Fars province. It wasn't hard to figure out that people over there were pissed off about the fossil fuel industry. That, or they were angry about the local rednecks who attached importance to tradition. Shiraz was an ancient town. Ancient with ruins, that was the Middle East. Like Europe, they had history. Being American, there's history, but it isn't the same.

Thinner, he thought, American history's the kind of history you could keep track of.

Keeler closed his eyes and fell into an almost immediate sleep. In it, he saw large fields, like he was above them and looking down. Not the kinds of fields they had outside the safe house in France, but the fields of his youth, American fields. The rural places he'd grown up in, from Arkansas to New York and back again, down through Louisiana and up to New Mexico and the Dakotas.

He woke up a few hours later when the door opened and Chet came in. Keeler heard him moving around and turned over to his side. The guy was rooting around for something on his side of the room. He said, "Sorry buddy, I need to turn the light on."

Keeler grunted and squeezed his eyes closed when the room went bright as a flash. After a couple of seconds it went dark again and Chet left.

Keeler still had an image of the target in his mind, seeing him screened on the back of his eyelids. *Tabrizi*, the surveillance photographs and videos. This Iranian guy in some shopping mall in the vast *Marne La Vallée Expo Center* complex, purchasing a pair of shoes in a store there. Eating a hot dog instead of the usual five star experience these people took advantage of. Maybe Tabrizi was a drag on the system now, with a small per-diem expense account while on business. Plus a French hot dog would have been pork. He wouldn't be the first so-called religious Iranian guy to indulge on the sly.

Keeler wondered what happens to a Revolutionary Guards officer who's wanted by the United States Clandestine Service? Do the Iranians protect him forever? The death sentence is real, not some bullshit like the mullahs put on Rushdie. Tabrizi had been on the run since 2007, eight years, a lifetime in spook terms. A person gets on Uncle Sam's list, and they don't get to see old age. You figure in that case nobody's going to want to be anywhere near the guy, for fear of becoming collateral damage in the hit.

Maybe why he had no bodyguards.

So, here's Farid Tabrizi now, a case officer with the Quds Force. Killing him was going to be an important signal to others, a reminder that when you pull the trigger on one of ours, you sign up for life as a walking dead man, just waiting for the day when someone like Keeler shows up to put a pillow over your face.

FIFTY

Tel Aviv, Israel

Hershkowitz was in his mother's apartment in Tel Aviv, drinking black coffee, listening to his assistant talking through a little bud stuck into his left ear. His mother was moving slowly around the kitchen, searching for flour and sugar. She tended to forget where she put things and then found them only to forget again. She needed the live-in help, but it was frustratingly tough to find someone at the moment.

Maybe something to do with the situation in Gaza, what everyone blamed for their problems.

His assistant was at the office. Hershkowitz's eyes and ears. Her voice narrated laconically, piped in through the earbuds.

"Yeah, I'm looking at the family's social network, it's currently spinning in a slow circle on the screen."

Hershkowitz grunted. She was talking about a model his people were making that could show you a person's social connections in 3D. Like, who they spoke to on the phone, who they had as friends on social media, who they lived near, everyone on their team or in their class, or who were regulars in their favorite bar.

The model looked like a complicated virus under the microscope, a multitude of spikes coming out of central nodes. Each node a person, each spike a connection. People literally gave that information away. Sometimes they paid to give it away. The world was completely insane.

He said, "You're talking about the old model. They're populating a new one, right?"

She said, "They've got the previous model on the left. The new one's already populating with data coming in from the photo scans and stuff. They'll make a comparative analysis later."

"Uh huh." Hershkowitz sipped coffee. As the data was generated in the Makhoul house, it was already streaming into analytic filters, like facial recognition systems. He could see it in his mind's eye, the social model changing slightly as new people slotted in, others shifting a little in the other direction.

Analysis of the family waste had confirmed the two parents and three children. If they were hiding this Jafar person, he wasn't shitting in the regular toilet. Hershkowitz's mother was looking lost, staring into the wall by the clock.

He said, "Mom, the salt's in the drawer right there," pointing at the place, watching his mother discover it gratefully.

The earbud made a sound like a bird, which meant someone was calling on the secure system.

He tapped at it. "Yeah."

"Mike it's Gabi." The deputy head of the Mossad's guttural voice put bass sonorities into Hershkowitz's ear.

"Go ahead Gabi."

"We have an update on this Egyptian, Hisham Al-Masri."

"The colonel."

"Yeah." Gabi said, "Our sources have him on the American desk, working out of Cairo."

Hershkowitz let that seep in. He was surprised by this,

considering the colonel had been in North Sinai. Hershkowitz was expecting there to be a Gaza connection, maybe a liaison with Hamas or PIJ.

He said, "On the American desk how exactly?"

Gabi said, "Supposed to be nominally in charge of negotiations with the Americans around anti-aircraft missile imports."

"That's not a full-time gig."

"No, but you know how they work. They grift and they graft. It's a thug's life over there."

Hershkowitz was thinking about the Ghost-Fish drone from El-Gora to *Midreshet*. An American connection was making more sense. "Your source is reliable?"

Gabi said, "A hundred percent. I'm personally involved."

Which meant that Mossad had a source high in the Egyptian Intelligence Service.

Hershkowitz said, "That clarifies things somewhat. He's got a license to roam because the Americans are everywhere."

"They're with you and against you, all at the same time."

"Which means that him going up into Sinai raises no eyebrows."

Gabi said, "But the connect to our mystery man Jafar puts him in our sights. Operational assumption. Hisham Al-Masri is rotten."

"And the Egyptians either know it or they don't." Hershkowitz paused for a moment considering the ways that this colonel could be handled. He said, "What's the next step, Gabi?"

Gabi's growl went one more octave down, becoming a sonorous bass line of words.

"I've already spoken with Bibi about it. This man's suspected to be running an agent in Israel and he's going down. We believe that it's best to let our Egyptian allies take care of their own, Mike. This is how we want to do it."

"What if the Jafar guy's a regular mukhabarat asset? I mean, we run against them, so it's not a surprise they're running against us."

"Sure, but unacceptable anyway. We'll seed his destruction into their system, make them find out he's rotten all on their own."

Which meant the Mossad would be organizing this man's downfall, set him up so that his own people took him out. In which case, his demise would be quite uncomfortable.

Hershkowitz had no issue with that. He said, "On my side we've got loose ends."

"Related to this Egyptian?"

"That hasn't popped up, but sure, it's a possibility."

The deputy director of the Mossad said, "That's all up to you Mike, seeing as you wanted it. You know where to find me."

The line clicked off and Hershkowitz was left looking at his mother again, over by the stove holding a box of spaghetti. She turned slowly to see him and looked surprised.

She said, "Jonathan."

He said, "No mom, It's Michael."

YASMIN WAS STILL IN BED. They'd put her in an apartment outside of Haifa in case she needed to get back to Nazareth quickly. The place was in a high-rise building overlooking the Carmel tunnels. She pushed the covers aside and sat on the edge of the bed, getting a view through the double-paned windows to traffic far below, noiselessly flowing. Vehicles carrying people into the city, cars sucked into the Chinese built holes bored deep under the mountains, some engineering miracle.

Thinking of Zeina, picturing her face, the way that she spoke.

No way that Zeina Makhoul was involved in something nefarious. That's what Yasmin's instinct told her. This woman was pure. So why would that guy have her photograph? She knew, as a military commander, sometimes the answer to a problem isn't complicated. Either the guy was a lover, or in love with her, or she was his target.

Remembering the name on his identity card, *Jafar*. Maybe she'd confront Zeina with that name if it came to it.

The thought occurred to her, what if Jafar was the father of Zeina's children? Stranger things had happened, people have affairs, they father secret children. Arab honor culture was real, letting a secret like that out into the open could have deadly consequences. Zeina and Mikhail Makhoul seemed the epitome of modern, but that didn't preclude a more traditional extended family.

In the case of something like adultery, it was entirely possible that some male member of the clan would take it upon themselves to repair the family's tarnished honor by murdering the adulterous woman. Fear of that was rational. Yasmin suddenly had the embarrassed feeling that she was intruding into someone's private life.

Is that what it was like to be an intelligence agent?

She'd been holding her breath and let it out in a long stream. The force of exhalation folding her back in bed. Thoughts of private lives turned fast to Tom Keeler. His face still clear in her mind, as was the feel of being physically close to him. But she wasn't. She was in Haifa, while he was an hour and a half away in Tel Aviv, what the two Mossad guys had said. Yasmin figured he'd been taken to the American embassy.

FIFTY-ONE

Hershkowitz's assistant had been downstairs in the parking lot, waiting for Yasmin. Now, sitting in the passenger seat as the assistant piloted the vehicle east to Nazareth, Yasmin watched her operate the steering wheel and foot pedals. Seeing her nibble the croissant followed by a long sip of a latte. One at a time, bite, sip, bite sip, bird-like mannerisms, like she was tearing off flesh with each peck.

Yasmin said, "So what's up?"

The assistant said, "Nothing, that's the problem. You'll see what I mean when we get there."

There meaning the safe house in *Nof Hagalil*.

Hershkowitz was already present, along with the two guys from the night before and a woman Yasmin hadn't met. The boss nodding to Yasmin as she came in the door with his assistant. He'd poured her coffee and handed her a donut before getting to business.

"What it looks like is, no Jafar of any kind in the family photo collection. No lead, nothing. Quite a few faces, the majority of them passed clean through facial identification, all above board except these." He handed a tablet device to Yasmin. "Look at those guys and tell me what you think."

Yasmin flicked through a dozen images, cropped and blown up from the scanned family photos. They were all men, some with mustaches, others with beards, a couple who were clean shaven. None of them looked remotely like the man she'd seen on the other side of that Egyptian infiltration tunnel.

She handed the tablet back. "Nothing."

Hershkowitz said, "I didn't think so. Those guys we'd already identified as foreign nationals visiting the family." He swiped across the tablet's screen. "The Makhouls have ties in Jordan." He tossed the tablet like a frisbee to the sofa. One of the guys caught it. "So here we are at zero. Not a person there who we don't already know, and not a soul who you might suspect of getting muddy in an infiltration tunnel from Sinai."

She said, "Which means what?"

He said, "Which means absolutely nothing. I think Zeina Makhoul knows this Jafar guy, he just isn't connected to her family, that's what. A different vector maybe but connected."

Yasmin wasn't dumb. She was aware that Hershkowitz was rhetorically getting her motivated for something. She said, "So you want me to do something."

Hershkowitz said, "Funny that you should ask. I was thinking about that. Zeina Makhoul hasn't done anything wrong, so we're not going to use coercion. Right?"

Yasmin resisted agreeing automatically, looking into Hershkowitz's face for signs of trickery. Nothing there but a blank look. She said, "Alright."

He said, "So if we can't use coercion, you'll need to go up there and talk to her again."

"Me?"

"She already knows you. You had chemistry."

Yasmin wasn't so certain. "Chemistry."

Hershkowitz said, "Yes. You're good at this. We're going to use the soft approach. Imagine I show up there with these goons." Indicating the others in the room. "She'd clam up. With you, who knows?"

Yasmin said, "And if that doesn't work?"

"Then we could end up on a wild goose chase." Glancing to his assistant for support.

The assistant unstuck her lips with a sound like a glued poster being pulled from a wall. She said, "which could be too slow, if something's going on that we need to know about."

Hershkowitz said, "We could learn about it the wrong way, in other words."

Yasmin's heart began to beat a little faster. What they were implying was serious. If they didn't find this Jafar guy soon, there was a chance that they'd end up finding him only *after* an attack. Because in Israel there was always an attack being planned. Their job was to prevent it.

She said, "So I go up there again, but I'm not playing nice, is what you mean."

The assistant said, "You can be nice, it doesn't matter, as long as you're direct."

Hershkowitz said, "Time to cut out the bullshit is what we mean."

BY THE TIME Yasmin showed up at the Polyphonic Project building, Zeina Makhoul's music appreciation session had finished. Yasmin found her in a common room drinking tea with half a dozen colleagues. She was able to observe Makhoul through a window in the door, and backed off to the lobby, figuring she'd wait for the coffee break to be over.

Ten minutes later, Makhoul came out of the break room

dressed in a coat with a handbag over her shoulder. She spotted Yasmin and stopped momentarily, clearly a little surprised to see her again. Yasmin did her best to make it smooth, all smiles, saying she was sorry for having missed the music appreciation session. That chilled Makhoul out some, buying Yasmin's excuses. She was going shopping. Yasmin started walking with her, trudging up the hill. She was keeping the conversation going, asking questions about the kids' session, feigning interest, the type of music that Makhoul programmed for the kids.

Once they were fifty meters from the building, Yasmin stopped walking and put a hand on Makhoul's arm. She was confident, even though the other woman was older, more mature, a prominent citizen with a family. Makhoul stopped, and they faced each other.

"Zeina, I need to talk to you. This isn't about music, or the Polyphonic Project. I think your work is admirable and interesting, but I was never here for that." Taking a moment to look in the older woman's eyes directly, seeing confusion like an adrenaline hit. The pupils dilated. Yasmin said, "Do you understand?"

A moped was buzzing up the hill slowly, coming towards them and Yasmin stopped talking, waiting for it to pass. A young man or teenage boy with another riding pillion. Both wore helmets with opaque face shields. The rider hit the throttle, and the two zoomed past.

Makhoul had frozen in place, body and facial muscles showing nothing but surprise. That changed. She blinked, comprehension developing. She nodded, her eyes darting around now at the surrounding cars. Yasmin understood what Makhoul was thinking. There wasn't a single Arab Israeli citizen who was unaware that they were surveillance targets of the security services. Arab Israelis had lived under military rule from the initial civil conflict in 1948 until 1966. Now they were a hell of a lot more integrated, but much of that integration was very recent.

Makhoul said, "Are you going to take me to interrogation or something?"

Yasmin said, "No, I just want to talk to you privately. Can we go to your house?" She indicated the area. "We can't talk out here, I'm sorry. I'll explain what it's about when we're in private."

Makhoul just nodded and began to walk. Yasmin caught up with her.

FIFTY-TWO

THE WALK to Makhoul's house took ten minutes. They didn't exactly walk in silence, but they weren't speaking either. Yasmin finding it weirdly calm, all the usual sounds a town makes, plus the rhythmic tapping of two pairs of shoe clad feet on pavement.

Makhoul didn't feel the need to pretend to be hospitable, but when they got there, she wasn't bitter about it either. She didn't start making tea, but she did offer Yasmin a glass of iced coffee from the refrigerator. Fiddling with the sugar and milk while Yasmin leaned back against the kitchen counter.

Yasmin couldn't help noticing the fancy organic milk from Kibbutz Harduf, a fifteen-minute drive from Nazareth.

Things had changed in Israel since 1966, before either her or Zeina Makhoul had been born. Back then the bitterness of civil war was fresh in everyone's minds. Yasmin knew that for Israeli Arabs, the security services had been seen as the enemy. Now that wasn't necessarily the case. Sure, there were ethnic tensions but a woman like Zeina Makhoul wasn't going to voluntarily switch from Israeli to Jordanian or Egyptian or Syrian rule, that was for damned sure.

She was Israeli just like Yasmin, neither of them able to choose where they were from, both in the same boat.

Yasmin accepted the glass of ice coffee and got out the photograph. "Tell me about this."

If Makhoul was surprised to see the photo, she didn't show it.

Makhoul said, "That's me and the kids, years ago." She glanced at Yasmin. "What about it?"

Yasmin said, "Who took the picture?"

Makhoul glanced at her for a second, then back at the photograph. "My husband took that picture. It's *Beyt Sayda*." She said, "you know, where Jesus did the miracle with the fish and the bread." She was confused. "This is what you wanted to talk about?"

Yasmin picked up the photograph, fanning it in the air. "This was found in Egypt. It was in the possession of a man who was using infiltration tunnels to cross under the border. We think his first name is Jafar, at least that's the name on his Israeli identity card. Does this name mean anything to you?"

Makhoul was shaking her head. "Jafar. What was this man doing with my photograph?"

"We don't know why he had your picture. We're concerned about it. I'm asking you to help me try to understand."

Makhoul looked at her. "I'm concerned too."

Yasmin said, "Think Zeina. Maybe somebody in your past, maybe a person you went to university with?"

Makhoul shook her head, looking at the photograph as if it could tell her anything. "Not that I remember, but *Jafar*," glancing at Yasmin. "You know that's a Muslim name."

Yasmin nodded. Not having considered that, wondering what difference it would make. She figured Muslim and Christian Arabs didn't mix that much socially, maybe that's why

Zeina thought it odd. But Makhoul had stopped moving, staring straight ahead, her face turning crimson.

"It's not Jafar." Looking at Yasmin again, eyes now seeking.

"What's not Jafar?"

Makhoul said, "The name of the man. It isn't Jafar, his name is Fares."

Yasmin said, "I don't understand what you mean. Who's Fares?"

Makhoul had her hands up cradling her face, looking at Yasmin through spidered fingers. "Oh my god. It's my cousin. My father's brother's son. It has to be him."

"I still don't get it."

Makhoul was nodding to herself; something having clicked for her.

"We were supposed to be married, but I refused. I haven't seen Fares for so long."

Yasmin watched the mental gears operating in Makhoul's head, waiting for her to process. She was getting over the initial shock of whatever it was she'd recalled.

Makhoul said, "Jafar must be his new name, the one he took." Looking up, realizing from Yasmin's expression that she didn't have a clue what that meant. She said, "Fares *converted*."

Yasmin said, "Converted to what?"

"To Islam." Makhoul was looking at Yasmin, almost condescendingly. She said, "You don't know. I'll explain. When they convert, the Imam gives them a new name, yes? A man carrying that photograph of me. Who else would it be. I'm sure it's Fares!" Really adamant now, her voice a little shrill and the color in her face rising. She looked angry. "I'm sure that's it. It's Fares and his new Muslim name is Jafar."

Yasmin wanted to cool Makhoul down, bring the conversation back to a calm level. She said, "Alright Zeina. That's very interesting and important. Do you know where he is now?"

Makhoul made a gesture with her hand, like tossing something into the wind. "I don't have any idea. He left the community."

Yasmin was thinking, if this Jafar guy was her cousin, why hadn't they found a photograph of him among the family pictures that were everywhere.

She said, "Do you have a photograph of your cousin?" Pointing at the family albums on the shelf. "Maybe in a family album?"

Makhoul shook her head. "No. We removed all traces of him. Fares' conversion was a betrayal, he was disavowed by the *hamula*."

Hamula, the Arabic term translated best as clan. But the word clan didn't quite capture its meaning. In conservative Muslim and Christian Arab communities, hamulas attract much stronger affiliation and identity than the state. You belonged to a hamula more than the country, and so did all of your extended family. Some hamulas could have thousands of members.

Makhoul's face registered shock. "I can't believe he carried the photograph on him. I had no idea. I haven't seen him for more than twenty years." Her eyes were green, Yasmin decided, pretty eyes that were brimming with tears. "I feel bad for him somehow, if that's all he had in his life."

Yasmin said, "Jafar is your age?"

Makhoul said, "Three years older." She averted her eyes, looking concerned again.

Yasmin stepped into her personal space and put a hand on her shoulder, "What is it?"

Makhoul said. "You should contact his mother. She might be in touch with him, but secretly, you know, because of the..." She lost her words for a moment. She looked up at Yasmin with red eyes, emotional about it.

Yasmin completed the sentence for her. "Because of the shame to the family?"

Makhoul shrugged, embarrassed. "Because of the men, how they would react."

Right, Yasmin got it. A hamula clan wasn't some kind of egalitarian organization as far as women were concerned. Even fathers didn't have a say in what happened to their daughters, married off to whichever first cousin had the most rights within the system. Which begged a question she hadn't asked.

She said, "Zeina, how did you get out of marrying him?"

"I got his sister to convince him that it wasn't a good idea, we used all kinds of tricks." A thought occurred to her. "You met Basima. She's always been my best friend."

Basima who played the harp, who had led Yasmin to Zeina Makhoul's house.

Yasmin said, "Basima's your cousin?"

Makhoul nodded. "She's Fares' sister."

Yasmin was aware of the team listening in. Hershkowitz and his people would find the conversation stimulating, to say the least. The teams would already be exploding into action.

She said, "This is going to start involving more people than just us, okay Zeina? You understand what I mean."

"I understand."

Yasmin left the house and walked down the hill. She was met on the way by a white SUV. Two guys in it. The passenger telling her to hop in, a couple of vehicles converging already on the Makhoul home. She climbed into the back seat and a bearded guy behind the wheel turned to give her an over-the-shoulder glance and said, "Good job."

The SUV turned onto a side street and Yasmin caught a glimpse of the moped she'd seen earlier, at least it looked like the same one. This time it wasn't two teenage boys on it, just one. The kid sitting there fiddling with something.

FIFTY-THREE

Jafar Al-Husseini was looking at the feed from the camera his guys had rigged on their scooter. Arab teenagers he hired as freelance thieves, they'd done a good job of this, maneuvering enough to capture video of the Jews without getting caught.

Now he was able to move through the footage slowly, frame by frame. There were enough focused images to make the identification. The bitch from Sinai talking to his cousin Zeina, the only woman he would ever really love.

Footage from another crew showed the squad swarming the Makhoul house. Another of their teams was at his sister's place. The guys now needed to put some distance between themselves and the Jews, it wasn't safe anymore.

For Jafar it was over. He'd have to move fast if he wanted a chance at getting out.

Security personnel would be on the alert in the entire country, including the territories. His face would be populating thousands of devices, sensor networks and integrated facial recognition systems. No airport, train station, bus station, gas station, highway, or border was available to him. Best he could do was wear a baseball hat and glasses, get into a car with the correct license plates and attempt to make it to the Lebanese border. There he'd simply have to hope that they'd save his ass, but there were no guarantees.

Problem was, he had nothing to bring with him, no gift, no story, and no accomplishment.

His contact in Lebanon had said the Hezbollah would take him but he had to bring a gift. Those were tough sons of bitches, and they didn't make promises. He'd have to get up there and make the call. They'd decide based upon the situation as it appeared to them. His contact told him that he'd be nothing there. Told him to lower his expectations and be ready to accept life as a free man. Jafar wasn't even a Shia Muslim, which made it even more difficult for him in South Lebanon.

However, the man said that if he managed to bring them a gift, or do something notable, he'd have chance at status, and a life.

At that moment, Jafar was sitting in an apartment in the shitty part of south Tel Aviv, watching young people down below. The light was beautiful, and the scent of the sea was in the air. The neighborhood was packed with bohemians in the kind of colorful clothes that they liked for their outdoor dance parties, the raves and the acid techno. The women showed a lot of flesh. The activity in restaurants cafes, and bars was frenetic, accompanied by the constant electronic thwap of modern music.

All the things that he hated about the Jews.

Even more so because he knew them.

Knew them because he was almost one of them, having grown up to some degree among them.

Of course, he'd grown up as Fares Khoury from Nazareth. The Zionists had selected him for one of their Arab Israeli integration programs. So, he'd attended Israeli schools up in *Nof Hagalil*, the fancy Jewish area.

Which meant that Fares had ingested the Zionist propaganda, entire courses dedicated to impressing the founding military mythos of the country into the youth. Fares had been just as impressionable as any other young boy. He'd eaten it up, even hoping to enter a fighting unit of the IDF himself.

One of his favorite stories had been the *legend of Petra*.

Back in the day, Jordan was an enemy of the Israeli state. The desert regions were particularly hostile, teeming with Bedouin who would gladly slit a Jewish man's throat. The toughest special forces operators were Sayeret Matkal, and legend had it that the last trial for initiates attempting to be accepted into the unit was an unofficial and highly dangerous solo trip through the Jordanian desert to Petra, a famous archeological site that no Israeli Jew should ever see.

The teacher had said that many had tried. He'd raised his hand and asked her, tried, and failed? She responded, *tried, and died*.

But he wasn't Fares anymore, he'd transformed himself into Jafar Al-Husseini by force of will. His mentor in the conversion was a descendent of the famous grand mufti of Jerusalem, Haj Amin al-Husseini. Jafar knew the Zionists well enough to hate them, but he wasn't stupid enough to underestimate their capabilities and motivations.

He'd move carefully and contact the brothers in Lebanon. But there was no way he'd go up there empty-handed. He'd need to bring a prize.

FIFTY-FOUR

T*ROYES, France*

Keeler was downstairs making coffee. The sun wasn't even up on the horizon yet and he'd already been outside, roaming the exterior of the house and looking into the fields and the trees around the property. Triggering Neilson's sensors, no doubt, the thought bringing a grin to his face. There was an artificial pond for cattle not far from the house. No cattle, just water with scum on the surface.

Chet came down, grunting a good morning greeting. Keeler poured him a mug of hot fresh bean juice.

Chet received it gratefully, sipped at the brew and made positive noises. He said, "Sorry about putting the light on last night buddy. Forgot where I put my toothbrush." He laughed hoarsely. "I couldn't hack not brushing my teeth man. They made us eat frog's legs."

Keeler said, "Who made you eat frog's legs?"

He remembered then that Chet had been out with Rodriguez the night before. Chet was standing by the table grinning, like he'd invented the idea of eating frog's legs. The mug of coffee was clutched in both hands, a black image of a dog printed on the white ceramic.

"You ever eat frog's legs man? They taste like *pond*."

"I asked you who made you eat frog's legs, Chet?"

"Spooks and the liaison guy. You think they eat that shit over there? I never saw a snail or a frog's leg over in the sandbox or nothing."

The sandbox was Iraq. Keeler said, "What's the connection between Iraq and frog's legs?"

Chet said, "One of them was Egyptian." He shrugged. "Not technically the sandbox, but same shit I guess." He sipped coffee and swallowed. "You think they eat frogs in Egypt?"

"The liaison guy was from Egypt?"

"Yeah."

Keeler drank coffee. Next time he'd add a spoon of ground beans to the pot. He said, "I don't know that they do eat frog's legs over there Chet. Probably a little dry for frogs. I guess they'd have them down in the Nile, but maybe not enough of them to make it an acquired taste."

Chet said, "That implies a whole bunch of frogs in France, given that it's a delicacy over here."

"True, we need to consult with a frogologist or something, get to the froggy bottom."

Chet laughed and flipped the kitchen light on. "You mind?"

Keeler didn't mind, but as the fluorescent bulbs clicked and crackled into action, illuminating the laptops and cables strewn around the table, a dim light began to pulse in Keeler's mind. Egyptians eating frog's legs. Stupid trivia populating the brain first: the French cooked them in butter. The amphibians themselves usually sourced from Indonesian frog farms, some hot and humid place. They'd come skinned and decapitated, basically from the waist down, legs and pelvis. The things would be fried in butter, adding cream with garlic and parsley thrown in at the end, salt. Keeler knew, having eaten it once with fried potatoes. The bones were thin, and you had to sort of spit them out as you ate, sucking thigh meat from the frog, using the tongue to get rid of the bones.

He said, "Tell me about the Egyptian Chet."

Chet took a big draw from his cup, nodding to himself as he contemplated the question. "What do you want to know Keeler? He liked eating frog's legs. The CIA people wouldn't touch them." He grinned, as if that was a clever thing to say.

Keeler didn't say anything, letting Chet understand that more information was required.

Chet said, "Rodriguez had to take them to dinner, like a diplomatic thing between Operations and the spooks. The Egyptian came with the spooks. The man wanted to eat frogs legs and snails I guess, like what you do when you come to France. What else is there, cheese? I was along for the trip, you know, riding shotgun for the boss."

"Did he like his frogs?"

"Oh yeah, the guy vacuumed that shit up. Drank a bottle of red wine just by himself. The CIA guys didn't imbibe and me and the boss drank beer."

"You didn't talk about the job I guess."

"No sir."

"Uh huh."

That dim light that had begun in the back of Keeler's mind was now flashing strobes at him. He blinked once, looking at Chet. "Excuse me a minute."

KEELER TOOK the stairs two at a time, without spilling the mug of coffee held fast in each of his hands. He stacked one cup onto the other and opened the door to Neilson's room with his free hand. The man was lying in bed, eyes open staring right at him.

Keeler said, "Rise and shine brother."

Neilson came up to a seated position and took the cup. "Thanks. I was in a dream man. Fog and stuff on a mountain, Taliban country. Remember Chapman up on Robert's Ridge, right?"

Keeler hadn't known Chapman personally, a pararescue combat controller who had gone above and beyond to bring the fight to the enemy on his own, even when his comrades had been put down.

He said, "Show me that picture you guys have of the target fifteen years ago or whatever, and the photo of him now."

Neilson sipped coffee, looked over the lip of his mug. "Right now?"

Keeler found his eyes were fixed on Neilson in a vacant murderous stare, how a lion looks at an antelope chewing grass, fixated on the feed and unaware of the impending fate.

Neilson's mouth had dropped open. "Okay, man. Relax."

Keeler said, "It isn't the time for relaxation Neilson. Get your shit in gear."

Neilson pushed the bed covers away, revealing hairy blonde appendages protruding from boxer shorts. He leap frogged onto his stool and set the mug of coffee down on the makeshift desk. Fingers flew across several keyboards, as other fingers and thumbs slid, clicked, and tapped at mouse buttons and trackpads. Pretty soon there were two images side by side on a large screen. One of a young man in his twenties, a headshot taken with an old film camera and scanned, the grain pleasing to the eye. The other was a recent photograph of the middle-aged guy holding a plastic carrier bag. He was in a mall, maybe some place in the Expo Center if the pic was recent. The image flat and textureless, desaturated, the angle coming from above, indicating a screen grab from a CCTV camera network.

Neilson said, "What do you think?"

Keeler pointed at the recent photograph. "We're up on their network feeds?"

Neilson flicked fingers over his controls and a live feed came up.

"We're inside their feeds yeah." Neilson showed the images again. "What about the resemblance?"

Now he saw that the place was a food court. The older photograph showed a strong hairline. The newer one showed an attempt to comb over thinning hair. If someone said it was the same guy, Keeler figured he'd buy it. On the other hand, if someone said the opposite, he'd buy that too.

He said, "Hard to tell."

"Yeah. That's what I thought too."

Keeler said, "Actually it's impossible to tell, not from those pictures."

Neilson said, "You've got a point there pal, the physiognomy changes. It's a big issue with facial, exactly why we're going for other biometrics now."

They both knew that a facial recognition match between a man in his twenties and one in his forties was worthless, easily a false positive.

Keeler said, "Let me guess, we've got no original DNA to match."

"Correct."

Which meant that the entire operation was premised upon the testimony of an Egyptian intelligence officer on the verification team.

Keeler said, "Where's Rodriguez?"

Neilson jerked a thumb behind him. "Got his own solo room back there, end of the hall."

FIFTY-FIVE

Rodriguez was sitting on the edge of a single bed looking into a phone screen when Keeler came in. He looked up, not happily. "What?"

Keeler pulled a chair out from under the desk where it was tucked. He rotated it a hundred and eighty degrees and sat backwards, resting his arms on the back rest. He looked at the Operations Officer for a long moment, thinking about him. Rodriguez had always been solid; every time Keeler had been in a situation with him. He was strong, like all of them, but he had a good way with the higher command and knew how to deal with the spooks they'd have to deal with down range. Rodriguez was blessed with the ability to get along with assholes.

Keeler said, "Chet told me about your frog's leg dinner party with a bunch of Egyptians last night."

"Chet tell you my bra size too?"

"Allow me to take a guess?"

Rodriguez just stared at him.

Keeler said, "One of the Egyptians was some slick guy in his late thirties. Glossy black hair and probably dressed like he was late for a dictator's daughter's wedding."

"Yeah, that describes every non-bald officer in the Mukhabarat."

"The guy's a muqaddam, equivalent to a colonel in our service."

"What are you trying to prove?"

Keeler said, "You know the way I was inserted here." He pointed a finger at the sky and made a gesture like helicopter seeds coming down out of a tree.

"Yeah. They made you do a HALO jump in the rain, alone. We all wondered who you'd pissed off."

"Well, I'm beginning to realize that I've pissed off one of our Egyptian allies."

Rodriguez rolled his eyes. "Is that right?"

Keeler let out an involuntary laugh, small, but there it was. He was thinking of the French connection, trying to remember what the colonel had said about his childhood in France. He'd said that the French were pigs, but they knew how to be rich. It was a decent line.

He needed to tread carefully. If, by some miracle or curse, this colonel was involved in the verification of their target here, the mission needed to be aborted immediately. At the same time, he wasn't naïve enough to think that an operation of this magnitude would get pulled on the say so of a simple operator in a special tactics unit.

Keeler said, "I need you to listen to me with an open mind."

Rodriguez repositioned himself so his back was against the wall, legs crossed. "Yeah, go ahead."

He told Rodriguez the entire story, starting at the beginning, walking him through the episode across the Israel-Egypt border with Yasmin. He left nothing out and went into appropriate detail, slowing down when he was talking about the *mukhabarat* officer and explaining what had happened, being careful not to exaggerate the intuitive dread he felt about their mission, not wanting Rodriguez to think he was over selling it.

To his credit, the Operations Officer listened without interruption. At one point making a lip-smacking sound like he had something to say, but closing his mouth and shaking his head, he'd wait for Keeler to finish.

RODRIGUEZ WATCHED Keeler talking his story. This guy was a respected special tactics operator. He wasn't the kind to just make shit up. The PJ speaking now with force and economy. Once Keeler had finished, the chair he'd been balancing came to a rest on four legs. Keeler's eyes drilled into his, red hot daggers, or irons, something sharp hot and hard, that was for sure.

Rodriguez let some time pass before responding.

He said, "I hear that. Damn." He put a finger in his ear, wiggling it around. Looking at Keeler, liking and respecting him, but not enjoying the pressure being exerted. He said, "You think this colonel is the guy got you deployed here. For what purpose exactly?"

Keeler said, "My intuition tells me that he'd rather I end up dead for some reason, which if true doesn't bode well for your mission, *sir*."

That was a little much for Rodriguez. "Your intuition."

"The gut, what keeps us alive."

Rodriguez said, "Your gut is speaking to you, telling you that my mission is compromised, and I'm supposed to just accept that. You know this shit doesn't work that way, right?"

Keeler ignored him. "I suggest that you thoroughly audit the chain of verification. Go deep into the Egyptian side, which of them knows what, how, where and from whom. That's going to be a daunting task in itself, sir. But if you can get that squared away clean, maybe it's above board. If the Egyptians start stuttering and making excuses, you'll know it's time to walk away."

Rodriguez didn't even begin to have access to the Egyptians. *Walk away.* Keeler would certainly know that the chain of target verification was the property of CIA. Rodriguez and Keeler were present as the JSOC element. Their job was execution, not evaluation of intelligence.

He said, "Have you taken LSD, captain?"

"Excuse me sir?"

"Are you *tripping*?"

"No sir."

Rodriguez breathed deeply and got himself into a professional frame of mind. He let his inner personnel manager take over and held up his hand.

"I hear you Keeler. This is relevant. You're asking questions that I can't answer. I need to take it up the chain. But you know as well as I do this ain't going to be an easy sell, given the players."

"All you can do is walk it up the chain Rodriguez, I know."

Rodriguez said nothing. Keeler had unrealistic expectations, but that was important in a special tactics operator, a guy who you relied upon for swift action. All the same, Rodriguez was afraid that in this matter, Keeler was going to be disappointed.

He said, "I'll do that immediately. But it's going to be a private conversation if that's alright with you, *captain*."

Keeler said, "Send it up the chain, sir, we'll see what comes back and plan accordingly." He swiveled and rose out of the chair, returning it to its place.

The door closed and Rodriguez found he'd been holding his breath. Looking now at the closed door, thinking about having a guy like Keeler coming at you in the dark, knife between the teeth. Good thing he's on our side. He took a couple of deep yoga breaths.

∼

KEELER WAS outside in the yard in the rain. He had the burner out, composing a message to Ruth. The Egyptian angle was coming back at them, big time. Maybe there were repercussions for her over in Israel.

He set the call forwarding app to use a caller ID from Canada and thumbed in a message.

'Cluster. Egyptian angle getting tricky. Take Kare.'

The burner vibrated in his hand almost immediately. He hit the call button to accept.

"Yeah."

"Tell me what that means." Ruth's voice, as concise and professional as usual.

Keeler paused for several seconds. His message to Ruth had been aimed at Yasmin. Which meant that his dick had taken control of his mind, not a good thing.

He wasn't some civilian.

A member of the United States Air Force couldn't casually speak to an Israeli Mossad agent about operational matters, even if he'd worked with her in the past. It didn't matter that he liked Ruth, or that he was romantically linked to her sister. He'd made a mistake by sending that message just now. The Mossad was an allied service, but they were definitely rivals.

It would take a serious emergency to justify the kind of coordination he'd erroneously initiated.

Ruth's voice came through again, incomprehensible because the phone was down at his side.

Keeler ended the call without answering. The rain wasn't

coming down hard, it wasn't even really raining, more like a fizz in the air. The far fields were being enveloped by a white mist. Even the hedgerows at the end of the yard were softening up with it. He removed the SIM card from the burner phone and broke it in half. He couldn't find a garbage can so he just swallowed it.

FIFTY-SIX

Nof Hagalil, Israel

Hershkowitz had the team gathered at the safe house, a mile or so from Nazareth.

He pointed at a large screen. Yasmin recognized Basima and figured the photograph beside it was her brother Jafar, younger in the picture, a barely recognizable version of the man she'd seen as an infiltrator.

Hershkowitz said, "Meet the Khoury family, Basima and her brother Fares." His assistant clicked a remote, expanded the image to include the parents. He said, "The father Jirjis Khoury and his wife Mariam." Zooming back to the two siblings. Hershkowitz looked at Yasmin, speaking to her as much as to the group. "Fares Khoury made a conversion to Islam and became Jafar Amjad al-Husseini." He regarded his audience. "Very original."

Yasmin interrupted. "I don't get it. If he converted and changed his name officially, why are we only learning about him right now?" She pointed at Hershkowitz. "What about your, *whatchamacallit*, social model? What happened with that?"

The assistant said, "It happens all the time. What we do is

called *social* mapping, and it's time based, how social is a connection that's been cold for five years?"

Yasmin said, "Family ties have more potential social endurance than say, the relationship you've got with the gas station attendant. Your high-tech system is overrated, I'm surprised you rely so much upon the models."

Hershkowitz held up his hand, his assistant stopping in mid flow and shutting her mouth.

He said, "Yasmin's right." Looking at Yasmin. "Now, we deal with it. Here's what we know: Until a few years ago, Al-Husseini rented an apartment in *Sakhnin*. He was a regular at the Salah al-Din Mosque. Anyone want to take a guess at the Imam's name?"

One of the special tactics women said, "Nasrallah."

A few people laughed. Hershkowitz shook his head. Yasmin was thinking about the conversion, often the new convert adopts the name of his mentor, the man who guided him on his journey into Islam.

Yasmin said, "Amjad al-Husseini."

Hershkowitz snapped his fingers and pointed at her. "You get the Rambo medal for today. We're treating Jafar al-Husseini as a person of interest to the security services." Pointing at the special tactics team. "One team will go up to Sakhnin. I want a second team on Basima Khoury and her family." Looking at Yasmin. "The house has been searched but Basima's refusing to talk. We don't have any warrant for an interrogation, so I want you to approach her."

Yasmin didn't understand that. "Why no warrant?"

He shrugged. "There's no proof that this Jafar al-Husseini has done anything wrong. The Attorney General says we'll need to bring him into custody before we can take his relatives in."

"What am I supposed to say?"

Hershkowitz said, "I don't know, figure it out. Get her to *tell you things.*"

He pointed at the two men standing in a doorway. "You two are on the Khoury parents." He said, "There's an international dimension that we're coordinating with Mossad. The picture is going to develop fast. We'll get our warrant from the AG, but for now that's the plan."

The meeting ended, the team breaking into constituent units, Yasmin was paired with the bearded guy who'd been driving the white SUV. He gestured her over to the dining room table, unloading a tactical backpack. Which, among other things, contained a weapon for Yasmin, a Masada 9mm handgun snug in a belt clip holster. She checked the gun and the two seventeen round magazines that came with it.

The man said, "Obviously you're there for the relational part with the sister. I'm just the dumb guy backing you up."

"The relational part isn't going to succeed, but I'll try."

"That's all we can ever do."

Yasmin said, "And I'm sure you're smarter than you look."

The guy laughed. "Thanks."

THE SUV DESCENDED at an acute angle, nose down. Yasmin felt like she was going to fall out of the vehicle, body straining at the seat belt. The guy at the wheel said, "Driving around here is crazy."

Meaning it was extremely hilly, even more so than the rest of the Galilee. Getting from Nof Hagalil to Nazareth, you went up and down huge hills. Looking at her companion, bearded guy in his thirties with good hair and a pair of designer sunglasses pushed back. He would have been in some kind of special unit during his army service, before getting the gig on Hershkowitz's team.

He said, "I'm Eitan."

"Yasmin."

"I know."

There was traffic on the main road, so he got cute and started navigating side streets. He hit the gas hard going up a narrow street at an almost vertical angle and the sunglasses fell into the backseat. "Shit." Eitan said, reaching his arm around in a failed attempt to snatch them.

At a more reasonable gradient, Yasmin unclipped her seat belt and went hunting for the sunglasses. A moped whine nearby made her glance out the rearview window. Two kids on a bike, pulling in from a side street, revving because of the sudden gradient.

She got back into the passenger seat and clipped in the seat belt, putting Eitan's sunglasses in a dashboard compartment. She said, "Keep them here for now."

He said, "Sure."

Ten minutes later they were coming up a winding road towards Basima's house. Eitan had the address programmed into his phone, navigating and driving at the same time.

He said, "We're almost there. After the intersection it'll be the next left, house is middle of the block right side."

Yasmin wasn't sure if she was supposed to do something with this information. The neighborhood was quiet, cars parked on either side of the road, other cars in motion. People waited at a bus stop. Coming up to the intersection, the light turned red. The slope wasn't insane but Eitan put the car in neutral and pulled the handbrake.

An old guy with a cane crossed the road. He moved slowly, almost painfully so.

Yasmin heard the whine of a moped engine and saw movement in the right side of her peripheral vision. Turning her head, seeing movement in the mirror. Eitan made a sound, between a grunt and cough. She turned her head all the way, looking almost behind her. Through the windows she saw the moped, very close, just to her right, the rider shimmying the bike through the narrow gap between the SUV and the parked cars.

Initially, it was just annoying teenagers on a motorcycle. But the bike was right there in her face, the kid riding pillion wearing a black tracksuit top with a stripe down the sleeve, his hands were gloved and gripping a handgun, the weapon up and barrel coming level. Yasmin perceived it as a flash of images, each one focused and isolated. The dark bore of the weapon. The two boys on the bike, faces behind mirrored visors.

She saw her distorted self-reflected in the visor. The kid pulled the trigger and the car window between them shattered.

The next moments passed without clear images, more like a stuttering strobe light in a darkness roiling with frenzied activity, where you can only half see what's going on. A hand reached in and grabbed at the lock switch on the inside of the door. Yasmin realized they were trying to get in the car. More gun shots, movement again to her right. She was reaching behind her for the handgun, clipped into the belt at her hip. The door opened and hands reached in, fingers grabbing at her, clutching onto clothing and yanking. She couldn't even tell how many hands, but it felt like many. The seatbelt kept her in.

The weapon came free. Yasmin, managed to throw herself back at Eitan, slamming against his body. She freed her legs from the foot well, getting a boot up to deliver a hard kick at one of the intruders as he came in trying to unlock her seatbelt. The kid lost balance, and she had the weapon up, pulling the first time and finding the trigger tough. The second pull was easier, the explosive gas helping get the firing pin fully cocked. Both rounds were true, one hitting him in the side, around the rib cage, the second round taking him under the edge of the helmet, where jaw meets neck.

Eitan, was having his own issues, she could only register a partial impression. Feeling his body against hers, struggling and fighting. She heard at least one more gunshot before hands were on her, and she lost the pistol. Struggling but powerless to resist the people pulling her out of the vehicle. At least three of them ripping her free and grabbing at her from all directions, containing her struggle.

A heavy thing like a fist struck her in the mouth, knocking her senseless. The next thing she was aware of was the hood shoved over her head. She was hit again in the cheek and a vertiginous moment later her face met the hard asphalt. Yasmin tasted blood and felt fragments of tooth against her tongue.

3
ADAPTATION

FIFTY-SEVEN

P*ARIS, France*

The colonel was sitting on a bench in the *Jardin des Tuileries*, slitting a baguette down the middle with his thumb nails. He'd done a decent surveillance detection route and ended up here after making sure that the CIA handlers weren't on his back. In fact, they seemed calm and friendly. He just had to assume that they were suspicious.

The Tuileries was also calm and pleasant, a tourist site that was large enough to do the job and remain peaceful. Women and children and ducks in the little pond, Frenchmen and other men. Old Europe, where they'd used their hundreds of years of massacre and bloodletting to buy some decades of peace.

Looking around at the tourists, the colonel was certain it wouldn't last. This wasn't any place to escape to. Which was one reason why the colonel had contacted a Russian FSB officer he'd met in Cairo during the negotiation over purchasing Tor-M1 air defense systems.

His message had been blunt and to the point. 'Good morning. I'm in Paris and require a clandestine meeting with one of your colleagues.'

The return message had been equally perfunctory. 'Tuileries, 2pm tomorrow.'

Hopefully Anastasia would appreciate his initiative. The colonel had a feeling that Cairo was not going to be a safe place for him for much longer. He was simply too afraid of rejection to ask her directly.

He spread the halves of the baguette and inserted wedges of Camembert cheese that he'd bought from a fancy *fromagerie*. He layered in two slices of French ham and closed the completed assembly into a sandwich. You could get a lot of goodies to eat in Cairo, but you couldn't get this for under a hundred bucks.

In Moscow you could eat caviar.

Studying the thing before taking a bite. Once you begin, it's hard to stop. Like war.

The human brain is a funny thing. You only slowly begin to realize what you are, what you've been doing, what you've become. The idea of a plan turns out to have been ridiculous, *the big plan*, even more so.

The thing with Anastasia had been weird from the start, but that was only possible to understand in hindsight. The colonel remembered the first time. Anastasia in a resort in Sharm El-Sheikh. She'd been there at the bar, choosing him, so he thought. Of course, she did.

Now that he thought about it, she managed to get information out of him even then, that first night. He'd used his status in the mukhabarat to impress her. She'd started calling him 'my colonel', and he liked that.

And he *had* liked that.

It had felt like sharing. He'd never married, so he had no confidante, just himself in his solitude. And then Anastasia, two years ago. At what point do you become a traitor? Probably at exactly the same point that you dedicate your allegiance to

Anastasia.

Now here he was in Paris. It felt cold here, like the kind of place where you just die. He felt very far away from home.

The flight from El-Gora had been direct to Wiesbaden Germany, an American airbase. He'd come into France on a TGV train. This was the European Union, no papers necessary, except for a German ID card with an Algerian alias that the Americans had given him, just in case.

The Americans were organized. He'd never seen anything like it, the little he was able to see. The Egyptian role had been target verification. Which made sense. The intelligence had come from the mukhabarat. Well, it had specifically been handed to the colonel by the major, and probably negotiated with the Americans beforehand by the general.

His job had been to physically deliver the goods. And then in their safe house he'd been the one to verify the target. The Americans had multiple video feeds going. An entire room of the apartment had been dedicated to screens and boxes and cables and pelican cases. The CIA men were very good at typing.

They'd shown him the images, and he'd verified them on behalf of the Egyptian mukhabarat. Not that he'd ever seen this Iranian guy before, he was just running through the paces, doing exactly what he'd been told to do.

The Americans had been watching him, looking at him and probably making some kind of guess, or projection of what was going on in his brain. The idiots didn't see through the disguise. He'd nodded wisely.

"Yes, that's definitely our man."

The CIA men had moved into action, happy now. Making calls and tapping their machines.

Their structure was highly compartmentalized, each team in its own orbit, linked only by intermediaries, like the Operations Officer he'd taken to dinner. He'd tried getting the man drunk the night before, but the American had kept the conversation away from professional matters, him, and his underling. The two Americans had been a little disturbed by the frog's legs in cream sauce.

The colonel ate slowly, watching the ducks. The cheese was creamy and rich with notes of mushroom sliding nicely against the ham's sweetness. A young man in jogging clothes stopped near the colonel's bench. He was panting, sucking from a water bottle with a built-in handle.

The man nodded at the colonel and grinned. He spoke in French.

"Good afternoon colonel."

THE RUSSIAN SAT down on the bench. He was sweating profusely and looked way too happy for the occasion.

He said, "So what can I do for you?"

The colonel said, "I want to be brought in. Cairo isn't safe for me anymore. I think they know."

The man nodded, sort of to himself. He glanced at the colonel. "Know about what?"

"About me and you." The colonel was a little surprised, suddenly feeling exposed. "You know."

The man widened his eyes. "Actually, I don't. I don't have any idea about me and you. We've only just met. I'm here because you requested a meeting. Sorry, a *clandestine* meeting."

The colonel said, "I should have gone through my case officer. You're not briefed on the situation, obviously. Probably above your pay grade."

The man nodded. "Yes, that's most likely the case." He stood up. "Have a good day colonel."

He watched the man jog away, looking carefree. Which is exactly the opposite of how the colonel felt. He felt like not only an idiot, but a soon to be dead idiot. It was only occurring to him now that Anastasia might not be Russian at all.

And if that was true, what was she? Who had he been supplying with information for two years? The colonel realized that it didn't matter. He'd go wherever she told him to go, but maybe he'd screwed up and she wasn't going to be happy at all.

FIFTY-EIGHT

It was no accident that Rodriguez had been promoted to Colonel. Neither was it coincidence that he had reliably served as JSOC Task Force Commander on dozens of missions, with notable exceptions, like the current mission, which was being led by CIA.

So, when he considered how to handle the hot potato that Keeler had thrown at him, he did so in a methodical way, running his thought processes through frameworks that he'd studied and absorbed, and sometimes even taught to others in regular stints at Fort Bragg. He even got sent down to Fort Benning occasionally and had been a guest speaker up at West Point twice.

Thinking about the Egyptian intelligence officer whom Keeler had run into, sort of coincidentally, or at least luckily. Keeler had thrown shade on the overall intelligence picture. He had argued that there was no such thing as a coincidence. He'd looked deep into Rodriguez's eyes and asked him if he'd ever seen a combat related coincidence.

Rodriguez had said, "What do you call it, if it's not a coincidence."

Keeler said, "Shit that happens."

The *shit happens* framework, a theory which Rodriguez had read somewhere and remembered agreeing with at the time. Which left him a little torn.

He'd promised Keeler that he'd bark up the chain to the Task Force Commander. But he wasn't entirely sure what to tell him. The guy was a senior CIA officer who knew the president personally. Rodriguez corrected himself, the former president. Whatever.

The Task Force Commander wasn't going to enjoy hearing this, but Rodriguez decided he'd have to hear it anyway.

THE TASK FORCE COMMANDER had a similar problem, but different.

His problem was similar because he too had to run the risk of pissing off a superior who wasn't going to like either the questions or any bad news arising from them. The differences were a little worse than the similarities. The main difference being that as a senior CIA officer, he was a couple of years deep into the relationship with this group of Egyptian intelligence officers in question.

He had a major role in the cultivation of *Kaleidoscope,* the covert operation to run a stealth regime change in Egyptian intelligence. He was committed to the mission of changing the Egyptian military culture for the better. That'd make better allies and a better world. The Task Force Commander was a believer. The other thing was that he answered directly to the CIA Director.

The conversation wasn't going to be easy.

Despite all that, he felt obliged to pass the information up the chain. If he got sunk as a consequence that was the price you paid for being professional.

All the same, a vaguely articulated thought did pass through his mind. The target was traveling under the alias of a dissident Iranian journalist based out of Istanbul. But he'd never seen photographs of the dissident journalist. The Egyptians had said the guy had gone to ground, living in fear of his life because of a fatwa. Consequently, there hadn't been any photographs of him taken since he'd gone into hiding.

THE CIA DIRECTOR was a political appointee who was losing his job. He'd be out of there on January 20th, regardless of anything else that might happen. His replacement had to get through senate confirmation hearings, but the incoming administration weren't waiting for that, they were already swarming over the executive suites at Langley, taking measurements and making plans with interior designers. The deeper levels of the bureaucratic institution itself were bracing for the shit storm, entrenching themselves and preparing to endure whatever attacks the deplorables were planning on mounting.

He recalled the zoom call with Tel Aviv, having enjoyed Ambassador Chambers' discomfort when Vicky Neuman tore him a new asshole. He listened to the Task Force Commander patiently, watching the man's face on his laptop screen. The Task Force Commander was adroit and adaptable and used information as a weapon.

On the other hand, the CIA Director knew at least one thing that his annoyingly competent subordinate didn't.

He knew that this Air Force PJ guy Keeler's participation had been an exceptional Egyptian demand. Exceptional because the Egyptian asset had threatened to abort the mission if the request hadn't been fulfilled. It'd been the Undersecretary of State for Politics who had ultimately signed off, arguing that the choice of a trigger man was always going to be sensitive.

The CIA Director was going home regardless, given the regime change in Washington. So, he didn't mind tossing the problem back to Vicky Neuman, not only the mastermind of this pet project, but the one who'd approved the extortionate request for this Keeler guy anyway.

∽

Neuman listened to the CIA director without interrupting. When he'd finished talking, she had only one question. "What are the options, Trevor?"

She was in her home office with a large tumbler of Blanton's bourbon, having been woken from a wonderful slumber a half hour earlier. The CIA director was a face on her laptop's screen surrounded by darkness, a single framed painting illuminated behind his head, looking like a portrait of a child, maybe a Gainsborough reproduction.

Trevor had done some blah blah, and then he'd done some fast talking. Now he was hemming and hawing and pouring himself a glass of Baileys, a liquid that Neuman was not amenable to drinking.

He said, "Two options that immediately present themselves ma'am. We go ahead with it or we don't. Breaking out the latter option we are either walking away from disaster or success, but we'll never know because it won't happen. Breaking out the first option, we get to actually *experience* either disaster or success, with only regret or jubilation as a result."

Neuman laughed. She took a hit of the Blanton's, letting the bourbon roll nicely over her tongue.

"You're so full of shit Trevor, I actually admire that in you."

"Thank you, ma'am."

"Alright you shit, I'll put it another way. What are the stakes if we screw up and the target isn't who the Egyptians claim he is?"

The CIA Director lowered the glass from his face. The Baileys had left a faint cream-colored mustache on his upper lip. He shrugged, "We wipe out some guy in Paris and the French get the message. Everything goes like it would have if the target had been kosher, except the dead guy doesn't mean shit to anyone who counts."

Even less of a stink than if they were successful. Not a bad outcome.

She said, "And we're back to hunting Tabrizi, even though it's not us doing it, it's the deplorables who get a second bite at the cherry."

The CIA director said, "That's another possibility."

Neuman said, "On the other hand if it works, we're the ones who got revenge for Karbala. We take out Tabrizi and in four years we're back on message with a major covert success for the presidential nominee to brag about in wonderfully vague terms."

He said, "You'll be there Vick, I don't have the slightest doubt about that."

"Not you?"

"Not me."

Neuman said, "What's the timeline?"

He said, "It's tight. They need a decision within the next hour, the mission is at a critical point."

She said, "Not enough time to really untangle this problem if it's something real. We won't get to the bottom of it within the hour, so we're just shooting in the dark, Trevor."

The CIA Director said nothing. Looking at her with that sharp-eyed squint. The Clint Eastwood thing that had gotten him up the political ladder. Neuman wasn't going to let him dictate timing, she waited.

He said, "They'll never tell us anyway, even if that *Mukhabarat* officer Al-Masri isn't kosher." He shrugged. "Worst-case scenario The Egyptians will shoot him in the head and dump him somewhere. Thing about Egypt is, problems don't come back to haunt you. They just get disappeared."

Neuman said, "I'll get back to you."

She killed the connection and shut the laptop, putting her weight on the chair's arms to relieve the pressure in her knees. She retrieved her glass and finished it. Turning to the door and walking through it, passing from home office to landing. She went down the stairs carefully and took a right to the kitchen, a room the size of most people's houses. Her husband Bob had an apron on, surprisingly.

She said, "What are you doing?"

"Making pancakes."

Neuman looked at the oven clock. "At two forty-two in the morning?"

Bob looked up. "Yeah, I got hungry since you weren't coming back to bed."

The kitchen was well equipped, and Bobby loved the copper pots and pans. He was running flour through a fancy sieve, Neuman figured it was supposed to avoid the stuff clumping in the batter. The oddly shaped bottle of Blanton's was on the marble counter. She fetched a tumbler and poured her husband a couple of fingers. When he'd downed it, she poured another and told him about the situation.

Bob was a political philosopher, and he liked to mix pears and apples in a compote together with brown sugar, butter, and a little lemon. The pancakes were perfect. Crunchy and thick but fluffy and light inside. The compote didn't need any whipped cream, but Bobby did scatter fresh blueberries when he plated his creations.

High end bourbon and pancakes, with a side of high stakes political intrigue. Three in the morning and here they were, living the dream.

Bob chewed with his mouth closed, lost in thought. He speared a blueberry and put it in through fleshy lips. Chewing, Neuman knew, twenty-two times before swallowing.

Bob said, "Do you remember the Red Prince?"

"No."

Bob licked his fork. "It was called the Lillehammer affair. 1973. The Israelis were going after the perpetrators of the Munich Olympics. Lillehammer's this town in Norway where they accidentally killed a Moroccan waiter instead of this guy they were after, the Red Prince, Palestinian terrorist name of *Salameh*. Worse than that, the Mossad agents were caught."

Neuman said, "So what happened in the end?"

Bob shrugged. "The waiter died; the Norwegians got pissed off. The Israelis had to suck it for a while, but they got their guys back after a year."

"And what does that teach us, Bobby?"

He ate a big forkful of pancake, clearly relishing the delicacy, sitting there with his plaid wool pajamas on under the apron, the man she loved. He said, "We're not the Israelis, and the French aren't the Norwegians."

She said, "Meaning no way one of ours would set foot in a French prison, even if everything were to go radically sideways."

He nodded. "Don't ever forget that we're the United States of America and they're all just a bunch of pissants in comparison. Geopolitically we're untouchable babe. Go for it."

Neuman nodded. "Right. What's the worst thing that could happen?"

Bobby giggled and cut into another pancake. "The worst thing that could happen already happened; you're getting a four-year vacation from government."

FIFTY-NINE

They'd run through the job sixteen times on the virtual reality set. This was the final pass before they did it in *real* reality, the way Keeler explained it to himself. Not that the VR looked fake, it looked amazing, but it wasn't real.

Three of them sitting there with the VR headsets on and a handheld device that you used for moving around in the virtual world. Visuals in the headsets were accompanied by audio. Neilson sat next to him, monitoring the session on his laptop, which is pretty much what he'd do on the operation.

The simulation started in the hotel's parking lot. The lighting was realistic and appropriate for time of day, season, and projected weather forecast. Keeler rode in the backseat, Chet driving and Billings up front in the passenger seat. Chet parked the car, and they came out of the vehicle, moving across the lot towards the hotel entrance, pace automatically calculated on the fly, the move more a drift than a walk.

Keeler didn't need to look to the left, because after sixteen simulations he knew that the group of three military aged guests in tennis outfits by the benches were part of the reconnaissance team. Him, Chet, and Billings walked into the building, the infiltration route already cleared and established. He didn't know if the hotel staff at the counter were occupied with a distraction team, but that wouldn't have surprised him.

The walk to the elevator bank was calculated at exactly thirteen strides across carpet. He was thinking, you don't trip over untied shoelaces in a 3D model, or a small renegade lapdog. A force protection team mingled with the civilian lobby traffic, their movements timed to Keeler's team, the precise choreography conducted in real time by an operator whose job was to coordinate observations from Neilson and his counterparts on the other teams.

The ride up to the fifth floor plus the doors opening took 6.5 seconds because there hadn't been any stops along the way. The last run through had taken more than half a minute because of two stops. Factors like that were randomized in the model.

The elevator doors opened. Fifth floor, a blonde woman in her mid-forties was lingering with a Prada shopping bag. Another team member, this one from recon. At the other end of the corridor was a second reconnaissance operative. The target's room was three quarters of the way down, number 230.

Chet took the lead. Walking calmly across the carpeting. Keeler tilted his head down and saw the paisley motif. A maid emerged from a room on the left, pushing a cleaning cart. The second reconnaissance agent began moving to deal with her. Chet arrived at the door.

Chet said, "You guys make sure you're not walking too close to me."

Neither Billings nor Keeler responded to his remark.

In the virtual world Chet moved the door key close to the lock mechanism. The latch snicked. Two seconds later they were inside a simulation of the room. The door clicked closed, Chet hanging back while Keeler moved past him, and Billings followed. The suite had two sections, the entrance with bathroom and a sitting area, and the master bedroom with a king-sized bed, desk, dresser for clothes and a couple of sofas in floral print.

Chet's voice over the communications system said, "Absolution."

A remote voice said, "Roger."

Neilson said, "Proceed."

In the model the simulated hotel room was empty, nobody in it. The killing wasn't going to be played out in the virtual world. As far as the simulated sequence was concerned, it was simply *assumed* to have happened.

Plus, they didn't have to wait the estimated three minutes it was going to take to kill the guy. The screen blinked and Keeler found himself crouched by the king-sized bed, where he was going to end up after suffocating Tabrizi with a pillow. He turned, seeing Billings' avatar, Chet standing behind her by the door.

Chet's voice over the communications system said, "Clearance."

A remote voice said, "Roger."

Neilson said, "Proceed."

Chet opened the door. Keeler followed Billings. Two men were at the end of the hall near the elevator bank.

Neilson said, "Proceed."

The two civilians were in their 60s, waiting for the elevator. Not your classic military aged males, someone who might play on the red team. The light above the doors blinked as the elevator reached the fifth floor. Keeler, Chet, and Billings lingered. In a situation like that you'd look at your phone, or just hang out. Waiting for an elevator wasn't the most suspicious activity, just socially weird sometimes.

The civilians were procedurally generated in this model. Keeler didn't know what that meant exactly, just that nobody decided if they'd show up or not, they were generated randomly by the machine, supposedly as unpredictable as life.

There were two elevators. The civilians entered one on the left and it took another ten seconds for the other one to arrive. The ride down took 21.4 seconds on account of a stop at the third floor. A woman entered the elevator, riding with them to the lobby.

Billings said, "That's going to be awkward."

Chet laughed.

After sixteen and a half run-throughs, a slight ache had developed at the middle of Keeler's forehead from the headset.

Neilson said, "Activity outside. Proceed."

Neither Keeler nor Billings asked what activity was outside, it wasn't their role to know about it. Their only task was to leave.

The scene in the carpeted lobby adjusted, in terms of motion. Civilian avatars moved at their usual, random speed, some hurrying, others getting in the way. The force protection team's movements gave the computer generated atmosphere a weird, edgy vibe. Crossing the carpet took the same amount of time as before.

A remote voice said, "Engaging."

Neilson said, "Proceed."

Three steps out of the hotel door Keeler understood the issue, looking left, seeing three avatars in French police uniform jogging across the grass. What were they doing there, random, or connected?

Neilson said, "Proceed."

The reconnaissance team in tennis gear were in motion, exchanging places with the force protection team, adjusting to the current situation. Keeler was looking straight ahead, seeing a vehicle parked at the other side of the walkway, blocking their exfiltration route.

He said, "On my 12, vehicle."

A remote voice said, "Noted."

Neilson said, "Proceed."

Chet and Billings continued moving forward towards the vehicle. From behind him, Keeler heard a flurry of thick metallic sounds. Silenced weapons pumping lead into French police officers, radical. Up ahead, three men coming out of the vehicle that Keeler had spotted. One of them moving to his right, two others approaching.

Neilson didn't say anything.

Keeler kept moving, following his teammates. Up ahead the men from the car continued getting closer. None of them were holding weapons, but that could change fast. He anticipated what might happen. The guy in front would be first, the sniper would probably go for a head shot. The others would follow quickly, crumpling like rag dolls to the ground. It didn't happen, the men kept on coming, someone had decided they were civilians. Maybe it was someone's birthday.

A silver Renault van pulled to the curb. Chet and Billings climbed into the back. Keeler kept on walking, arriving at another corner in the parking lot. A tan four-door Renault Clio. Keeler got into the passenger seat and Rodriguez pulled the vehicle away from the curb.

Keeler took off the headset. Billings had gotten a little sweaty and red in the face. Chet sucked coke out of a cup with a straw. Rodriguez had brought lunch from Burger King.

Keeler wasn't happy about the model they were using. He didn't like the fact that they skipped over the killing itself. It wasn't a huge deal, but it would have been better to add in some realism at that point in the sequence. People did all kinds of dumb shit when they were under pressure. Leave a latex glove on the floor, some other neglected item. Billings was looking at Keeler and he figured she felt the same way.

It was a team effort, in a big way. But everyone knew which two of them were going to kill the man in the hotel room. Actually, it was going to be one of them, Keeler. He'd never done it like that, premeditated and everything, hitting a guy who didn't pose an imminent danger. Rationalizing, the guy might deserve to die in an abstract way, but actually killing him wasn't going to be an intellectual exercise.

He said, "If we were going to shoot the guy in the head, would this thing model it?" Spinning the virtual reality headset on the table with a finger.

Neilson said, "Yeah."

Billings said, "Creative limits of the machine."

Rodriguez's phone bleeped in interesting ways. He brought the screen to bear and looked into it, squinting, and tapping a couple of times and staring more.

Neilson said, "It's not a limit of the machine, Billings, they just decided not to model it."

Nobody said anything because they all knew exactly why the killing wasn't being modeled.

Because it's not pleasant to look at. Those virtual sessions were recorded and reviewed by commanders in the military and intelligence services, plus the random senator or cabinet secretary. For that reason, the videos were sanitized.

Rodriguez put the phone down. Made eye contact with Keeler and shook his head, like no dice, the message had been up the chain of command and back and nobody was willing to give credence to Keeler's concerns. Keeler raised his chin a half inch in acknowledgment. The operation was on, but even if the game was a trap, he wasn't going to let his teammates fall into it without him.

Keeler leaned against Neilson, nudging him with an elbow.

Neilson said, "What?"

Keeler said, "Nothing."

But he meant more than nothing. Even if Rodriguez and the command above him weren't interested in the paranoid rantings of an experienced special operations officer, Keeler had no intention of showing up on the battlefield a hundred percent unprepared for disaster. Eighty percent unprepared was bad enough, but it was better than total blindness.

SIXTY

Neilson was sitting back on his single bed. Hairy blonde legs poking out of shorts. He was shaking his head and smiling, fingers stroking the mustache.

Keeler had just given him pretty much the same story he'd told to Rodriguez. He'd incorporated a couple of learning points and made adjustments. In any case, the narrative was solid. He could tell that from the mustache stroking. That was Neilson's tell right there.

Neilson cursed. "So…" he raised eyebrows. "They denied the appeal from the grunt on the ground, as usual."

"Correct."

"Interesting." Neilson scooted up and addressed the computers, tapping and swiping and doing knob turning types of actions. One of the screens in front of him displayed a dark stretch of road. "Check this out brother. It's from last night."

Keeler said, "That's the road out there?" Pointing towards the driveway.

"Right. I didn't make anything of it at the time. But take a look."

The screen showing the road, now blossomed with the twin lights of an approaching vehicle out of the dark.

Neilson said, "That's Rodriguez and Chet coming back from their outing."

The Peugeot 206 came past, showing dents in the infrared picture. Twenty seconds later another vehicle came into view, moving slowly. Neilson switched something on one of the boxes in front of him. The angle changed, another camera. The same vehicle moving past the driveway and then accelerating.

Keeler said, "Rodriguez is being followed, the tail slows down and then takes off after making the location."

Neilson was fiddling again. He said, "That's how it looks now, after what you've told me." He looked at Keeler, shaking his head like everything was ironic. "Last night it just looked like someone slowing down. Happens once in a while. I traced a couple of them. Both times it was a local who I figure knows the place, maybe wondering what kind of tourist rents it out this time of year."

Keeler said, "What about this car?"

Neilson was nodding. "I bounced it through the system. Belongs to a leasing company in Paris. I stopped there. But let's go deeper now."

He switched into another screen. Keeler could read French perfectly, as could Neilson. This was the Automated License Plate Recognition, the ALPR database. Keeler leaned in. The vehicle was registered to a leasing company out of a western Paris suburb. The vehicle had been leased two months previously, with the contract set to end in a week.

Keeler said, "That's a decent amount of prep time, if you were juggling a hundred eggs. Can you get into their records and find out who took out the vehicle."

"It's a holding company out of Belgium."

Neilson clicked and dragged, switched into other

applications, and entered keystrokes in furious bursts. Keeler was able to basically follow along. He was inside the French police Vehicle Tracking system.

Neilson said, "They use the ALPR database so that law enforcement users can make *pattern of life* maps. Basically, showing them where the vehicles go." He fiddled and fussed, bringing up a map with lines tracing where this vehicle had been.

Keeler leaned forward, trying to figure out what he was looking at. A map of the Paris region, with pink lines indicating the vehicle's path. It looked like a game of cat's cradle, except there were some lines that were much thicker than others.

He said, "They can't watch it in real time because there isn't any tracker on the car. What they can do is pick up the vehicle on traffic cameras, CCTV, security, dash cams." He looked at Keeler. "Shit like that. They collate the data and smooth it into a path. The thick lines are the more routine pathways."

Keeler leaned in, looking the spidery lines moving in and out of well-worn routes in and around the Paris area.

Neilson said, "This particular Ford Focus has a simple pattern of life. It rested most nights in an underground garage in *Bercy*." He studied the screen for a minute. "Mostly it isn't in use actually." He leaned in. Pointing and tracing. "There you can see them going out to the *Marne La Vallée Expo Center*. Parking on the north side."

He looked at Keeler, eyebrows raised.

Keeler said, "Bingo."

Neilson was looking at him. He said, "Egyptians?"

Keeler said, "I don't know who they are. Do you have a GPS tracker we can deploy?"

"Sure."

"So, let's go get up in their shit tonight. Put a tracker on that Ford. If something pops off, we'll know where to find them."

Neilson nodded. "Just us, without telling the others, or Rodriguez."

Keeler said, "Correct."

Neilson was watching him carefully. A good man making up his mind to take initiative against the wishes of command. Neilson's brows kind of creased and came together. His mustache wiggled and the corners of his mouth curled up.

"Let's do it."

SIXTY-ONE

It was a two-hour drive to Paris.

Keeler had the wheel, letting the Peugeot puff along at its comfortable speed. Neilson fooled with the radio, getting up a French rap station that Keeler was initially averse to. Thing was, he could understand the lyrics, and they weren't all that bad. By the time they arrived in the big city he wasn't actively hating the music.

Neilson had Keeler stop the vehicle under a twisting tangle of highway overpasses. The no-man's-land areas were packed with migrant tents, fires burning and human activity flourishing in there. Currently it was too dark to make out more than silhouettes.

Keeler said, "Why stop here?"

Neilson was busy with his laptop. "Oh, it's the same everywhere in Paris," he said. He tapped and swiped at the computer. "The vehicle's out in the 16th arrondissement."

All the way on the west side of the city.

Keeler said, "Let's go there."

"Okay."

Keeler piloted the vehicle through the narrow Parisian

streets, following the Seine and ending up in the rich part of town, on a tree-lined street with luxurious old apartment buildings on one side and the *Bois de Boulogne* on the other, a large park.

Neilson had him cruise slowly, looking into his laptop. The road was straight alongside the park, each block had a turn out for parking in front of the old buildings.

Neilson said, "Last traffic camera picked them up here." He looked up, pointing into one of the parking inlets. "Pull into that one."

Keeler pulled in and cruised slowly. He saw the vehicle at the same time as Neilson did.

Neilson said, "That's it."

The Ford Focus was a family sized vehicle in white.

Keeler accelerated past the vehicle and had to park on a smaller street around the corner. They walked back and examined the situation.

Keeler said, "Let's take a walk."

Since they'd driven up from one direction, they strolled in the other, eventually coming to an obvious destination. Set into the park was a circular drive on a slight incline. A night club, with a baby blue neon sign over the entrance declaring *Les Sauvages*.

Keeler giggled. "Classy." He said, "You go in and poke around, get your phone recording and find them. Let's see if my guy's in there."

Neilson laughed. "We can do better than that."

Ten minutes later, Keeler was sitting in the Peugeot looking at a tablet screen. He'd found a closer parking spot with a view to the entrance of *Les Sauvages*. Neilson was in the club with a description of the Egyptian colonel. At first, he'd simply ordered a scotch on the rocks, walking around with his undetectable body cam. They had a closed-circuit comms situation going as well.

Neilson's voice was coming through the bud in Keeler's left ear. "Check this out."

The video feed wasn't grainy, or low resolution like it might have been five years previously. Now it was high end, sharp as a tack and in full color. The club had a main space that Neilson was walking through. A dance floor where willowy shaped women gyrated under the attentive gaze of men in open collared shirts and hairstyles that had lost their shape with the evening's extracurricular activities. Around the periphery of the club were tables. Neilson did a thorough patrol. Couples, groups of men and women. Normal rich people having a good time.

Neilson said, "Main area. No obviously Egyptian looking people in sight."

Keeler said, "Go deeper buddy."

"Roger that."

Neilson cruised the club, another large space with a table at the end with four middle eastern looking men. "What about these guys?"

Keeler said, "Show me."

Neilson lingered, leaning in, and making small talk. Keeler was looking at Rolexes and French hairstyles. He certainly wasn't looking at the colonel.

He said, "I don't think so."

Neilson said, "They weren't speaking Arabic anyway."

A corridor accessed the back area. The video showing a bouncer, black guy, built like an MMA fighter, which he probably was. The guy was polite enough.

"No entry monsieur, couples only."

A statement that Neilson replied to with grace. He went back to the bar and ordered a scotch.

Keeler said, "Get in there."

Neilson said, "Yup."

He was a good-looking man, with a blonde mustache and a natural wave in his hair, like a surfer. Back in the day Keeler had seen him in action, somewhere in the Keys, if he remembered correctly. Neilson wasn't a big *approacher*. The other guys always liked seeing him get attention.

He went for the dance floor.

Keeler couldn't see him, but he could tell from the body cam's jiggling that Neilson was actually dancing. The willowy women from before weren't interested, maybe Neilson didn't look rich enough. But he did manage to get attention. It took a half hour to work the magic but work it he did.

Neilson said, "I don't think this is a regular club."

Given the back-room protection, there was a possibility that he was correct.

Keeler said, "Sex club."

The bouncer stepped aside.

Now, the decor turned red and dark. The camera adjusted. Keeler was looking at dark wood paneled corridors and flooring. Either side were private rooms. Everything tastefully decorated and comfortable, the floors covered in pillows and other soft looking objects. Truth be told, Keeler wasn't paying much attention to that because the human activity was way more interesting.

He could hear Neilson's voice through the earbud, deflecting the woman's requests with panache, making sure to do that tour, staying on mission. Keeler didn't envy him; the job was tough. Neilson worked it hard, getting body cam shots of male faces when he could.

Twenty minutes later he'd done full coverage and the woman he'd come in with was angry. Like, she'd been waiting for a guy to go back in there with and when she finally found one, he turned out to be lame.

Keeler sat back thinking about it. He said, "Break off Neilson. Go back out and get the middle eastern looking crew from before. Maybe our Egyptian's not with them tonight."

Neilson said, "Roger that."

He felt bad for Neilson. The woman was disappointed. Keeler leaned back and watched with amusement while his buddy worked hard at defusing her anger. The camera had a wide angle, which distorted the woman's face as she gave Neilson a hard time. The bouncer watched attentively, but Neilson was good, giving him no reason to intervene.

Keeler revised his opinion. While Neilson had been dealing with relationship issues, he'd backtracked the video and checked out the table of Middle Eastern looking guys with Rolexes. They had decent face shots of them all, good enough for facial recognition.

He said, "Correction. I don't want you to go back to that table. Let's pull out of the place."

They parked the vehicle in a spot with an observational view both of the approach from the club and the Ford Focus. An hour later the four men walked back to the vehicle.

Keeler said, "Moving as a group."

These men looked like operators, the way they walked.

Neilson said, "I'm looking at a mission-oriented team on a night out before the show."

Keeler said, "Not a bunch of Egyptians."

"Weren't speaking Arabic."

"So, what were they speaking?"

Neilson looked at him. "I'm not a linguist buddy, you want me to guess?"

They followed the Ford back to Bercy, but Keeler wasn't loving it. There weren't many vehicles on the road, so he kept a distance. The Ford disappeared into a parking garage. Keeler and Neilson split. A few minutes later the group emerged from an exit that Neilson was covering. Keeler had to hustle over to track them, since they'd already seen Neilson at the club.

The group entered a large Parisian apartment building a couple of blocks away and that was it. The door shut and Keeler kept walking. He looped back and around to find Neilson in the driver's seat of the Peugeot. Keeler leaned in the window.

He said, "No way to know which apartment they're in."

Neilson chin pointed at the building. "*Au contraire mon frere*. Apartment on the third floor, corner unit."

Keeler said, "What, it lit up?"

"Exactly."

Keeler nodded. "Feeling comfortable aren't they, our new friends."

"Indeed."

Truth was, Keeler was itching for a home invasion.

He said, "Wouldn't you like to bust in there with a couple of M4s and take out that team right now, Neilson?

Neilson cackled. "Roger that bud, but it ain't going to happen. Same as always, right? Chain of command. Give a man an inch, he'll take a mile."

Keeler said, "Do the tracker."

"Oh yeah."

Neilson jogged over to the parking garage with a little tool kit. He came back some time later and got into the passenger seat.

"Done."

Keeler put the car into gear and began the long drive back to Troyes. Neilson leaned over to turn on the car radio, but Keeler blocked him.

He said, "We've got two hours. I'm going to brief you on Plan B."

Neilson leaned back in his seat, eyebrows raising and a hand rising to his mustache. "What's Plan B?"

Keeler said, "At the moment this is just you and me. Tomorrow, it'll be just me in the field and you back monitoring and doing your electromagnetic shit, yeah?"

"Yeah." The guy gazing into the oblivion of a French night sky. Keeler liked Neilson.

He said, "You'll be the point man for informing the others, like Rodriguez." Keeler punched Neilson in the shoulder. "Not only informing him, but you'll also need to be convincing. We need him operational when the shit hits the fan."

Neilson said, "What's his role?"

Keeler said, "He's not operating. He'll be back getting the feeds and communications, but the guy's a natural born killer. His job will be bringing us an informer, or multiples."

"Egyptians."

Keeler shrugged. "Whatever they are. I've told him everything, but he's caught in a bind by the command structure, you feel me?"

Neilson, nodding. Every operator had to accept the flaws in how military command gets politicized. They were used to it.

He said, "I hear you."

Keeler said, "Those people in that apartment back there might get the first punch in, but this isn't a street fight Neilson. The sucker punch isn't going to win."

"A hundred percent. I'm all ears. We'll hit them on the counter."

So, Keeler told him the plan, the strategic set of actions and reactions that had been percolating in his mind for the past couple of days. The drive back seemed shorter now that his ideas were being formed into spoken words. Neilson even had some ideas of his own.

SIXTY-TWO

Northern Israel

Yasmin's eyes were wide open and all she could see was black. It took her a minute to get oriented, the smell was confusing, the scent of home. Until she realized that she was wearing a hood, which must have been recently washed with the same fabric softener that her mom used at home. The material was cotton, double lined for the opacity. The fact that it had recently been laundered in someone's house gave her mixed feelings. Aside from the young militants who had hijacked their vehicle and taken her and Eitan, someone's mother or wife had also been involved in the preparation.

Because guys don't do laundry, a universal rule that's only occasionally broken.

It wasn't always so easy to conceptualize the enemy, visualize what it was that you were fighting, besides guys that would just pop up and try to kill you. That was easy, the idea of the *terrorist*. But here she was wearing a hood prepared and laundered by someone's mother.

Since she couldn't see anything else, Yasmin pictured a laundry room, women washing clothes for men, plus the odd hostage hood. Maybe one of them had sewed it herself, or a dozen of them, like a cottage industry.

Yasmin focused, blind but not deaf or dumb.

They were riding in a vehicle, maybe a van. The road was increasingly bumpy. Yasmin was lying on her side, back up against the wheel arch. Her hands were bound in front of her, now almost completely numb from loss of circulation. Pulling gently at the wrists she found no play in the zip ties. She didn't want to move around, assuming that someone was in there with her. A man with a gun, prepared to use it. Maybe watching her for signs of consciousness.

The only thing left to do was be passive and listen.

Wheels over a rough surface, more irregular than asphalt. A dirt road, but one that was maintained. There were no voices, only the sound of tires rolling and the mechanics of the vehicle itself, the brakes and hydraulics and the engine humming along.

Yasmin had a couple seconds of despair and panic, a cold feeling that crept up all over her suddenly from the gut. Ice in the belly threatening to spread out and freeze her into complete paralysis. She couldn't let that happen. She took a deep breath. Her training and willpower began driving down that instinctive panic.

Yes, she'd just been taken by a team of Palestinians, presumably because they'd gotten close to this Jafar al-Husseini. And now she was in this situation, bound and hooded in the back of a van.

Thinking of his sister, Basima. She's the one who'd cottoned on to Yasmin first. Warned her brother and then stepped back into the shadows and let his crew get busy.

Most likely scenario was that they'd be trying to get her crammed into a tunnel under Khan Yunis or Gaza City. Somewhere subterranean, no light, terrible food with zero nutritional value, plus the potential for being abused by male militants with weird fantasies about Israeli women. Raped and toothless is how she'd end up. Yasmin cursed at herself.

I'm not finishing this life raped and toothless, unable to walk out of there on my own feet fifteen years from now, after they've finally made a deal, a thousand terrorist prisoners for me. Half the country resenting me for the rest of my life because of the hostage to prisoner ratio, like freaking Gilad Shalit.

That was not going to happen. She thought, *over my dead body*, literally, said it to herself a couple of times. *Over my dead body*.

The thought occurred to her *what would Ruth do?* Her big sister was a warrior.

Yasmin allowed the natural motion of the ride to move her imperceptibly, each bump extending her range just a little more. A small accidental contact is all she was looking for, feeling with her bound hands, seeing if she could bump into something with her knees, or a foot. She wanted to know what was around.

Besides the wheel arch and the edge of the van, apparently nothing.

Ten minutes later the van slowed. The driver turned off to the left, the force of the movement shifting her into the wall. The vehicle crawled for a while at a snail's pace. A few minutes later there was another turn, or maybe they were just pulling over to the side. It was hard for Yasmin to tell. The vehicle stopped moving.

A door opened up front, driver's side first. The air pressure adjusted in the van; the suspension croaked. The sound of boots crunching dirt. The passenger door opened, seat springs croaked again, right above Yasmin's head and the door slammed shut. No conversation, the engine hum was different now that the driver's side door was open. More footsteps in dirt or sand, the shuffle of something being dragged. A murmur of voices in Arabic, but not loud enough that she was able to comprehend.

Someone was breathing near her feet. Maybe Eitan.

She was going to say something, the words just getting to the tip of her tongue when the rear door of the van opened, and a strong chill blew in. The vehicle's suspension eased again as weight was transferred from the van to the exterior. One of their captors had just come out of the van. The rear door closed.

Yasmin moved her hands up and lifted the hood. It had been Eitan breathing. He was there just by her leg. Nobody else in sight. They were alone in the back of the van.

She kicked Eitan. "Hey."

He didn't say anything or move, but that was a performance. When her foot had nudged him in the back, his body had stiffened up. If he was unconscious, that wouldn't have happened.

She said, "We're alone."

Eitan said nothing for a moment. He lifted his hood and, glanced up at her. He said, "How long have you been conscious?"

"Just a few minutes. You?"

"The whole time. We've been driving for two and a half hours I think."

She said, "The north smells different."

"Yeah."

Eitan was examining their location, which made Yasmin pay attention. The vehicle was a work van, like something a handyman would like to have, the interior panels were sheet metal with fixtures for bolting on modular accessories. Like a toolbox or shelving unit. Now the interior was set up like for a moving van, a nylon strap was attached just behind her, the red material ending in a frayed knot. Other than that, she couldn't see any stray objects. Yasmin got to her knees, examining the fixtures.

One steel tab with a bolt hole had been bent outwards slightly.

Eitan said, "We need to try now."

She said, "I'm trying."

Yasmin got her hands up there, testing the protrusion on the zip tie, trying to get the steel in between her skin and the plastic. She was using her body weight, basically hanging from the thing, feeling immense pressure on her wrists but since they were numb, there was no pain. The plastic popped, and she collapsed to the floor.

The rear door opened. Yasmin froze, in an embryo position on the floor, hood halfway up her face. The sharp desert chill returned, like the breath of a demon close to the back of her neck. She could feel the light absorbing bore of a gun barrel between her shoulders, like a fuzzy electrical current. On the plus side her hands were in front of her, and whoever was looking in wouldn't be able to see that the zip tie was busted because her back was now to the open door.

The weight shifted. Someone heavy jumping into the back of the van. The sound of a fist hitting flesh, but not hers, Eitan's. He grunted and she could imagine him, teeth clenched and tightly wound. A male smoker's voice, baritone like a croak. "*Sharmuta!*" The Arabic term for a whore.

A thud and a groan, Eitan being hit with something.

Another man came into the van, the floor shifting under her. She resisted the instinctual tightening of muscles. Tried to unfreeze her mind, remain casual even now. There were two men in there. The other one moving. His boot brushed her foot. The one who'd called Eitan a *sharmuta* spoke again. "Take his other arm."

The van's suspension released. Two men dropping from the vehicle. Eitan was pulled off, a swish when they dragged him and a thud as he hit the ground. More came into the van, someone gripping her arms hard, two men. Yasmin kept the wrists together, the hood riding up now around her nose. They pulled her along the floor of the van, boots in front of her face. She pressed her head against the van bed, allowing the hood to come up over her eyes, a snatch of sky as they came to the edge. A weapon was slung over the shoulder of a man. Short version of an M4, IDF military issue, most likely stolen from an arms depot.

Yasmin allowed her head to drop towards her hands, letting the actions of the men dragging her seem to naturally move her into that position. She didn't know if Eitan was still there, or conscious. These people were taking them into some secure hiding place. The best moment to break away was now, between the transportation and the prison they'd prepared. Here was the weak spot, the transfer of hostages.

She blanked her mind, loosening the jaw. The muscles slack and ready, softer against the hard clutching of their fingers. She jerked her right arm against the weak spot in the grip, where finger and thumb struggle to meet.

The arm came loose, and with it came the man who'd lost his grip. Darting towards Yasmin to get her under control again. She used this, driving the sharp part of her elbow into his throat. The man on the left jerked her away but hadn't realized that her hands were unbound. Yasmin turned on him in a flurry of punches, using the fact that he was grabbing her left arm. The man not entirely understanding the situation, getting hammered and retaining his grip. A lucky punch hit him near the eye, and he let go of her, probably trying to get to a weapon.

She glanced back, seeing Eitan in a fight for the rifle, the barrel waving around crazily. He had the hood half off, but his hands were bound. The second man was coming at her now, Yasmin telling herself that there were three enemies. One of them still not recovered from the strike to his throat. She charged the man in front of her, lowering her shoulder and taking him in the chest.

The man lost balance, her attack unexpected. His eyes getting that shocked look. Yasmin got a knee hard into the groin and her hands all up in his face, scratching at him and fingers grabbing. The man went over on his back, and she was on him, pushing fingers in his eyes.

He screamed.

She got her head up, scanning. A deserted agricultural installation, hoop houses with torn plastic sheeting, the detritus of plants that had once been irrigated from the now shredded drip hosing, strewn like broken spaghetti. The cover she'd spotted wasn't a solid wall, but an opaque PVC sheet that they wouldn't be able to see through.

Yasmin was there in four strides.

A triple burst chattering from behind her, thinking the rounds weren't aimed at her. That they were going for Eitan. A section of sheeting got perforated just in front of her face, rounds ripping through the thin membrane. A bullet slammed into an aluminum hoop section to her left, dinging off into space.

Yasmin dove out of sight, her chin slamming into hard packed dirt.

Scrambling forward on knees and elbows, registering more gun fire through the hard throbbing chemical feed of adrenaline.

She got up and sprinted hard, giving it everything she had left. Ten seconds later she was at another hoop tunnel structure. Looking around, nobody coming after her yet. She paced, heaving, letting the heartbeat come down a little, getting her breathing right. The hoop tunnel was mostly intact, only one single gash opening up the roof, as if a huge talon had cut into it from above.

Yasmin set off, running steadily, her pace even now, ready for the long haul.

SIXTY-THREE

Palmachim Airbase, Central Israel

The big bald man sat in front, his tanned and liver-spotted head blocking Hershkowitz's view. Around him were a team of colonels and lieutenant colonels, rationing their attention to feeds, the large screen up front, and the smaller ones in handheld devices and laptops. Each man and woman having a function, the nature of which an outsider could only guess.

Much of it about communication, Hershkowitz reflected. Comms back and forth, signal and message. Signs blinking into a system of rationalized warfare. On a good day.

It had taken a while for his team to realize what had happened. The vehicle that Eitan and Yasmin had been using was the indicator. The SUV was immobile for long enough that someone had started paying attention. The three other operational teams were directed to the location. They reported back, Yasmin Shoshan and Eitan had been successfully kidnapped. It had taken ten minutes to get the roadblocks going, in some places longer. Too long. By then there wasn't a trace, just regular traffic so far, civilians pulled out of vehicles. The security services were keeping the area controlled anyway, it was still possible that they might find something.

The forensic team had discovered blood at the scene, DNA identification would take a few more hours, if it was Israeli blood there would be a match. Meanwhile, they'd expanded the operation. Almost three hours had passed since the kidnapping, and each minute made the likelihood of saving Yasmin and Eitan more remote.

Because of the resources required now, the Yamam and Shin-Bet had taken over the operation. Hershkowitz had his own team, but he was technically subordinated to the bald man up there, Commander "S" as he was known to the public, a straight guy for sure, wife and kids and a yard with a dog and maybe a private interest in archaeology. A political operator in the system, finishing his career in the next few years and already slipping and angling towards some kind of elected public office.

Luckily not a dick. He'd give Hershkowitz a little slack to do his own thing, as long as it wasn't going to involve invading Egypt or Lebanon. Gaza or the territories would be open season.

Up on the screen a new feed flickered in. An agricultural area in the north by the Syrian border, viewed from above. Hershkowitz read the data layer. This was a live stream from a Skylark drone. Coming over a small, forested area. A van and two men hanging out by the rear. A third man between them, collapsed on the ground, unmoving. The bald man hunched forward, speaking into a comms device, an aide right by his shoulder.

A voice came over the comms system. Gunshots detected by the sensors along the border. The audio waveform coming up on the top left of the large screen, the AI system identifying the round by its sonic signature. The ammunition was 5.56×45mm NATO, presumably fired out of an M4.

The skylark drone pilot lingered, the vehicle easing into a wide rotation. The men below noticed the drone and reacted quickly, not exactly panic, but they were definitely concerned. Hershkowitz glanced at the data, not even a thousand feet high. The skylark would make a loud harsh buzz, and a sure sign of incoming death.

The men hustled the body into the back of the vehicle. They leapt into the van and got moving, the rear door left open in their haste, swinging out with the jerking forward motion. The guy back there must have been unconscious or dead. The van squealed in a tight turn and entered the cover of one of those greenhouse things made of a hooped structure enclosed in opaque PVC sheeting.

A uniformed soldier working the computers said, "The Black Hawk is two minutes out."

A helicopter which would contain a team of commandos, basically whoever was available and nearby at the moment. Hershkowitz glanced at the screens, looking for information. It was a Sayeret Matkal team.

The dispassionate voice spoke through the comms. "Incoming vehicle southeast. Break off the Skylark, Hermes can cover."

The first feed changed, the small drone swooping to the new object of interest.

Hershkowitz wondered why they'd leave the current situation, but the second feed came online, maintaining the coverage.

The data feed indicated an armed Hermes variant, a larger RPA that would be neither audible nor visible to the men with the van. The perspective was wider, taking in more of the abandoned agricultural settlement on the northern border with Lebanon.

A new voice came through the comms system. "Second vehicle identified, approaching from the east."

On the other screen the skylark drone was now tracking a white sedan. The drone swooped in a curve, coming low over the trees, tracking the vehicle. The camera operator was able to zoom in tight, everyone in the command center looking directly at the occupants, the image surprisingly clear and stable. Five men, one of whom had a long gun.

The voice over the comms system, from whoever the drone was being controlled, stated, "Occupants armed. We're going to engage."

The driver's face was a grimace, clearly aware of the drone. He pulled the white sedan over, colliding with a large boulder. The skylark had rapidly gained altitude, maneuvering for the strike. They could all see the driver struggling with his door. The front end of the sedan had crumpled on impact with the huge rock. He was struggling to open the door. The Skylark's feed wobbled slightly, and a missile impacted the sedan. The car bloomed in fire and sparks, rendering the camera's image white.

The voice over comms said, "Squirter."

Which meant someone had successfully escaped and was running. The Skylark now higher up, the figure below had somehow made it out of the car, was now running but the terrain wasn't in his favor. Rocky and hilly. A second missile impacted near the man, and he was down, unmoving, and perhaps limbless, it was hard to tell.

Hershkowitz was wondering if they'd just killed Jafar al-Husseini.

Meanwhile, the Hermes drone feed had adjusted. A male figure could be seen below, running hard. The Hermes moved, coming in for a better angle. Another person running, both of them military aged males.

Hershkowitz read it, understanding in an instant the chain of events, reading body language and tension in the gait.

He said, "She's escaped, in there somewhere. Those guys

are hunting Yasmin." Not knowing why he was so sure but trusting what he saw and the judgements he made of it.

The problem was he couldn't see her. The Hermes was too far up and focusing on the men chasing her.

The bald guy was on the phone, Commander "S". He handed the receiver to an aide and turned slightly so that Hershkowitz could see his right eye. The profile was soft, padded with fat.

He said, "That was Mossad, it's a no on the Hannibal directive."

Hershkowitz was immediately relieved, Yasmin Shoshan was Mossad connected. They'd want her alive, wouldn't be ready to give up on that. Normally, in a case like this, the Hannibal directive would be considered. If the enemy was likely to take a soldier hostage, they'd simply kill everyone in the vicinity, so it didn't happen. This wasn't going to be pretty, but at least her own team was not going to cut costs and kill her.

SIXTY-FOUR

Yasmin was gasping for air, sprinting hard through the hoop tunnels until she broke out into an open area strewn with plastic detritus, like shredded tarps and black drip feed hoses. Beyond that was a small concrete structure set into lush vegetation. Maybe a pumping station for the irrigation system, she didn't know.

There had been an explosion, something serious. She could hear the drone overhead, one of theirs.

She was looking for a weapon, anything that might work. Going into the concrete building through an opening, dark now, looking around and finding nothing but rusted iron pipes, curving into the ground. A pumping station, like she'd thought. Yasmin saw a long thin pipe, connected into the main unit and extending vertically.

She was able to step up onto the curved metal and grasped the thin pipe, but it wouldn't budge. Tugging at the thing and realizing that it was deeply embedded. Yasmin was afraid that she was being too noisy. The drone was both reassuring and annoying. Reassuring because it was her people, annoying because it was noisy, and she couldn't hear if the men chasing her were nearby.

Of course, that went both ways; the drone buzz covered her own noise.

The drone meant help was on the way, but a team might take minutes or even more. Death was capable of arriving within seconds.

She stayed where she was in the concrete structure and waited. The drone buzz drifted away a little. Footsteps became apparent outside and Yasmin's heartbeat began to increase. She took deep breaths, hearing the movement. One guy, creeping through that shredded tarp material. He'd be armed, and alert.

But would he be a trained fighter? Probably not as well trained as she was.

She prepared herself for a non-stop attack on him. Hearing the guy get closer and thinking it was highly likely that he'd come check out this pumping station, just like she had.

Yasmin had been taught to enter a doorway in a very specific way. You don't go in barrel first, for example. You'd 'slice the pie', reduce the angles and keep the weapon at chest level, ready to engage but not over committed.

The guy came in weapon first, barrel moving through the doorway. He'd never been trained in urban combat. Yasmin grabbed at it with both hands, yanking. The weapon was slung, so the man was yanked with his rifle. She let him come at her and kicked him in the groin, since both of his hands were dedicated to holding onto the M4.

The guy grunted. Yasmin got a hold of the upper receiver. Since the weapon was attached to the man, she wasn't going to be able to get it away from him. She pulled at it and let him resist, still in pain from the kick. Once he was resisting strongly, Yasmin reversed the force and slammed the butt of the weapon into his face. He was knocked back hard. She kicked his feet out from under him and he went down.

Yasmin was on him fast. She made a fist and pounded his nose hard, getting a crunch and strong blood flow into the man's mouth. The guy sputtered, and she struck hard fingers into his throat. The other hand made a fist with the thumb on top, punching into his left eye and digging in, gouging, just like she'd been taught in Krav Maga training, although there had never been a practical demonstration of this exact technique.

Now she was able to tear the weapon away. She recognized the man's bearded face, one of the men who'd been back there when Eitan had been killed.

Yasmin put two rounds into his chest and a third through his face.

She moved out of the concrete structure breathing hard. The light from outside was blinding, causing an involuntary squint. Yasmin was suddenly aware that she'd come out too fast, without looking first. The shot came from her right and hit her in the left leg. A flesh wound, grazing the thigh, but the force of impact put her down. Next thing she knew there were two men on her, tearing the M4 out of her hands and dragging her with them.

Yasmin screamed, struggling and fighting to get out of their grasp but it wasn't working.

Her heart was beating loud in her ears, pounding. Until she realized that it wasn't her heart, it was a helicopter. She'd heard many, this was a Blackhawk, which would be carrying a team. She screamed out, giving it everything she had.

"I'm here, I'm here. Help me!"

The voice of course totally lost in the mayhem.

The men were struggling with her writhing, hitting her with fists to shut up and, moving her as fast as they could. The helicopter blades thumping insistently. Like it was on the ground.

Gun shots, triple bursts. Yasmin was hearing it, calculated methodical fire from disciplined soldiers, brothers in arms, coming for her. The men carried her into dense vegetation until all was dark and she was being projected towards a small structure, concrete, like the pump house.

A man beckoning frantically, looking up suddenly and his fat face exploding into a bloody pulp, the body gone to gravity. A heavy thing hit her in the head and that was it. A vertiginous capitulation and darkness descended over the world.

SIXTY-FIVE

A FEW MINUTES EARLIER.

Hershkowitz was in the command room, observing, but unable to act. Watching the back of Commander "S"'s head, the bald cranium getting red now. A high-pressure environment. The whole point was to coordinate with the actors on the battlefield.

Hershkowitz saw it like a dream. The command center, a hum of digital signals and wiring, like the brain of an alien colony.

An officer said, "Northwest one hundred meters."

The Hermes camera shifted, moving in on an area of lush vegetation between abandoned green houses. A large man in a striped sweater, pushing a cart of some kind. The image flicked out, glitching, rudely replaced by a helmet cam perspective, one of the soldiers in the Black Hawk.

A voice said, "The team is on the ground."

The image bloomed as the Sayeret Matkal fighter turned himself towards the exterior of the black hawk, the video feed showing the ground approaching fast. It wasn't the first time

Hershkowitz had been a spectator to combat like this, but it did take some re-orientation each time.

The Matkal guy was jumping off, behind teammates hustling out of the chopper, the camera zig zagging as he sprinted to cover. The men in front of him maneuvering in their way, a ballet oriented around weapons. What pointed at what, the system of clapping a hand on a buddy's shoulder, moving around as a team.

Battle choreography.

Someone up ahead was running. A flurry of gunshots, the reports harsh and thick out of the helmet mounted camera's audio system. Now there were two enemy corpses out by a stand of olive trees, just men in civilian clothing dead and bleeding out from accurate head shots. Two soldiers calling out coherently, battle speak, glimpses of a Sayeret Matkal operator hurling a flash bang in through an opening. Some small concrete structure, like where you'd keep cows or sheep or whatever.

Hershkowitz was no expert in agriculture.

Interior of the structure, dark without electric light. Moving forward, past several masked IDF commandos. Another man's corpse on the ground, some dead guy wearing a Mickey Mouse t-shirt, head shot leaking into a large puddle underneath him. In the corner of a darkened room, soldiers standing around a square hole in the ground.

Hershkowitz's heart sank, literally into his bowels, what it felt like. He was looking at steel ladder rungs built into the shaft. Yasmin was gone into the tunnel, the worst possible outcome. She was in enemy hands.

He couldn't help himself, leaping forward to grab the mic from one of the commanders in front. Screaming. "Get her out. Go in there and get her out!"

Nobody listened to him.

An argument was going on up front. Commander "S"

refusing to allow the men to enter the tunnel. Voices were raised a female aid shouted to her colleague, excited. The tunnel robot was ten minutes away, canine unit wasn't going to get there on time. Hershkowitz turned away from the scene, catching his assistant's eye.

Her face was the color of cold ash, she averted her gaze.

Murmurs from up front. Commander "S" was getting agitated, poking at something on the console in front of him. The screen was filled with new imagery. Helmet cam feeds from the Sayeret Matkal team. Approaching the squirter, the guy who'd fled the white sedan before it had been obliterated by the Skylark drone strike.

The guy was moving, the lower part of his left leg had been blown off, lying there on the red dirt with the boot still attached to his foot. The Matkal operator was closer now, near enough to identify Jafar al-Husseini.

Hershkowitz moved forward, speaking to Commander "S". "That's Al-Husseini. We need to keep him alive."

The bald general barely nodded. "Of course."

Two paramedics were already kneeling over him, applying a tourniquet. Al-Husseini's face was a bewildered mess, yellow from the loss of blood, eyes darting around. Hershkowitz was thinking about his sister, Zeina Makhoul, and the cruel journey this guy had made from his origins in an upstanding family to this, an amputated terrorist bound for a Shin Bet interrogation chamber. After they'd rinsed him, Al-Husseini would be tried in court, as an Israeli citizen.

No doubt the sentence would be twenty years to life, given that he'd caused an Israeli woman to be abducted into Lebanon.

His assistant was proffering the phone to him.

She said, "Gabi."

He took the phone. "Yes."

The deputy director of Mossad said, "We need to talk."

A high ringing feeling kicked up at the top of Hershkowitz's head. A feeling, or a sound, something cold and unbearable.

He said, "Okay."

Gabi said, "I'm just outside. Come please."

The phone clicked off, and he handed it back to his assistant. She brushed hair out of her face. Hershkowitz looked away, a slight throbbing sensation had begun between his eyes.

SIXTY-SIX

Hershkowitz exited the facility, squinting for a bit and seeing Gabi out there, keeping to the shade smoking a cigarette. A large man with an entirely bald head. The guy had been shaving it since as long as anyone could remember. At least since their early days in the army, but maybe even as a teenager.

Gabi was blunt. "So, they've taken Yasmin Shoshan."

Hershkowitz said, "Yes."

A straight answer, looking the devil directly in the eyes.

Gabi's ride was a gloss black Volvo with smoked glass. The passenger window was cracked and Hershkowitz could see someone in there, white hair, maybe a guy on the phone.

Gabi said, "This is going to get messy. You understand that." He was tapping the cigarette nervously, even though there was no ash.

"And?"

Gabi tilted his head to the Volvo. "Come on."

Hershkowitz had a funny feeling. Walking to the car, following Gabi's heavy frame. The Mossad man all in black. He opened the rear door and Hershkowitz got in. The prime minister was on the phone, didn't even glance at him. Bibi must have been here monitoring the situation, probably demanded that Gabi bring him over to the command center.

Gabi got in behind the wheel, his weight tipping the scales slightly.

Bibi was making noises and saying things like yes, and no, and later, and I'm not sure about that. He ended the call and looked up at Hershkowitz. The PMs face was yellow, he wore a black blazer, and a white-collared shirt with no tie. He had makeup on, and his hair was sprayed in place. For a second this startled Hershkowitz until he considered the media engagements the PM was always doing.

Bibi said, "I'm not doing another Gilad Shalit."

Hershkowitz said, "No."

Bibi nodded. "You've been a good guy Mike, but now you've screwed the pooch."

"I know that."

"Right, so you're going to have to fall on your sword for me. You'll do fine if you go with the program."

Hershkowitz said, "What's the program?"

Bib said, "I want her back." He was looking at Hershkowitz directly in the eyes, and Bibi's eyes were reddened and weird. Like his face was a mask, and another person was inside it. "I don't want her back in pieces, or in years, I want her returned immediately. This is messing with other things we've got cooking Mike, at a regional level so I want exactly *nothing* to happen."

Hershkowitz got it. The new American administration, the secret plans for a regional accord. Nobody wanted conflict at the moment.

The PM said, "Everyone wants her back, if you've got some magic wand let me know."

Gabi's voice from the front. "We've got a hit on six Iranian officers operating out of Syria. IRGC people, three of them at the Brigadier General level. We've had an operational plan for two years, updated according to changes on the ground. Our assets are still in place, the operation's a go, we just haven't had a reason to proceed."

Bibi said, "And many reasons *not* to proceed."

Hershkowitz took a second to digest this. six IRGC officers was quite a lot of enemy weight. If Mossad had them caught in the sights, this was big news. And then he understood the issue.

He said, "You take them out we'll be starting World War three."

Bibi said, "Correct. Which is why you're going to be in charge. You don't kill them, you *grab* them."

Gabi said, "An adjustment to the plan has been made. It's riskier but it should work."

Hershkowitz said, "And we trade for Yasmin."

Gabi said, "If Nasrallah and the mullah's go for it."

Bibi grunted, like he agreed with the question. He said, "It'll have to happen fast, the negotiation."

Hershkowitz understood the gambit. He was meant to command this mission, for which he'd be publicly castigated as a rogue officer. He'd resign or be fired in disgrace. Hassan Nasrallah would go for it because the Iranians would make him release her. The IRGC paid the bills for Hezbollah.

As long as the Iranian officers were important enough, it would work.

Bibi said, "If we do it right, it won't be some public thing that we brag about Mike, nobody will ever know except us and them. You'll go to your grave as the guy who got Yasmin Shoshan taken hostage. You understand that."

Hershkowitz understood. He nodded. "Will Yasmin know?"

Bibi said, "Absolutely not."

Gabi said, "She'll just get out of the dungeons, that'll be enough for her."

Hershkowitz didn't ask if they had a Plan C. Bibi always came up with some arcane plan.

Gabi handed over a file. "It's a combined operation with AMAN operatives and our people inside. You pull the trigger from unit 201's headquarters and it'll happen over the next forty-eight hours. This will blow our whole penetration there, so it's a loss on the accounts. We're deep in the red on this Mike."

Hershkowitz looked over the operational plans. It took fifteen minutes to fully understand what was going to happen. He wouldn't have to do a thing, just be a figurehead in charge and take the fall for it. Not only him, the whole 201 team.

He said, "You're disbanding 201?"

Bibi said, "Already history." Looking hard at Hershkowitz. "Are we good?"

Hershkowitz said, "Let's do it."

Gabi said, "Good, now get out of the car."

THEY WALKED BACK to the command center together. The building itself almost looked temporary, a corrugated steel roof and ugly concrete exterior. The landscaped grounds had only sparse growth.

Gabi stopped him outside the door.

"Before you go commit suicide, I want to untie one little knot."

Hershkowitz said, "Give me a cigarette."

Gabi extended the pack, Marlboro lights. Hershkowitz lit up.

He said, "So what's up?"

Gabi said, "Your Egyptian friend, Al-Masri, the colonel."

"What about him?"

"I'm giving him as a gift to our friends in Cairo. I wanted to know if you had objections."

Hershkowitz said, "None."

The deputy director of the Mossad turned to go. He said, "You were a good commander Mike, I'm sorry that you went out like that."

Gabi walked to the Volvo. The PM had raised the window. Now it was just dark reflective glass.

SIXTY-SEVEN

ÎLE-DE-FRANCE: *The Parisian Metropolitan Area*

The simulated operation had started in the parking lot, but reality was a bitch. In other words, a two-hour drive from the outskirts of Troyes to the *Marne La Vallée Expo Center* in the Parisian ex-burbs. Three vehicles in a convoy. One, a Ford van that Neilson drove with a long-haired knob twiddler, a dedicated nerd for the mobile command-and-control hub, coordinating between operational teams. Keeler was in the back seat of a Renault Kangoo driven by Chet. Billings was riding shotgun up front, both of them chewing gum and deadpanning. The third vehicle was Rodriguez in a newly acquired Mercedes S class.

Billings said, "Why are the French so monoculture on the coffee?"

Chet said, "What do you mean, monoculture?"

"Like they've got this single-minded idea of coffee as this uninteresting black liquid excreted by some indifferent machine into a small little cup. Then they sip at it, like two sips and it's done. That's it, they leave."

Chet said, "You mean, like espresso. You're complaining about espresso."

"If they made espresso that would be a good thing, they don't. They make a kind of gross nothingness."

Keeler watched her. Billings was animated, screwing her face into expressions of disgust, waving her hands around, fingers in claws. She was nervous, maybe she'd taken a pill.

Come to think of it, Chet was a little spacey too.

Chet said, "So what, you're advocating better European coffee, or like, Starbucks?"

Billings sank back into the seat. "More like Starbucks. I want coffee to die for, flavors and stuff like cream and chocolate all over it."

Keeler watched the landscape get chewed up by the middling engine of the Kangoo. Chet was a solid driver, keeping two kilometers below the speed limit in the slow lane. Once in a while a vehicle would shoot past in the left lane, absurdly fast. People in a rush seem to favor Audis for some reason. Weird how they thought going faster was going to help in some way. You'd get there two minutes earlier maybe, or you'd die or get maimed, and then what?

Keeler carried a wallet with two thousand euros in cash, otherwise his pockets were empty. The same was true of Chet and Billings. Made him feel like he'd been purified for a ritual killing.

Personal items including identification documents were in the Mercedes with the Operations Officer.

Chet parked the vehicle. Keeler caught his eye in the rearview mirror. Chet nodded.

"Alright."

Keeler exited the Kangoo and stretched. The hotel parking lot wasn't exactly the same as the simulation. The puddles were different, real when you walked in them. He looked at his fingers, thinking about the pillow. Maybe holding the guy down first while Billings did her thing with the needle. The sun poked through cloud for exactly three seconds, consumed by the uniform whiteness as quickly as it had appeared.

Chet closed the door. The keys would be inside under the floor mat, waiting for another man to come and drive the vehicle away. Keeler had never worked this way before, on a mission like this, in the civilian world with so many moving parts. People on specialized teams whom you didn't know, maneuvering around you, aware of their cog and the one they locked in with, but no other view of the machinery.

He followed Billings and Chet towards the hotel entrance. A man in a severe suit locked the trunk of his car, an old classic Citroen in shiny black.

In the simulation they'd been drifting. Now he was walking, feet hitting the asphalt, over painted lines, and remnants of the recent rain. To the left up ahead by the entrance, the group of three military aged guests hadn't yet arrived. He was expecting them in their tennis outfits, faking a casual conversation. The reconnaissance team would have already scoped out the scene. Their mission was to put eyes into corners before Keeler's team moved in.

Oh yeah, the group of military aged men and women dressed for luxury sports began to converge, maybe thirty seconds off schedule, arriving from a couple different directions, so casual. At this point everyone maintained radio silence.

They weren't convincing actors to Keeler's directorial eye. Stiff and trying hard to look happy. The tennis rackets were an issue, the team didn't look like they were actual tennis players. Tennis didn't have to be the best day of your life. If he was the director of this performance, he'd have told them to chill out and not try looking so ecstatic, like life was an endless weekend. It made them look creepy.

One of the guys put his heel up on the bench and bent over to grab his toes. If the infiltration route had already been cleared and established, the guy deserved the stretch.

Chet moved to point, and Keeler and Billings fell into position behind him, a phalanx as they crossed the doorway into the hotel. A seam line with cameras, Keeler thought. The threshold of significance. To the right was a distraction team taking up the head space of receptionists. Three of them today, unlike the two they'd had in the simulation. An operator caught his eye, black guy wearing a golfing cap, unprofessional.

The carpet didn't exist in reality, it was wood, not exactly polished, more like 'treated', natural looking grain, like walking across the roof of a ski chalet. The timing was correct, thirteen strides to the elevator bank. Nobody tripped over a shoelace. The force protection team looked completely obvious to Keeler, but they didn't look American. Come to think of it, neither had the reconnaissance team in tennis outfits.

They'd looked French.

Not that Keeler could know, it was a judgement call. Anyway, it'd be weird to have a hotel full of American operators, too distinctive. The force protection people were pretty good at blending in. One tall guy moving from the restaurant area towards the entrance, crossing through the space near the elevators.

A young woman walked, eyes searching, like she's on her way to find a toilet but gets distracted by someone she recognizes. They meet and exchange words, like they're friends but not lovers.

Colleagues.

A man walked past and handed Keeler a late generation iPhone. Keeler pocketed the device, which wasn't a phone but a stun gun. Billings had also received a package that she secreted in a pocket.

The elevator door opened, and Keeler took the lead with Billings and Chet right behind him. He hadn't seen a dog yet. A bunch of older ladies with leopard print shopping bags were seated next to a huge window looking out to a wood chipped garden. The elevator door closed.

Chet sniffed. Billings looked wide awake, making eye contact. Keeler looked at her and didn't turn away, her eyes were good, clear, and un-drugged. The air pressure had increased as they rose. A camera was affixed to the ceiling at the rear corner. The elevator stopped at the third floor. Keeler glanced at Chet, who raised his eyebrows. The doors opened and two men stepped in.

Billings and Chet remained motionless, almost defensive. Keeler moved back, putting his butt against the rail. He nodded at the man in front, who gave him a fake smile. White teeth, dark black hair combed in a side part, blue eyes. The other man was bald, shaved head, the skin red and shiny. He was a large man. Both of them wore workout gear, towels wrapped around their necks. Like they were on their way to the gym, not coming from it.

But coming from the third floor. So, they were either buddies or a couple.

The bald guy lifted a hand to the control panel and punched the button for the twelfth floor. The word 'gym' appeared above the number twelve in raised letters. The man with black hair spoke to his friend in Russian. Something about idiots. Keeler had a little Russian language, maybe an eighth of a conversation worth. Picked it up hanging out with a bunch of Ukrainian mercenaries in Tangiers.

The big bald man laughed. He said something obscene, turned to look straight at the polished steel elevator door. Keeler made eye contact with him, and the Russian kept it for a long moment, before glancing back to the front.

The fifth floor came, and Keeler figured this would be the time. The two Russians would part for Keeler's team to exit the elevator. They'd be walking through a sort of hostile corridor. The doors would open, and they might find enemy combatants out there in the corridor. There had been radio silence until now, which didn't mean that anybody was still alive on the other side of the operation's comms network.

He looked at Chet, the man was jacked up on adrenaline. Billings had sunken into herself, like an animal coiled into its shell, ready to spring. Keeler had no doubt that she was a fierce fighter, the woman was small but thick with muscle, like a little ninja. She'd be an expert in unarmed combat. Put holes in a guy before he could even think about her coming at him.

SIXTY-EIGHT

The elevator shuddered to a halt, slowing intolerably on servo motors. Hydraulics pushing hard at incompressible liquid, doing the heavy lifting. The door opened, and the Russians parted, turning slightly. Keeler moved past them with an easy mind, no spider sense was kicking off, no pheromonal secretions alerting him to imminent danger.

The real corridor was carpeted in red. The walls creme fabric with thin gold stripes printed vertically. The simulation had featured a middle-aged blonde woman up in there with a Prada shopping bag. Reality was a thin young woman in a black dress wearing sunglasses so big they made her look like a bug.

Billings and Chet came through. The Russians stayed in the elevator, like the two were going to the gym. Or they had just sent a message. *We're here*, and you don't know if that's significant or not. In other words, intimidation. But as they say, no news is good news.

The thin woman in black was talking on a phone, French. She was moving towards them aimlessly, as if the conversation was distracting. In the other direction was a man wearing a blue baseball cap hanging out by the exit. Chet took the lead down the corridor. Keeler half expected a maid to come out with her cleaning cart. That had happened on a few of the virtual run throughs, some looping action that had been programmed into the pawns. The second reconnaissance agent maintained his position.

Chet arrived at the target's door.

He had a key card up and ready, moving it to the lock. The latch snicked and Chet opened the door. Holding it for Keeler to come through. The entrance was similar to the simulation except for the colors and the furniture. They hadn't accounted for a console table with a black stone bowl for pocket litter. Currently the room's occupant had dropped the key card in there with his phone and a pack of mint gum. Keeler walked through into the bedroom area. The target was lying on the bed in boxer shorts and a t-shirt. From that angle he was all belly and bare feet, with hairy hands holding up a phone.

The man was up quickly, alarmed and mobilized in rapid but aimless movement. Keeler registered his approach, sort of fast but less a practiced attack than a panicked flurry of limbs and bare feet. The man was all flesh and body hair. His skin was very pale. Keeler moved quickly into his personal space, introducing all kinds of stability issues to the game.

He grabbed him under the left armpit and put the stun gun against his chest, delivering a million volts at 3 amps. The target's body convulsed, and Keeler caught him, easing him onto the bed.

Looking down at him, conscious but stunned. Either Farid Tabrizi, hero of the Islamic Revolution, or a dissident journalist name of Pejman Kazemi, only time would tell.

Chet spoke and his voice came both live through the gas mix of real air and electronically through the earbuds. "Absolution." There was a latency of several milliseconds, which gave a metallic robot tone to the voice.

A remote voice said, "Roger."

Neilson's voice said, "Proceed."

Billings took a knee and got out her kit.

Keeler bent over the target, looking into his eyes. Fear seemed to be the predominant emotion at the moment. He'd seen blind fear often, but this guy's concern wasn't a hundred percent animal. Looked like he'd been prepared for the possibility of this moment.

Keeler put his hand on Billings' shoulder, she looked up at him.

He said, "What's a dose where he can still speak?"

"Huh?"

"I want you to make him relaxed but not paralyzed."

She said, "This won't do that."

"So, hold off a minute."

"What?"

Keeler said, "You heard me. I need to talk to this guy first." He lied, lifted his eyes to the ceiling. "Special orders just came in, sorry."

Chet said nothing, probably hadn't heard the exchange. He was watching from the door. The target was moving. Keeler put a hand on his chest, towering over him there on the bed.

Keeler spoke in French. "What's your name?"

The guy's eyes were moving in a crazy ping-pong pattern. His body actually shivering in fright. He said, "Pejman Kazemi."

The pronunciation was a little different from what Keeler had used back when he was reading the Kazemi's articles. He said it. "Pejman Kazemi, I like that name."

The man said nothing.

Billings said nothing.

Chet stood at the door. Keeler could see his feet shifting nervously.

He leaned on the target, putting his weight on him. Physical pressure adds a lot of stress. People don't tend to be very good at coming up with convincing lies while under stress. He said, "Give me the names of three members of the Islamic City Council of Shiraz. Say it slow so I can understand. I don't speak Farsi." The man looked confused. He said, "I don't know how to ask you this in your language buddy, I only speak French. You want to help me out here?"

The guy, Kazemi or Tabrizi, was out of shape, chest heaving from the stress of his situation.

Keeler said, "Maybe this will help. We're here to kill you. You might want to get your shit together and answer the question."

The man licked his lips, pupils were dilated, he looked crazy.

He said, "Shiraz." Eyes wandered to Billings and back. "Doumani, Mousavi. Uh, Naseri and Darvish. Cyrus Pakravan." His eyes pinged around the room and found Keeler's again. "I don't know many of their first names."

Keeler had memorized the list. Kazemi's pronunciation wasn't the same as what he'd internalized, but it was close.

He said, "Good job. Now tell me this, how many barrels of oil were produced in Khuzestan, Iran, in 2011?"

The man looked at Keeler hard now. He coughed and smiled, somehow reassured by the question. He said, "Good question. Nobody knows the answer because they don't release the data at a provincial level. Obviously, you've read my article."

Keeler nodded. "Yeah, I have."

Billings was standing now, staring at Keeler. She spoke in fluent native French, the operational tongue. "What the hell are you doing?"

Chet was staring at them but hadn't yet moved from his assigned position by the door. A good soldier.

Keeler said, "We're aborting the mission. This guy's not Tabrizi. He's just a journalist we've been set up to kill. The mission's compromised. Maybe they just wanted us to kill this guy, I don't know if they've got any more surprises planned."

"Who's they? Who set us up?"

He shrugged. "I don't know exactly. Does it matter just now?"

Chet said, "What's going on?"

Billings and Keeler ignored him.

Billings said, "You serious?"

"Yeah. I'm serious." He looked at her, not saying something dumb, like 'trust me', simply standing and looking at her. The journalist's chest was moving beneath Keeler's hand, and he took the pressure off.

Kazemi said, "You're what, DGSE?"

Direction Générale de la Sécurité Extérieure, French version of the CIA. It wasn't a bad idea if that's what the guy thought.

Keeler said, "Just shush for a second. I'm trying to make it so you don't die, give me a minute."

Neilson's voice came over the comms system. "Status?"

Chet's hand went up to his earpiece, about to hit the comms switch and say something. Keeler put his hand up and pointed at him. Chet's hand stayed down.

Keeler tapped the ear bud. He said, "Golden Gate."

An arbitrary signal, but the one he'd agreed upon with Neilson to signal Plan B. Neilson would now compartmentalize the communications, keeping the loop tight within the kill team circuit. Rodriguez, Neilson, Billings, Chet, and Keeler. He would also be coordinating with the intermediaries for other cells of the team. Neilson would be opening a private line to Rodriguez, giving him instructions that Keeler had dictated for him to memorize.

Chet said, "What are you doing?"

Keeler looked at Billings.

She said, "We're aborting the mission, apparently." Billings pointed at Kazemi. "What about him?"

The question was leave him or take him. Was he in danger even if they left the room? The answer was definitely. There was no telling who might countermand Keeler's executive decision. People aren't generally very pleased when the hit man decides he's not doing the hit. Keeler didn't care what anyone thought, he'd already been convinced the operation was rotten, it had only needed confirmation.

He said, "We're taking him out of here." Looking at the journalist. "Now you need to have some faith in me, pal."

Keeler released him and Kazemi sat up on the bed, still heaving with anxious energy, having a very bad day. Chet was having a conversation with the air, something happening between his ears, probably speaking with Rodriguez who'd just been briefed by Neilson. Hopefully nobody would do anything stupid.

Keeler said, "We'll be leaving the room and traveling to a secure location. I don't know what's going to happen on the way, but you should know that my friends and I will protect you. We may be attacked by people who mean harm. In that case we will do them harm, without limits. Do you understand what I'm saying?"

Kazemi said, "Yes."

Keeler had been thinking about Kazemi's meeting with the guy from the Iranian embassy. He said, "Who's the Iranian guy you met in the conference center?"

Kazemi said, "Faravahar, this is the reason I came here."

"Keep talking."

Kazemi looked bewildered. He hadn't yet totally cottoned

on to his existential problem. He said, "He's a source. I'm a journalist."

Keeler said, "What do you mean by a source exactly. This is an Iranian embassy official."

"Yes." Kazemi put his hands up into air quotes. "Sports and culture advisor." The hands came down, and the journalist assumed a cold tone. "He's an Al-Quds officer and I'll bet you it isn't long before he defects. Maybe he's trying to see who will give him the best deal, the Israelis, or the Americans."

Keeler nodded. "Did he pay for this?" Making a hand gesture to indicate the suite.

"He's a dissident, using his budget to screw the mullahs."

Keeler said, "Yeah, I don't think so pal. It's you who got screwed."

Kazemi shut up, a look of despair rippling across his face. He'd been thoroughly bamboozled by the Al-Quds people, as had the Americans.

Billings said, "He needs to change clothes."

The stink was getting obvious, even to Keeler who tended to ignore that kind of thing. A thousand volts will certainly make a man shit his pants.

He chin pointed at Kazemi. "Go change your underpants and put some clothes on, you can take a 30 second shower if you need to."

The man scampered off. Keeler noticed the digital clock on the bedside table. The illuminated numbers shivered and turned to zero. Which meant the power had been shut off. They hadn't noticed because Kazemi had kept the lights off in his room. Bad vibes.

Neilson's voice came over the comms system. "Time to move."

Chet looked at Keeler, who nodded. Chet looked at the floor

and spoke to the comms unit. "Moving out in less than a minute."

Neilson's voice said, "Mixed situation."

Meaning there was some information but also some lack of information, making situational awareness difficult. In the bathroom Kazemi ran the water for twenty seconds. He came out in a collared shirt and V-neck sweater, looking like a terrified subterranean rodent.

There was a gunshot out in the hall, muffled by the closed door.

SIXTY-NINE

KAZEMI'S EYES were open wide, glossy like a child's. Weird because otherwise he looked like an unhealthy middle-aged man who lived with more than his share of stress.

Keeler said, "What's the deal, they made a fatwa against you?"

The journalist was used to the idea. The corners of his mouth raised, some humor back where the fear wasn't allowed to penetrate. He said, "Yeah, a few of them actually."

Keeler said, "They'll have to come back another time, bud. No fatwa today, alright?"

The guy nodded. "Great."

Chet made eye contact with Keeler. Billings said, "Let's do it."

Chet spoke into the network, "Clearance."

Neilson's voice said, "Proceed."

Chet opened the door. Keeler pushed Kazemi in front of him, following Billings. A man lay on the carpet by a cleaning trolley. A red stain was developing in the center of his white t-shirt. A sports jacket sprawled open; its wool cloth pleated like a curtain. Kazemi had to step over the corpse on the way to the elevators. Keeler kept a hand on his shoulder.

The thin woman with bug eyes was mouth breathing, a couple of yards from their path. The man with the blue baseball cap was over the other side of the target's room door. Fifteen steps and they were turning to the elevator bank, tucked away inside a short corridor. Elevators, a couple of leather benches, a plant, and the emergency exit.

A sound from behind them, down the hall. A door opening. Keeler swiveled to the threat. The door swinging inward, creating a slight depression. The man in the blue baseball hat was already moving, no weapon drawn, but his bare hands were curled into useful appendages. He wouldn't necessarily be armed. His body blocked Keeler's sight, but something entered the doorway from within. Keeler could make out only hair curlers and a flash of pink. The man in the blue baseball hat speaking now to the woman, his voice inaudible at the distance.

Neilson's voice said, "Proceed."

Keeler turned back to the direction of travel, Kazemi had followed Billings and Chet. They were already a couple steps further in than Keeler. He didn't see it at first, Billings was the one to react. He caught sight of something moving on the other side of Kazemi, a quick flash of agitation, the air seemed to freeze, becoming still. Sounds became background concerns and his vision pinched into an acute frame of focus.

Keeler pulled the journalist back. Billings was up in the intimate space of a tall man, a bristle of short hair and unshaven cheek. She was stabbing a syringe into the man's throat, pushing him back against the wall, using her thick muscled legs to hold him in there. The guy not making a sound, maybe in shock.

Chet was down, flailing on the ground by the elevator, recovering from something. A second man darted from the door marked *sortie*, the emergency stairwell. He was reaching back, gun hand seeking the solid reassurance of a personal weapon. Definitely the wrong way to come through a door. The error made it easier to break him down technically.

Keeler was up in his personal space, timing the movement to interfere with the man's action clearing his weapon from behind his back. Keeler pinned the shoulder to the wall and used his right hand to deliver a million volts of electricity to the enemy's neck.

The man spasmed, face instantly contorted, lips back over the teeth, tongue in there all rigid and stiffened by shock. The body hit the ground, convulsing. The confusion and anxiety levels would remain elevated for an hour maybe.

Billings jumped back, getting out of the way as her adversary slid down the wall, losing his strength. It would take a minute for the *succinylcholine* to diffuse sufficiently through the blood stream and paralyze his muscles, but a work in progress can already be functional. The man's arm was twitching, a pistol still clutched in the hand. The fingers seemed unable to move independently, having already succumbed to the neuromuscular blocking drug.

Keeler had to exert a little energy, taking the gun from the man's involuntarily clutching hand, a Sig Pro in 9mm. Checking the action and doing a quick search for ammunition, finding two magazines tucked into a slick belt holder. No identification, no pocket litter. No way of knowing who this person was. Billings had been equally busy looting the man whom Keeler had put down.

Chet cursed, not just a single word but an entire foul phrase. His nose was bloody and broken. A black eye would be forming later on. Keeler hadn't been there, but it seemed that Chet had been overcome by the first man to come through the emergency exit door. Keeler could imagine it, guy comes through with a drawn weapon, Chet reacts, maybe gets a chance to deliver damage. The guy puts a knee into Chet's face, but then gets a load of Billings coming at him like a wildcat with a loaded syringe.

Chet opened the stairwell door. He had blood on his face, pooling at the corner of his mouth, wiping at it with a shirt sleeve. Billings went through into the stairwell, weapon raised and clearing the area.

When she nodded Chet said, "Moving."

Keeler directed Kazemi through the doorway. Kazemi keeping his eyes forward, not staring dumbly at the men Keeler and Billings had put down.

Neilson's voice said, "Proceed to the twelfth floor."

Keeler thought, *'why the twelfth?'* but he followed, a hand on Kazemi's shoulder, the feeling of it now natural. He was able to sense the other man's level of tension. By the time they got up to twelve Kazemi was winded, the fringe of black hair at the nape of the journalist's neck wet with perspiration. He leaned against the concrete wall catching his breath. The remaining hair on Kazemi's head was plastered in strings to his scalp in a smear of sweat, droplets forming on his forehead and in the dense growth on his upper lip.

Keeler said, "You're not a big fan of rowing machines are you."

Kazemi shook his head and made an exhausted approximation of a laugh. He said, "I promise to do better in the future, sir."

Chet said, "Twelfth."

Neilson's voice said, "Enter the gym, other side of the weight room you'll see a door. Go through it. A raised tunnel accesses the next building over. Force protection is being diverted."

Chet said, "Copy."

Keeler had given Neilson a complex set of instructions

regarding Rodriguez, in the event that this assassination job went sideways. Keeler hoped that the Operations Officer would be busy with his assigned task.

Neilson's voice said, "Word from Ops Officer. He says *pineapples*."

Which was exactly what Keeler wanted to hear, like there was a mind reader haunting the ether.

∽

THE RUSSIANS WERE over in the corner by a rack of kettlebells, other side of a water cooler and a radiator with a mirror above it. The floor was soft black matting. The bald Russian had an extra yoga mat for his activity, while the other guy was leaned back against the wall drinking from a plastic cup. The bald man was in the end stage of a Turkish getup. What looked like the heaviest weight available was attached to his fist, arm raised in an iron vertical line with the spine. He was a strong boy, muscle fibers inflated, and skin reddened by exertion, veins popping out of his forehead as he completed the rep. His buddy took a seat on a rowing machine, sweat drenched head wrapped in a white towel.

Keeler nodded as they walked by. The door on the other side of the weight room was locked. Chet dropped to a knee. Keeler turned to face the room, his back to the lock picking, looking at the Russians who were staring. Keeler winked. The weapon was tucked safely into his waistband, a SIG Sauer SP2022 chambered in 9mm, an old familiar friend he was quite fond of.

Chet said, "Go."

Keeler backed through the door and closed it behind him. The Russians kept on looking and then he turned and was out of their line of sight. Maybe the bald guy would call it quits, or maybe he'd get all excited and do an extra set.

The tunnel was a floating corridor over the green pastures of Expo Center grass. Down below was nothing much, a gray day, parking lot visible in both directions. In between that was grass and concrete, people, and their things, like dogs and bikes and a coffee truck. It almost looked as if nothing was happening, which was clearly not true.

Keeler saw it differently, an augmented reality. The world becoming threat and non-threat. His training had embedded some weird mental machinery that reduced complex stuff into blunt objects, blobs of decision.

SEVENTY

The floating corridor ended in double glass doors, like the window to an aquarium, inside of which a whole different world was being lived. People talking but their words silent. A couple dozen people in there moving in multiple directions, busy, like it was break time in a business conference, trestle tables out in the vestibule. Office people, happily using toothpicks to spear food held in napkins, pop it in the mouth and chew, some of them speaking around it, verbalizing, and eating at the same time.

Chet slammed a shoulder through the door, a guy who'd be more than happy using an MRE spoon to fish food out of a military issue tri-laminate bag. A female office worker dropped her shrimp toast on the carpet, staring. Chet didn't even notice her; the guy was suffering from some form of tunnel vision. Keeler knew why the woman was surprised, the blood on his buddy's face.

Other side of the conference room there were choices to make. One, a fancy wood door, swung in to reveal an acoustic paneled auditorium. Conference attendees were in there as well, settled into the seats, focusing on lunch or looking at phones. Right side of that area were double doors looking like they'd lead to a corridor or maybe another stairwell.

A small man in a tennis outfit came through the door, hand obviously holding a pistol in a track suit pocket, keeping it from falling out. His eyes sought danger, and found Chet, settling on him before raking laterally to land on Keeler, locking in there for a minor examination. The man didn't flinch, eyes roaming away from Keeler, seeking threats. He nodded briefly at Chet and held the door open.

Keeler passed close to him, the man's skin dark and glistening with sweat, smelling of coconut oil. The man was breathing through his nose, flaring with each inhalation before dilating with the expired air. Good situational awareness.

The man pointed and spoke in French. "Go to the end."

At the far side of the corridor was a young woman with nervous energy, someone who might have been the man's girlfriend or sister. She waited for Chet at a doorway, holding a Glock flat against her chest in the Sul position. The woman preceded Chet, leading the group into a stairwell. Keeler was in back but caught glimpses of her hustling down the stairs in gym shoes and dark blue camouflage patterned yoga pants.

Kazemi tripped and Keeler was there, picking him up off the floor. The journalist was sweaty, giving off a vinegary scent of fear. The man in the tennis outfit was right behind Keeler, moving down the stairs backwards, covering threats.

The ground floor had a glass vestibule, leading out to the lawn below the elevated walkway they'd taken earlier. The woman avoided the outside, leading them further downstairs, into the subterranean levels and ending at minus two. A low-ceilinged parking garage, accessed around a cinder block wall. The place stank of gasoline, diesel, rubber, and plastic. LED lights and stained concrete.

Keeler figured, maybe a vehicle, but the woman was jogging

across the lot opening another door. Hurrying, but not yet in a rush. Keeler wondered about her threshold for panic.

The squeal of tires sounded from above. The man in the tennis outfit pushed past Keeler, into another staircase vestibule. The woman and others were waiting near a service door. The man bent to insert some kind of specialized key and open the door.

He stood up. "In here."

Same order as before, the woman jogging ahead of them. Chet following her, then Billings leading Kazemi, no longer as winded, in the rhythm now, maybe even excited. Keeler kept in touch with the journalist, hand on his shoulder, knowing how it is for civilians, the sudden shock of trying to stay alive.

They were jogging through a harshly lit tunnel, a round passage with ducts and electrical conduit cable, water, and sewage pipes, basically an infrastructure extension passage to which they'd added a footpath. Probably a tunnel used by the cleaning and maintenance staff so that their existence and necessity wouldn't disturb the busy millennials above.

The woman was moving up a set of concrete steps below a steel pavement grate. She raised her arms, lifting the grill and shifting it to the side. She took another step up, the top half of her body now in daylight. Keeler and the team stood below, waiting for her to clear the route. A different exfiltration plan than Keeler and the hit team had memorized.

The woman's head wobbled, the side of it making a fast wave inward, distorting the shape. There was a sharp report from a distance. The woman instantly dead as she fell back against Chet. The sudden force pushed him off balance, a foot slipping and the other leg collapsing with the weight of the corpse. He tumbled in disorder.

Keeler vaulted over Chet, seeking to get up and out and engage. Some animal instinct had kicked in fast, registering the direction of gunfire and making the decision to move. Once he emerged fully into the daylight both the front and back of his mind were on the same page.

He barely registered the sound of an incoming round, whipping air as it twisted by.

What he knew, you could move quickly through a line of fire and only a very good shooter would track you fast enough. He was out of that opening in a curved sprint, having seen the brick building just in front of him, no windows, maybe a maintenance shed, maybe a place where they housed machines or tools.

He slammed against the wall two yards from the corner and gave it a moment, to see if the enemy would precipitate. The edge of the building exploded, sheared away by a heavy bullet. Keeler ducked out and identified the source of fire, an SUV parked fifty yards away. He saw Billings exiting the underground passage. Keeler took a knee behind what was left of the wall and put five rounds into the vehicle, not trying to be tricky, just firing methodically, each shot spaced out a quarter of a second apart.

Billings got in behind him and clapped a hand on his shoulder.

Keeler sprinted at the SUV, hearing Billings' weapon spit lead to cover him. He was identifying figures inside the vehicle. Keeler ran with the weapon up, sighting and moving while shooting. The rounds coming from Billings made the windshield quiver. Keeler could already see one man with multiple gunshot wounds.

A bullet whipped past his ear making a crackling sound. Keeler moved laterally, skipping to his left. He sighted at a shape in the back of the vehicle. Glimpsing a long gun barrel, firing into the darkness, and moving forward, running at it, and squeezing off two more rounds.

Two males in the back, slumped against each other like drunk cousins, corpses now. Both could pass for Middle Eastern or Hispanic ethnicity. The vehicle itself didn't look too bad. A Mercedes SUV, evidently not well armored. Chet was hustling Kazemi across the grass. Keeler opened the rear door and pulled the dead enemy operators out of the vehicle, dragging the corpses into the grass one by one.

Kazemi and Chet got in the back. Billings had the driver's body out now and had taken his place. Keeler took the passenger seat.

"What about our friend with the tennis outfit?"

Billings said, "Not coming." She looked at him and shrugged. "Cleaning up or something. I don't know."

The situation compartmentalized, as they say.

The engine was still running. Billings glanced in the rearview mirror, searching for Chet, and finding him. Keeler looked back, saw that he was occupied with the long gun, what looked like a Heckler & Koch G36 platform with heavier and longer barrel, set up for sharpshooting.

Billings shouted back. "Chet."

Chet's eyes flicked up, and he reached to tap his earbud, the designated comms man for the team. He said, "We're in a vehicle. Get us out of here."

Neilson's voice said, "Copy that. I have position for you. Move southeast and go straight through the intersection. Entrance a kilometer south of that."

Billings got the vehicle moving. The stereo system was putting out French rap music. Keeler shut it off. On their left side was a forest and, on the right, the green grass of the Expo Center, buildings rising out of shrubbery about fifty yards away. Up the road was a turn, beyond which it wasn't possible to see.

Neilson's voice said, "Hold position." The tone sharp.

Billings applied the brakes and for a second they sat in the vehicle, unmoving. The sound of police and emergency vehicle sirens could be heard now, along with the raucous shrieking of crows.

Neilson's voice said, "Law enforcement moving through exfiltration path. Hold."

The wait was exactly thirty seconds, but it felt longer. Keeler didn't enjoy sitting motionless in the car waiting for whatever Neilson was looking at. Probably an overhead feed from a DJI Mavic drone or something. He could feel eyes hiding behind corners, in the trees maybe. A creepy intuitive feeling that sitting still wasn't going to be a good idea.

Keeler said, "Drive into the woods."

Billings said, "What?" Searching around, trying to figure out what he was talking about.

Keeler said, "Left, do it now."

She saw it, the gap in the trees, a path for forest management vehicles to enter. Log piles to the right of the entrance, detritus from a chipper, almost degraded to mulch. Yeah, this was the way in. Billings realized it too, hitting the gas and swinging around in an arc, guiding the SUV into the space, and now rolling through an autumnal wood.

Neilson's voice said, "Sorry we're dealing with an..." The voice cut off mid-sentence.

Keeler looked back at Kazemi. "You have a phone?"

"No."

Keeler grunted. He remembered the black stone bowl in the journalist's Hotel room foyer. He'd left the phone there.

Kazemi said, "All this for me? I'm feeling a little overwhelmed by the attention."

Keeler said, "It's for us. You were just supposed to be the initial sacrifice."

Billings snorted. "Shit man."

Neilson's voice said, "Issues with..." and cut off again.

There was an issue, an attack on their communications, maybe the enemy was in their networks. Keeler sensed it, like the bad guys were pulling some kind of digital hood around them. If they were cutting into their operational comms, the enemy could equally be capable of tracking the vehicle.

Keeler said, "Stop the vehicle. Everyone gets out."

Billings braked when he opened the door. Keeler continued moving, stepping back and glancing at her as she killed the engine. She nodded, kicking open her door and moving out. Keeler got Kazemi out of the car. Chet exited the other side, carrying the rifle. He scuttled into cover behind a mature birch, getting the weapon up and swiveling his head, scanning the terrain. Keeler shepherded the journalist into the woods. Stopping him behind an almost identical tree. The forest was one of those European planned projects, trees evenly spaced and uniform in circumference.

SEVENTY-ONE

WHINING FROM ABOVE THE TREES. Micro servos hitting high gear. Quad rotor zip.

Chet said, "Drone."

Billings said, "Is it ours?"

Keeler said, "Take it out Chet."

The thing was hovering above the vehicle. Chet raised the rifle, bracing his arm against the birch bark to steady the gun, barrel pointing maybe eighty degrees. The G36 was running a suppressor. The gun popped, and the round made a loud *clack*, a direct hit on the drone which tumbled through branches. Keeler could hear a vehicle approaching, not the engine but the rolling tires on rock and dirt. He pulled at Kazemi and led the group away from the Mercedes. The enemy was closing in, probably had the vehicle's position, maybe theirs, time would tell.

Fifty yards away was a good spot, dense thicket sunken into a waterlogged area. Not precisely a swamp, but certainly cold and wet. He pushed Kazemi in.

"Get in that thick brush and stay down." He pointed at Chet. "You're with him. Give me that weapon." Pointing at the

H&K rifle. Chet glitched momentarily before handing the rifle to him. Keeler handed Chet the pistol, slapping it butt first into his outstretched hand. "Keep out of sight and wait for the call."

"What's the call?"

Keeler ignored him. Stupid question. The call was the call, it wasn't going to be complicated.

Kazemi was ankle deep in cold water, looking bedraggled but not unhappy. *Alert*, Keeler thought. The guy looks good, maybe the most exciting day in his life. Billings checked her weapon. Keeler jogged back towards the vehicle. Ten seconds later he stopped and turned. Chet and the journalist were out of sight, the boggy area was blending into the forest. Billings took a knee behind him, seeking eye contact.

She chin pointed ahead.

The Mercedes was forty yards away. Another twenty yards beyond it was a second SUV, creeping up in a slow roll crunching wood and clumps of leaf and grass.

Keeler said, "We're going to take them out."

Billings said, "You betcha."

No other vehicles in the vicinity, just these guys in a silver SUV, a Lexus maybe. No more drone rotor noise either. It was possible that these people were alone. Keeler was hoping to nab one, take him back to play question time.

He waited until the SUV had ceased moving. The Mercedes they'd been in was now between the silver vehicle and themselves, concealing himself and Billings. Keeler crept forward, to a depressed stream bed. A good place to make a lateral move, pinching in on the enemy. He looked back and locked eyes with Billings.

She'd be onboard with the program. Keeler had the long gun, so he'd hit them first, taking out as many as he could while she charged under his cover.

She used hand signals, and he responded with a thumbs up.

He signaled for her to think about keeping behind the engine block. Billings nodded.

Keeler got prone and performed a low crawl on elbows and knees, getting wet and muddy in the trickling stream, ignoring it. A minute later he figured he was good, risking a peek up over the low steam bank. The new vehicle was stopped behind the Mercedes. He'd been correct about the make, Lexus, not a subtle car.

Keeler made sure the weapon was prepared. Standard magazine capacity for the G36 was 30 rounds. He estimated that fifteen had been discharged, hopefully not more. He selected for single shot, noting that the weapon had either semi-automatic, or full auto. Thinking, 'that would be nice'.

The sight was some kind of French thing, a SCROME model. Keeler laid the gun into dry leaf, using the bank and digging a knee into the mud to settle himself. The silver SUV had four occupants. One of them was out of the car now, rear door swung open. The two in the front were in a conversation. Billings could probably take them through the windshield if the vehicle didn't have armored glass.

He'd go for the two in the back.

One man still sitting in the rear. Keeler sighted on him, going for a chest shot. He practiced moving between the seated man and the standing. Brushed the trigger and figured it'd be a question of one entire second. He returned the crosshairs to the man in the back seat, who had now kicked his door open, preparing to exit. Keeler shot him in the small of the back. Swinging the weapon to bear on the standing man, now jolted into a crouch and moving fast.

Keeler tracked him, another half second, or five of the man's frantic steps. Keeler was unwilling to fire yet, wanting to get a good shot in. The man was in motion, scuttling like a crab. He waited for the figure to clear a small tree, leading him in the sight by about four inches. His finger squeezed another round and a millisecond later the man staggered and pitched to the side.

Keeler came to a knee, tracking back with the rifle to the men in the front seat. The driver was upright and moving, other side of the vehicle. Billings was putting rounds through the windshield, presumably into the man in the passenger seat. Keeler looked back to the driver, who was no longer where he had been.

Billings had cleared the Mercedes and was now sprinting forward, angling for a better view of the enemy. Maybe she hadn't noticed the driver. Keeler saw him coming up on her flank. Billings, now between him and the enemy. He tracked the G36, raising the weapon slightly and sighting for the driver, a matter of seconds really. The man was in his sixties, gray hair and clean shaven with a silver mustache. Problem wasn't getting him in the sights, it was the fact that Billings was in the way, making the shot risky.

Billings moved clear and Keeler pulled the trigger, hearing a loud shot and momentarily confused until he realized that he and the driver had fired at the same time. His shot was suppressed, and the driver's pistol made the louder report. Keeler was up and running, seeing Billings on her knees. The man with gray hair was sprawled into a fallen tree, the head shot had taken half his face and splashed it into the dirt, his skull violently misshapen. Billings was slamming a hand into the dirt, spitting out blood and saliva, cursing.

Keeler got her into the recovery position. Pulling up clothing, searching for the gunshot wound and finding it on the outside of her left breast. The wound wasn't leaking blood, and he didn't see an exit out the back. The bullet had remained inside her body, a very bad situation. Billings was already having trouble breathing, the blood coming out of her mouth bubbly and frothing.

She was going into shock. Billings said, "What?"

Keeler shouted. "Chet." That was the call.

He turned to Billings. "Nothing, we'll get you out now."

She was going to die within five minutes.

Chet came sprinting over. He took a good look at Billings. Keeler shook his head, like no it wasn't going to end well.

They carried her into the back seat of the Lexus. Kazemi was quiet, but he helped. His eyes bulged and darted around. Keeler got behind the wheel, handing Chet the long gun. He maneuvered the vehicle into a K-turn and drove carefully out of the forest, not wanting to appear rushed, moving out the same way the vehicle had entered.

The forest path led to a blocked off entrance. The gate nothing more than a log on chains. Chet jumped out and lowered the barrier. The vehicle bumped over it and came through onto a small road, what they call a *departmental* in France.

Keeler got Neilson's voice in his ear. "We're on a private circuit."

Keeler said, "Go ahead."

"Rodriguez has issues. There aren't good options at the moment."

"No force protection?"

"Nothing that can be diverted, everyone has issues right now. I'm headed over to help him."

Keeler said, "I'm a couple minutes out from the Expo Center, on a departmental road moving southwest."

Neilson knew where they'd been a few minutes earlier, the exit out of the Expo Center and then the forest they'd turned into, avoiding the French law enforcement presence.

He said, "Yeah, I got you now. I'm seeing a suburban train

station at *Fontenay-sous-Bois*. Maybe three minutes away. One of you could get up to *Bobigny* and support the boss."

Keeler looked at himself, Billings' blood all over him. He was entirely unpresentable for public transportation. A vehicle was approaching on the departmental road.

He said, "Hold for a minute Neilson."

Keeler waited for the vehicle to get closer before swerving to block the road with the big Lexus SUV. He was out of the Lexus and approaching the driver's side window of a small Citroen. A terrified woman behind the wheel, frozen in shocked paralysis. The blood, and the pistol pointed at her head.

Keeler spoke calmly to her in French through the half-opened window. "Madam, I don't have time to explain but you'll need to get out of the vehicle. I'm with counterterrorism and there's an immediate need for your car."

The woman was trembling, obviously not believing him. Keeler opened the door and took her arm. No time to wait. She came out shaking, a mousey haired woman in her forties, wearing glasses and an earth-colored sweater.

She said, "What do you want?"

"The car."

SEVENTY-TWO

It wasn't as if Keeler had carefully thought this through.

Now he was wondering what to do with this woman. She couldn't travel with Chet because he was already weighed down with taking care of Kazemi and Billings, who wouldn't be alive much longer.

He said, "Get into the passenger seat."

She said, "What are you going to do?"

Keeler was impatient.

He hunted around in the car. Her phone was clipped into a holder on the dashboard, a wire running into an adaptor plugged into the vehicle's cigarette lighter socket. Keeler took the phone and the handbag on the passenger seat. The woman was nervously standing by the passenger door.

He said, "Get in. I'm not going to hurt you."

She gave him a blank look, panicked and incapable of reacting.

He pulled the car keys and jogged back to the Lexus, clutching her bag because he hadn't gone through it to check for another phone or something. Chet had a face like a question mark.

Keeler said, "Listen carefully. You're going back to Troyes. Neilson booked two cabins in a motel called the *M'sieur-Dame*. It's close to the place we stayed. Don't go near that house, you hear? It's compromised."

Chet was French fluent. He said, "Roger that."

Keeler said, "Neilson hit me on a private line. Rodriguez needs backup, I'm going to be it. You hunker down at the motel and wait for us. Get some food and whatever else we might need."

Chet nodded. "No problem." He looked up. "Oh shit."

Keeler turned. The woman was sprinting into a fallow field, stumbling over the deep ruts in the churned earth. Beyond the field were electricity pylons and more fields, probably with small roads between them. She'd end up getting attention, but by the time that mattered Keeler would be done with the vehicle.

Chet was moving into the driver's seat. Keeler made eye contact with Kazemi through the windshield, gave him a nod, hoping it'd help with his confidence.

The whole thing was touch and go at the moment.

He went back to the Citroen and threw the handbag into the back. He got the little car going. Keeler swerved around the Lexus and started on the departmental. He tapped the ear bud.

"I'm moving. Where am I going exactly?"

The car had a mapping device built into the dashboard. Keeler drove and poked and tapped it, following Neilson's instructions, trying to get the thing pointed in the right direction. The map on the Citroen's dashboard said twenty minutes to get up to Bobigny. Keeler drove as fast as he felt was possible, given the circumstances. He didn't want to attract the law.

Fifteen minutes into the drive, Neilson had arrived at the destination. The line between them was open. Hearing Neilson get out of the vehicle, cursing. Gunshots from what seemed to be a short distance, but still outside. Neilson was already breathless with adrenaline.

He said, "Some shit going down here. I've got a Glock. Are you still unarmed?"

Keeler said, "Picked up a Sig. Got maybe thirty-three rounds." The precise number just tumbling out of his mouth. He hadn't consciously kept track of the rounds fired but he had two spare magazines and something like three or four rounds in the weapon.

Keeler heard Neilson and could tell he was moving at a jog. The thunking sound of him running, the communications device jiggling up and down in his ear.

Neilson said, "I'm going in now. Left my guy in the vehicle with the gear. I think Rodriguez is inside but there's been no comms for maybe ten minutes."

More gunshots. The whole thing completely disorienting since Keeler was driving while listening to this in one ear. This kind of gunfight was going to attract the law, for sure. A few seconds later there was an outrageous burst from what Keeler surmised was a semi-automatic. It sounded thin to his ears, but that was just the comms unit microphone.

Neilson grunted and cursed. Gun fire from up close, which was Neilson firing his Glock. The metallic thunk of rounds popping off.

Bobigny was a gray suburb with concrete apartment blocks stacked like dominos, one after the other. He turned into the grid. Big apartment blocks giving way to smaller two-story residential buildings, a couple of streets of houses with enclosed yards. He clocked a van parked up at the side of the road, just before the mapped destination. Keeler moving the Citroen closer, slowing down to identify the van model.

He said, "You're in the white Renault Trafic."

"Yeah."

Keeler said, "Any weapons in the back of the van?"

"No."

Keeler pulled in behind the Renault. He checked the Sig Pro and got out. A long-haired thin guy was in the driver's seat of the van looking pale. Keeler glanced at him and nodded. He could understand, a knob twiddler, not a fighter. Sometimes you needed them. The guy pointed towards a building about fifty yards away. Neilson was outside, back to the wall. As Keeler got closer, he saw a body in the stairwell, fallen in an undignified position.

Neilson said, "That's one of ours, I believe. Although I am unsure if he's an American."

Rodriguez's mission had been to secure the colonel for an interrogation. Looked like that had gone sideways, like most everything. Keeler took a look at the corpse, a thick muscled man in his mid-thirties. He figured it was one of Rodriguez's guys.

"Where's Rodriguez?"

Neilson said, "He's inside. Pinned down."

Keeler said, "What's the issue?"

Neilson said, "You take a step in there and they're putting bullets down the hole. If we had a tank, we could hit em from the side, take out the whole building. Otherwise, we might need a team to get up on the roof. I could keep plugging from here and distract them."

Keeler darted in and grabbed the dead man's boot. He dragged the guy out, drawing two shots from above, raising concrete dust where they impacted on the stoop.

Keeler checked the dead man for identification, got a French identity card in a wallet stuffed with pocket litter. Nothing American about him. Maybe CIA was using mercenary cut-outs for deniability.

Keeler said, "Get some distance from the building. Cover

this entrance in case they squirt. I'm going to hit from another direction. Anyone comes out you clip them. Do we know which apartment?" Neilson said, "Up on the second floor. Apartment on the right."

"Why hasn't Johnny law showed up yet?"

Neilson grinned. "French no-go zone. I think even the gangsters are afraid of us."

Keeler nodded. Wise gangsters. He slipped along the building's facade. Making the corner and planning the next step.

SEVENTY-THREE

An hour earlier, the colonel had been lying on the single bed looking at his phone. He had his own room in the apartment, the other two CIA men sharing the second bedroom. One of them was always on duty so they took turns with the bed.

He'd noticed that each of them made the bed meticulously, immediately after rising. The pillows got turned over and plumped, the sheets were straightened, and a bed cover draped over the mattress. These were good boys, disciplined soldiers for America.

Still, it was an alien thing, something that the colonel wasn't truly able to understand, how two grown men in their forties could share a bed like that without feeling the humiliation of insult to their rank. These weren't rookies, they were field agents at the peak of their powers.

Not that any of this really mattered, he was feeling down in the dumps. While he hadn't been under the illusion that Anastasia was in love with him, he did think that she had at the very least some affection for him. Two years isn't a lifetime, but it's not nothing either.

After the meeting with the Russian in the Tuileries, the

colonel had recognized his mistake. Anastasia wasn't a Russian agent; she was something else. What exactly, he couldn't know. Maybe Israeli, or someone else. He didn't want to consider that she might be Iranian, but there it was, the suspicion existed.

He cursed at himself, a colorful string of words in Arabic.

The text message thread remained exactly as it had been for quite a while now. The last message from Anastasia had been received back in the Sinai, what seemed like a long time ago. Since the meeting with the Russian he'd sent two messages and nothing had come back.

He gave in to the urge and hit the call button. Putting the phone to his ear and letting it ring. Since he was calling from within the messaging app, it didn't matter that the phone was using a French SIM card. She would see that it was her colonel calling.

No response.

The colonel let it ring for a minute and the call ended by itself.

'Call not answered', was the notification he received.

He tossed the phone onto the bed and got up, padding to the kitchen across the wooden floor in his socks. They had a Nespresso machine set up with a bowl full of capsules. The colonel chose a green one first, watching the machine squeeze bean juice out of it into a glass latte cup. He used a second capsule, this time brown, adding milk and plenty of sugar to the drink and taking it back into the bedroom with him.

The phone screen was lit up as he came in, blinking out to black. Someone had messaged or called. The colonel set the coffee cup down on the wooden desk by the window. He fetched the phone and got the messaging app up.

Anastasia had sent a two-word message. 'Get out.'

The colonel felt as if his heart might burst from his chest.

SEVENTY-FOUR

Keeler was creeping around the back of the building, seeing a ground floor entrance and a window looking into someone's kitchen. He tapped on the glass, trying to get attention. Nobody. Keeler used the butt of the Sig Pro to break the glass. He reached in and opened the window. A half minute later he'd rolled through and was sitting on the sink. Keeler could already see the elderly lady in the other room, sitting on a recliner.

He came in and stood in her living room. Knowing how he looked, bloodied and big. The woman was in her eighties at least and had the palest skin and the whitest hair he'd ever seen. She was almost translucent, wearing a pink and blue lace dress and very pragmatic white shoes. The house was decorated with complicated porcelain plates on the walls and framed oil paintings of dogs.

He said, "Those your dogs?"

The woman nodded.

He said, "But no dog now."

"No monsieur. It wouldn't be fair to the dog, at my age."

"You'll live another hundred years, madam."

She said, "I've lived many dog lives, so I'm not afraid, monsieur. I will not be terrified."

"That's a good attitude. I need to get up to the apartment on the second floor. The one where the bad people are staying. What's the best way?"

She pointed up. "Just above my daughter's room."

"Maybe." Thinking she meant the location of the apartment.

She said, "My husband fought in Algeria."

Keeler said, "Tough war."

She was pointing up. "My daughter's room."

"Gotcha." She wasn't just tripping, there was something to be seen in her daughter's room. Woman like that, with the dog pictures and the plates, you had to take her seriously.

He moved past the recliner, entering a narrow corridor at the end of which was a small room with a single bed, the daughter's room. He was immediately drawn to the closet. Thing about buildings like this, the closet was usually the weakest link, in terms of the construction process. This closet was stuffed with bed covers and quilts and a broomstick without a broom. The shelf was loaded with plastic bags of Tupperware. Keeler displaced the contents onto the narrow bed. The shelf came out easily.

The small dining area had six sturdy chairs. The woman was watching him. It was weird, her body didn't move, nor the head. Only the eyes were tracking him.

He said, "Do you mind?"

"You can use the chair, and you do not have to put it back. I am entirely capable of putting it back."

Back in the daughter's room, he set the chair into the closet and was able to get up in there and examine the ceiling. Looking up, it was obvious why the woman had mentioned the daughter's room. The original ceiling was rotted away, covered now with painted cardboard. He pulled it down, looking now at ceiling joists. The daughter had probably climbed up in there as a kid. It must have been totally fun.

He tapped the earbud.

Neilson's voice came through. "Status?"

Keeler said, "Get Rodriguez in the loop."

Neilson said, "One second."

Rodriguez's voice came through. "You sonofabitch."

Keeler said, "What's your position?"

"Up on the second floor. We've breached the apartment but I'm two men down and pinned in the kitchen. They've got three or four men back in the main bedroom and another guy out on the landing, messing with my rear."

Keeler got a good grip on the joist and hauled himself up to access the ceiling void.

He said, "Copy that. Maintain and stand by."

Now he realized what that woman had been talking about, pointing up to the other apartment. This wasn't some big apartment block. It had once been a single house and the second floor wasn't sealed off the way it would have been, had it been two separate dwellings. Keeler was able to pull himself in and access the space between walls. He got up in the cavity, just about able to move around into the tight space.

He said, "Rodriguez, when I say *milkshake* I want you to cover me." He had no idea where the word milkshake came from, some deep part of the back of his mind maybe, he was a big fan of them.

Rodriguez said, "Where are you?"

"I'm coming from another angle, actually I don't know exactly but you cover me when I say the word. I'm serious, I'll be coming out blind and naked brother."

"*Milkshake*. Copy that. I'll send hellfire into the bedroom."

"Neilson, you need to storm the stairwell on my call."

"Copy that. Do or die on *Milkshake*." Keeler could hear the humor in Neilson's voice, this guy was gold.

Now, he was looking at a vertical option and a horizontal option. Up in the building's innards, maneuvering around joists and pockets of insulation. Lucky it was November not August, it'd be stifling in there. He figured, go horizontal and see what happens. He managed to balance, walking along the joist, following it in towards a tight wall cavity. Now he could hear voices. Two gunshots, muffled by the sound insulation. The voices coming from somewhere in front of him. The cavity was stuffed with slag wool insulation that had lost its shape. Keeler started ripping it out. Wanting to get in there.

A minute later he'd made the space necessary to slide into the cavity, aware that the project was completely insane.

The voices were closer, louder. At least two men. He could hear them clearly. Their language wasn't English or Arabic. Which reminded him of what Neilson had said back at the nightclub, when Keeler had asked what the men had been speaking. *I'm not a linguist buddy, you want me to guess?* It made him laugh now, stuck in the wall as he was.

No plan, just a guess and a gun.

The wall was plasterboard, simple as that. On the other side of it were voices, conversing excitedly in neither English nor Arabic. One of those voices was close. In fact, the guy was speaking just now, a long flow of whatever language it was. Keeler was so close to the wall that he could hear the vibrations from the man's voice. This somatic proximity allowed him to visualize the man's shape, where the guy was. The enemy was leaning back against the wall, sitting on the floor, like relaxing or something. Maybe recovering from a wound. Keeler pushed at the plasterboard with a finger, it moved inwards slightly. A single thin board. Cheap construction.

Keeler visualized the guy's head, just knew it was there from the way the board buzzed as the man spoke in his alien language.

He got into position, thinking fist and foot, one after the other. Just do it.

He said, "*Milkshake.*"

Gunshots from somewhere to his right. He figured Rodriguez and the other guy.

Keeler put a fist through the plasterboard, aimed just to the right of where he knew this guy's head was. The instant his big fist was through he grabbed at the head, getting a hand full of already struggling face, locking it in. He put his left through the wall. Same thing but better, the guy had turned his head away from the right hand. Keeler got fingers into nostrils and an eye socket, pulling the man into the disintegrating wall. He kicked hard with a steel-toed boot getting in there and ripping through the plasterboard at the bottom.

There were gurgles and shouts from the other side. More gunshots. Maybe this guy was having his little moment and his buddies weren't even aware, occupied as they must be with Rodriguez's covering fire. Maybe Neilson had broken through. Time to find out.

Keeler pulled the guy through the wall, holding his head now in both hands. The wall was destroyed, coming out in chunks. He dove into the room, coming up in a roll. The Sig Pro was up and ready. He felt his awareness heightened.

Two enemy combatants in the room, each of them holding a shortened Heckler & Koch MP5, taking turns firing around the doorway. The man closest to the door was clueless, but his buddy was reacting to Keeler's presence by turning and almost losing his balance in the process. Keeler remembered the face from Neilson's body cam. He moved forward aggressively and shot him in the head at point blank range.

The second guy staggered back; a natural reaction given the

situation. He moved into the doorway and thus entered the line of fire coming down the hall from Rodriguez. A volley of rounds tore into him, and he was down. Keeler spun back to the man he'd pulled through the wall. The guy was struggling, having fallen through back into rafters. Keeler hauled him up into the room.

He clipped the guy behind the ear with his pistol, putting him out.

More shooting from down the hall. Keeler risked a look, seeing Rodriguez's back as he stormed the position at the stairwell. Neilson's voice yelling up.

The apartment stank of death. Keeler looked into the other room, a pile of bodies in the corner. Rodriguez came back, pulling Keeler out of the room.

"This was ours, a CIA safe house for the verification team. The Egyptian's gone and the two CIA analysts are dead."

"You've had contact with the Task Force Commander?"

Rodriguez was getting his breath, overexcited by the tangle. He said, "Assets on the ground are tied up." Making eye contact. "Complete shitstorm. We're not the only ones with bodies."

Keeler said, "And?"

"Five hours." Rodriguez was wounded and didn't know it. His chest was leaking through the shirt. He followed Keeler's gaze. "Ah, shit."

Keeler said, "I'll look at that en route. Five hours to what?"

"Not sure, although it's not going to be your people."

Which meant not JSOC, but operators with the clandestine service. Keeler had mixed feelings, plus five hours could be a very long time.

He looked at the unconscious enemy captive, lucky to be alive. But then again, not so lucky because Keeler required information, and he wasn't going to ask politely.

He said, "Let's load up the bodies."

A proposition met by a staccato hail of gunfire from outside. Keeler took an oblique angle, looking out the window. A hundred yards off, a police patrol vehicle was reversing in a hurry. It was hard to see precisely what was going on, but out of the alleys on either side of the road poured what seemed like dozens of young men and boys, masked and hooded, throwing stones at the police car. Keeler's sharp eye picked out two adults, tall, bearded men with stiffly erect postures and firearms held low against the leg. Ringleaders who could put a burst into the vehicle's hood and make the cops run.

Neilson had his long-haired geek bring the van up so the bodies could be transferred more easily. Rodriguez knew which of the dead to take, leaving behind the rest. The gangsters watched from a distance, probably unsure of exactly what they were looking at. Keeler figured they were confused about many more things than that.

Upstairs Rodriguez got busy setting incendiary charges. Keeler placed three of them in the Citroen. As the van drove away thermite reactions ripped out behind them, destroying biological traces, hopefully without harming a hair on the head of the lady living downstairs.

SEVENTY-FIVE

Rodriguez had bullet fragments in his pectoral muscle, not a direct hit, more likely a consequence of a bullet striking a brick or concrete wall and shattering in proximity. Which meant a certain degree of surgical precision was necessary. But that wasn't going to happen real soon.

The back of the van was crowded. Keeler had bound their captive with duct tape and thrown him on top of the two dead CIA men. That might not have been pleasant, but it was just a prelude to the pain that Keeler intended on bringing.

The rest of the van's interior was dedicated to the equipment that Neilson had installed and the space that Keeler was using to treat the Operations Officer.

The medical kit was decent, but Rodriguez knew not to expect the turkey with *all* the trimmings, there was going to be discomfort. The van rocked and rolled. Keeler steadied himself, cleared the blood from the affected area, staunching the flow without too much difficulty, no major blood vessels nicked or arterial damage. He had Rodriguez supine with the torso and head elevated, toggling between an irrigation syringe and the forceps, digging in, using a flashlight between his teeth to hunt the metal fragments.

Rodriguez made a sound like a hippo in heat. It would have been more convenient to have a set of hemostats to lock onto the fragments, given that each time the forceps slipped off with the vehicle's bounce, it caused a new set of nerves to be violated.

Rodriguez didn't scream, he resorted to animal sounds, grunting, and holding on tight, nails digging into Keeler's leg, a length of rope between his teeth, hissing and groaning. The van slowed and then sped up a little. Eventually it stopped. Keeler wasn't paying attention to the journey, too occupied with Rodriguez.

He said, "Two more to remove boss, as far as I can tell. You'll feel better soon."

Rodriguez said something obscene about Keeler's close relations. The last bullet fragment came out, a thin piece of copper jacketing, sharp as a newly cut razor blade. Keeler let it drop to the van's floor, already awash in blood and other bodily fluids excreted by the dead, the wounded, and the terrified enemy captive. He sanitized the wounded area, applied a compress and wrapped an Israeli bandage around Rodriguez's torso.

"Good to go."

Rodriguez said, "Thank you." He moved out, impatiently getting back to command.

Keeler took a break outside the van.

Neilson had brought them to an underground parking garage. He'd spiraled down a ramp from the exit to subterranean level minus two. Keeler saw two men on each side, facing out, armed with MP5s. He figured this was a vehicle switching facility maintained by the United States clandestine service, which had them in most capital cities.

It'd be a real parking garage for ninety-nine-point nine percent of the time.

At the moment, the garage smelled like gasoline and diesel, which was a whole lot better than the back of the van. Neilson said that the replacement vehicle was en route to their location, ETA: 20 minutes. Keeler wasn't going to wait that long to squeeze the prisoner.

What he wanted now was the Egyptian colonel. He got Neilson's nerd to help him drag out the bodies. Once they were transferred Keeler got in with the bound man and shut the doors. He put on the overhead light and looked at the guy in the dim glow. The guy looked back; duct taped mouth bubbling as he did some heavy breathing through a clogged nose.

KEELER RECOGNIZED the man from the nightclub, still wearing a Rolex, his French haircut a little sticky. Nobody had checked his pockets. Keeler found a wad of Euros, much of it in hundreds. No identification documents.

He said, "You're what, Iranian?"

The man looked at him with large brown eyes, mouth duct taped and incapable of speech. Keeler was looking for something simpler, a nod or a shake. He grabbed at the man's nose and broke it, twisting it violently for about thirty seconds while the man moaned and writhed in pain.

He let go of the nose and watched the guy try to breathe through it now. The guy's eyes bugged, face in contortions as he attempted to suck air through the constricted passageways. Keeler recalled the two CIA men, now corpses. Wherever back home was, there were people who weren't even aware of the bad news coming at them.

He said, "You're what, Iranian?"

The man nodded. Keeler ripped the duct tape off his mouth, eliciting a storm of gasping and air gulping. Keeler was straddling him and could feel the guy's entire body convulsing in relief. He waited for the breathing to get more regular.

He said, "I just want the Egyptian."

The man laughed. "The traitor. Who wants a traitor?"

"You think it's funny? I do."

The man said, "I also want things."

A negotiator.

As far as Keeler was concerned, this wasn't going to be an actual conversation. He reached into Neilson's tool kit and removed a set of needle-nose pliers and a large screwdriver. The man's eyes followed his actions.

The mouth began shaping up to say something, but Keeler put the screwdriver in, prying the mouth open while he got the tapered jaws of the pliers around the right central incisor. The guy was blubbering and salivating and trying hard to speak around the tools currently inserted into his mouth. Keeler put his left forearm over the face and leaned in hard, using it as leverage to rip the tooth out by the root. The man screamed for all he was worth, spittle flying. Keeler held the tooth up for examination. The object was impressive, with the long single root intact.

He said, "What was it you wanted, teeth?"

Blood boiled out of the Iranian's mouth. He turned to spit it out. Keeler grabbed him by the chin, bringing the head around. The man was trying to speak.

Keeler said, "What?"

"What, what do you want?"

"I want the Egyptian."

The man sobered. "The Egyptian's gone." He was looking at Keeler with glossy eyes. The face pale, mouth open revealing the disturbed dental work. "The Egyptian." He rolled his eyes. "A traitor. Nobody trusts a traitor."

Keeler said, "Let me be clear. I want this Egyptian. You are now the property of the United States of America. The information coming out of your mouth might save American lives. This would be a good thing for you, in the next years of your captivity. If you fail to divulge useful information, it will not be good for you. You've now transitioned to a simpler life with fewer choices."

The man's eyes cleared suddenly, as if remembering something.

He said, "Kill me now. I'd like that."

"I'm sure you would."

The guy licked at the hole where his tooth had been.

Keeler wanted answers to his question. He had this insane urge to get his hands on the Egyptian colonel and felt the barriers of normal behavior breaking away in front of him. He snagged a section of electrical cable that Neilson had neatly stowed around a peg on the wall of the van. He wrapped each end around a fist and looped the cable around the man's neck.

Keeler began bearing down, tightening the cord and restricting airflow. His face was inches away from the man, already turning red.

He said, "Where did the Egyptian go?"

The man was hardly able to speak. Incomprehensible sounds coming out of him.

Keeler was aware of the way he was behaving, like a *berserker*. He was in that mode, because it was unavoidable. At some point in life everyone needs to accept themselves. Keeler had passed that milestone a while ago. He was going to kill this guy, squeeze the life out of him.

Neilson was speaking to him. "Quit it."

Getting an arm around Keeler and pulling him off. Keeler threw an elbow into his friend's face. Bearing down on the Iranian Quds Force agent.

"Tell me where the Egyptian went."

He slacked off on the electrical cable, allowing the man to feed off a slim sip of air. The guy sucked it, the oxygen filtering into his system.

The man said, "We were sent to kill him and the Americans, okay. He wasn't there, so we killed the Americans."

Neilson was pulling him back again. "That's good, buddy."

Keeler let go of the guy. Releasing him from the constricting cable, the man gulping and gasping air.

Neilson said, "Come out of there man."

Keeler came out of the van and took a deep breath. The air in the garage was fetid, but a hundred times better than inside the tight space with its death stench. Neilson was sitting on the edge catching his breath, the beginnings of a black eye forming from the elbow strike.

Keeler said, "What'd you think, I was going to kill him?"

"Yeah, it did look that way."

"You hurt?"

Neilson ignored the question.

A vehicle approached, coming down the ramp. Squeal of tires and another Renault Trafic van was pulling around. This one black. Two men in the cab, three men coming out of the back. Rough looking guys with black beards who were clearly not American. Like the CIA was sourcing local operators. Rodriguez went over, speaking French and gesticulating, giving instructions.

Rodriguez pointed at Keeler and Neilson. "Get in the van. We're out of here."

They'd rally at the *M'sieur-Dame* motel in Troyes, wait for the CIA backup team and then follow an exfiltration plan out of the country. Kazemi might be taken to the USA, who could tell. The Iranian agent would most likely end up in a black site somewhere in the Middle East, a place firmly under Uncle Sam's thumb, like Jordan. Interrogators would mine him for everything he had and then let him rot or let him go, nobody could tell.

Keeler's Plan B had sort of worked, it was now being adjusted. The United States military machinery was taking over and once that got into gear nothing could stop its relentless swarm.

SEVENTY-SIX

The colonel looked up at a blue sign affixed to the building, above the brasserie. *Rue des Lilas, 19th Arrondissement*. He knew Paris well, particularly this part of it. The plan was to get to the *Parc des Buttes Chaumont* and find a spot to think, somewhere relatively out of sight. He'd come out of the *Porte des Lilas* metro, and nobody had looked twice at him since.

He bought a smartphone and a pre-paid SIM at a kiosk, planning to use the phone as a burner, needing the apps a device like that could offer. Before leaving the safe house, he'd wiped his old phone and destroyed the SIM.

Once he'd slipped out of the safe house, he'd just started walking. The CIA men hadn't come after him. He'd made it to a suburban rail station and worked his way into the city improvising a surveillance detection route. Nobody had followed.

Anastasia's message had been both very clear and obscured in mystery. He'd read in it a clear and present danger. Beyond that he was still in the dark. The other thing was that the thought of going back to Egypt had somehow become impossible. He had just enough awareness to understand how badly his bridges had been burned.

And it had all happened so fast.

There was a cafe in the *Parc des Buttes Chaumont* that he used to enjoy as a teenager, during the years that he'd lived in the 16th arrondissement. He found a seat in the back and unpacked the smart phone and SIM, getting everything set up. The waiter came, and he ordered coffee.

He had the remains of his cash envelope from the Americans. In addition to that he had funds stashed in Switzerland, plus a nice nugget of crypto currency. A twenty-four-word seed phrase that he'd memorized was all that was required to access more than a million dollars' worth of the stuff.

The sun was getting low. The colonel paid for the coffee and began walking west, across the park. The walkways winding down around the rock formations that gave the place its name. It would be easy to find a place to stay in the *Goutte D'Or*, a bustling immigrant neighborhood where he'd disappear into the human tangle. Certainly, going for the border was a bad idea at the moment.

In any case, he had to consider where to go.

The colonel was walking past the *Place du Colonel Fabien*, the old Communist Party Headquarters, when he caught a glimmer of apprehension, noticing a man across the street, back maybe twenty meters. The man wore a red turtleneck sweater under a dark brown blazer. It was the color that had stood out, making the colonel remember seeing the guy earlier in the park. Then, he'd been eating an ice cream, looking at the water flowing out of the butte.

The Communist Party Headquarters was on the colonel's left, the strange architectural formations standing out in the neighborhood's boxy conformity. He spotted a second man in front of him on the right. The guy wore a dark blue bomber jacket, not a military item but a fashion version, with a logo at his breast. A cold feeling gripped the colonel at that moment.

Both men were of a type familiar to him, dark hair cropped short in the military style of an Egyptian Mukhabarat officer.

Of course, he couldn't be a hundred percent sure. He might just be batshit crazy.

The other thing he started thinking about was the possibility that they were presenting themselves for him to see, attempting to deflect him left onto *Boulevard de La Villette*. The double wide artery with a strip of trees and vegetation in the middle. A core element of his youthful experience, the Belleville section full of Chinese prostitutes, shamelessly parading. It was once exhilarating to return to the geographical comfort of Paris, and at the same time dreadful seeing his compatriots arrayed in a net formation that could only have one purpose.

They were going to capture him. That was their plan. If they wanted to kill him immediately, he'd already be dead, of this he was fairly certain. He didn't plan on making it easy.

The colonel didn't take the left. He sprinted into the intersection, going for the metro station entrance on the other side of the circle. The sudden movement forced a car to put on the brakes in panic. The crunch of another hitting the rear end was followed by drivers leaning on horns, Paris style. The man in the bomber jacket was in motion, angling to cut off the colonel across the busy traffic circle. A man in a gloss black Mercedes cursed at him, the car stopping inches from the colonel's knees.

He was across the road and running for the stairs. *Metro Colonel Fabian*. The man in the bomber jacket not so far off. The colonel got ahold of the banister and vaulted over, hustling down the stairs to the interior of the metro. Thankful for the twenty minutes per day he did on the bike after yoga, back in Cairo. He glanced behind him, catching the mukhabarat agent's silhouette at the top of the stairs.

The colonel didn't have a ticket, so he jumped the turnstiles, squeezing in through the closing flaps. Waiting on the platform, feeling all kinds of butterflies. The train was two minutes out and nobody came after him. Why?

The train arrived, the metro line actually perfect for what he wanted, heading up past the Stalingrad station, he could get off at *Barbes*, another crazy neighborhood packed with Algerians. It took five minutes to get there. The train emerging from underground and now elevated above the city. The gray life happening below. Five hard minutes, each one a kind of stress torture. He steeled himself, now questioning his intuition. Had those men actually been following him?

Out of the train at Barbes, moving into the crowd, hustling downstairs to street level. Parisian rush hour now, people returning home from work or school. An older guy bumped him on the way down, apologizing politely. The colonel felt an itch on his right buttock. He snatched at it. Down at street level, under the railway trestle. North African men called out, selling cigarettes. Others hanging out and smoking. A Senegalese man had a cart roasting chestnuts.

The colonel felt something sort of *bend* inside of him. An internal weakness. He noticed the onset of disorientation, before it fully overcame him. The man from the stairs who'd bumped into him and apologized. He was now taking his elbow and guiding him to the other side of the trestle. The colonel found that he couldn't actually move on his own anymore. A second man had his right elbow. A van waiting. The door sliding open and then he was inside.

A familiar face looking at him from the gloom. A mukhabarat officer he'd come up in the ranks with. Now looking at him with disgust.

The officer spoke to him in their native tongue. "Hisham Al-Masri, you stand accused under the highest authority of the Egyptian General Intelligence Directorate of committing acts of treachery against the Arab Republic of Egypt." The tone became less formal. The man growled. "You'll beg for death."

The man who'd stuck him with the nerve agent was in the van with them, the seats installed so that they faced each other. He leaned forward to look at the colonel, pale blue eyes behind wire-rimmed glasses. The man spoke in Hebrew, a language that he had very little familiarity with, having taken only the required courses during his training. Which wasn't a problem since the words were simple.

"Yasmin Shoshan sends her best regards, colonel."

The colonel faded, losing consciousness until there was nothing.

SEVENTY-SEVEN

Seddiqine, *South Lebanon*

The sound of the keys woke her. Yasmin observed the guard through partially closed eyelids, wondering if he was bringing her food or if they were going to chop off her head today. A range of possibilities all playing in her mind. Maybe they'd allow her to wash for the first time.

The man unlocked the barred cell door. Yasmin had been asleep on the thin and dirty mattress. The place was not a room, more of a niche carved out of pure rock, dripping with humidity. It was cold and clammy, but she was alive, and that's what she held on to. She repeated the mantra in her head, what kept her going. *At home they'd do everything in their power to get you back. They'd give a thousand captured enemies for you. You're invaluable, they'll never give up on you, not ever.*

The guard held the door open. They spoke to her in bad English.

He said, "Come."
She said, "Where?"
He said nothing.

The man didn't look any more threatening than usual, well

built and tall, carrying a newer AK-12 model. Which put the guard firmly within the Hezbollah elite, most likely a Radwan Forces commando.

They'd taken her down into the tunnels under South Lebanon, that much was obvious. Yasmin had regained consciousness to find herself strapped to a stretcher and unable to move. She'd been carried by four men, jogging at a no-bullshit pace. It was an entire journey in the tunnels, she wasn't certain, but she estimated the trip had lasted maybe two days. They'd switched out the men every four hours or so, a new crew ready to take the weight.

At the end of the descent there had been two women in a room to greet her. They wore full Islamic head coverings, the hijab, plus black abaya robes, and silently stripped Yasmin of her soiled clothing. They'd thrown a thin oversized t-shirt at her and that's all she'd had ever since. Mostly, she huddled under the cheap fleece blanket in her cell.

Yasmin had no idea how deep they were. She figured it'd be deep enough that they felt safe from Israeli sensors. Maybe a hundred meters, maybe less. She wasn't an expert.

The guard was holding the door. She hadn't ever seen his face because he wore a mask at all times. But she'd seen the eyes. He took turns on shift with one other man, shorter but stronger. Yasmin felt like she knew something about this guard by now. Human connections were strange that way. The other thing she experienced was being vulnerable and alone. She was by herself in a serious way. This was neither solitary confinement in a regular prison, or the solitude you get in nature. It was her alone in a dungeon while above ground people lived their lives without any inkling of what was beneath their feet.

Yasmin and them, that's how it was. The masked enemy seemed content to make monsters of themselves, but they were human just like anyone else.

She rose and exited the cell. The guard let her pass. The living area was two small alcoves bored into rock. The cell where she was kept, and a small nook with a bucket toilet. A guard sat on a chair at all times, looking at her through the barred door. A camera had been mounted to the wall directly facing her cell. The red light constantly on, watching her and recording.

The guard pushed her in a different direction this time. A walk of several minutes that passed through two blast doors. The way this man looked at her, and held his weapon, he wasn't trying to get friendly. He'd kill her in an instant if he thought there was a chance of her getting away.

Stockholm syndrome was some bullshit. She wasn't identifying with him. This wasn't Scandinavia. She did like the weapon however, the AK-12 was a friend to whomever got it in their hands, that was the cold truth that she'd been taught.

Yasmin had been in Gaza. She'd seen the tunnels there. This tunnel system wasn't anything like that. In Gaza, the tunnels were constructed from prefabricated concrete arches. They had workshops where the forms were molded and packaged for assembly underground. Here the tunnels were bored out of pure rock. The difference was in the medium. Gaza was all sand, and therefore the tunnels needed reinforcing. South Lebanon was mountainous.

They entered an expansive room with a domed ceiling. A camera had been set up on a tripod, two lights either side of it aiming at a beige sheet that had been stretched across a section of rock wall. A small stool was placed in front of the sheet. To the left of that setup were two tunnel entrances. The schematic diagram would look like a central subterranean hub with three spokes kicking out. Looking at the camera equipment, Yasmin quickly understood that they were planning on making a hostage video. She didn't see any surveillance cameras.

She'd seen plenty of hostage videos over the years. They weren't so much a sign of life as psychological warfare designed to create confusion and uncertainty among the Israeli public, elected officials, and the military. Once the video was shot, these people would broadcast it over the internet and she'd be a celebrity at home for all the wrong reasons, for the rest of her life.

Yasmin didn't want to be a celebrity.

Right now, it was just her and this guard. He pointed at the stool.

"Go."

The man was keeping his distance. Yasmin got it; they wanted her hands free in the video, which is why he hadn't zip tied her. He looked nervous however, alert, and probably under the weight of a great responsibility. It was extremely unusual for these people to get their hands on an Israeli hostage. If anything happened, he would face serious questions.

She moved past the camera, thinking about how it could be destroyed. Yasmin calculated that she'd have about five seconds before an intervention, probably less. It wasn't going to be enough, and even if she managed to destroy the equipment, there'd easily be another camera available.

The beige sheet was crudely stuck onto a rough stone surface with duct tape. Which gave her an idea. If you can't destroy the means of production, destroy the product instead.

She didn't think about it too hard, going on pure instinct. Yasmin walked to the wall and head butted the rough cut stone as hard as she could. Her front tooth had already been chipped earlier, and now she simply didn't care. She went for the nose, break that, and make it look awful. The appendage would be fixed if she lived and if she didn't live, there was no point in having a nose.

Make herself impossible to look at.

Yasmin got two good head butts in, forcing herself to do it before any pain snuck through. The impact knocked her silly but she managed a third one, slamming herself into the rock wall, getting a good solid thunk in the face, but then losing her feet, involuntarily crumpling to the ground in a stunned tangle of limbs.

For some reason the guard's reaction made her laugh. He started acting all panicked, fumbling over her and calling out for help. Which is what gave Yasmin the best idea she'd ever had. There wasn't any CCTV in there, and she was alone with this guard. It was entirely possible that these people hadn't prepared for taking a hostage, this was an improvised operation. Which meant that she was able to improvise as well.

A second man rushed into the room. The guard jabbering at him about her hitting her own head on the wall.

She hadn't spoken Arabic to them yet, so when she started yelling they paid attention.

Yasmin propped herself up on an elbow. "He raped me. He's lying. I was violated and then he smacked my head into the wall."

The second guy was holding a clipboard, not necessarily a guard. He seemed shocked at what she was saying. The man's gaze swiveling from Yasmin to the guard. Who tried to interject a denial.

"That's a total lie, she did it to herself."

Which didn't seem like a good answer. The second man looked at her again.

Yasmin doubled down, locking in the eye contact.

"Is rape your policy? Are you a bunch of rapists?" No response. She increased the pressure, getting her voice to a high shriek. "Is this what you stand for?" Turning to the first guard, who seemed taken by surprise. Pointing at him. "Rapist, murderer!"

The guy could have calmly rebutted her accusation, but he didn't. He raised his voice and got all defensive when his colleague started asking questions.

"She's lying." Turning to the second man. "Can't you see that she's lying?"

The second man spoke for the first time. He said, "Shut up." Looking at Yasmin. "What happened?"

She began to cry, the tears coming so easily now that she wished them out. A flood almost instantly soaking her face. They say that a good actor can do it on command. The technique is all about summoning some kind of ancient trauma. Yasmin found it pretty easy to call that kind of emotion up. She was surprised at herself. Blubbering and telling the tale.

The first man tried to interject by the second guy stopped him again. They started arguing.

Yasmin said, "Please, examine me. You'll see that I'm telling the truth."

The second man wore a pistol in a holster at the hip. Yasmin put her focus there, watching the weapon approaching through a veil of blood that now covered her face. Seeing the pistol bobbing in front of her as the guy came forward. She was acting all listless, going for the broken doll look, but ready to act when necessary.

She said, "Look what he did to me." Keeping the voice soft and victim like.

The first guard said, "She's a lying zionist whore."

The political officer said, "Shut up, idiot." He crouched over her. "Where besides the face?"

She said, "You know where."

The guard said, "Lying bitch."

The political officer leaned further in, the pistol grip almost coming into reach. It was going to be a matter of her getting hands on it. Maybe she'd punch him in the balls and go for the weapon.

That possibility drifted away when he pulled back from her. He said, "Get Nour."

Yasmin heard the guard speaking into a communications system. It was an intercom attached to the wall at the far end of the space. And she realized that the intercom system was hard wired so that electronic signals interception would be impossible.

'Nour' was a woman's name, and Yasmin understood the situation. The political officer wanted a woman to examine Yasmin because, as an observant Muslim man, he wasn't permitted to do so.

Which made this Nour person potentially interesting from a survival and evasion point of view.

SEVENTY-EIGHT

UNDERGROUND FACILITY, *Mount Meron, Northern Israel*

Hershkowitz sat one row back from the control panel. Silhouettes just in front of him, three females and a male, conscript soldiers in uniform. The monochrome images from infrared cameras lit three large screens on the front wall. On the left side was a drone's eye view over a walled compound within a Damascene neighborhood.

The middle screen showed the world from the gun turret of a Blackhawk helicopter. The chopper was looking at the back of two other Blackhawks in tight formation moving up the Lower Galilee towards the Golan Heights.

The sun was already below the horizon, but full darkness was about an hour away.

The screen on the right showed the view from a body-cam embedded in the button of a shirt worn by their agent, a man whose identity Hershkowitz wasn't ever going to be allowed to know.

The location in question was an Islamic Revolutionary Guards Corps annex near the Iranian embassy in Damascus. The agent moved down a corridor bathed in the harsh glow of fluorescent light strips, the wide-angle lens showing the ceiling and floor, the image distorted around the edges.

'Bug's eye view', Hershkowitz thought.

The man reached a door and his hand extended to open it, pale and hairy with a thin bracelet. The conference room was hazy with smoke, emitted from the cigarettes of maybe a dozen men gathered around a table laden with lemonade bottles, coffee cups, ashtrays, and wired communications terminals.

The men were a mix of gray beards and younger officers, plus assistants. This was the main operational node for the IRGC efforts in Syria, from where command and control was exerted over their activities in Lebanon and along the southern Syrian border with Israel.

Hershkowitz found himself holding his breath and inhaled through his nose, exhaling through his mouth, regulating the respiratory system again. This was it, the moment they'd been waiting for, and he wasn't going to be the only one who'd held his breath.

He already recognized several personalities from the deck. The body-cam feed had been frozen and fragmented into small boxes, each containing a usable shot of a man's face. The recognition systems crawled over features, doing their thing, the calculation of relative distance, nose to lip, edge of mouth to the corner of each eye, interior corner of an eye to a nostril, and so on. It was called a facial identification matrix and each human being on earth has a unique version.

Names were being called out as the IRGC officers were verified. One by one they were identified and named until a younger officer in the front row held up his right hand for attention, finger raised.

He said, "We have them."

A woman next to him clicked several keys on the console in front of her.

She turned to look back at Hershkowitz.

He said, "Do it."

She said, "Tango One go" adding the Hebrew language version of 'safe travels', *Behatzlachem*.

∽

SIX AIRCRAFT from an F-16 fighter jet squadron crossed into Lebanese airspace from the Mediterranean Sea. The journey to Damascus took almost four minutes. Three of the F-16s were tasked with electronic counter measures, while the remaining three sent small diameter GPS guided glide bombs into a building about three hundred meters from the Iranian embassy compound.

The target had been chosen as a credible decoy. A building housing several Hezbollah officials in Damascus. Two of the glide bombs came in through the second-story window on the north side of the building, the third came in on the right and missed the window completely.

The drone's eye view was looking down at the scene. The third glide bomb had hit first. Slamming into a corner of the building and exploding, sending broken concrete and metal fragments cascading into the street. It was an accident, but Hershkowitz had no doubt that civilians were down there paying with their lives.

He watched the remaining split screen images along with the others in the command room. The nose cameras from the remaining two glide bombs showed the building approaching rapidly, then the entry in through the two windows followed by a bright flash as the explosion overwhelmed the image sensor and the camera was vaporized.

The screen reverted to a static hiss.

The drone's eye showed fire and smoke.

There would be sirens and ambulances, and all kinds of hysteria. Maybe even a couple of dead Hezbollah officials, along with their families, or local mistresses.

More to the point, the Iranian officers were going to react.

Attention turned to the body-cam on their man in the IRGC conference room. The camera had no audio capabilities, but the men in the conference room were now clearly agitated, suddenly busy and in motion, probably feeling the tremors of the explosion, hearing the bangs, and approaching sirens.

Bodyguards entered the room, and the Iranian officers began to move, standing up from the table and being hustled out, presumably to the compound's bomb shelter.

Which is exactly what the Israelis wanted them to do.

A new video feed came up on the screen, replacing the Blackhawk helicopters. It was mounted on a body-cam worn by one of their people in Damascus, currently riding in the back seat of a van marked with the logo of a Norwegian NGO specializing in water sanitation.

None of the passengers were members of the NGO, and the van was a fake. These were mission oriented Sayeret Matkal operatives who only cared about the objective.

A female soldier up front clicked keys and spoke into a headset.

"Received." She looked up and back at Hershkowitz. "The targets are moving to the shelter. We're going to lose the video from our man inside."

SEVENTY-NINE

It took the woman named Nour five minutes to arrive.

While they waited, the guard and the political officer did not converse. Which was a plus-one for Yasmin's chances of dividing and conquering, at least that's the way she was thinking about it. She had been playing half-dead. Letting herself drool blood onto the rough stone floor, moaning once in a while. The guard lit a cigarette and the other guy made him put it out.

These two were not friends.

Nour entered the room from one of the tunnels to the left of the beige sheet. Yasmin wasn't looking, but heard the quick footsteps and the breathlessness in her voice as she spoke.

"What's going on?"

The first guard started to speak but the second man cut him off.

"Go examine her."

Nour approached, and Yasmin was ready, turning to clutch her arm and speaking softly in Arabic, not much above a whisper.

"I need to clean myself. Please don't let them see me when you examine my body. Don't let them dishonor me further."

The woman said, "Get up." She addressed the men. "I need to examine her in private."

Yasmin allowed herself to be lifted by Nour and one of the guards, letting her body remain limp. Once on her feet, she leaned on the woman, only now allowing herself to take a look. Nour was shorter than Yasmin, with more girth and heft. She wore a hijab that covered her hair, framing her face in brown cloth. A floor length plain black abaya obscured her body's shape.

Nour took her into one of the other tunnel entrances, the political officer following them closely. An alcove had been carved out of the rock. Nour pointed to a thin mattress lined with pillows. It was both a resting area and a sleeping nook. Yasmin sat down on the mattress and Nour drew a curtain closed.

Yasmin's heart began to beat more rapidly. This was it; she wasn't going to have another chance. At least the curtain seemed to shut properly.

Nour got down on her knees and prepared for the examination. Yasmin could hear the political officer on the other side of the curtain. He was pacing back and forth. Yasmin let Nour lift the t-shirt, exposing her groin area.

Yasmin said, "Did they tear my underwear? I felt it rip when they assaulted me."

Nour clucked her tongue, like she didn't believe Yasmin. The woman was almost exactly where Yasmin wanted her to be. Another few seconds. She needed her a little closer.

The political officer in the corridor spoke loudly. "What are you doing?"

Nour said, "What do you think I'm doing. Go away."

The man leaned his mouth close to the curtain. He spoke quietly. "I'm not talking to you, I was talking to the idiot." He continued speaking, moving away from the nook. "Put that down you moron."

Yasmin blocked his existence from her mind. At the moment there was her and Nour in there.

Nour said, "Remove your underwear. I'm not going to do it for you."

Yasmin reached down and her hands were directly below Nour's head. The movement required for removing her panties necessitated a lifting of the knees and a few moments in which her hands were obscured from Nour's view.

She said, "Excuse me sister, what's your name again?"

Nour began to speak, and Yasmin used the opening of the woman's mouth to begin her gambit. Yasmin's left hand had crumpled the underwear into a ball. Now, she raised it to Nour's mouth and jammed the fabric in, sneaking her panties through Nour's teeth. At the same time, her right hand braced onto the back of the woman's plump neck, preventing recoil.

Yasmin shifted rapidly, just like in the Brazilian Jiu Jitsu lessons, wrapping her legs around Nour's soft body, locking her in place as she adjusted, snaking and fastening her arms around the woman's neck, cutting off the air supply as she held in the gag with a hand clamped over the mouth.

Nour struggled and moaned, but she was unfit. Yasmin had her easily under control. It took several minutes of for the woman to asphyxiate. Yasmin maintaining the intensity and pressure, trying to relax her own breathing. The death was terrible, Nour's body clenched in spasm as she struggled to live. The organism holding on until there was literally nothing left to live on, no oxygen to the brain and eventually an evacuation and release, the control function finally extinguished.

Yasmin couldn't satisfy herself with simply choking Nour

out, she had to make sure the woman died. The death rattle was final, and gave Yasmin the shakes.

She focused on what needed to happen, the exchange of clothing. Yasmin pushing aside the horror and the other thoughts of future outcomes, concentrating on the task at hand and her own breathing. There were more threats out there and she needed to go from one to the other, like a sequence of linked problems.

Now came the hard part. The political officer had already moved back up the corridor.

His voice was close through the flimsy curtain fabric. "What's going on?"

Yasmin had heard Nour's voice only once, it was a soft voice, feminine and slightly husky. She had the dead woman in the t-shirt and maneuvered the corpse onto its side, facing away from the curtain opening. Yasmin adjusted the hijab and took a deep breath.

She did her best to replicate the woman's tone. "She's unconscious. Come, I need help getting her up."

Yasmin turned her back to the entrance, leaning over Nour's body. Hoping that there would be only the one man.

The political officer said, "Is she decent?"

Yasmin said, "Yes, come."

The man pushed aside the curtain. The optics must have been correct because a second later he was there beside Yasmin, shoulder to shoulder, crouching over the body. Nour's hair was long and covered the exposed face. Wrapped in the oversized t-shirt, the corpse was a good enough bait.

The pistol jabbed Yasmin in the hip, and she moved into action.

By the time she had extracted the weapon from its holster, the security officer was only beginning to realize the ploy. Like, he hadn't imagined what could happen. A common issue in military affairs, lack of imagination.

It all happened within a single second, at least that's what it felt like. Yasmin moving to her left to gain a little space. Two hands mobilized, one to unsnap the holster, the second to draw the weapon. The man jerked to his right, finally realizing what was up, but Yasmin was ready. She moved with him, using the man's desperate movement to push him back into the rough stone wall. She jammed the pistol into his belly as hard as possible and squeezed the trigger once.

The report was muffled by the political officer's muscular build, but loud enough that she was certain the guard down in the main room would notice. The man slid to the floor, a pained expression on his face. A low moan emerged from his mouth. Yasmin put a knee on his neck, and pulled a thick pillow over his head. She pushed the pillow down and buried the weapon into it, firing at point blank range. The second shot was better suppressed than the first. Fluff from polyester filling floated in the air and the man went completely limp.

The head wound leaked into the stone floor, blood already running in a rivulet towards the corridor.

Yasmin stood and straightened the abaya, adjusting the hijab. She felt the high tenor of adrenaline pumping through her system, the heart beat thumping in her ears. She swept past the curtain into the corridor, unsure of what she would find.

The guard with the AK-12 was down in the room with the camera setup.

She called to him. "Come, help us with her."

The man was sitting on the stool they'd setup for Yasmin to occupy during the hostage video shoot. He was reading from the political officer's clipboard. Maybe it was a script they wanted her to narrate. He looked up at her and she beckoned, not wanting to get closer. The tunnels were dimly lit, and she figured the current distance was about the limit.

Any closer and he'd be able to see the difference between her shape and Nour's figure.

She said, "Come!"

He stood up, and she went behind the curtain, waiting for him. She let him come, hearing the footsteps. The guy was totally unsuspecting, but he did call to the political officer by his name.

"Hamed."

Like he wasn't going to take orders from Nour.

Yasmin couldn't do Mohammed's voice, so she was very tempted to step out of the curtained nook and just shoot the man. She didn't give in to the temptation and was rewarded when he put his head in through the gap between curtain and stone wall.

She came down hard with the pistol, slamming the heavy steel barrel into a spot just above and to the right of his ear. The guard collapsed, falling like a rag doll onto his dead friend. She used another pillow to muffle the shot, executing the second guard and shielding herself from the back splatter.

Yasmin stood up, a little shaky on her feet. Unbelievable. A pile of three corpses on that narrow bed. She needed to get out of there.

The tunnel entrance would be guarded. This was going to have to be quick and violent. She moved and planned ahead. Kill the guard if there was one. Steal a phone and get to safety. If she got that far into the escape, then she'd be able to contact someone in Israel through WhatsApp or another method.

She figured it would take her people a half hour to come and get her. Hopefully not more than that.

EIGHTY

Hershkowitz accepted a plastic cup of instant coffee from his assistant.

The operators in Damascus were into the tunnel they'd prepared near the Iranian security compound. The body-cam showed an infrared view of the backs of three Sayeret Matkal men who were huddled at a subterranean wall. On the other side of that wall was a bunker full of Islamic Revolutionary Guards Corps officers and their hangers on.

The camera had audio, but transmission was complicated by the depth.

The F-16 sorties had continued. Syrian air defenses were weak, a result of the continuous destruction of anti-aircraft batteries by the Israeli Air Force over the years. You couldn't let these people get S-300 systems dug in around Iranian proxy armies or the IRGC itself.

As far as anyone knew, the Iranian officers were sequestered in their bunker, which had been the object of intense IDF intelligence planning for the better part of two years. The Iranians couldn't have known that the Sayeret Matkal team was preparing to inject a gaseous substance with a close molecular relation to fentanyl.

The reinforced concrete wall had been carefully excavated over several months to prepare for its demolition. They had two tiny holes punched through with receptacles prepped to receive the nerve agent once the command was given.

The Sayeret Matkal operator came through on the comms, voice tone calm and clear.

"Preparations complete, ready for substance insertion."

The woman up front looked at Hershkowitz. He nodded at her, sipping from the coffee cup, and getting a good hit of sugar.

She spoke into the headset. "Go ahead, you have the green light."

"Received."

A flurry of activity followed. The team pulled masks over their mouth and nose. Each operator carried a compressed air tank for the job. They'd be able to last about an hour without needing to breathe atmospheric air unless there was a firefight in which case the timeline would be shortened.

The whole idea was that there would be no firefight.

Simultaneous to the operation on the ground, the Blackhawks were cleared to cross into Syria. The Sayeret Matkal men at the bunker would need to extract the captives to a spot chosen in an eastern suburb of Damascus. The choppers would exfiltrate from there and that would be it.

A second squadron of F-16s was to provide additionally decoy activity against a Syrian military base in the west. Two Heron drones were up for surveillance support and potential intervention as and when needed.

The operator on the ground spoke now from inside the mask.

"Substance deployed."

It took only five minutes for the fentanyl like gas to have its effect. While they waited, the Israelis had no way of knowing if it was working on the inside of the IRGC bunker. They'd tested it enough times to know that so far it always had. The gas was calibrated to incapacitate, not kill. They had physical profiles of the officers, in the trials they'd run the subjects had always survived.

The minutes clicked by in silence until finally the woman up front said, "Time."

The operators on the ground moved back, revealing the stretch of cement wall already degraded by a rectangular groove into which an explosive putty had been pressed. The section of wall blew in and the operators rushed forward.

Headlamps illuminated a dust filled interior chamber with a pile of maybe a dozen unconscious bodies. The team identified the key figures one after another. The operator calling the names in and sending face shots to be checked against the recognition systems.

Hershkowitz watched the war machine in action. He'd been among those operators in his younger days. Different unit, but the thrill was the same. An incredible feeling when it went your way, and nothing worse when it didn't.

This time the angels were with them.

The Sayeret Matkal men brought Iranian officers out of the bunker. The camera cut to another body-cam attached to an operator in the van. The IRGC men were being strapped to stretchers and lined up. Five minutes later, the rest of the squad was out, and the vehicle was on its way.

Three minutes from the rendezvous and Hershkowitz's assistant appeared in front of him with a very weird expression on her face.

He said, "What?"

She was holding out a phone, as usual. She said, "It's Gabi.

Yasmin Shoshan just called her sister. She's in fucking *Seddiqine*!"

He didn't completely understand what she meant. "They located her?"

"No." His assistant said, "They didn't locate her, she's escaped. Yasmin's saying that she's hiding in the back of a pharmacy there. A team is on the way to extract her."

"A pharmacy?"

"There's only one pharmacy in Seddiqine Mike, they know where she is."

He said, "Shit."

Hershkowitz looked up at the screens above the command center's console. He was initially thrown into confusion. What were they supposed to do with the Iranians now that Yasmin was out? The whole point had been to use them as a very tough negotiation card. The answer came to him of its own volition however, after only a second or two of reflection.

They'd make sure Yasmin returned home, then they'd see about the Iranians.

His assistant said, "What are you going to do?"

"Gabi's managing the extraction in Lebanon, right?" She nodded. He said, "We'll see what happens once they get to her. What's the ETA?"

His assistant put the phone up to her ear. "What's the ETA for the team to reach her position?" She looked at Hershkowitz. "Fifteen minutes."

In a few minutes, the incapacitated IRGC officers would be loading onto an IAF Blackhawk for transportation to perfectly humane accommodations, for the time being. Even now those Iranian bodyguards who hadn't taken shelter would be beginning to figure out what had gone down.

His assistant looked at her phone again. She tapped the screen and put it to her ear. "Yes." Hershkowitz watched her listening, looking away from him to the screens up there and nodding to whatever it was she was being told. She said, "Yes," and handed the phone to him. She mouthed the words 'Gabi'.

Hershkowitz put the phone to his ear. "Yes."

The deputy commander of Mossad said, "I've just spoken with our American friends. We'll take these Iranians regardless of anything else. I see that the operation is going well, and we want you to continue."

The call ended and Hershkowitz handed the phone back to his assistant. Up on the left side of the screen a new video feed had replaced the drone's eye view above Damascus. The new image was from the gun turret of a Blackhawk, flying low over the dark Syrian landscape. The Damascene plain was relatively high at around six hundred meters. The Ghouta region was fertile and green, a nice place to live, sometimes.

The residents would be getting an earful. They'd be wise to stay indoors because the helicopter crew wasn't going to be shy on the trigger finger tonight, there was too much at stake.

Hershkowitz looked away. There was always too much at stake. For the first time since all of this had begun he felt a sense of relief. The persistent pressure was going to end, and he'd be going home. Maybe it was time to get out of town once he'd found a helper for his mother.

He'd buy a place up in the Galilee, maybe join in on an ecological project with people that made pottery and raised goats for milk and cheese. Thinking of Yasmin huddled in the back of a pharmacy over in some Lebanese village. That was one seriously impressive woman.

EPILOGUE

RAF Mildenhall, England

. . .

Keeler only heard about Yasmin's escape two weeks later.

They'd exfiltrated him back to Mildenhall, England directly after the Paris thing. Nobody was particularly pleased about what had gone down in Paris. It had been a big old FUBAR situation and even though he'd mitigated the damage, you didn't get medals for that.

Instead, what he got was calculated indifference and some kind of holding pattern. It was cold and dreary up in Mildenhall, and Jodorowsky had him training new guys in the field. Which meant he was almost permanently wet and cold.

He'd messaged Ruth a day after getting to base, and she'd called back, explaining how Yasmin had been taken. It seemed dire to Keeler, and he felt a kind of hole open up in him. There wasn't much to talk about, so that was it. When a girl you've got feelings for is stuck in a Hezbollah dungeon, there are two ways of dealing with it.

Some guys would go all out and worry. Others would figure that there wasn't anything he could do about it, so it was better to just wait and see.

Keeler wasn't doing either of those two things. He was actively scheming on getting there and going into South Lebanon to bring pain to whoever had Yasmin and get her out. What Ruth had told him was that in Israel, the whole episode was shrouded in grim secrecy.

She'd said it was bullshit, and he agreed. He'd already asked twice to be assigned in some way that would help get her out.

Problem was that the command seemed to have guessed this would be his reaction, so Jodorowsky was keeping him busy with the new guys in the rain. They still owed him a week and a half of R&R.

. . .

THE SUN WASN'T YET up, and Keeler had just come back from a night out in the woods. He got back to his temporary lodging facility and threw his gear on the floor. Wet pack, a jacket, and gloves, socks and boots. All of it went on the floor near the bed. The weapons and other sensitive devices went on the bed.

The room had a desk, upon which sat a phone he'd bought. The message symbol was blinking at him.

Keeler picked up the phone and read the message: *Y for K. Cluster. You owe me 252 hours.*

He actually laughed. Looking at the message. It had been received the day before. Yasmin was out. Keeler whooped and dialed the number. He hit the call button and walked to the window. The sun might have been coming up, but you wouldn't know it from the endless drear of condensation on the inside and persistent drizzle outside.

Yasmin answered on the third ring. The throaty morning voice that immediately sent Keeler's neuro chemicals racing around the system.

"Hello?"

Keeler said, "How did you do it?"

"Do what?"

"Get out of there."

Yasmin didn't speak immediately. Keeler knew that the question wasn't tactful, but he figured; coming from one combat soldier to another it was a normal thing to ask. Get the elephant out of the room before anything else.

She said, "How would you have done it?"

"If I saw half a chance I would have gone full berserker. I would have made it happen."

"Despite the bodies."

"Affirmative."

She said, "Yeah, so I made it happen."

He said, "I'm glad. What are you doing now?"

She said, "Thinking about breakfast, you?"

He said, "Thinking about you, little sparrow hawk."

Yasmin said, "You owe me two hundred and fifty-two hours Keeler."

She sounded serious.

He did the calculation in his head. A week and a half of rest and recuperation. She was having fun with math. Keeler was looking outside, through the rain blurred window glass. The fields beyond were just a soft green shape in the weak light filtering through English clouds.

He said, "I'm working on it."

For a while Yasmin said nothing and Keeler was content to look at the window and have her breathing and living on the other side of the line.

THE END

AN EXTRACT FROM STRAIGHT SHOT

CHAPTER ONE

A MAN WAS WALKING the platform, scanning the train as it crept into Alencourt station. I was sitting at the window, watching him as we got closer. The brakes shrieked. The guy moved slow and stiff, his head swiveling like a searchlight as the train inched past. Looking for someone. He walked against the train's direction, while his head rotated back with it, holding each window in place as his eyes examined it, then circling back to scan again, as the next car came abreast.

The train approached; we got closer. I could see his eyes darting around, while the head moved smoothly. Then the eyes found me, but settled below my eye line. Like he wasn't interested in my face. Then the guy lifted his gaze to mine and we were looking directly at each other, engaged. The train was moving painfully slow, so there was plenty of time to get a good look.

Looked like he had recognized me, but I didn't know him.

Then the train stopped with a delayed lurch, and I saw him back off and disengage. Around me passengers were already dragging their bags and children off luggage racks and train seats. Soon they were flooding the platform and the guy was gone.

I was halfway to the entrance hall before I saw him again, over by the ticket desk, trying not to stare at me. He was maybe nineteen or twenty. Close small eyes and a tiny chin, like a rat. Dark hair buzzed to a number two, stripes shaved into one side. Like the Adidas logo. I went over to the information board and examined him in the glass reflection. He couldn't stop himself from looking at me. Not a professional. Some kind of petty criminal maybe.

I looked up at the clock over the information booth. Quarter to noon, Saturday, June 23rd. It was my first time in France.

The station was busy. People dragged wheeled suitcases around, ran for trains. Footsteps slapped on the concrete, echoing around the big hall. Mothers and Fathers pulled their kids. The rat-faced guy I'd never seen before was just standing there looking at my back. I supposed he was planning to mug me.

The entrance to the street was a wide stone arch leading to two-way traffic and a park on the other side. There was a kiosk in the park with newspapers and magazines and a big coffee cup on the roof. I figured I could cross through the traffic and wait to see if the guy came after me. On top of that I could get a cup of coffee.

I jogged across, weaving between taxis.

I ordered coffee at the kiosk and watched the entrance to the train station. Nobody came, nothing happened. I stretched out and yawned. My joints cracked. Twelve hours on the train. The coffee was dark and bitter. It came in a small paper cup. I drank it in two sips, crushed the cup in my fist and threw it into a garbage can. I didn't see anyone coming after me.

The weather was grey and so was the town. Grey stone.

Poured concrete fixtures. Warm droplets of moisture hung in the air, threatening rain.

I noticed the second guy right off the bat. He must have circled around the park to flank me. This guy was bigger than rat-face and wore jeans with a thin leather jacket. He looked like a young thug. Same age as the first guy. The second one had wet looking hair combed in a side part.

So I figured the first guy would be coming up behind me. They had wanted me to notice the second one. That was the strategy, distract, induce panic, come at me from both sides. I'd been out of the military for only a week. Their little strategy wasn't going to work.

The park was carved up into little walk-ways. I went off the footpath and cut across the lawn. Using peripheral vision, I clocked rat-face coming off the street and passing the kiosk. He and his leather jacket buddy were moving in sync, wedging me in. Dense evergreens crowded the path where it sunk down in a dip a dozen yards away. The dip would do. I figured less than twenty seconds casual walking.

Laurel bushes blocked out the light. The dip was an intersection. A spiderweb of narrow walkways converged in its hollow. But the two guys were gone. I stayed there for a couple of minutes to see if they would come. Maybe they were waiting me out. But nobody waits more than a minute. A minute's a long time if you're waiting. Young thugs in particular are impatient, nervous and jumpy. You can always wait them out. The two guys didn't show.

I exited the park and crossed over to the sidewalk. The town center was old and busy. The kind of old that gets preserved by committee. Busy with regular people doing regular things that hadn't changed all that much in a couple hundred years.

Twelve hours on the train made me want to stretch out. To walk. To loosen the hips and the knees and ankles. But first I wanted to stop by the town hall, see if I could find any record of my mother's family. She had been French, and spent her summers in Alencourt. I was curious about that side of my family because as far as I knew, my mother hadn't ever come back to France after moving to the United States.

The center of town was a big old medieval square with an ancient church right in the middle of it. The town hall was on the edge of the square. I told the old mustachioed guy at reception what I was looking for and he pointed across the square. He had to push his glasses down off his forehead to look at me. Blue eyes magnified and focused. He said that records were kept in the library, which was on the other side of the church. The old guy looked at his watch and shook his head, chances were the library was already closed for lunch.

But it wasn't quite closed. I got in the door. A young woman wearing a floral print dress was flipping over the closed sign at the front desk. I made it to the counter a split second before the sign flipped and put my hand next to it. Which made her look up. I gave a winning American smile. The librarian was in her twenties, strawberry blonde hair, long nose, high cheekbones, slim.

I said, "You're closing for lunch."

"Yes Monsieur."

"Can I bother you for half a minute?" I smiled.

"You can bother me for half a minute." She smiled back.

So I told her about my mother and how she had spent summers with family in town. I asked the librarian where I could look if I wanted to find traces that her family might have left.

"Your family."

"Excuse me?"

"You said you wanted to find traces of your mother's family, but it's your family as well."

Which was true, and maybe a better way of putting it. The librarian asked me to write down my mother's name and date of birth. She told me to stop by in the afternoon, say five. She said she'd see what she could dig up. But there were no guarantees. Some traces remained over time, others got wiped away. Depended on a lot of things.

I wrote the name down, *Delphine Vaugeois*, and the date of birth. Then I thanked the librarian and walked out.

Five hours. Enough time to have lunch, check out the town, take a walk, stop by the library and then get the late train out. Maybe there was a sleeper. I was headed South. Spain or Portugal and the beach. Figured I'd stay there for a month or a year, or however long it took to get bored of the beach. For the moment I was thinking about food and more coffee. Otherwise I felt good.

Off the church square, I turned into a series of narrow, crowded streets. The old town. Shoppers jostled in line for the butcher or the baker. The scent of fresh bread and coffee had settled. I squeezed through a knot of people outside the bakery and felt a push from behind. Turned to look. It was the second guy, with the leather jacket and the wet looking side part. I could smell the stuff in his hair.

So these clowns had waited for me. I had to give them points for persistence. But, what made them think I was a good mark?

Up ahead on the left was a little side street entrance, even narrower than the one I was on. I looked to the right, across the street. A new guy. Same age as rat-face, similar style. The local young thug look, but this time with longer hair in a pony tail and a manicured stubble beard. These guys were easy to spot because the rest of the crowd was older and dressed conservatively. The pony tail guy was dressed in a track suit like the rat-faced guy from the train platform.

So now there were three. The first guy with the rat-face and

Adidas stripe shaved into his head, leather jacket side-part from the park, and pony tail with the facial hair.

Their plan was simple.

Leather jacket side-part was pushing up behind me so I'd move forward, out of the bakery crowd. The new guy with the pony tail was there to push me left, into the side street. I figured rat-face would be waiting there. So that was their plan. They would pen me in and try to rob me. I thought, *welcome to France*.

I stopped abruptly and let leather jacket side-part guy walk into me belly first. I felt him grab my shirt above the waist. Which was a mistake, because I used his grab to pull him closer than he wanted. I stomped on his foot with my left heel and crushed his instep. The guy grunted, surprised. The stomp made him lean forward and I whipped my right arm back and nailed him in the nuts with the heel of my hand. I pulled away from his grab and felt the back of my shirt tear as he bent over and fell.

Which pissed me off somewhat. The shirt was new.

The third guy was moving from my right, trying to corral me towards the side street. His pony tail was pulled back tight. His little stubbly beard was carved into a thin shape on a weak face, but he had stunning bright blue eyes highlighted by dark eyelashes, like a male model. He was reaching into his pocket with his left hand, and I was on him in two steps, shutting him down. His right fist came up in a wild flail with no momentum. I stepped into the swing and at the same time transferred body weight from rear to front leg. I bent the knees, sinking low. Moved in close and punched my right elbow into his solar plexus.

The tip of the elbow made contact with a click. He went down in a sprawl.

The solar plexus is a bundle of nerves right above the

abdomen, where it meets the chest. It's near impossible to actually hit the solar plexus because it sits too deep inside. But, if you get low and aim up, kind of diagonal, you can impact the nerves enough to fire off impulses to the target's diaphragm. When you get it right, the shocked nerves overstimulate the diaphragm, which contracts. The target thinks that they are suffocating.

Which is what happened to the pony tail guy. I didn't swing my elbow in, I punched it out. The pointy part hit him right in the chest hollow. I followed through like he was made of paper. He hit the ground and started to spasm and gasp. He'd survive. In a few minutes the diaphragm would relax. But he'd get all clammy with cold sweat for at least an hour.

Two down, one to go.

I turned left to face the side street. I was right about the rat-faced guy, the number two haircut man with the Adidas stripe and small, close set eyes. He was coming out of the side street in short steps. This was someone who didn't do enough walking. Too much sitting around playing video games. I detected hesitation. His plan wasn't working out. He hadn't wanted to do it in a crowd.

He had a knife in his right hand. The blade was a Spyderco one handed opener. All steel. Pretty nasty. But the steel handle isn't much good because it gets slippery when wet. And if you're not planning on getting a knife wet, you shouldn't be taking out a knife. I stepped in quick and caught him off balance. He found himself too close-in to use the blade. I could feel the guy's breath on my face, onions and spice. He had a panicky expression, lips drawn back in a distorted scowl. People aren't generally comfortable with getting up close and personal.

I took control of his knife hand and twisted. Living beings move away from pain. So the guy tried to get away, but I kept the pressure on, pushing him back towards the side street. He groaned. His eyes rolled back in small sockets. The Spyderco clattered to the street. I adjusted my body weight and twisted quickly, pushing the trapped hand back towards the arm and up. The little scaphoid bone in his wrist snapped like a dry chopstick. He gave a little shriek.

Shouldn't have taken the knife out.

There was another high pitched shriek from my left. Which turned out to be a uniformed policewoman blowing on a whistle. We made eye contact. Hers were hazel with green flecks. She had a police cap on. Her pony tail came out the back. She had little stud earrings, made a couple of steps towards me and grabbed my shirt. "Stay there."

I relaxed and let my hands hang down, unthreatening.

CONTINUE READING. GET YOUR COPY OF STRAIGHT SHOT ON AMAZON!

Hello Friend,

I hope that you have enjoyed this book.

Please consider leaving a review on the book's Amazon page.

I love communicating with readers, and **I send a free Tom Keeler novella to anyone who joins my monthly Newsletter.**

Sign up at jacklively.com

See you there,

Jack Lively

SWITCH BACK

It's been two years since Tom Keeler left the military, but a combat medic never forgets his pilot. So, when he hears that Mallory's got terminal brain cancer, Keeler drops everything to see her one last time. But then he runs into a beautiful journalist, who's trying to escape cartel assassins out to kill her. Keeler's up for the challenge, but he can't get Mallory or her family involved, because the cartels never forget. So he's got to compartmentalize. On one hand there's a woman who's life needs saving. On the other, an old buddy who's life can't be saved. And this is Texas, on the hottest day of the hottest month of the hottest year that anyone can remember.

ALSO BY JACK LIVELY

The Tom Keeler novels can be read in any order.

Straight Shot

Breacher

Impact

Hard Candy

Berserker

STRAIGHT SHOT

After surviving combat tours in Afghanistan, Iraq, and northern Syria, Tom Keeler receives his discharge from the United States Air-Force special tactics squadron. He's planning a long vacation, beginning with the town of Alencourt, France, where his mother spent summers as a kid.

Keeler's in town for less than an hour and three men try to kill him. Nice place, nice try.

Those aren't the first men who've tried to kill Keeler and failed. He could just walk away, get back on the train and take it from there. But Keeler finds himself drawn back to Alencourt. Perhaps it's the beautiful French policewoman, Cecile Nazari, who tells Keeler that the attack was a case of mistaken identity. Or maybe, it's the fact that the people who attacked him might be the same people who left his French cousin in a wheelchair.

Or maybe it's the connection Keeler finds between these attacks and reports of asylum seeking girls from the Middle East going missing in the area.

Whatever the reason, Keeler becomes interested in what's going on, which isn't great news for the bad people preying on the weak and defenseless.

They thought they could get away with murder, but they never counted on coming up against Keeler.

BREACHER

Tom Keeler is on his way to Seattle after working on an Alaskan fishing boat for the salmon season. Keeler might have been done with Alaska, but Alaska wasn't done with him. People are following him and demanding attention, but he's not interested.

Jane Abrams has got big problems to deal with. Her son's gone missing and the police are useless. She wants Keeler's help, but doesn't know how to ask nicely.

The people pushing Abrams around step over the line, threats turn into actions and pretty soon there is a real situation. It isn't only the problem with Abrams and her son. Very bad things are happening up in Alaska. Keeler's not looking for a mystery to solve, but he's not going to walk away either.

Breacher is a pulsing thriller that sinks its hooks in from the beginning and never lets up until the last page.

They thought that owning the town gave them special privileges. But they never planned on coming up against Tom Keeler.

IMPACT

Tom Keeler's been down in the Florida keys taking leisure seriously. But his old military buddy has an issue with a tornado in Alabama, so

Keeler comes up to help. Pretty soon he's promising a distraught tornado survivor to deliver a special family heirloom to the town of Promise, Indiana.

As soon as Keeler rolls into the town of Promise, things get complicated.

Linda Cartwright's a happily married woman, and then somebody tried to kill her on her own front lawn. Keeler's ready to help, but Cartwright won't talk about it. When she disappears, Keeler suspects that Cartwright's in over her head. She's a tough lady, but even tough nuts crack.

And it's not only Cartwright, bad things are happening to regular folk, all over the town of Promise. People just disappear, and nobody seems to be able to do anything about it. Except for Keeler. Because he knows, behind every bad deed is a bad person. And when bad people are getting away with bad deeds, Tom Keeler's always going to be ready to make a strong impact.

HARD CANDY

Tom Keeler is on the southbound train to New York City. He's been in Canada and it's colder than a witch's tit up there. What he really needs is lunch in Chinatown. But now, that's not going to happen. The train gets stuck in a blizzard and Keeler's stranded in the town of Kitchewan Landing.

Luckily the diner's open and the beautiful train conductor Mini DeValla isn't going to say no to a free dinner.

But DeValla recognizes a passenger from the train, a man who doesn't want to be recognized. The man with the familiar face isn't the only stranger in town. There's a business conference up in the hills of Kitchewan Landing, featuring a man who just might be the richest man in the world.

DeValla and Keeler are going to find out that there's nothing more deadly than a man with nothing to lose. Tom Keeler has to solve a mystery that starts in the small town of Kitchewan Landing, but reaches all the way to the dizzying corruption of financial and political global elites.

BERSERKER

BERSERKER takes place in 2016, a few weeks before the events in Badlands.

Tom Keeler is in Ankara, Turkey, on a joint CIA / JSOC mission. A routine signal from a safehouse is missed and he's the one sent to check it out.

Things get a little tricky from there.

The missed signal leads Keeler on a devastating journey into the heart of the Syrian civil war.

He needs to beat the clock and get to a wounded comrade before it's too late. At the same time, multiple intelligence agencies are drawn to a mysterious woman, who might or might not be related to the most wanted man on the planet.

BERSERKER sees Tom Keeler join forces with resilient allies, fighting the toughest of enemies in the fog of war.

Get ready for an intense experience!

ABOUT THE AUTHOR

Jack Lively was born in Sheffield, in the UK. He grew up in the United States of America. He has worked as a fisherman, an ice cream truck driver, underwater cinematographer, gas station attendant, and outboard engine repairman. The other thing about Jack is that since he grew up without a TV, before the internet, he was always reading. And later on, Jack started writing. All through those long years working odd jobs and traveling around, Jack wrote. He'd write in bars and cafes, on boats and trains and even on long haul bus trips.

Eventually Jack finished a book and figured he might as well see if anyone wanted to read it.

Tom Keeler is a veteran combat medic who served in a special tactics unit of United States Air Force. The series begins when Keeler receives his discharge from the military. Keeler just wants to roam free. But stuff happens, and Keeler's not the kind of guy who just walks away.

Jack Lively lives in London with his family.

For more information go to:
www.jacklively.com

Badlands

Copyright © 2024 General Projects Ltd.

Badlands is a work of fiction. Names, characters, businesses, organizations, places, events, and incidents either are the product of the author's imagination or are used fictitiously. Any resemblance to actual persons, living or dead, events, or locales is entirely coincidental.

All rights reserved. This book or any portion thereof may not be reproduced or used in any manner whatsoever without the express written permission of the publisher except for the use of brief quotations in a book review.

ISBN: 978-1-0686930-1-4

General Projects Ltd.

London, UK.

www.jacklively.com

Made in the USA
Monee, IL
04 July 2024